GREEN VALLEY SHIFTERS COLLECTION 1

BOOKS 1-3

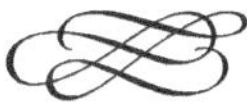

ELVA BIRCH

ZOE CHANT

A QUICK GUIDE TO GREEN VALLEY

Green Valley Shifters is a series of gentle, funny, found-family standalone short shifter novels with single dads, spinsters, and sweet second chances - plus adorable children and pets. This collection includes the first three books, *Dancing BEARfoot*, The *Tiger Next Door*, and *DandeLION Season*. Each book can be read independently, but you may enjoy them most in order, as these characters come back!

Get signed and sketched paperback copies at my webpage!

Patricia runs the local preschool. **Lee** is a bear shifter and his daughter is Clara. Find their story in Dancing Bearfoot (Book 1).

Andrea is Patricia's assistant at the preschool, and a hawk shifter. **Shaun** Powell is a tiger shifter, Trevor is his precocious lion shifter son. They meet in The Tiger Next Door (Book 2).

Tawny is a local spinster who meets big city lion shifter **Damien**, the father of Shaun and Shelley, in Dandelion Season (Book 3)

Shelley, a lion shifter herself, comes to Green Valley in Bearly

Together (Book 4) and finds single dad **Dean**, a bear shifter, and his son Aaron (with two As!).

Local prankster **Jamie** returns from firefighting in Alaska to run into new resident **Devon**, a lynx shifter raising his kid sister, Abby, in Broken Lynx (Book 5)

Fire chief **Turner**, a moose shifter, meets his destiny when he rescues **Linda** Powell, Shelley's mother, from a stray dog in A Green Valley Christmoose Disaster (Book 6)

DANCING BEARFOOT

CHAPTER 1

*L*ee lay awake for a long moment without opening his eyes, not ready to be awake, and not sure why he was.

"Someone is watching us," his bear supplied, wary and grouchy.

Lee opened his eyes at last, and found the cause of his uneasy feeling staring at him across the empty spread of bed. Blue eyes that matched his own were framed with white-blonde curls that were nothing like his own dark locks.

"I start preschool today," Clara told him, matter-of-factly. "I dressed myself. But I couldn't tie my shoes." The offending shoes, a worn pair of sneakers with pink cartoon bears, were laying on the bed between them. The knotted laces showed her efforts.

Lee groaned, and looked at the clock on the bedside table. "It's five in the morning," he explained.

"I don't want to be late."

Lee refrained from trying to explain details about time to a four-year-old, and resigned himself to getting up. He snagged a pair of pants from a moving box and padded barefoot across the thick carpet to sweep Clara up and toss her effortlessly onto the wide bed while he got dressed.

She giggled and tumbled, then sat up seriously. "Will my new teacher like me?" she asked anxiously.

"You don't need to worry about that, cub!" Lee was quick to assure her. "You're going to have a great time. Aunt Bella says it's the best school in the whole town."

Like the concept of time, it was pointless to add that the entire town was only thirteen hundred people strong, and there had not been a choice at all. If the preschool did not work out, he could pack them back up and move them to another town, but Lee was weary of moving, and tired of cities. He already loved the house they had found, and the quaint little town of Green Valley. His bear loved the wilderness that was only a short wander out his backdoor. If the preschool didn't work out, maybe he would just hire another nanny and keep Clara home. He was suddenly hopeful that his daughter wouldn't get along with the teacher.

"Would you like a special breakfast?" he offered, to distract her. "You can help me wash dishes, afterward."

Clara's face lit up. "Yes! Pancakes! With blueberries! Can I make the bubbles for the dishes?"

Lee helped Clara off the bed and took her little hand in his own. "Pancakes it is. And you can make all the bubbles, because it's your first day of preschool." He wondered when she would grow up enough to realize that washing dishes wasn't really the treat he made it out to be.

He was still looking for a reason not to like the preschool as he drove the beater company truck he had borrowed from his construction company up to the quaint little house. Despite his efforts, and Clara's insanely early wake-up, they were still running late. It had started to snow, and he didn't want to push the truck too fast on the slushy streets. It had also, somehow, taken twenty minutes to get Clara into her winter coat and out the door, despite her eagerness to go.

He unstrapped Clara from her carseat and followed her with growing reluctance up the snowy steps. He wondered if he should have insisted she wear her winter boots, rather than the pink bear tennis shoes, but she scampered up and was pushing open the door before the snow had a chance to stick to her legs.

The door opened to a tiny Arctic entryway. Clara would have pushed further on, but Lee noticed the rack of coats and stopped her. "Here, honey, let's take off your coat."

She squirmed and fussed while he unzipped her and hung her coat on an empty hook.

It was warm, noisy chaos behind the second door. Children laughed and played at activity stations around the room, and someone was playing a cheerful song on a slightly tinny upright piano. As the musician, unseen, ended with a flourish, some of the children clapped in delight.

He wasn't ready. He'd been a fool to think he could do this–to leave Clara with some stranger for so many hours? He would just tell the old woman that he'd made a mistake, that Clara would be too anxious, that... he cast about in his mind for some excuse. That he'd forgotten her lunch? He settled a scowl on his face; that was often enough to send weak-willed people running, and maybe she wouldn't ask why he was withdrawing Clara from her class.

But Clara, not at all bothered by the noise, was trotting forward, her lunch clutched in one hand and the other pulling him reluctantly forward. "Her name is Miss Patricia," she said enthusiastically. "Aunt Bella said so."

Then "Miss Patricia" was bouncing out from behind the piano, and Lee's excuses died on his lips.

The gray bun and glasses he had imagined were nowhere to be seen. The tiny, ancient woman he had envisioned bore no resemblance to the blonde goddess who was smiling down at his daughter. She was tall and curvy, with big, brown eyes and straw-blonde hair loose to her shoulders. Energy radiated from her, and Lee felt like the floor had fallen away.

"You must be Clara," she was saying. Her voice sounded very far away–the sounds of the room had tunneled away in the shock of seeing her.

"I am," Clara said confidently. "I'm four. I brought my lunch."

"Let me show you where to put that," Miss Patricia said, and as she straightened, she met Lee's eyes.

Lee had never believed in soulmates; he thought the whole idea of a destined mate was ridiculous, made up for people who need comforting fiction to get through their lives. But the teacher's eyes, infinite pools of brown warmth, were the first place he had ever felt truly at home. The bear in him rumbled in delight.

"You must be Mr. Montgomery," she said, and her voice was as rich as her eyes, with the subtle Midwestern accent that he hadn't known he adored.

Lee realized she was holding out her hand, and had no idea how long it had been there. "Lee," he said swiftly, reaching out too fast to shake it. Touching her skin was like being struck by lightning, and he had to make himself let go after a handshake that was too long and trailed away into simply holding onto her. He had never wanted so badly to kiss a complete stranger.

"Lee," she said, with amusement. "It's nice to meet you."

Then Clara was slipping out of his other hand and following the golden woman away. She moved like a dancer, all grace and efficiency of motion. If she filled out her flowered country shirt nicely, she filled out her simple jeans even better, and Lee was mesmerized to watch her bend over to show Clara where to put her lunch. Down at their level, she suddenly became a magnet to the children, and was swiftly swarmed by small people demanding her attention.

More attractive than her curves and soft hair—which were enough by themselves to send Lee into a stupor of desire—was an air of gentle affection that glowed around her. Her sweet smile and careful handling of the childrens' attention was enchanting to watch. She knew just which ones needed a little playful redirection of their energy, and which ones needed a gentle nudge to boost their confidence. Her movements were never sharp or angry. Her attention flowed between them seamlessly, and the entire room was warmed by her simple presence.

Lee did not realize that he was standing there, staring stupidly, until Clara trotted back to him and pulled on his hand. "Papa, you're supposed to leave now."

Lee felt his cheeks heat unexpectedly– he couldn't remember the last time he had blushed–and knelt to give Clara a swift hug. "Have a fun day, cub," he told her, and then he turned and fled in a rush of confusion.

~

*P*atricia knew that the first day of preschool after any break–even just Christmas–was always as much about the parents as it was the children. Few of them were really ready to say goodbye, and they dealt poorly with the children who were clingy. But so far, only one child that morning needed any serious distraction, and she was enchanted with the class rabbit in short order.

Harriette Ambler, as expected, was the worst of the mothers, a perfect storm of condescending and demanding. Her son, Trevor, was a meek little angel, but to hear Harriette talk–right in front of the poor boy!–he was a perfect devil, and she clearly doubted that Patricia was up to the challenge for a second semester. She elbowed a little girl out of the way in order to get Patricia's attention, and detailed the contents of his lunch (which were also written on the outside of his lunch bag), and insisted that he was not to participate in rough play or, from the sounds of it, anything fun. Patricia managed to catch Trevor's eye while his mother was turned away, and rolled her eyes at him with an exaggerated shrug. She was rewarded with a shy half-smile, swiftly hidden as Harriette scolded him for slouching.

"I'm sure we'll manage, Harriette," Patricia assured her buoyantly. "We'll see you at two!" Then she was able to herd Trevor off to a painting station and walk away to the piano. Left without an audience, the infuriating woman finally left, and Patricia launched into a cheerful song to celebrate.

The last parent on Patricia's list and the only one that she didn't already know was Leland Montgomery. In some ways, he was exactly as she expected–and in some ways nothing at all as she'd envisioned.

His sister, Bella, had explained that he was a single father, and Patricia braced herself for a spoiled or neglected child and a harried father who couldn't even be bothered to arrange his own child's education. She was unsurprised that he was running late, and came out from around the piano braced for excuses and unpleasant conflict—he would either be the kind of single father who hated women for hurting him, or the overprotective sort who would never believe their child had flaws. Either way, being late would already put him on the defensive.

The first shock was his size. He made the schoolhouse feel small with his great bulk. He played football in high school, she guessed, with those fabulous shoulders. He probably worked construction now. A glance out of the window confirmed that guess— a battered company truck was parked in front of the school.

But he didn't look like a blue-collar worker, despite the worn plaid shirt and the big hands. He looked like a model playing at being a lumberjack, with fine cheekbones and piercing blue eyes. A mop of thick dark hair above glowering eyebrows looked as artful and deliberate as the stubble across his chiseled jaw. It was the kind of face and build that made Patricia's knees feel weak, and she had to focus on the daughter—or embarrass herself by drooling, or possibly fainting dramatically at his feet. Since she was far too large and awkward to look good fainting, Patricia was happy to exchange smiles with the little girl instead.

Clara was as adorable as only a four-year-old with curls could be. Her chubby-cheeked smile of trust and excitement was the whole reason that Patricia had become a teacher. Meeting her father's watchful gaze gave her whole new reasons for other things, and Patricia had to reach deep to find the calmness to say, "You must be Mr. Montgomery."

"Lee," he said shortly, with a scowl, and he reached out to give her hand a shake. The touch of his hand on her own was like jumping into a cool swimming hole on a sweltering day, all shock and relief and excitement at once. He had calluses that confirmed her guess about his occupation, big, strong, rough-fingered hands that made her own feel small and dainty. She forgot to let go until it had become awkward.

"Lee," she repeated like an idiot, savoring the simple syllable. "It's nice to meet you."

Fortunately, Clara broke her stupor with her childlike enthusiasm, and Patricia was able to peel herself away from the gorgeous man to show her across the room to where the child cubbies were so she could stow her lunch.

"It has my name!" Clara exclaimed in delight, and she could point out all the letters. "I have two As," the little girl assured her solemnly. "But they aren't together."

That drew the attention of a little boy named Aaron, who pointed out that his As were together, and then they were the center of a swarm of children who wanted to meet the new girl. Coming from such a small town, the rest all knew each other already.

"We just moved here from the city," Clara told them. "Our house is falling apart, but Daddy will make it like new."

That prompted questions about the city, and Amber begged Patricia to read the City Mouse book, and somewhere in the chaos Clara slipped away to see her father and shoo him out the door. Patricia didn't watch him go, but could feel his exit from the room as if he'd taken all of the light with him. She had never been so disappointed to see a parent leave and wished for a foolish moment that Clara had been more needy and given him reason to linger longer.

CHAPTER 2

*L*ee had no intention of being late to pick up Clara.

It had been embarrassing enough to arrive late dropping her off, but more than that, he could not wait to see Patricia again. He caught himself rubbing the hand she had held throughout the day, and thinking about that laughter in her eyes and the way her mouth moved when she spoke. His bear grumbled impatiently inside, eager to be in her magnetic presence again as soon as possible.

His was the first vehicle parked in front of the old schoolhouse, and he had to make himself wait until the hands on his watch showed that he was only a few minutes early. Just as he unlatched the rusty door to the borrowed truck, another car drove up, and he paused so they could pull in beside him. The woman who exited the unreasonably shiny purple Chrysler had fluffy hair more suited for the 80s piled on top of her head, a cellphone in one hand and was wearing high heels that were utterly silly in the slushy snow. As Lee extricated himself carefully from the truck–she had parked foolishly close and slightly crooked–he must have growled a little, because he suddenly had all of her unwelcome attention.

Blue eyes widened, and her existing conversation miraculously became unimportant. The cellphone was being tucked into a designer purse as she met him at the front of their vehicles.

"Oh heavens," she said breathlessly. "I didn't leave you much room there, did I." Observing this somehow entailed squeezing right up next to him and leaning past him to examine the gap.

"Nope."

Lee hoped that the brief answer would suffice for conversation, but the woman clutched her hand to her chest as if she had committed some heinous offense. "I'm so sorry!" she said dramatically. "It's such a new car, you know. I'm just not sure where I am when I'm driving!"

Lee refrained from noting that she was clearly not sure where she was when she *wasn't* driving, and backed off a step to retain some personal space. "It's fine," he said shortly, hoping to get past her.

She seemed to think his acceptance was license for further conversation. "I'm Harriette," she introduced herself, holding out a hand to shake that Lee could only helplessly compare to Patricia's. It was a tiny, limp hand, with overdone nails, flawlessly smooth skin, and none of Patricia's warmth or strength. "You must be Mr..."

"Montgomery," Lee said shortly, deliberately not offering his first name.

Harriette paused a moment, expecting it, and finally moved on, not yet relinquishing his hand. "Mr. Montgomery," she savored. "It's *so* lovely to meet you! You've just moved in, then?"

Lee recovered his hand, and nodded. He was disappointed that his usual scowl was not having the usual effect.

"I work in real estate," Harriette explained without invitation. She looked thoughtful and then guessed, "You must have bought the old Lawson place!"

"Yes." Lee wondered if he could elbow past her without being rude, as another car pulled up, then another, disgorging a flurry of mothers who converged on their space. Harriette looked affronted, but managed to turn it to her advantage by introducing him to the gaggle of women as if she were in a privileged position of knowledge.

"This is Mr. Montgomery," she told them, as if they were long-time chums. "He's bought the old Lawson place."

"Oh, the old Lawson place," a brunette with a short bob said eagerly, pushing forward to hang on his handshake. The wedding ring on her hand didn't seem to deter her from all but drooling on him. "That's such a lovely *big* house. A shame they let it get so run down."

"I'll be restoring it," Lee felt conversationally obligated to say, and this prompted an interested murmur, with speculative looks at the battered company truck. He was beginning to regret his choice to put on nicer clothing to pick up Clara; his efforts to make a better impression with Patricia were having the unfortunate side effect of making him look monetarily desirable to the housewife brigade.

To his relief, the door to the farmhouse opened then and a herd of children padded in coats and boots and overseen by a watchful assistant that wasn't Patricia came scampering down to interrupt them. He was able to pick Clara out of the crowd and swing her into his arms. "I like preschool," she said cheerfully.

"What a charming little girl," Harriette gushed at him, entirely ignoring the little boy who had come up to hand her the craft they had created that day. "She's so adorable!"

"We got to paint, and there was music and there is a rabbit and Aaron has two As together in his name and we sang songs and I wrote my name on this for you!" Clara's monologue was a welcome excuse to ignore Harriette, which Lee cheerfully did. He considered the gauntlet of other women eyeing him speculatively between him and the schoolhouse, then decided that retreat was to be preferred to attempting to see Patricia. He brushed past the obnoxious little woman and went around the truck to tuck Clara into her carseat. He would catch Patricia another time.

His bear growled discontentedly at him as they drove away, leaving Harriette with a deep scowl in front of her shiny purple car.

CHAPTER 3

*P*atricia glanced out the window just in time to see Lee's pickup pull away. A pang of disappointment hit her, but she quickly pushed it away. That gorgeous man probably didn't even remember her from their meeting that morning. She, on the other hand, felt like her entire world had shifted in some way.

"Patricia, you fool," she chided herself, picking up the litter of toys left out by the window. "Love at first sight only happens in fairy tales." She, on the other hand, was a grown woman, far too old for such nonsensical ideas. She was just a little lonely and had reacted unreasonably to a particularly handsome man with a wonderful handshake.

"Isn't he a *dish*," Andrea said as she came back in, echoing Patricia's thoughts. The last child had been attached to their parent and the final car was pulling out of the driveway. "And that didn't escape the attention of any of those vulture mothers."

Patricia chuckled. New single men in town were always the object of a lot of attention, from women both married and not, and Lee was the type to get a lot of interest; he seemed to be poor, but was plenty good-looking enough to make up for that.

She looked up from the basket of toys to find Andrea looking at her appraisingly. "What?"

"You like him!"

Sometimes Andrea's powers of observation were uncanny. Patricia had accused her of witchcraft in jest once or twice, but the longer she knew the small, vibrant woman, the more she began to wonder.

This was another case of her guess hitting close to home, and Patricia felt her cheeks heat. "I... er... he's very... we've only barely met!"

Andrea smiled smugly and tossed her sleek, dark hair knowingly. "And you're far too pragmatic to believe in love at first sight."

Patricia had to laugh at herself. "I am," she insisted. "I know better. Besides, he's the father of one of my students. How inappropriate would that be?"

"No more inappropriate than any of the married women throwing themselves at his feet in our parking lot," Andrea said with a roll of her eyes. "Promise me that if the opportunity presents itself, you won't chicken out."

"There won't be..."

"Promise!" The top of Andrea's head might barely hit Patricia's collarbone, but she was all fire and vinegar.

"I promise!" Patricia said meekly.

Andrea gave her a skeptical look, then accepted Patricia's word with a solemn nod. "I'll hold you to that."

Patricia knew that she would.

Later that evening, as she tied an apron around her waist at her second job as a waitress, Patricia tried to convince herself that it was a moot promise anyway.

It wasn't like they were going to have a lot of opportunities to interact outside of a strict teacher-and-father relationship. By the time Clara graduated from preschool, he would undoubtedly have been snagged by one of the many interested women in town; he was too handsome to go with a cold bed for any longer than he wanted, and what did she have to offer him other than that? Though Green

Valley wasn't a wealthy town, there were certainly citizens with more means than she had. Harriette, for example, had made a respectable pile of money in real estate. The idea of Lee with Harriette set Patricia's teeth on edge, and she didn't think it was only because the odious woman had made most of that money selling family farms to developers who were planning to put up cheap condos. She was trying to buy the schoolhouse Patricia taught preschool in, and rumor had it that the horrid woman had just taken earnest money for a quaint landmark farm that she planned to have leveled to make a series of cheap, cookie-cutter houses—part of her self-announced plan to make Green Valley a bedroom community for the nearest city.

Patricia was still steaming over that idea and fantasizing ways she could buy out the schoolhouse herself as she made her rounds of the tables at Gran's Grits, the smaller of the two diners in town. The dinner rush, every one a familiar face, was a welcome distraction from her thoughts.

When she heard the bell at the door ring again, she automatically narrowed the possible customers down in her head; they were too far off the highway to attract many strangers. "Evening, Stan!" she called over her shoulder, and she was turning with a menu in hand even as she realized something was different. She knew what she would see before she actually did—was it his wild, clean smell? Or some hint of his strong step on the floor? She had to make herself not stare; Lee was somehow more handsome even than she had remembered, and once again, Clara saved her from making a fool of herself by giving her a safe place to look. Her hands knew to grab a second menu, and she was able to joke, "How nice of you to bring your father out to dinner, Clara," as she led them to a table tucked into the corner. Her hands only shook a little as she passed the menu to Lee.

"Papa can only cook pancakes," Clara explained candidly.

"Well, our special tonight is..." for a moment Patricia's mind blanked completely. 'Me on a platter, would probably be inappropriate,' she reminded herself. That wasn't what Andrea had meant about taking an opportunity that presented itself, anyway. "Chicken pot pie," she remembered just before the moment got awkward. "I recommend it."

"You're my teacher," Clara said, with her face crinkled thoughtfully as Patricia helped her clamber onto a booster seat.

"I work here, too." She gave Lee a wry look and joked, "Being a preschool teacher in a town this small for three days a week doesn't exactly cover the mortgage." She immediately wondered if it was inappropriately frank, aware of the discretely (and not-so discretely) curious looks they were getting from other tables, and vowed to be more professional. "Can I bring you some drinks?"

Lee glanced at the laminated menu. "Iced tea," he selected. "And milk for Clara."

Patricia escaped to the kitchen.

Fortunately, Old George, the order cook, was the large, quiet, non-judgmental type, and he didn't say anything about the fact that she splashed cold water on her hot face before she dispensed the drinks and headed back out to the dining room to take their order.

"Does the popeye have spinach?" Clara wanted to know when she delivered their drinks.

"Pot pie, Honey," Lee corrected.

"Popeye," Clara repeated carefully.

Patricia exchanged an amused look with Lee before she could stop herself, and only blushed a little before explaining to Clara, "No, no spinach. It's a pie crust with a cream sauce and pieces of carrot, peas, potatoes, and chunks of chicken. It has mashed potatoes on top!"

"They have hot dogs," Lee suggested, looking at the child's portion of the menu.

But Clara had been convinced. "I want popeye!" She handed Patricia her menu imperiously.

"Two orders of the special, on your fine recommendation," Lee agreed, and he gave Patricia a smile that made her insides melt.

She took the menus and retreated to put the order in and pick up a tray of plates for another table.

"Gina says Harriette says he bought the old Lawson place," Norman told her as she refilled his water and asked after his satisfaction with the meal. He could always be counted on for good gossip through his daughter. Patricia hadn't checked Lee's address in the parent database, but she gave a healthy amount of doubt to anything that came through Gina. Particularly if it came by way of Harriette.

At another table, old Mrs. Fredricks cackled and beckoned Patricia close so she could stage-whisper, "He's gorgeous, honey! If you don't give him your number, I will!" Patricia laughed at her, and gave her a hug around the shoulders because she was already leaning in.

~

*L*ee tried hard not to watch Patricia waltz around the little diner too obviously, but it was a small room, and she filled it with her golden presence. The tenderness and warmth he had witnessed with the preschool children apparently extended to people taller than three feet, and he found himself growing envious of her easy affection.

He had never been grateful for how slow Clara usually ate before, but this time, he could have kissed her for dawdling. Half a plate of pot pie became the occupation of an hour, then two. A spilled half-glass of milk took up another several minutes, and Lee considered spilling his own drink in order to watch Patricia kneel to clean up the mess with her forgiving laugh again.

The other diners gradually trickled out, until they were the only occupants of the cheerful room.

"I've never had so many dessert orders," Patricia told him, as she brought him the bill with two cello-wrapped mints. "Everyone in town wants to stay to see the most interesting little girl," she teased Clara, but she gave Lee a little half-glance that suggested it wasn't Clara who was really getting all the attention. Her cheeks colored, and she added professionally, "I'll be your cashier when you're ready to go."

Lee was used to women trying to flatter Clara to get his own attention, and he was used to them falling all over him even without her. Patricia, on the other hand, gave every indication of being attracted to him, but offered no hint of pursuit. She flirted more with the last old man to leave than she did with him, and her attention to Clara seemed completely genuine. It made the bear in him want to chase her more than ever, but he was absurdly uncertain how to do that. This was a problem he'd never encountered.

So he just watched her clear tables as he got Clara into her coat and boots, and after agonizing over the tip for a moment—would too much seem like he was trying to buy her?—he left her exactly a 15% tip on the credit card receipt, calculated to the penny.

At the door, he paused. "Thank you," he said.

Clara echoed him as he struggled to find something to add. "Thank you, Miss Patricia!"

"You're very welcome," Patricia called back. "I'll see you tomorrow!"

Then she was bustling away with their bill and the last glass, sparing him any conversation at all.

His bear wanted to chase her quite literally, but he reined in the beast and took Clara by the hand. He could be patient. He would have to be patient.

CHAPTER 4

The cheerful chime of the door alarm got Patricia's heart racing every time it sounded, even though she knew it was more likely to be one of their familiar regulars, and looking around so quickly was only giving herself whiplash. She brought extra napkins to Norman, whose hands shook more than he liked to admit these days, and gathered the dirty dishes off of Mrs Fredricks' table, shaking her head at her foolishness.

She forced herself not to look when the bell rang again as she was taking Stan's order, faced away from the door, but she couldn't keep the ridiculous hope from rising in her throat.

Turning to discover Lee standing at the entry with Clara's mittened hand in his own made her blush, and smile too broadly, and then nearly sneeze trying to get her face back under some kind of control.

"Good evening," she sang too loudly, bringing them menus and gesturing to the same table they had sat at before. "I'll be right back to tell you our specials for this evening."

She fled to the kitchen, where Old George cracked a rare smile at her when she couldn't remember what Stan had ordered.

"He came in last night, too," the cook rumbled. "Looked disappointed you weren't here."

"He's a single guy who can't cook," Patricia explained. "There aren't that many choices in town!"

George shrugged and started making Stan's usual, sending Patricia back out with a plate to deliver.

Patricia got it to the destination without problem, trying not to turn herself too obviously so that she could watch Lee's table out of the corner of her eye. She took a deep breath, then brought an iced tea and a milk to Lee's table. "We've got a chipped beef with toast tonight," she said. "It's one of George's specialties."

Lee looked bemusedly at the iced tea.

"I, ah, should have asked if you wanted that again," Patricia said, suddenly realizing that it had been presumptuous of her.

"Oh, I do!" Lee said quickly. "It's good tea. Very lemony. Not too sweet."

"There's sugar, if you want it sweeter," Patricia said, pointing out the very obvious sugar caddy at the far edge of the table, then felt ridiculous, because he'd just said that it wasn't too sweet.

"Right," Lee said.

Clara, who had been stacking her coat and mittens in the empty chair beside her, chose that beautiful moment to say, "I could add sugar to my milk!" She reached eagerly for the tin.

Lee snagged the sugar caddy and brought it out of her easy reach. "I don't think so, kitten. Milk doesn't need sugar."

"Aaron's mom says you need sugar," Clara said candidly.

Lee and Patricia both choked on their laughter, and couldn't quite meet each other's eyes.

Patricia cleared her throat, casting about for a safe topic. "We do have fresh brownies made, for dessert."

"If you eat your dinner," Lee added quickly, as Clara bounced at the idea.

"A hot dog!" Clara declared, handing the menu to Patricia. "I'll eat the whole thing!"

"I'll take the special, and hold us two brownies," Lee said, and then he did meet Patricia's eyes.

It was like basking in sunlight; his gorgeous blue eyes were something she could drown in, if she let herself. *Don't flirt, don't flirt,* Patricia told herself ferociously, though she wasn't able to keep herself from blushing. She had seen how the preschool moms had pounced on him, two days in a row now, and how coldly he had reacted. "Sounds great!" she said with a big, friendly smile that didn't invite anything more, and she didn't come back to the table until she had their plates ready.

Lee tried several times to strike up conversation, to Patricia's surprise. She answered his questions about Green Valley as simply as she could and found other tasks to pursue, reminding herself fiercely that she shouldn't attempt to draw him out, trying to balance a light friendly air with her ridiculous desire to throw herself down in his lap and beg him to kiss her.

Gran's Grits closed early, specializing in breakfast and lunch with dinner as an afterthought, so Lee and Clara were once again the last customers. Clara held true to her promise to eat the whole hot dog, but slowed drastically halfway through the big brownie. The ice cream it had been served with melted into a puddle, but she continued to nibble at it as Patricia cleared away Lee's desert plate and she brought him the copy of his receipt with his credit card.

Their hands touched as he took it, and Patricia froze. He didn't move his fingers, and when Patricia dared to lift her gaze to his face, he was looking at her with a curious, intense look. She was keenly aware of where their skin was just touching, and it wasn't until she realized that she was trembling a little that she could let go of the tray with the copy of the bill. He wasn't expecting her sudden movement, and it fell a few inches to table with a clatter that startled Clara, who had been starting to doze off in that glaze-eyed way that children could manage while still sitting upright.

"I'm tired," the little girl said plaintively, and the moment was shattered.

Lee's attention was all for Clara again, and Patricia fled to the kitchen while they bundled up in their coats and left.

CHAPTER 5

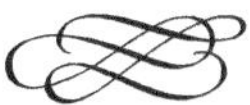

*J*ust as Lee turned off the power sander, the sound of the doorbell jarred him out of his working reverie. "Coming!" he hollered, navigating the maze of sawhorses and power tools to get to the big receiving room.

The house was a chaos of moving boxes and construction sites. Fully half of the house was still being refinished, with painter's tape on all the trim and plastic taped over the old fireplaces. Only Clara's bedroom and his own had been fully finished, as well as the bathrooms for both of them, and the kitchen downstairs, which had been gutted and combined with servant's quarters to become one big open, airy space with a breakfast nook. The outside looked worse, with the siding power-washed but not repainted before the winter had settled in. Two of the windows in the unfinished wing were boarded up. The roof was due for a full replacement, but had been temporarily patched and tarped in places, giving the house a look of utter disrepute.

Lee's frustration at being interrupted in his work turned to fear when he flung open the door and saw Patricia standing on the porch, the limp form of Clara over one shoulder, draped in a puffy orange and blue down coat dusted with snow. Behind her, big, fat flakes of snow were blanketing the yard and obscuring the view of the valley.

"Clara," Lee said, fighting past the paralyzing fear. "Clara?"

"She's fine," Patricia said swiftly, and Clara stirred and mumbled, putting her arms more firmly around her teacher's neck. "She just fell asleep on the way over."

"It's not time to pick her up yet," Lee said lamely, checking his watch to confirm. His heart rate eased only slightly at the relief of his daughter's safety; being this close to Patricia made him feel all undone and filled with need. His bear growled inappropriate suggestions at him.

"It's snowing like the apocalypse," Patricia explained, carrying Clara in gently. When Lee went to take her, trying not to be distracted by the delicious warm scent of snow melting in Patricia's hair, Clara buried her head further into Patricia's shoulder and protested wordlessly. "We canceled the last half of school today. I tried to call, but it went straight to voicemail. The roads were getting so bad, I wanted to get her home while we could still make it."

Lee remembered the blinking red battery symbol on the phone when he'd hung up with his sister Bella. He hadn't put it back on the charger. "We haven't gotten a landline yet," he said apologetically.

"You, ah, seem to have a bit of a work in progress here," Patricia said diplomatically.

"Clara's room is finished," he said defensively.

When another attempt to remove Clara from Patricia's shoulder met sleepy protest, he said, "Bring her this way," just as Patricia said, "Maybe I should put her into bed..."

The grand front steps had not been refinished yet, but the upper hall had been, and Lee was gratified when Patricia stepped into Clara's room and said with a little gasp, "Oh!"

Lee had spared no expense on the room, and had let Clara take a role in the decoration. She had picked a mermaid theme, one that Lee wholeheartedly approved of. The walls were teal blue and white, with decals of tropical fish, coral, and sunken treasure. The bed had a shell-shaped headboard, and a shimmery bedspread of blue. A windowseat as broad as her bed was cluttered with seashell pillows and an enormous knitted red squid. Short bookshelves lined one wall, filled with books and coloring books and bins of crayons and blocks. There was a dollhouse in one corner, and a riding-size excavator and dumptruck, but the current feature of the room was a battered moving box with a door and several windows cut out. Childish artwork adorned every wall and part of the roof, and a small table (another moving box) was inside and spread out for tea with a lace tablecloth. Across the room, white doors were open to show a walk-in closet and a glimpse at a private bath.

Patricia took her armful to the bed as Lee drew the curtains shut, and she peeled off Clara's boots and laid her down. Lee, watching her helplessly, could only marvel at how perfect and wonderful it was to watch her draw the blankets up over his daughter, smoothing the comforter up around her shoulders as Clara gave a contented sigh and snuggled in. He flipped the light switch, and Patricia padded her way out by the light from a muted blue nightlight.

The click of Clara's door closing seemed to be a changing point, and if Lee had been painfully aware of her nearness in any other way, he was suddenly keenly aware of her as only a woman now—his woman. His soulmate. They were alone, in his house, and she was standing close enough that he could smell the delicate scent of her shampoo. His erection was making his utilitarian jeans uncomfortable, and he had to wrestle back the bear who was singing in his head that she was his, and to take her now.

If I make a move now, she'll run, he thought. *She needs a... subtle touch.* "I could... ah... show you the rest of the house," he offered.

Patricia looked up at him and bit her lip, her eyes shy but steady. "You could show me your bedroom," she said in a rush.

It was all the invitation Lee needed; his heart filled with triumph. He enfolded her into his arms and kissed her.

CHAPTER 6

If Patricia could bring herself to be jealous of a four-year-old girl, she might have been jealous of Clara. Her bedroom was like walking into a fairy tale fantasy, and filled with things that even grown-up Patricia would have enjoyed playing with. Four-year-old Patricia would have had raptures.

Twenty-six-year-old Patricia was having raptures at the closeness of Lee, instead. He was wearing only a tight t-shirt that hid nothing of his amazing physique, and he smelled like sawdust and sweat and manliness that was deeply distracting. Patricia tucked Clara in and retreated from the bedroom, Andrea's admonition ringing in her mind.

This was an opportunity. This was *the* opportunity. There would never be another opportunity so opportune.

Was she reading his signals wrong? Was he really attracted to her? She thought she caught his gaze lingering, wondered if he didn't smile at her just a touch more than the conversations they had deserved, but maybe she was misreading the situations.

The door to Clara's room shut with a tiny click, and they paused together. "I could... ah... show you the rest of the house?"

The way he offered, so tentatively and hopefully, gave Patricia the rest of the courage she needed. She made herself hold his gaze and brazenly offered, "You could show me the bedroom."

She had a split second to wonder at her own forwardness, then he was kissing her, pressing against the length of her, his embrace like a bear's as his mouth found her own.

Her doubts vanished with his kiss—kissed her with his whole body and being, and Patricia felt like she was being swept away in a river of passion. His erection was hard against her through the fabric of his jeans. She clutched at his shoulders helplessly, tipping her head to take as much of his kiss as she could. They collided with the wall of the hallway, and broke apart, shushing each other and giggling.

"The bedroom," Lee said breathlessly. "This way..."

They kissed and grabbed the entire length of the unadorned hall, plucking at each other's clothing as they went and running into the walls twice more before Lee opened the door to his own bedroom and they fell inside.

His hands were big and callused, but gentle and nimble, and Patricia's shirt was off before they'd made it halfway to the bed. She had his belt unfastened and was working on his jeans by the time they'd made it to the wide bed, and they paused a moment together, gasping for breath. Lee's gaze could only be classified as 'appreciative,' and Patricia didn't even try not to stare back. If anything, the tight t-shirt had only been a tease, and the physique beneath was even more delicious. His shoulders were thick with muscles, and his core rippled with abs. And as amazing and gorgeous as his body was, it was his face that continued to draw her back. He was beautiful, and his eyes were adoring in a way that made Patricia weak and wet.

"I'm not usually like this," she said, swallowing. She'd made her last boyfriend wait three weeks of dating before she'd taken off her shirt. What was it about this man that made her so crazy?

"I'm not, either," Lee said, and just the sound of his husky voice made her knees tremble.

Then he leaned in and kissed her, and it was a different kiss than the first–less passionate, but more controlled, deeper, and more meaningful. Patricia lost herself entirely in it, putting her arms around his neck and letting him lay her back down onto the silky bedspread.

He released his kiss, only to move it to her neck, which left her writhing in helpless excitement, and resumed undressing her. He unclipped her bra first, slipping it off her with reverence, and then slid a finger into the waistband of her jeans as he kissed the breasts he revealed, toying with her a moment before unbuttoning and slowly– so slowly!–unzipping her jeans. Patricia whimpered and clutched at his thick hair and broad shoulders. She wanted to beg him to hurry, but was enjoying the build-up too entirely to truly protest.

He shimmied her out of her jeans with no effort, stroking her thighs and kissing her tummy as he did so. Patricia couldn't help but squirm and screw her eyes shut to try to stem the overwhelming cascade of sensation. She must be wet right through her simple cotton panties–there was no way he couldn't notice how excited she was.

Then he paused, and her eyes flew open as he shifted on the bed. He was suddenly not moving slowly at all, but tearing off his own jeans, and releasing the huge erection she had felt earlier. She was glad that her eyes were open for the reveal– he was magnificent!–but also rather alarmed. It didn't look geometrically possible for it to fit within her. Then he was tearing her panties off and growling like an animal, the weight of him deflecting the bed around her as he straddled her, and she wanted nothing more than to take the entire thing right then.

"Please," she murmured, and he was burying himself into her with one long, slow thrust, filling her with his length and heat.

*P*atricia arched up into his advance, gasping and clawing and begging in a way that lit Lee on fire. His need for her was deep and wild, but he concentrated on her pleasure first, and was rewarded by her blistering orgasm and moan of delight within a few careful thrusts. Her cry was passionate and she tensed beautifully before relaxing in the wake of her release. He kissed her neck and shoulders, pinning her under him on the bed, but had to slow himself to an agonizingly slow speed, or risk cutting off their fun too soon with his mounting need.

She kissed him back, then rolled until she was straddling him, her luscious breasts swinging in rhythm as she took him deep inside her.

She was glorious, riding above him, matching his leisurely speed until he had wound himself into a frenzy. "If you don't stop, I'm going to—"

She only sped up, the vixen, and clutched at his shoulders as she achieved another moaning, arching orgasm, and her pleasure was the inescapable catalyst of his own sexual climax. He flung his arms out and clutched at the blankets on either side as she rode him wildly and they both came with abandon.

Patricia collapsed atop him, and Lee continued to thrust slowly in the afterglow of his pleasure until the last ripple of the orgasm was finally played out.

"Oomph," she said finally, voice husky near her ear. "I'm too heavy to lay on you like this."

In response, Lee wrapped his arms around her and held her close. He loved the feel of her curves against him, the silky touch of her skin along the whole length of his body, and wasn't willing to let her go quite yet. She didn't struggle, only gave a blissed-out sigh and snuggled closer.

"I'm not usually like this," she said, as she had earlier, and Lee chuckled.

"I'm not, either," he agreed.

But then, it wasn't every day that he made love to his soulmate, either. He rolled over so that they were side-by-side on the bedspread, and he could look directly into her face.

"This... is terribly unprofessional of me," she confessed.

"Are you sorry?" he had to ask.

Her face took on an impish expression. "Not in the slightest."

He had to cup her face in his hand and kiss her again, to see if he could taste the laughter on her lips. She kissed back with all of her earlier passion, and Lee knew that he could be ready for her again in short order. She was the most perfect armful that he had ever held, and there was a feeling of loss when she slipped away from him and went rummaging for her clothing.

"The bathroom is through that door," he indicated, and he sat up in the bed just to appreciate her graceful pad across the plush carpet.

Then he flopped back across the bed. He had to tell her. He had to explain that she was the one for him—the only one. She was his everything, for all that they'd only known each other a few short months, and he wasn't willing to let her get away.

He'd have to tell her about being a bear.

That was where he tripped up. It was an impossible conversation to have.

"I'm a bear shifter," he imagined himself saying. "I can turn into a grizzly bear." She would laugh and not believe him. Would he have to shift, and prove it? Would she react with terror and flee him? Faint on the spot? He just couldn't imagine Patricia fainting. Shooting him, maybe—she looked like the kind of farmgirl who had handled a gun before.

He'd never told anyone before—not even Clara's mother. Guilt and confusion chilled him, and he found himself rising and going to one of the unpacked moving boxes. A pile of framed photographs were stacked near the top—photos of Angela, and Clara as a baby. He hadn't been able to bring himself to hang them yet, using the state of the rest of the house as some kind of excuse for not hanging things here in the bedroom yet. He tried to tell himself he liked the austere bareness of the off-white walls with the pearly-gray carpet.

Mostly, he couldn't bear to have Angela looking at him from those walls.

This was a new house, a new start. He wanted this to be his house with Patricia, though he hadn't known that until he met her. But wasn't it unfair to Angela's memory to cut her out? Wasn't it cruel to Clara to have her mother excluded from their family walls? It felt like a terrible disservice to his brief years of marriage, and even now, years later, he had difficulty separating his grief and his guilt from his memories of joy.

CHAPTER 7

*P*atricia gave a little gasp as she went through the empty walk-in closet to the master bath. From the little hallway, it opened up into an oasis of marble and chrome. The shower door was pristine, clear glass, and there were two showerheads, one from each side. Beside it was a jetted bathtub in the corner, big enough for several people at once. A counter with two sinks ran the length of the room just opposite, and the toilet was tucked around a discrete corner. Big windows opened out over a winter wonderland of trees and snow-covered lawn.

She turned on the water and watched the windows fog with steam. It was enchanted, magical, like making love to Lee had been.

And just as impermanent.

She would shower and get dressed, then go home and then they would pretend this had never happened. It was the best possible outcome.

She showered swiftly, though she wanted to savor the delicious heat and roomy shower. Lee apparently had only a single kind of shampoo/body wash, and Patricia had no regrets lathering herself in the manly scent.

She dressed as efficiently as she had washed, but left her socks off rather than try to pull them on over her wet feet. She was drying her hair with one of the big plush towels (there was no sign of a hair-dryer and Patricia was loathe to snoop through his drawers) as she walked back to the bedroom and she had to pause in the doorway with her breath caught in her throat.

Lee was sitting at the edge of the bed looking away, his big shoulders bowed. There was a framed photograph in his hands. Patricia couldn't see the subject of the photograph, but she could guess: Clara's mother. Had she been the first since...?

The scene felt painfully intimate, and Patricia wrestled with her desire to go immediately comfort Lee, and the sad understanding that she could not, and that she was simply not part of Lee's intimate sphere. She wanted to be, she realized keenly. It wasn't just that she was irresistibly attracted to this man; she would have admired him with half the looks just for his handling of Clara, and every time they spoke, she found something new to like in him. She wanted him on levels that she'd never experienced before, and always thought she never would. Her friends would talk about true love and settling down, but she had never wanted to, until Lee. Now, unexpectedly, she wanted nothing more.

She chewed on her lower lip, then crept backwards several steps. If she couldn't be his everything, she could be the best for him that she could at least, and that meant letting him keep his dignity. She started humming, and was whistling by the time she came back into the doorway so that he had a chance to toss the photograph back into the box and sit up straight.

"What a shower," she gushed, as if she hadn't witnessed a thing. "That whole bathroom is a work of art. You must have spent a fortune on that room alone!"

He looked uncomfortable—Patricia couldn't decide if it was because he knew he'd been caught in his moment of vulnerability, or because she was talking about money again like an idiot.

She clamped her mouth around her desire to babble moronically and tried to simply appreciate the view. That wasn't too hard—he was lounging in unselfconscious nudity, and his muscles were ripples of masculinity under a layer of perfect, barely-tanned skin.

She was sorely tempted to tear off her clothing and go diving back into that bed again.

"I should... ah..." Not undress and throw myself at him again... "Be leaving. Before the snow gets too deep to get home."

Lee was standing up now, and he was as impressive upright as he was reclining across the sheets. "I fear you are too late for that," he said apologetically, with a gesture towards the window.

The snow was coming down in a soft curtain now, too thick to see even to where the driveway curved. Patricia's car was already blanketed in nearly a foot of snow. "Oh gosh, it's pretty," she said. "Like a dream." Lee was close behind her, smelling like sex and forest and wildness, and he was part of the whole crazy dream.

He put his hands on her shoulders—hands, strong hands, *sexy* hands, and said in a voice like chocolate, "I suspect you are stuck here for a little while, at least."

"Papa! Papa!"

Clara's voice from down the hall had them scrambling apart. Lee dressed himself so swiftly that Patricia was still trying to figure out what to do with her own hands when he was back in his clothing and striding out the door.

"Miss Patricia brought me home!" Clara said enthusiastically when they met in the hallway, her blonde curls rumpled from her nap. "And it's snowing white! It never snowed white at home!"

Patricia chuckled. "It didn't snow *white*?"

"Only gray! Everything was dirty!" Clara seemed utterly nonplussed to find that her teacher was still there, hair still damp from a shower, and took her hand with authority. "Can I need a snack and go play in the white snow?"

"I think that's a remarkably good idea," Lee agreed. "Let's go show Miss Patricia the kitchen."

CHAPTER 8

$\mathcal{L}$ee and Patricia walked with Clara between them down the stairs and back to the sprawling kitchen. He couldn't keep himself from glancing over, watching the profile of her smiling face as she entertained Clara's endless prattle.

His mate.

There was bone-deep contentment just being close to her, knowing that she was his. All of his earlier concerns and worries were swept away in the simple peace of her presence.

Her delight in the kitchen was almost (but not quite!) as rewarding as her delight in his body had been. Clara gave her a gabby tour, opening every cabinet in her reach and pointing out all of the others.

"The blender is there, I'm not allowed to touch it and it's very loud. That's a mixer! I'm allowed to play with the plastic things in here."

Patricia was a rapt audience. "Oh, that's lovely! What a beautiful plate! Such soft towels!"

She said more seriously to Lee, "This kitchen is a cook's fantasy, Mr. Montgomery. If I had designed my dream kitchen straight from scratch, it could not have been more perfect." She actually squealed a little when she saw the heavy-duty mixer.

"I've never used it, but I asked our cook to make a list of everything he wanted in a kitchen," he explained, half-apologetically as he stacked up a few dirty dishes from lunch that he hadn't washed yet.

"Your cook had excellent taste," Patricia said, with delight.

"In all things but choosing to stay in the city," Lee agreed. "We'll have a housekeeper in a few weeks, I hope," he added apologetically, aware of his dirty lunch dishes and the sawdust footprints he had tracked into the kitchen.

Clara got herself a plate with a pile of peanut butter and an apple, which Patricia cut into careful wedges for her, exclaiming over the high-quality chef's knife. Clara settled herself in the booster cushion at the kitchen table.

"There is a formal dining room," Lee explained. "But we're still waiting for the dining set to be delivered."

When Clara had finished eating, graciously sharing her last two slices with Lee and Patricia, she insisted on showing Patricia the rest of the house.

Their last stop was after a full circle back to the dining room. "We'll eat here when we have a table," Clara explained, tugging Patricia through the doorway. Lee followed them. "This is my favorite room! Except for my own room. And Papa's room. And the kitchen."

"I can see why," Patricia said without sounding patronizing. It was a big, empty room with a hardwood floor. The only furniture was a built-in sidebar and a single padded bench that had been put there temporarily. "It's such a lovely, big room. It's perfect for dancing! I bet you dance here all the time."

Cornflower eyes blinked up at her. "I don't know how to dance."

"Don't know how to dance?" Patricia looked genuinely alarmed at the idea. "How can you not know how to dance?"

"I never took classes for it." Clara looked at Lee for guidance.

Patricia's laugh was reassuring. "You don't need classes, sweetheart! You just dance from inside! Everyone is born knowing how to dance!" She held out her hand to Clara. "Come dance with me!"

Clara hung back. "There isn't any music," she said, but she looked hopeful, and interested. It gave Lee a pang of guilt. Perhaps he should have insisted on lessons earlier.

Patricia pulled her phone out of her pocket, opened the music program, and put it on the sideboard. The music was terribly tinny, and it sounded like an old-time radio. She offered a hand to Clara.

This time, Clara took Patricia's hand, and a slow smile bloomed on her face. "Can Papa dance, too?"

"Of course he can!" Patricia met Lee's eyes with dancing mischief and held out her other hand to him.

"Oh, no, I..."

Patricia was already pulling Lee into the middle of the room.

"No, really, I can't..."

"It isn't rocket science," Patricia promised laughingly. "You just move around to the beat!"

Clara was willing to do what he was willing to do, so Lee followed Patricia's lead obediently, suspecting at once that she was making things more ridiculous than they needed to be. They bounced and wiggled and twisted their hips–shy at first and awkward, then looser and more joyous to match Patricia as she teased and encouraged them.

They did silly moves–twist and the moonwalk–and Patricia showed Clara the first two ballet positions to a pop version of the nutcracker.

The phone went to a slow ballad, and Patricia showed Clara how to waltz with her little bare feet on Patricia's bare feet.

Delighted, Clara danced a round of the room with Lee in the same fashion, and then gave him over to Patricia expectantly.

Lee took one hand and put his other at her waiting waist, suddenly feeling awkward. "I really don't dance," he protested, despite their antics of moments ago.

"Not on my feet, you don't," Patricia laughed at him. Her cheeks were bright with exertion, and her hair was drying from her shower in soft, golden waves around her face.

She led him patiently around the room, praising his rhythm, and correcting his form. He stumbled over her feet several times, but she only laughed off his apologies. He grew braver as they danced, holding her closer and finding it easier to sway to the beat. The smell of her, and the warmth of her close against him filled him with contentment and joy.

He could have continued to hold onto Patricia much longer, but Clara wanted another turn balanced on his feet, and he carefully cavorted her around the room again, feeling more effortless about it with every bar of music.

Finally, Lee and Patricia collapsed together on the bench by the wall. The intimacy and energy of the dancing made it natural to sit leaning close together, and he wove his hand into hers without thinking about it. Clara continued to jump and spin in giddy delight.

"Never danced!" Patricia said, shaking her head in astonishment. "You're a natural," she praised.

"I want to dance for always," Clara said, pure joy in every line of her body.

Lee didn't realize he was scowling or squeezing Patricia's hand too tightly until he caught her quizzical look, but he wasn't prepared to explain why the simple statement hit him so hard.

"It's almost time for dinner," he deflected.

"Can Miss Patricia stay for dinner?" Clara stopped dancing and asked, her voice already taking on a whine in preparation for a fight.

"Miss Patricia is stuck here for the night, sweetie," Lee explained. "There's too much snow outside for her to drive home." He gestured at the window, where the evening gloom had a strange snowy brightness.

Clara squealed in absolute delight, flinging herself into Patricia's lap for a big hug and then leaning across her for a bonus hug from Lee. "She can stay in Aunt Bella's room," she suggested happily, sprawled bonelessly across their laps with the ease of a small child.

"Yes, of course," Lee and Patricia said in unison, just a little too fast. They glanced at each other and Lee felt a smile tug at the corner of his mouth. Her answering smile was a delicious promise of things to come.

Lee had never been so grateful to the weather.

"Let me cook for you?" Patricia offered, untangling her fingers from Lee's. "As a thank you for your... hospitality." She blushed beautifully.

CHAPTER 9

atricia had not exaggerated her appreciation for Lee's kitchen. Everything was thoughtfully laid out on broad counters. A whole series of beautiful knives, perfectly sharpened, was just out of easy child's reach, and she had her choice of gorgeous hardwood cutting boards.

She found a beautiful set of high-end spices, and was unsurprised that none of them except the garlic had been unsealed. The refrigerator revealed a gallon of milk and a wealth of condiments, but few useable perishables. A few plastic take-out containers were stacked in one corner. An investigation of the pantry discovered a selection of canned vegetables, pastas, and staples. Patricia suspected by their perfect organization that they had not been touched. An untidy row of macaroni and cheese boxes suggested what they usually ate.

After puzzling over the ingredients for a while, Patricia put together a spaghetti sauce from a can of tomatoes, some frozen breakfast sausages, and a sad forgotten bell pepper from the bottom of the crisper. Clara danced around her feet while she cooked, asking to see and smell everything, and Lee sat at the table, watching her move around the kitchen with unsettling—but strangely comfortable—attention. She boiled the noodles, and toasted garlic toast under the broiler.

He set the table, with Clara's help, and when she set the plates in front of them, they both gushed their pleasure and delight. She sat at the third space at the table, and they merrily shared the meal together.

"I had no idea there was anything so... edible that could be made from these ingredients," Lee confessed, mopping the last of his sauce from the plate. "I'm not sure how to thank you."

Patricia loved how relaxed his face was. There was no trace of the scowl that seemed to be his usual default expression with other people, only warm smiles and dancing blue eyes. "Maybe tomorrow you can make me pancakes," she suggested. She smiled at Clara. "I've heard so much about them."

"It's a deal," Lee said.

Sharing in Clara's night time routine seemed perfectly natural. The little girl had her own mermaid-themed bathroom, with a shell-shaped tub just her size. After a bath heaped with bubbles, she toweled herself off and insisted that it was Miss Patricia who helped her into her fuzzy-footed pajamas.

"I wish I had footy-pajamas with kitties on them," Patricia said with only mostly-mock envy.

"What do you sleep in?" Clara asked innocently.

Patricia had to bite her lip and studiously not look at Lee. She couldn't exactly admit she liked to sleep naked.

Lee didn't help matters. "Good question, Sweetie," he said, straight-faced. Humor danced in his eyes. "What DO you sleep in, Miss Patricia?"

Patricia was beginning to suspect that there was pure mischief behind the scowl that Lee had cultivated. Well, two could play that game. "Not a stitch," she admitted brazenly, looking right at him. "I figure if I can't wear fuzzy-footed kitty-cats, why wear anything?"

Clara seemed nonplussed by the idea, but Patricia took great glee in watching the tips of Lee's ears turn pink.

It was Lee that tucked Clara into bed, and Patricia retreated to the hall so they could read their favorite book together and share a quiet, murmured conversation before Lee pulled the covers up to her chin, kissed her on the brow, and turned off her bedside light.

He shut her door with a careful click, and Patricia's heart melted at the tender look on his face. He loved that little girl more than the moon. The look didn't fade as he held Patricia's gaze, and the moment grew more tense.

Patricia found herself blushing. "This is... er... familiar. Didn't we do this just this afternoon?"

"I hope we'll do this many more times," Lee said, voice husky as he gathered her into his arms and kissed her.

Patricia's heart leapt in her chest at the idea. He wanted to see her again! This wasn't a one-freak-snowstorm affair, but maybe something more... She caught herself short at the idea. Just because he wanted to continue their relationship didn't indicate he meant that relationship as more than just a comfort of the body. She was probably just... convenient.

"I think you should get into what you sleep in, too," Lee suggested, and his kiss slipped down to her neck. Patricia stopped thinking about pesky relationship thoughts and let him lead her down the hallway to his bedroom.

"Won't I be sleeping in Aunt Bella's room?" she suggested mischievously, pausing at his door.

Lee drew back from kissing her and scowled in a now-familiar way. "Do you *want* to sleep in Bella's room?"

Patricia wrapped her arms around his neck. "Not in the slightest," she laughed at him.

To her astonishment, he picked her up, without the slightest hint of effort, and carried her to his waiting bed, nudging the door shut behind him with one foot.

He undressed her efficiently, but paused at each layer of clothing. "Is this what you sleep in?" he would ask.

Patricia pretended to consider it. "A little bit less," she encouraged.

He kissed her, wherever was closest, and peeled off another

layer. Patricia couldn't decide if she was glad for the Midwest winter encouraging her to wear so many layers, or if she cursed it.

But the time he got to her underwear, she was quivering with anticipation and desire. He slid a finger into the waistband. "Is this what you sleep in?" he asked, mouth close to her stomach.

"A little bit less," Patricia said breathlessly.

He drew off the simple white underwear—she was too distracted to wish she had dressed with more care that morning, but how could she have anticipated this kind of a snow day!—and kissed her mound, tongue flickering inside her and making her arch up in an agony of desire and need.

"Oh, *Lee*," she said, and she loved the way his simple name tasted in her mouth almost as much as she loved the way he felt teasing her with his tongue.

He coaxed a long, delicious orgasm from her with his lapping thrusts, and when she could see straight again, Patricia tipped up on her elbows and demanded, "And what do you plan on sleeping in, Mr. Montgomery?"

Lee pulled his shirt off with one deft move. "I like your choice of attire," he said with a slow, sexy smile.

Patricia helped him pull off his pants and free the erection that she'd been dying to see again. She wrapped bold fingers around it, and delighted in the involuntary gasp that he gave. She stroked it gently, and explored it with fingertips, observing which motions set his jaw to clenching, curious to see how much teasing he could take.

He growled at her, finally, and tilted her back onto the waiting bed with a slow, tender pressure.

Patricia lifted her hips to meet him, and he slipped into her waiting entrance, filling her slowly, irresistibly, until she cried out and clawed at the blankets in an agony of delight.

He brought her to orgasm, then slowed as the ripples of pleasure ebbed away, thrusting gently and smiling in self-satisfaction as she recovered. She had to laugh at his expression, then pulled him down and tumbled sideways with him until she was on top and could take control of the situation herself. There was so much strength in him, that he had to let her do it, and she was equal parts delighted by this and challenged by it.

She straddled him with authority, riding him enthusiastically, but careful not to let him get too close to release. He held her waist, explored her swinging breasts, and even reached up to cradle her face as they pulsed together. Patricia forgot her plan to keep him thirsting for her, and lost herself in the flames of passion, cresting to another orgasm just as he sped up and took his own final pleasure, hot seed erupting in her.

They lay together, gasping for breath and balance, for a long, delicious moment. He continued to caress her, bringing the love-making to a beautiful trailing end that Patricia had never known could be.

"Tell me about yourself," Lee said, stroking her hair. "I want to know everything."

Patricia stirred so that she could look at him in surprise. This wasn't the kind of intimacy she had expected from him. It wasn't the sort of opening that usually came with casual sex. She squashed the idea that he might be thinking about something more than casual sex. That would be ridiculous.

"I grew up in Green Valley," she said finally. "A country girl to the heart. I went to the twin cities for college, took some dance classes, got a teaching degree, had to come running back."

"You took dance?"

Patricia wasn't sure how she should take the surprise in his voice. "Not that you'd know it from our dancing this evening, I know," she laughed sheepishly, choosing humor over getting offended, though it occurred to her that it would be easy to take his words the other way. "I don't have the figure for it, of course, but I love the art."

Lee was quiet, so Patricia had to fill the silence with something or think too hard about what couldn't possibly be.

"I started the Hands and Hearts Preschool after a few years of teaching middle school. There's not much of a market for it, of course—I've only got eight full-time students this year, and that's two more than last. It doesn't do much more than hire Andrea and pay the classroom rent, so I waitress on the side. I'd make more at

Hardy's, but the skirts they make the staff wear there wouldn't reflect well on being a preschool teacher, so I work at the cafe."

She was babbling about *money* again, Patricia realized. Before she could stop herself, she had asked, "What about you? You aren't just a construction worker with McDonald Company."

CHAPTER 10

$\mathcal{L}$ee tried not to squirm. He had known this question was coming, and he wasn't sure how to handle it. Money was one of those tricky subjects that seemed to embarrass her when she brought it up, and while he knew that she didn't have much of her own, he knew that earning her own was a matter of pride. "No," he admitted.

"So... you own it?"

"No, I own the company that owns it."

Patricia thought about that. "That's some conglomerate, right? D.C.L? D.M.L?"

"D.L.C. Contracting," Lee said, then added. "And no, I own the company that owns that. Also, a factory in Milwaukee and a small financial firm in Duluth."

"Oh," Patricia said dryly. "Only, a small financial firm, though."

Lee did squirm then, relishing the feeling of her bare skin against his as he did. "Well, medium-sized, I suppose. Large for Duluth, maybe."

Patricia buried her face in the pillow and Lee was alarmed when her shoulders began shaking. Was she angry? He put a tentative hand on her shoulder, and she lifted her face from the pillow to let a whoop of laughter out.

Bemused, Lee watched as she chortled with abandon, laughing until tears rolled down her cheeks. "I had no idea financial firms were so entertaining," he said, mystified, and he recognized that he was frowning at her.

"They aren't," Patricia agreed, wiping her cheeks. The exertion of sex and laughter made her face glow. "It's just... I..."

She had to smother her hoots of laughter in the pillow again, while Lee helplessly patted her, not sorry for the excuse to keep his hands on her. He eventually had to laugh with her, even though he wasn't sure of the joke.

She finally managed to get her breath under control and told him, eyes dancing, "I brought you scholarship paperwork."

Lee felt dim. "Scholarship paperwork?" She wanted him to sponsor a scholarship?

"Well," Patricia explained, looking sheepish now. "You drove that beat up truck, and Clara was wearing short pants and no boots. I thought you might have trouble covering the tuition."

Lee cast his memory back. Clara had been so adamant about her choice of pants and shoes that first day. He hadn't considered that they had been her favorites for some time, and that she had grown in that time and that although they were clean, and hadn't been cheap, they were starting to look worn. "I let Clara pick her own clothes," he explained, sounding more defensive than he meant.

"It's okay," Patricia said hastily. "Most kids have favorites! You just... don't look like a millionaire, you know." She propped up on an elbow and gave him a stern look that was belied by her dancing eyes. "And you don't tip like one, either. 15%? *Really?*"

Lee put his hands behind his head and played along with a lofty sniff. "I'm not a millionaire, I'm a billionaire. And I should have tipped 10%. We had to wait a good five minutes for a refill on that milk we spilled."

"You're lucky I didn't land that second glass in your lap," Patricia countered with a sniff of her own.

"You could have licked it up, if you had," Lee suggested. "That would have gotten you a better tip."

Patricia giggled and sat up so she could hit him with the pillow. "Dirty mind!"

The pillow hit was all the invitation that Lee need to sit up and wrestle her back down onto the bed with kisses and caresses. Patricia kissed back, unquenched passion in her mouth and hands, until she had to break away from him in giggles again.

"What's so funny?" Lee asked, kissing her ear.

"Harriette Ambler!"

Lee pulled away in puzzlement. "What about her?"

"She fancies herself the local robber baron," Patricia explained. "She works in real estate, and she's going to be devastated to realize that she's a pauper compared to you."

Lee shuddered. "That horrible woman with the bright purple Chrysler and the impractical shoes."

"That's the one. I hope she decides being second best in a town this small is intolerable and leaves before she does more damage here."

"Damage? More than being an eyesore with that car?"

Some of the life unexpectedly drained out of Patricia—everything about her was so irrepressibly expressive that Lee could practically read her moods in the pores of her skin.

"I mentioned she was in real estate," she explained sadly. "She specializes in selling off historical properties to developers. She has aspirations of making Green Valley a bedroom community for Milwaukee. There's talk that she's buying old Gertie's farm to put in a membership warehouse, and she's trying to buy the schoolhouse I rent."

"I'm a developer," Lee reminded her, driven to honesty by Patricia's transparent distress. "But turning Green Valley into a sea of cheap apartments and box stores is an appalling idea." He didn't have to exaggerate his reaction.

Patricia's head tilted as she focused a thoughtful gaze on him. "You didn't bulldoze this old place to build something new and perfect."

"I love old buildings," Lee explained. "And I moved here so that Clara could grow up in a small town, not an extended city suburb. I want to build her a treehouse, and let her run wild in the woods when she's older." If Clara was a shifter like he was, that would be more important than he could easily explain.

"I hope Green Valley still is that small, quiet town when she's older," Patricia said, settling back into the pillows.

"I could make sure that it is," Lee was spurred to declare. "I can keep developers from buying any more here, and stop construction on anything that's in progress. There are some restoration projects two towns over that could suddenly need the company resources more urgently. If they aren't mine, I know people who can get them moved. I know the company owners of two of the major membership warehouses and could convince them to look elsewhere for their expansions."

Patricia sat up again, astonished eyes dancing and a new, hopeful smile tugging at her lips. "You can DO that?"

Lee gave a practiced nonchalant smile. "It's done."

"I never thought I'd find that kind of power sexy," Patricia said, new laughter in her voice.

"But..." Lee prompted her.

Patricia rolled onto her hands and knees and growled playfully through her loose hair, "It's the sexiest thing I've ever heard in my life. Roar!"

The growl, and her seductive look, brought his bear roaring to the surface, and Lee growled in reply before he could stop himself. If anything, she looked aroused by his response, and snapped her teeth suggestively at him. He could no longer keep his hands off of her, and reached out to gather her close.

*P*atricia tumbled into Lee's arms with delight, relishing the strength in his shoulders and arms. He lifted her to straddle him with ease, and she could already feel him engorging again, his thick member rising to brush the insides of her thighs as she playfully nibbled at his neck and ears.

He rumbled right back at her, and his hands at her waist pulled her closer, until he was teasing her entrance. Before he claimed her, though, he rolled her over so that he was spanning her, kissing her neck and her jaw, keeping himself tantalizingly just out of reach as he caressed her skin and bit at her collarbone as if he were barely in control of himself.

Patricia groaned and caught herself clawing at his shoulders desperately—she couldn't think around the desire that was welling up in her. She writhed, pressing her hips up at him, and he teased her more, pressing at her waiting, wet lips but not entering.

"Please..." she heard, and realized it was her own voice, rough and needy.

When he finally took possession of her, filling her deliciously, she had to bite her lip to keep from crying out in abandon. The taste of blood was iron on her tongue.

Then he was kissing it off of her, his tongue tangling with hers as he filled her and retreated, thrust after thrust, her orgasms a dizzy cascade of pleasure.

Lee stopped and withdrew abruptly, breathing hard and clawing the sheets. Patricia soothed him, stroking his sides and kissing his face while he regained control of himself. Impulsively, she tumbled him over and took the top position, precariously near the edge of the bed. She gasped as Lee took them one circle further, catching her and flipping her over to kneel in the plush carpet at the edge of the bed. She was sprawled leaning over the bed, and he was kneeling behind her, pressing irresistibly at her nether mouth. She was still unexpectedly hungry for him, even still hazy from her orgasms.

He pressed into her slick waiting lips with a little groan of passion, and they were moving together as one, relishing this new position of possession and release.

He came at last, just as Patricia discovered new heights of physical joy, and the sheets were dragged from the bed by their grasping hands.

For a long, gasping moment, they simply collapsed there beside the bed, tangled in sheets and sweat and the sweet fluids of their lovemaking. Slow hands trailed over each other; Patricia could not get enough of the hills and valleys of his muscles, even so fully sated as she was.

"And you think you aren't a dancer," Lee said near her ear, and there was something that Patricia couldn't identify in his voice.

She had to giggle, languidly, and answer, "I said everyone is a dancer at heart. Especially when the music is right." For now, the music was his heartbeat, hammering near her ear and rattling through her own body because they were so tightly entwined. He squeezed her breath away, then gently untangled her from the sheets and helped her up.

Patricia flowed up into his arms and kissed him, feeling graceful and liquid. "I noticed that your shower has two showerheads..." she suggested. She didn't want to stop touching him, and didn't, through an entire steamy shower. They soaped each other, and rinsed each other, and dried each other, carefully, then fell naked into bed where they snuggled in to snatch a few precious hours of sleep.

～

*L*ee woke to an armful of delight. His bear was as contented as he was, for the first time in a very long time, and he still felt deliciously sated after their active night.

Patricia stirred, and mumbled something into her pillow.

"Hmmm?" Lee asked her, cradling her close.

"Pancakes," Patricia repeated. "You promised pancakes and I'm *starving*!"

He was too, now that she had vocalized it, and it was possibly the only thing that could have driven him out of bed. He reluctantly let go of her and rolled out of bed.

Sunlight was streaming through the gap in the curtains, and Patricia put a pillow over her head when he opened them wide to look out. The snow had stopped during the night, and the entire world was blanketed with white, downy serenity.

"I think it snowed two feet," Lee said in wonder.

"Pancakes!" Patricia reminded him from underneath her pillow. She was probably used to snow.

If the snow didn't impress her, the pancakes did. Lee managed not to embarrass himself, mixing the ingredients and cooking them each on the skillet to golden perfection.

Patricia, dressed in her own jeans with one of Lee's big shirts belted over it, repeatedly expressed her delight, and ravenously downed a stack smothered with syrup.

"I told you they were good," Clara said smugly. But she had to be coaxed back to her chair to eat them several times—she was more enthralled by the snowy scenery out the window, and the prospect of playing in it.

They had barely put down their forks before she was dragging them to the door to go out, not even interested in making the bubbles to wash up.

But when the door finally closed behind them, Clara wasn't sure what to do, and she stood on the porch in her crinkling snowsuit blinking at the bright vista.

"Let's make a snowman!" Patricia suggested at once, and waded fearlessly out into the snow.

Clara took Lee's gloved hand and followed her, floundering in the tall snow. She helped roll up the snowman's base, and patted it carefully into shape, slowly taking the role of director as the snowman grew too tall for her to reach.

"The head is crooked!" she pointed out, after it had been heaved into place.

Patricia struggled to remedy that to his daughter's satisfaction, while Lee went back into the house to find a scarf and hat. "We need a carrot for the nose!" Clara called after him imperiously. "And coal for the eyes!"

"I don't think we have those things!" Lee warned her from the porch, but he gamely went inside to try to find them.

Cubed frozen carrots from a package of mixed vegetables weren't going to meet her demands, he decided, so he brought a piece of scrap trim for a nose and two washers from his workbench for eyes. An extra scarf from Clara's closet was obtained, and one of his own baseball hats, when he couldn't find an extra wool hat.

When he returned, Clara and Patricia were standing back from the snowman, looking at it critically. Lee's offerings were considered by his daughter carefully, and deemed acceptable.

The resulting snowman was still lopsided, but Clara gave a pleased smile, and agreed that he would do. "I like snow!" she told Lee seriously. "I want it to snow always!"

"I'm going to remind you that you said that someday, and you'll deny it," Lee predicted.

Patricia laughed, of course, and dragged Clara off to make snow angels.

The sound of their laughter together was impossibly familiar, like Lee had been waiting his entire life to hear it.

CHAPTER 12

*P*atricia looked up at the sky, sweeping her arms to make angel wings in the fluffy snowbank.

"Like this?" asked Clara.

Patricia had to struggle to sit up in the loose snow. "That's perfect, Honey! She looks beautiful!"

"How do I get uuuupppp?" Clara wailed, giggling and thrashing.

Chuckling, Patricia went to help her up, then tossed her, shrieking with laughter, into another snowbank, then dived in after her. Laughing and swimming through the snow together, Patricia tickled her and rolled her in hugs.

They lay cuddled together for a long moment once their laughter had worn out.

"Do you think my Momma is an angel now?" Clara asked, unexpectedly.

"I bet she is," Patricia said carefully, sitting up with her. "The most beautiful angel ever."

"She was beautiful," Clara agreed. "I've seen pictures."

Patricia glanced over to where Lee, out of earshot, was clearing off her car and shoveling around it. "You don't remember her?"

"She died when I was a baby," Clara said gravely. "She was sick for a long time and they couldn't make her okay."

Patricia hugged her tight. "I'm sure she loved you very much and was sad to go."

"Papa was very sad, too," Clara observed, and Patricia had no answer for that.

They sat together in the snow for some time, watching Lee together. Far away, there was the grating sound of big equipment along the road. "What's that?" Clara asked.

'The sound of the end to my winterland fantasy,' Patricia didn't say out loud. "That's the snowplows! They are down there clearing all the snow off of the roads so that it's safe to drive again!" It was already above freezing, and the snow was warm and soft. Perfect for... "You know what we should do?" she said quietly near Clara's ear.

The little girl froze, sensing a conspiracy. "What?"

Patricia made a snowball in her gloved hands and looked suggestively at Lee, whose back was to them.

"Oh!" Clara said loudly, then clapped a mittened hand over her mouth. Over it, her eyes danced in anticipation and she nodded.

Together, they made a small arsenal of snowballs, gathered in Patricia's hat. If Lee noticed their preparations, he gamely pretended not to, so that when they staged their attack with a warrior's whoop and a flurry of ill-aimed snowballs, he was taken entirely by surprise and staggered back under the onslaught.

Patricia got at least a few good snowballs to hit him, and a few of Clara's landed close enough to splash him as they fell apart.

"I'm under attack!" he hollered gamely, pretending to be mortally wounded. "Yetis from the north with their deadly snowballs!" Undeterred, he scooped up an answering round of snowballs, hitting gently, but with far more precision at Clara's shoulders. She laughed and ran behind the car. Patricia ducked one that would have hit her face, and returned one to his chest, exploding in powder.

As she retreated behind the car with Clara, Lee called, "Get her,

Clara!" and the traitor unleashed an enthusiastic rain of tiny snowballs on her unexpectedly.

"Whose side are you on?" she demanded, turning back to find herself cornered by Lee. She couldn't help giggling and being a little deliciously terrified as he descended on her, sweeping her up in his arms and tossing her into a snowbank with ease. "I won't go down easy!" she protested, and she tossed a snowball right into his face as she laughed and struggled up.

Clara danced around at his feet. "Toss me, Papa! Toss me!"

Lee obliged, then gave each of them a hand as the rumbling machinery in the distance grew louder, and a truck with a plow and the markings of Lee's business appeared at the curve of the driveway, pushing a modest wall of snow before it. Clara took each of their hands as Patricia tried to smooth down her parka and look a little less like she had just been rolling in the snow with unprofessional abandon.

"Do you have to go now?" Clara asked, carefully pulling them back from the big truck.

Patricia met Lee's eyes briefly and had to look away. "Yes, Sweetie," she said, trying to mask her regret. "It's time for me to go to my home now that the road is clear."

Clara let go of Lee's hand to wrap both of her arms around Patricia's knees. "I hope you come back soon," she said mournfully.

"So do I," said Lee, unexpectedly, and Patricia looked up into his face in surprise and sudden joy.

"Well," she said, smiling slowly. "I'll need to return your shirt."

CHAPTER 13

Patricia dumped the blocks back into the big bin, enjoying the noisy percussion over the radio that was playing refreshingly grown-up music as she and Andrea cleaned up the room and prepped for the next day's work.

"I'm so glad you took my advice," Andrea said smugly, tossing another stray block from where she was sweeping behind the craft tables.

"Which advice was that?" Patricia feigned innocence.

"The advice about Clara's gorgeous dad," Andrea said, not fooled. "Look at you! You haven't been this happy and relaxed since you opened this circus!" Another block arced to follow the first into the bin.

"I probably shouldn't," Patricia confessed, smiling foolishly and denying nothing. "It's not exactly professional..."

Andrea snorted. "It's not like you're *his* teacher," she said dismissively. "And it's not like you were even chasing him like half the rest of this town, either."

Patricia found that she was hugging the teddy bear she had just picked up and put it back on the bench with the others before she could indulge in dancing around with it. "No, but..."

"No buts!" Andrea said, flinging another block across the room. This one missed and bounced onto the floor. "You deserve a little happiness," Andrea said emphatically.

"Well, keep quiet about it," Patricia said. "I'm sure it will be over with the semester, and the last thing I want to do is give those harpies more to gossip about."

"Too late for that," Andrea said with no sympathy. "Mrs. Harrison saw you leaving his place last week, and told her hairdresser, who told Sabrina, so now everyone knows. You should have seen the way Harriette was glaring at you when she left with Trevor."

"Uuuugggghhhh," Patricia moaned. "I was hoping not to get *her* attention."

"She's got to have some vent for her frustration. Sabrina says that her real estate deals are falling through like it's going out of fashion, and she's lost buckets of money because Gertie wouldn't sell. So what have you found out about Clara's mother?" Andrea dumped her dustpan into the trash and came to lean in towards Patricia conspiratorially.

If the idea of Harriette's jealousy had left Patricia feeling cold, the mention of Lee's dead wife left her chest aching. "She died when Clara was a baby, and she was sick. That's all I know." It was a lie of omission. She also knew Lee still loved her.

"You haven't found anything other than that out in nearly a month?" Andrea scoffed, clearly not impressed with her investigative skills.

"Lee doesn't really want to talk about her, and it's not an easy subject to bring up with him. Not that we're doing a lot of... talking."

Andrea giggled in appreciation for that, and then suggested, "What about Clara? Doesn't she know anything about her mother?"

"Are you really suggesting I pump a four-year-old for information?"

Andrea's green eyes sparkled with mischief. "Why else even be a preschool teacher? The little devils are ripe for providing the very best in high grade gossip. Wave a cookie in front of their nose, and they'll bring you all the skeletons from the closets."

Patricia clipped the lid onto the last toy bin and shoved it into place. "You're unbelievable, Andrea," she said with a reluctant laugh.

"Fine, fine," Andrea said, returning the broom to its corner and flipping the switch for the overhead lights. "I'll have to do my own investigation, then."

"Have fun, Sherlock," Patricia retorted. "But don't drag me into your sordid curiosity!"

She turned off the last lights and pulled the door shut behind her. She was curious, yes, but the ghost of Angela was too painful to face, knowing that Lee still loved her.

~

*P*atricia had all but forgotten Andrea's threat to investigate, so she was surprised when Andrea pressed two printouts into her hands during a lull in the preschool set up. At first, it made no sense to her. The first was a flyer for a prestigious ballet, a waifish figure in white standing on toe. The name, Angel Barrette, meant nothing to Patricia.

"What's this?"

"That's Clara's mother," Andrea said, something like smugness at the corners of her mouth.

Patricia blinked and looked again. Angel — Angela – was the perfect ballerina, all swan-graceful and delicate strength, and she was headlining the flyer for a prestigious company show at an uptown stage that even country-girl Patricia had heard of. Patricia swallowed and found that her grip was beginning to crinkle the edge of the printout. She flipped to the next page, a tearful obituary for a beloved wife and mother, famous dancer, darling daughter, and, from Patricia's swift skim, well-named Angel.

"I found her on the Internet," Andrea said. "Took some digging, let me tell you. Different last name, most of her stories are about her gazillionaire daddy and his stock-topping companies. Which, by the way, when were you going to tell me that your boyfriend was a billionaire?"

"He's not my boyfriend," Patricia replied automatically. Her heart was sitting in the bottom of her stomach. She'd never thought that Lee was particularly serious about her, but she never thought he might be comparing her to *this*. Angela was perfect. The obituary made her sound like a saint. She volunteered for charitable events, and there were testimonies from her fellow dancers that she was dedicated and talented, never using her family connections for unfair advantage. A husband, Leland, and a baby, were bare mentions.

She thought about sliding around barefoot in Lee's empty dining room, teaching them both to dance, and felt like a fraud. A giant, clumsy, curvy, fraud.

How could he let her make a fool of herself that way? How could he sit there and let her gush on about dancing, when he knew that what she was doing was some backwoods country chicken dance compared to what he was used to?

"Patricia? Honey?" Andrea's voice was anxious, and seemed to be a hundred miles away.

Patricia very carefully put the papers down on her desk and stood up, grateful when the bell at the front door gave its cheerful jangle. "The students are coming," she said, shoving aside the turmoil in her belly. "Let's get to work."

Patricia had never been so glad for a busy day in her life. The children were fractious, and there were more messes and accidents to clean up than usual, giving her a good excuse to put her head down and work hard, ignoring Andrea's worried looks and her own heart for the scissors and glue of the classroom.

"No, no, I'm sure," Lee said, glad that he was on the phone and not at the office in person. He knew he was smiling foolishly, and he couldn't seem to help himself, but the topic and the person at the other end of the line were anything but a smiling matter.

"This is a big deal, Lee," Dan told him, puzzlement clear in his voice even with the shaky cell connection they were on.

"You have no idea how big," Lee agreed. "But it means a lot to me, and you know I'll turn you a good favor down the road."

"I trust you," Dan finally said reluctantly. "But it means a lot of changes in our production schedule while we find another suitable property. They're going to want a good reason for this at head-quarters."

"Tell them it was an Indian burial ground," Lee said flippantly. "Or that you struck quicksand."

There was a moment of silence. "Did you just make a joke?" Dan asked incredulously.

Lee wondered if Dan could hear the grin on his face. "No, I don't do that," he said, as seriously as he could muster. "Just tell them the real estate agent was wearing impractical shoes and you couldn't strike a deal."

"I think that little country town has gotten under your skin," Dan said, and he chuckled. "Every woman wears impractical shoes."

Lee thought about Patricia, sliding barefoot around in his dining room with her big, clunky snow boots by his door. "Not every woman," he said. When they hung up, he slipped the little box he'd been toying with out of his pocket. It was black velvet, and he flipped it open with one thumb to check the contents again. It wasn't a huge glittering diamond like the one he'd given Angela, but he couldn't picture anything like that on Patricia's practical hands. This was a simple band, in braided shades of gold, with chips of rubies and diamond flush with the surface; nothing that would snag on craft supplies or mittens.

He would ask her tonight–, tomorrow morning, over pancakes. He'd let Clara help him with the proposal, then that afternoon during her nap, he would come clean with Patricia about being a shape-shifter. Maybe the ring on her finger would help her accept it a little more easily if he explained how it came with the idea of a mate.

He snapped the box shut and put it back in his pocket, picking up his phone instead. There were more calls to be made, and then there was something else he was finally ready to do.

~

*P*atricia could not get the picture of Angel out of her head. She toyed with the idea of canceling her evening with Lee, but couldn't find a good enough excuse. Besides, though her heart ached, the rest of her longed to be with him. She yearned for him in a way that she'd never desired another man. Every time they made love, she felt more connected and closer than she'd ever been to anyone, and it filled some hollow inside her that she'd never recognized was there.

She paused, with her hand raised to knock at the front door, in a moment of unexpected clarity. She loved him. It wasn't just that she wanted and lusted after him, she loved him, to the bottom of her heart, and she wasn't sure what to do with the overwhelming emotional backlash of that realization.

Clara opened the door before she could collect herself enough to knock or turn and flee, and Patricia forced herself out of her daze to smile down at the adorable girl.

"I saw you drive up!" Clara sang, bouncing forward to grab one of her hands, careless of her bare feet in the snow on the porch. "Papa said you would read me a story before bed!"

Patricia had just enough time to kick of her snow boots before Clara was pulling her up the stairs by one hand. "Alright, alright," Patricia had to laugh helplessly.

Lee was standing at the top of the stairs with small pink slippers, looking harried and handsome. "You aren't supposed to go outside barefoot," he told Clara, but his eyes were only on Patricia, and he smiled in a way that made her toes tingle.

'Don't fall for this man,' Patricia reminded herself, far too late, and then she was being swept down the hallway towards Clara's room.

To her surprise, framed photographs now lined one wall. Clara was pulling her along too fast to look closely at them; she only got glimpses of a stately ancient collection of grim-faced ancestors in furs and jewels, giving way to more modern tinted prints and finally color plates.

"This is my mother," Clara said with unexpected gravity, pausing only at the last pieces. There were several that Patricia recognized now as the dancer from Andrea's printout. One was a formal dance portrait, with a dramatically lit stage and a slight figure in classical tutu and pointe pose. The next photograph was a light-haired woman in a fur coat seated at the edge of a fountain holding a bundled baby. Lee, looking younger, was smiling over her shoulder. Golden sunlight sparkled in the water and made a halo around the woman's head. She really did look like an angel.

"She's beautiful," Patricia said, honestly, hoping her heartbreak wouldn't be heard in her voice. This was a woman no one could hope to compare to, especially not a country cow like herself. She steeled herself to stick to her plan. This night was a final goodbye. She had to get out before she lost too much of herself to a perfect dream she could never really be a part of.

Clara seemed to accept her statement as fact, and said cheerfully, "Let's go read *Give a Mouse a Cookie!*"

That, with the careful scrutiny of every page and all the hugs and blanket arrangements required, took all of Patricia's attention until the door latched behind them, and she and Lee were once again standing together in the hallway.

This time, however, she could feel the oblique attention of Angela's portrait, judging her from a swan-perfect pose.

If Lee had tried to kiss her there, she might have balked, but he only took her hand, tenderly, and led her further down the hallway, past the end of the portraits, to his room.

"Patricia," he started to say, but she couldn't handle words.

Instead, she reached up and put arms around his neck, kissing him with all the love and passion he had ignited in her. If she was going to say goodbye to him tonight, she was going to do it properly, and put this all behind her when she left in the morning.

CHAPTER 15

*L*ee had changed his mind again. He couldn't wait to ask Patricia to marry him, he would ask her tonight, so that he could get past the terrible looming reveal. And he couldn't ask her to marry him until she knew the full truth about him, so he had to... had to...

Any plans he had made unraveled and fell apart when she put insistent arms around his neck and kissed him like the world was ending.

The feeling of her body against him, strong and yielding and so perfectly rounded in all the right places left him unable to form words, even if her mouth had allowed it. He slipped arms around her, and kissed back.

They undressed each other slowly, not willing to break the kiss more than was required for pulling shirts off and maneuvering tricky zippers and belts. Lee didn't think he was imagining the different tenor to their dance—less laughter and enthusiasm and more desperation. Did she know, somehow, what he had planned? A trickle of doubt crept in—would she be able to handle the knowledge of his shifter side? What if she didn't want to marry him... then she was putting tender hands on either side of his face and murmuring as she rested her forehead against his. His bear, with none of his own inner doubts, knew what to do with his mate, so close, and so naked, and so did his body.

He lifted her onto the bed with another kiss, his hard member pressing at her lower mouth, but not demanding entrance, only reminding her of his presence.

His attention was for her lips and mouth, swollen already with his kisses, and her beautiful face—every freckle beloved. He wanted to tell her how much he loved her, but his mouth was busy, kissing the line of her jaw and the edge of her ear. He nibbled at her lobe, and she writhed below him, pressing upward at him with a low moan.

He held himself back and kissed down her neck, finding pale skin that rarely saw sunlight, and the fine blonde hairs that had escaped the braid she was wearing today. Her arching collarbones got his attention next, feathered with kisses and licks as he finally let himself explore down her chest to the breasts that were quivering below.

Patricia gave a musical breath of desire and pleasure, arching into his questing mouth. She was so woman, so full and waiting and wanting, and her breasts were big, beautiful handfuls and mouthfuls of joy. He nibbled and kissed and licked, and she gasped and groaned and tangled her hands in his hair.

Finally, when their desire was at a fever pitch Lee had not thought was possible, he let himself enter her, finding solace and relief and raw animal need at the sensation of being buried deep inside of her.

They finished together, almost musically, and lay entwined while their heartbeats slowly returned to normal.

Lee felt completed, as if his entire life had been a song waiting for its harmony, and now she sang with him.

"Patricia," he said, brushing her hair back from her face when he'd finally caught enough of his breath. "I have something I need to tell you."

Silence answered him, and a glance told him, unexpectedly, that she was asleep, long eyelashes splayed over her cheeks.

Lee found himself smiling and snuggled closer. He wasn't worried about what she would do anymore. Whatever happened, she was his mate, and he could be patient. He fell into the easiest sleep he could ever remember, and dreamed at once of wandering the woods with a golden bear at his side.

CHAPTER 16

*P*atricia woke slowly, comfortably sore and clinging to sleep as long as she could. She was warm and safe, curled up against something plush and large. She wiggled closer, not wanting to wake up and face the inevitable goodbye, and recognized through a fog that it didn't exactly feel *plush*, but coarser, and longer, and it was larger than a pillow or a person. She wrinkled her brow in confusion, the unexpected discovery waking her further. She was in bed with a fur coat? Even breaths raised the bulk beneath her out-flung arm, and she realized with alarm that it was too big to be Lee, even if he had, for some bizarre reason, gotten up in the middle of the night to put on a large buffalo coat.

She withdrew her arm cautiously, rolling away with care, and raised her head enough to see, in the early dawn light coming through the window, that there was a bear sprawled across the bed, enormous head on a pillow, sheets tangled in its back paws.

As collected as Patricia liked to consider herself, the shock drove a scream from her lips before she could remind herself that waking it was probably a bad idea.

The mountain of bear snorted and rumbled, and Patricia, naked, propelled herself back out of the bed and cast around helplessly for a weapon of some kind, any kind. Bereft of anything useful, she leapt for the curtain rod over the big window, and managed to pull it down with a crash as the bear woke and rose, blinking sleepy eyes at her from its vantage on the bed. Could she make a break past it for the door without it intercepting her? Patricia wondered. And where the hell was Lee?

Even as she summoned that thought, struggling to rip off the curtains that were weighing down the curtain rod she was trying to use as a makeshift weapon, the bear made a strangled noise of alarm and surprise.

That was it, Patricia realized. It was awake now for good, and she was armed with a crappy brass curtain rod and a few yards of white tapestry. She was going to be bear breakfast, and the curtains were going to be completely ruined from the blood. At least she wouldn't have to go through the ordeal of saying goodbye to Lee...

From down the hall, undoubtedly wakened by the racket they were making, Clara's shrill scream pierced the scene. The bear's head pivoted towards the door, and Patricia leapt for it without thinking. She was naked, and didn't think the curtain rod would survive one good blow from the bear's paws, but she wasn't about to let it go after Clara. Her only hope was to frighten it off, so she gave a blood-curdling warcry and jumped onto the bed with her curtain rod raised above her.

It was caught by a hand—a human hand—and somehow, through a blur that Patricia couldn't follow, it was Lee kneeling on the bed before her; the bear was nowhere to be seen.

"Patricia! Patricia, it's okay! It's me! I'm sorry, I've been wanting to tell you..."

Patricia's pulse hammered in her ears, adrenaline coursing through her like fire. "Tell me what?" she managed. "Bear. There was a bear..."

"That was me," Lee said, ridiculously. "I'm the bear. I'm sorry, I didn't want to surprise you like that. I must have done it in my sleep. I was just... comfortable."

Patricia stared. "You were... comfortable? You know, most

people, when they get really comfortable, they accidentally fart or something. They don't... turn into bears."

Lee blinked at her, then burst out laughing.

Patricia tried to maintain her stern visage and failed in the face of his laughter, falling forward with limbs that were suddenly utterly weak and shaking, face first into the bed, howling with hysterical laughter.

"Papa?" Clara's frightened voice and timid knock from outside of the door made them both sit up and silence their laughter.

"It's okay, kitten!" Lee said at once. "Nothing's wrong. I just..."

"Farted!" they said together, giggling like loons.

Clara was silent outside the door for a moment. "You woke me up! We have to make pancakes now! I'm getting dressed!" she said accusingly, and then they heard her little footsteps stomping back away down the hallway.

Lee rolled out of his side of the bed and grabbed the clothing that waited there. "You heard the little tyrant," he said, then sobered. "I did want to tell you a little less... uh..."

"Alarmingly?" Patricia suggested. "In a less heart-attack inducing fashion?" As weird as it seemed, now that the adrenaline was ebbing away, the idea of Lee being a shapeshifter was somehow comfortable. It was a tiny affirmation of all the magic she had clung to believing in since she was a small girl, and it suited Lee. All of his serious demeanor and secrecy, all of his riches and his enormous palace of a house; it fit that he was a shapechanger prince from a fairy tale.

'And you aren't a princess,' Patricia reminded herself, sorrow-fully, pulling on her jeans and t-shirt. "So, is it some kind of curse or something?" she asked, as if it was perfectly ordinary.

"No," Lee said slowly, shaking his head. "I come from a line of shifters. There are a lot of around. I picked this town because it's usually... friendly to our type."

"That... explains some things," Patricia said, thinking about some of the odd people she knew at the diner, and the way she sometimes felt like there were topics that went silent when she approached, and so many of the stories she heard as a child that she had dismissed as fantasy.

"There's something else," Lee said hesitantly, coming around the end of the bed. He was wearing his pants, but not his shirt, and Patricia looked at his sculpted chest instead of his dear face, bracing herself for the rest.

CHAPTER 17

$\mathcal{A}$s reveals went, Lee suspected that it could have gone better. Still, Patricia seemed to be taking the shock in stride. She hadn't jumped out of the window, at least, and once the hysterical giggling had passed, she seemed to be surprisingly accepting of the whole thing.

"There's something else." Lee made himself keep going, knowing that if he lost momentum with this whole confession, it was only going to be harder.

Patricia made a conversational noise as she buttoned her shirt, smoothing the front down over her luscious breasts.

"Shifters... we have this thing, a mate, a *soulmate*. There's one person we're meant to be with, one perfect partner, that we—"

"I know." There was a serene smile on Patricia's face, still and deep, with an odd flavor that Lee couldn't put his finger on.

"It's just... this mate—"

"It's okay," she interrupted him swiftly. "I understand. I... already knew."

Relief flooded through Lee. Of course she knew. She had to know. How could she not have felt the incredible bond that they shared. He smiled, suspecting it was a ridiculously soppy smile, but he couldn't help it. "I'm so glad," he said simply.

"Clara's expecting pancakes," Patricia reminded him. She was so delightfully down-to-earth.

Lee swept up his shirt. "Yes! Pancakes!" He would stick to the original plan. A ring with her pancakes, and he'd have Clara there for the moment; all of the most precious people in his life together at once.

He rehearsed the moment in his head as they walked down the stairs to the kitchen, and imagined the words and Clara's laughter as he mixed up the pancake batter and heated the griddle. He was wrapped up in his busy mind until he brought the first stack of cakes to the table—and found Clara setting it for two.

"Where is Miss Patricia?" he asked, suddenly aware that she wasn't there, that he couldn't sense her nearby.

Clara looked at him with big blue eyes, alarmed at his surprise. "She drove away!"

Lee let the plate of pancakes fall the last few inches to the table and land with a clatter. "When? Where?"

"In her car!" Clara supplied helpfully. "She said she had to go."

Lee ran the distance to the front door in a matter of seconds, but the car was long gone, tracks in the snow showing her hasty escape. He stood there with the door open, cold air swirling over his bare feet. The sound of a car near the tree-shrouded bottom of the driveway gave him a moment of hope, but it moved away down the road.

He'd read her wrong. Finding out he was a shifter had changed her mind about him. Mate or not, she didn't want the complication that he was in her life. This was their goodbye then; a cold, empty driveway and uneaten pancakes. Lee stood there until Clara drew him back inside by the knees, complaining of the cold that he didn't even feel anymore.

*P*atricia flew down the driveway much faster than she knew she should, trusting her Subaru to stick to the road and power her through the wet, drifting snow.

"I ought to have waited for the snowplows," she thought to herself, pulling out into the slushy, snowy road with the barest hint of a pause at the bottom of the driveway.

The snow had cleared and the clouds lifted, but given the tears that clouded her vision, Patricia knew she should pull over. She slowed to a safer speed, but there was no clear shoulder here in the hills. She wiped her face with the back of her coat sleeve, biting back a sob.

If she had doubted that Lee was still in love with his dead wife, his words had erased that.

A *soulmate*, a perfect partner.

She couldn't compete with that.

She turned the defroster higher as the window began fogging in the cold and she realized it wasn't all her own tears obscuring her view. Behind her, headlights through the snow she was kicking up showed a car coming right up on her tail, driving close in the poor conditions.

Distracted from her own thoughts, Patricia scowled at the other car in the mirror, dark in the poor morning light. It wasn't driving well for the winding road, and was crawling up at her trunk without care for the slippery conditions. She tapped the brakes just enough to light up her taillights in warning but not to slow, and was equal parts alarmed and relieved when they backed off just a little and pulled into the oncoming lane—it was a stupid move in a place with no shoulder and no clear line of sight to traffic that might be coming from ahead, but at least she wouldn't have them tailing her all the way into town.

"Idiot," she muttered to herself, slowing to give them the best chance they could around the curve.

She was looking forward, focused on looking ahead for oncoming traffic and keeping her Subaru in its indistinct lane as the dark car passed, throwing snow into her windshield.

Momentarily blinded, Patricia went too far into the soft snow at the edge, and lost whatever control she'd had. Tires spun in the soft snow, and her car tottered at the crest of the shoulder before finally plummeting into the ditch beyond. For a moment Patricia thought she could simply ride down, hoping against hope that she wouldn't hit a big tree at the bottom, but it was too steep, too slippery, and the world went into a crazy spin as the car finally rolled down into oblivion, the airbag exploding into her and slamming her back into the seat.

CHAPTER 18

*L*ee tried not to mope, eating too many pancakes with Clara and feeling the burn of the jewelry box in his pocket. His daughter, at least, seemed oblivious to the fact that everything had gone perfectly sideways, and chattered gleefully about imaginary friends, and her plans for the weekend, which seemed to involve a ball with a prince, a baseball game, and a big party for her stuffed animals, all hosted in the swimming pool, apparently.

He was carrying the dirty dishes to the sink, not even cheered by Clara's requests to make the bubbles, when the doorbell rang.

He almost dropped the plates, and Clara went scampering for the front door.

"Slow down, kitten!" he cautioned her, putting the plates down on the counter before he followed her. Relief flooded him. Patricia had come back. She had just needed a little space to get used to the idea, and let the whole crazy idea of shifters and soulmates settle in.

Clara got to the door just before him, and flung it open. They both froze, confronted by the entirely unexpected sight of Patricia's preschool assistant Andrea, standing naked on the porch with her arms wrapped ineffectively around herself.

"Patricia needs your help!" she demanded, with no explanation of her nudity or how she'd gotten there—there was no car in the driveway behind her.

Lee only stared for a moment before moving aside so that she could come in. "I... uh..." There was no standard greeting for naked women in snow.

"You are not the only shifter in town," Andrea said dryly. "Though you may be the most unobservant."

"I'm... uh... sorry?" Lee grabbed the closest thing that might fit her, waffling a moment between Clara's little coat and his own quilted flannel shirt. The first might actually be closer to her diminutive size. He decided on the flannel, suspecting she'd prefer more cover.

Andrea took it in stride. "I know that I was always around a powerful distraction," she shrugged, accepting the shirt. "But *she* is in trouble now."

Shock gave way to a calm readiness. Whatever his mate needed, Lee could feel his bear preparing to supply it; it felt like adrenaline, but more focused. "What happened?"

"She drove off the road," Andrea said, a glint of anger in her golden eyes. "I was flying over and saw the whole thing. A car passed her on a blind corner, and she veered into a ditch about a mile just down the road."

"You left her there?"

Lee didn't think about how accusatory he sounded until Andrea rebutted angrily, "I couldn't get the door open, and I wasn't doing her much good, naked in the snow. I'm a hawk, not a bear."

Moving automatically, Lee was already pulling on his boots and shrugging into a parka with purpose.

"It's the curve past the guardrail right before town," Andrea said, nodding decisively at him.

"Clara, stay here with Miss Andrea," Lee commanded with a growl, reaching for his truck keys.

Clara had born witness to their odd exchange with eyes like saucers, certain something was afoot, but not sure what to do with it. She looked trustingly at Andrea, not in the slightest bothered by the fact that she had arrived naked, and nodded. She darted for one swift hug from her father, her arms wrapping briefly around Lee's leg. When Lee knelt to hug her back, she solemnly said, "Make Miss Patricia be okay."

It was that simple, in Lee's mind. He was going to go get Patricia and make her be okay. Even if she wanted nothing to do with him now that she knew his shifter secret, he had to save her. "You bet, cub."

Then he was out the door, bolting for the truck.

Behind him, Clara fixed Andrea with a curious gaze. "Can I make bubbles for the dishes?" she asked.

CHAPTER 19

*P*atricia woke slowly, aware first that her hands were cold. She moved to tuck them under her blanket, then realized that she wasn't in her own bed, that she was suspended by seatbelt straps upside down in the crushed cab of her car. Something on the dashboard was beeping weakly. Anger gave her false warmth as she remembered the dark car that had foolishly passed her, and she struggled out of the seatbelt before she could suspect she might be injured and possibly shouldn't move before she had determined the extent of her damage. Pain radiated from her left ankle, and the ache in her shoulders made her suspect she would find that she was black and blue, but Patricia's quick assessment was that she didn't have anything worse than a sprained ankle.

She wiggled it experimentally and had to bite back a cry. Maybe a broken ankle.

She righted herself in the wrong-side-up cab, and began to struggle with the car door.

The latch still moved, but the metal was crushed into a form that didn't allow it to open, despite Patricia straining against it with all her strength and weight. Somehow, the glass was still in place, though it and the windshield had shattered in place. She'd have to break out of one of the windows, she decided, winded, but the idea made her ankle throb. She found one of her gloves, which had been in the passenger seat, and switched them between her cold hands, trying to decide which would be easier to get out of. The enclosed space of the car was beginning to make her feel trapped.

She curled up on the upside-down roof of the car and closed her eyes, feeling tears well up. She took a deep breath, trying to damp down her terror and think of something peaceful. Lee's face came to her imagination immediately, and the feeling of his arms around her. She pushed it aside fiercely, reminding herself that the relationship was not going anywhere. He'd had his perfect partner already, and she opened her eyes, prepared to kick out the front windshield with her good foot.

Suddenly, Lee's face wasn't just in her imagination, but at her door, worry in every line of his face. "Get back," he yelled through the glass, and she obediently backed as far as she could into the inverted roof of the passenger seat.

Through the frosted and spider-webbed glass, she watched his figure blur and stretch and bend into the shape of a big, dark brown bear. His clothing ripped away into shreds. A huge paw crashed through the window, easily breaking the weakened glass with a ear-splitting crash. Not finished, the bear growled and fumbled at the door, finally ripping the entire thing off of the mangled car and throwing it away into the slushy snow. Cold air swirled into the car, and she crawled carefully over the broken glass towards the bear, grateful for her sturdy jeans and coat.

He was human by the time she had wiggled her way to the door, and strong arms pulled her out the final bit.

"Are you hurt?" he asked anxiously, holding her closer than was strictly necessary.

"My ankle," Patricia admitted, and she was amused when Lee shivered; all that remained of his clothing was a puddle of ripped cloth at their feet. Even his boots had been rent from the ferocity of his transformation.

"I can carry you back up to the road," Lee said firmly.

"You're naked," Patricia giggled hysterically, looking at the steep snowy slope up to the road. It was astonishing how far she had rolled in the car. "You don't even have boots."

"Not like this," Lee said, and right under her arms, he shifted again, flowing into his bear form.

This close, right in his arms, it was completely different than watching it through an obscured window or simply waking up to it. His entire mass changed as a thick coat of fur seemed to come from nowhere, growing into long fur under her very fingers. She had to let go of him as he rose above her, and gasped in pain as she put weight onto her bad ankle. As large as the bear had seemed that morning when they met in bed, he was much larger looming right over her on hind legs. He must be eight or nine feet tall, Patricia realized in awe. Then he was dropping to all fours next to her, growling conversationally as he came to lay directly in front of her.

When she hesitated, uncertain, he raised his head and whined like a dog, twitching his massive shoulders at her suggestively.

It was still a rather good climb onto Lee's back, but the long, coarse fur gave her plenty to hold onto. Patricia swung her good foot over the ridge of his back and was astride. Lee gave a growl of warning and surged to his feet. Patricia clung tight, and as he began to climb up the slope, had to lean forward further and further, until she was basically lying against his shoulder, arms reaching as far around the bear's neck as she could. She continued to lie this way once they had leveled out on the road, cheek pressed into his fur. It was surprisingly comforting, riding in this fashion. He smelled like forests and wild things, and oddly just like Lee, and the rough fur felt just right under her fingers. The rhythm of the muscles striding beneath her was reassuring, and the snuffling growling noises he made as he walked were somehow familiar.

For just a moment, she was a princess in the fairy stories, rescued by her very own bear prince.

Then they were at his truck, and he was lying down again so she could dismount, carefully, hopping on her one good foot. She was opening the truck door when he was behind her as a human again, lifting her up onto the creaking bench seat.

"I should take you to the hospital," Lee said, sliding in beside her after a moment.

"You're naked," Patricia reminded him.

"They've probably gotten odder patients at the hospital," Lee said, but he looked embarrassed as well as cold. He cranked up the heat.

"Just take me to your house," Patricia said. "It's a weekend, and they'll only tell me to elevate it and get x-rays Monday when the walk-in clinic is open. It's not an emergency, and I'd rather call the car insurance company from your quiet house than a crowded ER."

~

*L*ee growled, but decided that Patricia was right. He didn't relish the idea of arriving at the hospital in his current state of undress, and Patricia didn't seem badly hurt. He turned back up the road towards his house rather than continuing into town.

"I'm... sorry I scared you," he said, after a long moment of silence spent squirming on the cold bench, trying to find a way to keep his seatbelt on without it pressing into his chilled flesh.

Patricia shifted on the seat, fumbling with her boots. "You didn't scare me," she said with surprise. "I was glad to see you, and being a bear shifter was particularly useful of you."

Lee could only sputter at that. "Useful?"

"I doubt even you could have torn off that door without a little help," Patricia said. "And while I'm sure I wouldn't have died there, I was getting cold and... alone."

"You're not afraid of the bear part of me," Lee said, puzzled by this reveal.

"You're clearly still *you* as a bear," Patricia said practically. "You were far more interested in helping me get out of the car than you were in, say, eating me."

"But... this morning?" Lee felt thick-headed, like he was missing something critical.

"It was a pretty shocking way to wake up, no doubt," Patricia said. "Is that what you were apologizing for? It's not like I blame you for not telling me earlier. It's a pretty big confession. 'Hi, I'm a bear sometimes.'"

"But you don't mind that I'm a shifter." Lee couldn't wrap his mind around the idea.

Patricia shot him a sheepish smile. "I'm a little envious," she confessed. "It sounds rather wonderful."

Lee chewed on that for a few moments. "Then why did you leave?"

Her stillness radiated unhappiness, and Lee had to force himself to watch the road instead of immediately reaching to comfort her.

He navigated a slippery curve before she finally answered slowly. "It was what you said about soulmates. I... know you still love your wife, that she meant everything to you. I know you'll never feel that way about me, that I can't be *that*." There was a little hitch to her voice that cut Lee to the bone. "I don't want to be that woman who can't separate sex and love, but I couldn't keep loving you the way I do knowing that what we had was just a pale shadow of what you'd had."

Lee slammed the brakes on, pulling the truck into the snowbank by the side of the road with a curse that had Patricia clinging to the handholds and looking at him with saucer eyes. "You thought I was saying that *Angela* was my soulmate?"

Patricia blinked at him. "Of course..."

Lee leaned his face on the steering wheel, cursing again. "I am the biggest idiot in the entire Midwest," he said, refraining from ripping the entire steering wheel off and throwing it out the window in frustration. He took a series of deep breaths, and unpeeled his fingers from the wheel. "I loved Angela," he said, then thought that might be a poor place to start, but it was an important detail. He met Patricia's eyes; they were full of tears. "But what I felt for her, it's no less than what I have in my heart for you. I never believed in soulmates before I met you. I thought it was a comfortable fiction, just a fairy tale."

"Like shapeshifters?" Patricia muttered. She rubbed the tears away from one cheek and Lee had to put a hand against her face and rub the other dry with a tender thumb.

"When I saw you, I knew it was all the truth. You were meant for me. Every part of me loves every part of you."

Patricia sobbed, but her face lit up behind the tears. "I never believed in love at first sight," she said in a small voice. "And I thought you couldn't possibly feel that way about me..."

Lee unclipped his seatbelt and fought free of the frigid contraption so he could slide across the benchseat and scoop her into his arms. She escaped her own seatbelt to meet him halfway, and lifted her mouth for his kiss with the same hunger that was coursing through his veins. Cold as he was, he burned for this woman, his perfect mate.

Their kiss was a tangle of tongues and a release of fears and despair, deep and long and lingering. If it hadn't been for the gasp of pain that Patricia gave when she moved her foot wrong, Lee was not sure how long they would have stayed there in the frosting truck cab.

Instead, he pulled back, then began cursing again as something occurred to him.

"What is it?" Patricia asked in alarm.

"Your ring," Lee told her. "It was in my pocket, and must be back with my ruined clothing at your car."

"My... ring?"

"Will you marry me?" It wasn't even close to the way he had planned to ask her. "You're mine, and I want everyone to know it."

The glowing smile she gave him, and the kiss that followed was answer enough.

Patricia gave Lee her parka to get into the house; he wrapped it inelegantly around his waist as an attempt at modesty. Both Andrea and Clara seemed more bothered by the way that Patricia was limping than by Lee's state of undress.

Andrea, to Patricia's surprise, was wrapped in Lee's oversized clothing. She looked between them, more puzzled than suspicious. There had been no other vehicle in the drive. "You're a shifter, too?" she guessed.

Andrea grinned. "You always said I had eyes like a hawk."

Patricia groaned. "This explains so much."

"Clara and I are making cookies," Andrea said with a nod towards the stairs. "I think Patricia needs a detailed checkover," she suggested. "Make sure she doesn't have any scrapes she doesn't know about."

Clara thought that was a fine idea, and brought Lee a first aid kit from the downstairs bathroom that he slung over one shoulder.

"You should both take a hot shower, too," Andrea suggest unsubtly. "To warm up, you know. We'll be down here making cookies for a long time. Don't rush, or anything."

Patricia could only sputter helplessly at the suggestion, but Lee seemed to think it was a perfect idea. "I want to check your head for lumps," he said, tightening the parka around his waist.

Then he swept her up into his arms over her protests, and carried her up the stairs.

"Have fun!" Andrea called up after them.

Patricia thought she would be too embarrassed to do anything, aware that Andrea was downstairs knowing exactly what was happening, but when Lee put her gently down on the wide ledge of his bathtub, nothing else seemed to matter.

He shed the parka so that his check-over of her was done entirely nude, and took his duties very seriously, undressing her slowly and looking over every inch of skin as it was exposed. The cuts from glass, all minor, were gently cleaned and antibiotic cream was applied. The bandages Lee had were all princess-themed, and carefully applied over a handful of abrasions. He explored her skull with probing fingers that lingered in her hair more than strictly required. Together they found a few tender spots, but no rising lumps.

"You're going to have a black eye," he informed her, sweeping her hair back from her face.

"I don't have to look at me," Patricia said, aware that her smile must look foolish.

"You'll still look beautiful to me," Lee said with a kiss.

The kiss only delayed their first aid for a moment, then it was time for the part that Patricia was dreading. He pulled her first boot off carefully, and the second even more cautiously. It hurt, but not as badly as Patricia had feared it would. The ankle was angry and swollen, but she could, at his insistence, move it through its entire range. Lee bound it up snugly with a bright pink stretch-bandage, and helped Patricia carefully wriggle out of her jeans to complete their inspection. There would be bruises where the seatbelt had kept her in the seat. "I should probably stay out of swimsuit competitions for a few weeks," she joked, poking at one of the bruises that was already starting to purple.

"You were lucky," Lee said grimly. There was a scowling ferocity to him that Patricia now recognized was driven by his grumpy bear.

"It's passed," she soothed him, caressing his shoulders. "I'll be fine, just forget it."

Lee responded, his nudity making his sudden arousal apparent. "Forget what?" He lifted her up into his arms again, and carried her to the bed. They were both still chilled, and he swept the comforter up over them and dove in. Wrapped in its warmth and darkness, they explored each other's bodies blindly. Lee was surprisingly delicate for his size, taking painstaking care not to jostle her ankle.

It took only moments of delicious discovery to warm up and thrust the blanket off, and Lee gently kissed her from jaw to naval, then straddled her, his erect penis promising unspoken pleasure. When he hesitated, Patricia pulled him down onto her, careful to keep her injured foot out of the way. His entrance claimed her, and her heart sang when she remembered that he felt for her as she did him.

Soulmates. *Mates.*

They were perfect partners, and they fit together like interlocking puzzle pieces, entwining as only two things destined for each other could.

His touch made every square inch of her skin burn for him. He drew her up to heights of pleasure she'd never known or even imagined, then fell with her in the warm afterglow.

Later, in a haze of sated exhaustion, Patricia let Lee tuck her under the comforter with her foot propped up on a pillow. She fell asleep to the smell of cookies and the sound of a shower running.

When she woke a short time later, she found herself alone. There was a glass of water on the bedside table, and a few over-the-counter pain pills that she gratefully took. A package lay on the other side of the bed, wrapped with a paper bag and tied with what appeared to be a sash from one of Clara's dresses. A cane leaned against the side of the bed.

Curious, Patricia unwrapped the crinkly package, and unfolded a length of fuzzy material, printed all over with pink kittens and mittens. A small black box fell out of the folds, and she scooped it up with trembling hands. It opened with a snap and revealed a sparkling ring, with rubies and diamonds flush to an intricate braid of multi-colored gold. She pulled it out of the velvet case and slipped it carefully onto her ring finger, marveling at the fit and sparkle and grinning fit to split her face. For some foolish reason, she wanted to cry, and to distract herself, she turned to inspect the cloth it had been wrapped in. It took her a moment to figure out what it was, and when she did, she burst out laughing.

Andrea laughed as well, when Patricia made her way down to the kitchen wearing both gifts and limping on the cane. "Is that a pair of footed kitty pajamas?"

Lee insisted that Patricia sit down at once, and fussed over elevating her foot. Clara brought her an ice pack from the freezer and carefully perched it onto the ankle, while Andrea brought a plate full of cookies.

"Where on earth did you find these?" Patricia asked Lee. She felt like she was wrapped in downy feathers, the fabric was so soft and fuzzy, and she was deeply cozy and warm. Was this what being a bear felt like?

"It was a special order," Lee said, smiling at her from across his own plate of cookies. "My tailor thought I was nuts, but he put it together anyway."

"I love it," Patricia said, deeply content. Looking around the kitchen, at Clara's eager face, her best friend's laughter in the air and her mate looking at her with love and adoration, she could not imagine a happier ending in any fairy tale ever.

EPILOGUE

"I'm not used to having anyone take care of me," Patricia confessed, letting Lee pile pillows under her ankle. "It's not even broken."

Lee scowled at her, a dear, familiar expression. "It's sprained," he said fiercely. "And you aren't staying off of it at preschool!"

"I make Andrea do most of the work," Patricia promised, touched by his care.

"How was it?" Lee asked. "Really, are you careful?"

Patricia put a hand over his, and was caught by the still-unexpected sparkle of gems on her finger. "I really do take it easy," she laughed. "And things are going smoothly. The new car handles great. Harriette is still missing and Trevor's living with his Dad now. That was half my stress!"

She was rewarded by an easing of the lines in his face, and then Clara was scampering into the living room, carrying a tray with a variety of Lincoln Logs on it. "I baked you cookies!" the little girl announced, and she solemnly gave one to each of them, and then took them back, declaring, "They have to cook more now."

She was gone as quickly as she'd come in, and Patricia exchanged an amused look with Lee that faded to alarm as something occurred to her. "Should I be worried about Clara turning into a bear cub some day at preschool?" she demanded. She couldn't imagine explaining that one away at storytime.

Lee shook his head. "Some shifters are born shifting, but my family has always come into it at puberty. It varies."

Patricia raised an eyebrow at him. "As if puberty weren't complicated enough," she said wryly.

"Are you reconsidering?" Lee gave her ring a tap.

Patricia gave him a searching look, trying to decide if he was really worried, or if he was just teasing her. She smiled. "You can't scare me off that easily."

"I'll have to try harder," Lee said with a sigh, and Patricia knew he was needling her.

"I can't imagine you being harder than you were last night," she whispered suggestively.

He grinned back. "I'm sure I can *rise* to the challenge."

THE TIGER NEXT DOOR

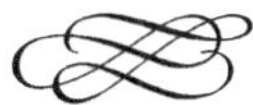

CHAPTER 1

"Mr. Powell?"

Shaun rubbed his face and reminded himself that glowering at the intercom was ineffective. "What is it?" he asked shortly.

"It's Mrs. Powell ... Er, Mrs. ex-Powell... Ah..."

"Harriette."

"Yes, Mr. Powell."

Shaun momentarily wished his office had an escape exit. Wasn't there some sort of requirement for that kind of thing? But they were dozens of floors up, looking out over Minneapolis, and vanishing out the window to scale a fire escape was unlikely to happen. Why couldn't he have a more useful shifted form, he wondered. Something that could *fly*.

His inner tiger gave an unamused snort.

"Mr. Powell?"

"Send her in."

Shaun had been expecting... something. A phone call? A demand for more money?

He hadn't been expecting Harriette to visit at his office.

And he definitely wasn't expecting the little boy who was holding her hand.

Trevor.

Whatever regrets he had about his brief and stormy marriage to Harriette, Trevor had never been one of them.

Trevor must be five now, and Shaun had seen him just twice in the past two years: awkward visits on his birthday. Trevor had been understandably shy and confused about him, and Shaun went away wondering if it wasn't kinder to step back and let him build a healthy relationship with whatever partner Harriette had last found to replace him.

He scowled and returned his gaze to Harriette. She must have some wild demands if she was dragging Trevor in for leverage.

"What can I do for you?" he asked. It *must* be money.

"I'm not here to ask you for anything," Harriette said, in that terribly reasonable tone she'd always had. "I'm here to give you what you keep asking for."

Shaun scrambled to think of anything he'd asked for since the divorce. His lawyer had tried to convince him to fight harder against her ridiculous financial demands, but Shaun had only wanted one thing — and Harriette's lawyer had been able to get *her* full custody of their son. His work and hours were 'incompatible' with raising a child.

"This is about the house in Green Valley?" Shaun guessed. "I got the foreclosure warning. I'm not sure how you bypassed the fund I set up to pay for that. Did you think it wouldn't count towards child support this way?"

"Don't be stupid," Harriette said. That was the Harriette from the end of their marriage. The cutting one who had already found something better to move on to. "I'm bringing you Trevor."

Shaun wasn't sure who to stare at.

Trevor was gazing at the fishtank, ignoring his parents' conversation. His blond hair was several shades lighter than Shaun's. Harriette had taken to dyeing her hair the same shade as Trevor's instead of her natural brunette, which was downright eerie.

Harriette put the papers she was holding down on Shaun's desk and plucked a pen from his holder. "I had my lawyer draw up the papers. You wanted him, you got him."

Shaun glanced at Trevor, his heart hurting for the boy. How brutal could it be, hearing Harriette give him away like he was nothing?

Trevor didn't seem to notice, staring enraptured at the fish.

Shaun stood and drew Harriette as far away from Trevor's hearing as the office could manage. "You mean you found someone new and he's an impediment? What happened to the real estate guy who loved kids?"

"That's none of your business," Harriette hissed. "Just sign the papers. It's what you want anyway."

Shaun stared at her, trying to remember that he'd found her beautiful once. She was so strong-willed and sure-footed, with her perfect make-up and sultry smile. Shaun only now really realized how much of that was an act.

She had never really wanted Shaun, only the successful investment company he was building. And once she'd set her sights on him, Shaun hadn't stood a chance.

"What about the house in Green Valley?"

Harriette shrugged. "I don't care. Trevor's got some stuff left there."

How had he thought she was sensitive and sweet?

"I go to preschool in Green Valley," Trevor said shyly, joining them.

Harriette ignored him. "Are you going to sign it or not?"

"Do you like your preschool?" Shaun asked gently.

Trevor seemed to perk up. "Yeah! There's a rabbit, and Miss Andrea can juggle. Miss Patricia plays piano."

"It's great," Harriette said dismissively. "Papers?"

"I'm not signing anything my lawyer hasn't looked at," Shaun said firmly.

Harriette's eyes narrowed. "Then I'll take him with me," she threatened. "I'm leaving the country, and with full custody, I don't have to clear that with you."

Shaun's stomach clenched and his tiger growled.

He looked down at Trevor's anxious face, remembering the scant armful he had been as a baby, and the fascinating expressions Shaun had spent so much time gazing at. Trevor had been taking his first steps when Shaun's marriage began to fall apart. After a few months of separation and a divorce that cost him hundreds of thousands of dollars, Harriette had taken their son to the quiet town of Green Valley; in no small part, Shaun knew, because it was just beyond a comfortable commute for visits.

Shaun had lost two years of Trevor's life. He'd gone away a toddler and stood before him now as a little boy. He could almost see the shape of the man he was going to grow up to be in the steady gaze and the set of the chin.

Trevor reached up and began to pick his nose.

"I'll sign," Shaun said quietly.

"Are we going back to Green Valley now?" Trevor asked in concern, looking from Harriette to Shaun. "I don't want to miss preschool."

"*You're* going back to Green Valley," Harriette said dismissively. "I'll be happy never to set foot in it."

She watched in triumph as Shaun read over the contract and signed it. He wasn't a lawyer, but it was a simple document compared to their divorce, and it said what he most wanted to see: full custody. No strings.

Harriette smirked.

"I saw the part about the settlement payment," Shaun growled. "So there's no need to feel smug. I'll have the secretary write you a check on your way out."

It would have been worth twice as much, to have Trevor back.

"What about preschool?" Trevor asked again. "I don't want to miss it. On Monday we're making Easter baskets."

"I... guess we're going to Green Valley, then," Shaun said in bemusement. "We'll check out the house and get it ready to sell and then we can move back here to the city together."

Harriette took her copy of the contract. "Whatever you want," she said dismissively. She gave Trevor a cursory hug. "Don't muss my hair," she warned the boy.

Trevor, realizing something was going terribly wrong, began to cry and cling to her. "I don't want you to go, Mummy. I don't want to live in the city. I want to go to preschool and stay in Green Valley."

Harriette peeled him carefully off. "You're going to live with your daddy now. We talked about this, remember? Be a brave, good boy and say goodbye now."

Trevor, chin trembling, let her go.

And then she was gone, leaving the best thing she'd ever done behind.

CHAPTER 2

"Can I get a refill?"

Andrea jotted down notes as fast as she could, cursing the fading pen and the textured napkin as she tried to remember the sequence of events she'd figured out while she was waiting for Stanley to pick from the menu that hadn't changed in twenty years.

"Order up!"

Damn. What had she figured out for the villain's motivation? She'd thought of a way to bring the cat back into the plot, hadn't she? She added a few question marks and a scrawl that might have been "cat" and "motivation for villain?" That would hopefully be enough to jog her memory later.

"Order UP!"

Andrea startled. Old George rarely repeated anything he didn't have to. Andrea tucked the pen and napkin into her apron, hoping that it would be readable later.

She swept the food from the kitchen window onto her tray, grabbed the water pitcher with her other hand, and nearly delivered the order to the wrong table.

"Patricia is a better waitress," Marta told her with the candor of someone who was past thinking what people thought of her as she accepted the plate of hash and eggs. "Doesn't this come with toast?"

"Patricia is a much better waitress," Andrea agreed with return frankness. "But she rolled her car and sprained her ankle, and Gran doesn't have much of a hiring pool to draw on, so you're stuck with me for a few weeks." She refilled Marta's water glass without sloshing too much of it onto the laminated tabletop.

Marta laughed with appreciation. "Probably more than a few weeks," she said speculatively. "With her new billionaire boyfriend, she doesn't have to wait tables for us commoners."

"Oh, you know Patricia," Andrea laughed. "She's not suited to being a kept woman. She'll be back at Gran's Grits before you know it, making me look bad again."

Marta kindly did not mention that Andrea was doing a perfectly fine job of looking bad without Patricia's comparison, and Andrea didn't add that she really needed the paycheck and hoped that Lee would convince Patricia to stay off the ankle as long as possible.

Andrea pretended not to see Devon wave his empty glass at her as she scooted back to the window.

"Marta needs toast," she reminded the short order cook.

"Waitress is supposed to do that." George wasn't actually that old, but he shaved his head and had a short, grizzled beard in salt and pepper, and since no one could remember a time without him around, he wore the nickname well. "Did Stanley ever decide?"

"Oh, crap," Andrea said, fishing into her apron pocket. She found two crumpled napkins of notes and an order ticket. "The fish lunch special," she said triumphantly, putting it into George's hand. "No salt on the fries."

"Go give Devon a refill, here's the toast you were supposed to make." George didn't sound happy about it, but Andrea gave him her best 'I'm-an-airhead-please-don't-fire-me' smile and cheerfully marched the toast back to Marta's table.

"What were you drinking?" she asked Devon, taking the glass and straw.

Devon looked at her like she was an idiot. "Iced tea."

"Oh, right. Soda machine's down."

"Maybe write that down on a napkin?" Devon suggested caustically.

Andrea blushed as she stalked away. Since she probably wasn't going to get a tip anyway, she did a second-rate job stirring in the sugar, knowing it would be a gritty sludge at the bottom. Patricia probably stirred it until it was completely dissolved and remembered the lemon every time.

Andrea picked the last, ugly lemon slice from the bowl and tried to position it to look its most hideous.

When she went to refill glasses of water throughout the small, dated diner, the regulars smiled and shook their heads at her.

"How's the book going?" Stanley asked her as she put his fish down in front of him.

"Oh, you know. I've got some ideas. Working away at it." Andrea didn't want to admit that the book was still mostly napkins and notes.

Somehow, when she started writing, tired from a day working at the preschool and an afternoon waiting tables, it didn't seem as captivating as she imagined it would be while she was otherwise busy. And at home, there were dirty dishes waiting for her to wash, and laundry in a heap by the washer, and spring was starting to melt the snow and expose all the things in her yard that needed to be picked up.

Somehow, she managed to instead spend an hour writing instructions to her aunt about unclogging her toilet, with pictures and diagrams, instead of adding actual chapters.

And there was the sky, begging for flight.

"Well, you just remember us, when you're a famous writer," Stanley told her warmly. "You remember Green Valley and all of us who cheered you on."

Andrea smiled and patted his hand, to be rewarded with a largely-toothless smile. "I could never forget," she promised.

CHAPTER 3

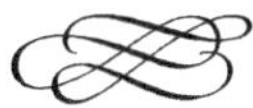

$\mathcal{P}$ulling up in front of the house in Green Valley, Shaun vowed to sell the place at whatever loss it took as soon as he could settle the back payments with the bank.

They arrived too late for Trevor to get to preschool, which had resulted in broken-hearted weeping that cut Shaun to the bone, leaving him ill-disposed to like anything about the sleepy little town.

It was an old building, like almost everything in Green Valley, with nothing particularly graceful to recommend it. It was grand, compared to the other, smaller houses, but needed a coat of paint and new windows. The yard might have been nice once, but was badly overgrown, and the swing set in one corner was rusty and looked like a good source of tetanus.

The house was offset on the property, so close to the neighboring house that you could undoubtedly see straight into their rooms.

Indeed, the whole neighborhood lacked anything resembling privacy. The narrow, waist-high hedge between these two was as much of as any of them had; most of the lawns simply ran into each other, occasionally with a line of decorative rocks or a flowerbed to designate the boundary. The proverbial white picket fence that ran along the sidewalk was more of a statement than a notion of separation.

Several of the neighbors were out, surreptitiously eyeing him as they planted flowers and raked up last year's leaves.

No space to run, his tiger told him sadly.

"We're probably not going to stay long," Shaun warned Trevor.

Trevor had exhausted himself crying on the long trip once Shaun had told him they wouldn't be able to make it to preschool, and he only shrugged miserably now.

"We'll stay the night, maybe two," Shaun tried to explain gently. "Then we'll pack up all of your stuff and go back to Minneapolis."

Trevor looked at him with big, broken eyes and didn't ask about preschool.

"We'll get you signed up for a great school there," Shaun said anyway. "With lots of kids your age that you can make friends with."

Trevor went back to inspecting his feet and Shaun pulled out the house key and tried to unlock the deadbolt.

The key wouldn't turn.

He pulled it out and checked the tag. This was the right key.

It went easily back into the lock, but no amount of wiggling it seemed to budge the bolt.

Then Trevor turned at the sound of a creak and began to tug at his hand. "Miss Andrea! Daddy, that's Miss Andrea! She lives next door!"

Shaun looked down at Trevor first. It was as animated as he'd been since Harriette had first dragged him into his office, and it gave Shaun the first ray of hope since that moment.

He turned to identify the source of Trevor's excitement, and found a woman standing at the gate next door.

She had long dark hair that made her look even shorter than she actually was, and warm caramel skin. She was wearing a dark tank top that showed off a glorious amount of cleavage, and a light-weight sweater was wrapped around her waist.

Most arresting were her eyes, golden and fierce even across what passed as a lawn at this house.

Inside him, Shaun's tiger gave a primal growl and Shaun was shocked by the unexpected, instant desire that coursed through him.

He had heard of the mate instinct; it was sometimes romanticized as love at first sight, and Shaun had always dismissed it as a fairy tale out of hand.

Now here he was, feeling helplessly swept up in his tiger's lust and longing.

This is not convenient timing, he told his tiger. He was keenly aware of the public scrutiny along the block, and of Trevor, who was trying to drag him over to the hedge as Miss Andrea walked towards them in response to his call.

Then they were standing just across the hedge from each other and Shaun was glad of the shrubbery between them, because otherwise he might be compelled to act on his tiger's strong impulses.

Up close, she was even more gorgeous, and she smelled like wind and just faintly of sweat, which made his tiger roll in ecstasy.

"Hi Miss Andrea," Trevor said, bouncing on his toes.

"Hi, Trevor," she answered kindly, and having her look at the little boy for a moment gave Shaun a moment to try to collect himself. "We missed you at preschool today."

"I missed making Easter baskets," Trevor said mournfully.

"Don't worry," Andrea said cheerfully. "I made an extra one just for you."

At Trevor's slow, grateful smile, Shaun might have kissed her even without his tiger's instincts trying to drive him into inappropriate actions.

Then she returned her gaze to Shaun and extended a hand. "I'm Andrea. I'm the assistant at Hands and Hearts preschool. You must be Trevor's dad."

Shaun gave her the swiftest handshake he could manage; the touch of her fingers was absolutely electric, and he wanted to simply cling to her in abject desperation. "Shaun," he finally remembered to say, once he'd taken his hand back. "Shaun Powell."

"Shaun," she repeated, smiling at him. Then she blinked and shook her head as if she were waking from a dream. "So, Shaun. Are you moving in or out?"

Trevor looked up at him sadly.

"In," Shaun said promptly. "We're staying through the end of the semester."

He wasn't sure whose smile was most rewarding. He held up the deadbolt key. "If I can manage to get *into* the house."

CHAPTER 4

$\mathcal{I}$t was swelteringly hot, considering how early it was, the midwestern sun beating down from a cloudless sky. The snow from the week before had melted entirely.

Andrea peeled off her sweater as she walked. The tank top underneath wasn't preschool appropriate, but it was a lot more comfortable. She tied the sweater around her waist, tugging it as tightly as she could because she knew it was only the matter of a block of walking before it would slither itself loose again.

Fortunately, the preschool was only a few blocks from her house.

Everything in Green Valley was a few blocks from her house.

Andrea squinted into the sky. Heat this early meant the summer was probably going to be brutal.

She was thinking about applying for work at one of the local farms for the summer, but the idea had about as much appeal as asking for more hours at Gran's Grits. Work at the preschool was her favorite job, by far, of all the opportunities before her, but it barely paid her utilities and insurance during the winter, and there was only another month before it broke off for summer.

If she could just turn her writing into something that could cover those summer months…

Andrea sighed. She loved the idea of being a writer, but if she had to be brutally honest with herself, she knew that she was failing at it, like she'd failed at her dog grooming business, and at landscaping architecture school, and even at being a cashier at the local grocery store.

Fly...

If only it were that easy.

Fly...

When she was feeling most insecure was when she most craved the peace and simplicity of the sky, and the wind under her wings as a hawk. But half of Green Valley was still blissfully ignorant of the shifters that lived among them.

So she trudged along on her own short human legs, getting damp with perspiration at the waist and cleavage, constantly tugging on her sweater to keep it at her waist.

As she finally turned into her front gate, she looked next door to find a car parked in front of Harriette's house.

It wasn't Harriette's ridiculous purple car, but it was an equally ostentatious luxury vehicle.

Andrea's heart sank. She was hoping that Harriette's flurry of packing and hasty retreat had been an end to her undesirable neighbor. She would miss having Trevor next door to slip cookies to, but not his aggravating mother.

Now she must be back with some new guy – some guy with lots of money, just the way Harriette liked them.

But there was no sign of Harriette, nor any sound of her strident voice. Trevor was standing dejectedly with a man in an understated suit who was trying to unlock the front door.

The squeak of her gate got Trevor's attention. His face brightened and he tugged at the man's hand. "Miss Andrea! Daddy, that's Miss Andrea! She lives next door!"

After gazing down at Trevor in surprise, the man turned with a scowl and Andrea sucked in her breath as his steel gray eyes met hers from across the yard and her world fell away.

Somehow, she walked in a daze to meet him as Trevor dragged him to the short hedge that separated their property.

Up close, he was even more arresting than he'd been standing on Harriette's – on his – front step. He filled up his suit deliciously, all broad shoulders and narrow hips and other features that Andrea was already trying to write descriptions for in her head.

He was straight out of a bedside romance novel, with his perfect jaw and neatly trimmed dark blond hair. His eyes were gray and tragic, and when he touched her hand in a perfectly cursory hand-shake, Andrea felt like she might actually faint.

"There's a trick to the lock," she was able to say, when he confessed his inability to unlock the house. She sounded shrill to her own ears, nervous and juvenile. "I'll show you."

For a moment, the hedge confused her, and Andrea had to draw a breath and decide whether to hop over it or walk the long way around back through her gate.

Decorum, she decided, and backtracked around on the side-walk, hitching her sweater tighter.

Trevor, bouncing in excitement, met her at the property corner and gave her an eager hug. Andrea knelt to give him a full embrace. Trevor was one of the students who drank up affection like a thirsty sponge, constantly seeking approval.

Besides, hugging him gave her a moment to try to collect her thoughts before she stood back up and faced Shaun.

Her hawk was singing non-stop in her head the entire time. *Ours, ours, ours, ours.*

I can't think when you do that, Andrea protested.

We don't need to think. Just knock him down and get him out of those clothes.

There is a 5 year old right here. To say nothing of the gossipy neigh-bors who were avidly watching all along the block.

Her hawk settled with a flip of wings, but Andrea knew that she wouldn't be put off for long.

What is wrong with you? Andrea asked silently as she accepted the key from Shaun, with the barest tingling brush of his fingers. "It's a little sticky, but you also have to pull the key back out the tiniest bit to get it to turn, so don't just force it."

He's ours, he's ours, he's our mate! her hawk trilled merrily.

In the middle of demonstrating the trick, keenly aware of how close Shaun was standing in order to observe her, Andrea suddenly froze. *Our mate?* she echoed incredulously.

Ours, ours, ours, her hawk chortled.

Andrea made herself finish turning the key and the deadbolt shot back. "Nothing to it," she said weakly. "I babysit Trevor all the time, so I know all the tricks."

"Thank you," Shaun said, and even his voice was perfect, musically gruff. It sent little shivers down Andrea's spine.

Trevor wriggled past them into the house. "I can show you my room, Daddy!" he said eagerly. "And my trains! I have…" the rest of his excited babble was lost as he scurried inside.

Andrea remained on the porch as Shaun started to follow him, then paused and turned back to her.

"Would you like to… ah… come in?"

"Yes," she said helplessly.

She wanted to follow this man anywhere he led her.

CHAPTER 5

Shaun held the door open for Andrea and stood carefully out of the way. It took every ounce of his self-control not to reach out and touch her as she passed; the silky fall of her hair was tantalizing.

"There's a light, probably," he said, looking for the switch next to the door.

"Over here," Andrea supplied, showing him where it was, half-hidden behind the heavy curtains.

There was a moment of confusion over who was going to turn it on, both of them reaching towards it when they thought the other wouldn't. Andrea flipped it on after a false start.

Shaun gave a sheepish chuckle. "You know my house better than I do," he said.

"Shall I give you a tour?" Andrea offered lightly.

"Much appreciated," Shaun accepted.

They stood looking at each other for just a moment, and Shaun thought that her face looked even prettier flushed.

Was she aware that they were mates? If the stories were true, humans usually felt an immediate attraction, but without an animal breathing down her neck like Shaun's tiger was doing to him, it probably didn't feel much more than an unexpected wave of desire.

It occurred to him that he was going to have to explain to her that he was a tiger shifter, if he wanted to try to tell her about the mate instinct.

As Andrea led him through the living room, through the kitchen, pointing out the utility room and the tiny downstairs bathroom, he stared at the back of her head with consternation. How did you even start a conversation like that?

Weirder still, he *wanted* to tell her.

"Come see my rooooom," Trevor hollered, already halfway up the stairs.

"Be right up," Shaun promised.

Andrea continued around more quickly, pointing out the pantry under the stairs, and the formal dining room, filled with the ugliest, uncomfortable-looking dining set Shaun had ever seen. It all looped back to the living room, and they were standing at the bottom of the stairs.

"The... ah... bedrooms are up there, of course," Andrea said, chewing on her lip.

"Come see my roooooom," Trevor called.

Don't let her leave, Shaun's tiger insisted.

As Shaun was trying to figure out any excuse to get her up the stairs, Trevor added, "Miss Andrea! Miss Andrea, I made a house and you have to help me with the roof!"

Not sure if he should be insulted that his son didn't think he was capable of the task, or just grateful for his interference, Shaun let Andrea walk up the carpeted steps first. When her sweater slithered from her waist, he was rewarded with a view of the most gorgeous ass he'd ever seen, cupped in paint-stained blue jeans.

He caught the sweater before it could reach the steps. "Got it," he said cheerfully, and did not offer to hand it back to her.

With a blushing backwards glance that suggested she'd seen through his ruse, Andrea finished her ascent to the top floor. Shaun followed two steps at a time and reluctantly gave her back her sweater.

"Come, come look!"

Trevor proceeded to show him into the messiest room that Shaun had ever witnessed.

A sheet over a table, clipped to chairs, formed a house in the middle of the room, decorated with pillows and stuffed with buckets of tinker toys and stuffed animals and… toys that Shaun couldn't even identify.

Completely unruffled by the mess, Andrea helped Trevor secure the loose edge of the sheet, and they spread the chairs to make it big enough for Shaun to fold uncomfortably into.

"I should probably get home..." Andrea started to say, but Trevor took her by the hand and dragged her into the house, to Shaun's delight.

"You have to *test* it with us," Trevor insisted.

It was a very small space, and although she was a small young woman, they all had to sit quite close together to fit. She and Shaun carefully did not look at each other, and he wondered if she was as hyper-aware of his closeness as he was of hers.

Trevor, utterly delighted by their attention, proceeded to show Shaun each of his most prized possessions.

Shaun was flattered to find that some of the gifts he had sent were favored toys, and puzzled to discover that old packaging and scraps of ribbon and scribbled receipts were equally important to Trevor. He and Andrea indulged the boy's imagination and let him playact that he was a 'seller,' demanding pretend money for each treasure that he handed them.

Shaun was willing to pay any price the boy named, but Andrea bargained with him shrewdly. "I'll only pay one thousand dollars for that book," she teased. "Look, it has teethmarks on it!"

"I chewed it when I was a baby," Trevor conceded. "Okay, it's free."

Shaun felt a stab of guilt. He should have *been* there when that happened. He should know these stories already, not be watching his new neighbor out of the corner of his eyes for all the clues he needed.

"I have to stretch out," Andrea said, just as Shaun recognized that his muscles were protesting the uncomfortable position he was trapped in. "This is a little boy tent, not a grown-up sized house."

They all crawled out carefully, Shaun trying not to stare at Andrea's perfect, curvy body as she navigated the cramped space.

"We should buy you some new shelves to put this all on," Shaun said, looking around at the disarray of the room as he finally managed to wriggle from the sheet-constructed house without collapsing it.

Trevor yawned, and Shaun remembered how long their day had been. Did Trevor still take naps? There was so much he didn't know. A glance at his watch showed that it was later than he had expected; outside, the sun was fading fast.

"Want some dinner, kiddo?" he asked.

Trevor brightened. "Yeah, I'm hungry."

"I should get home and get my own dinner going," Andrea said, sounding shy.

"Can Miss Andrea have dinner with us?" Trevor begged.

"Oh, I couldn't," Andrea said. "You weren't expecting a guest. You just got here!"

"We'd love to have you," Shaun insisted, even as he realized he had no idea what the kitchen held.

Andrea looked up at him, and her look was complicated and full of longing. "I..."

"Pleeeeaaaassssse?" Trevor managed to pack about a dozen extra vowels into the plea.

Shaun was somehow relieved to find that Andrea was no more immune to Trevor's big-eyed entreaty than Shaun was.

"I'd like that," Andrea agreed. She smiled. "I only had sandwich ingredients at home anyway."

Shaun smiled back, and stood chivalrously aside to let her go first.

At the top of the stairs, Trevor slipped his hand into Shaun's, and Shaun looked down at him in surprise; the act of trust hit something inside that he hadn't expected.

They followed Andrea down to the kitchen.

CHAPTER 6

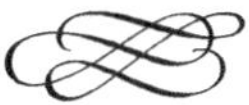

Shaun slammed the refrigerator door shut immediately after opening it and cleared his throat. "That's going to require an exorcism," he said.

"What's an exercise em?" Trevor asked.

Andrea smothered her laughter, wondering how Shaun was going to tackle the topic as he met her eyes with a briefly panicked expression.

"Bleach water," Shaun improvised sensibly, rather than trying to explain demonic possession. "The fridge needs lots of bleach water. Let's see what's in the pantry."

The pantry had a family-sized box of macaroni and cheese that made Trevor's eyes light up with glee.

"It's not fancy, but it's the kind with the sauce in a foil package, no questionable milk or expired butter required," Shaun said, reading it thoughtfully.

"It sounds delicious," Andrea said without lying. "As a connoisseur of boxed food and canned soups, I can assure you that is very high end."

"What's a can of sewer?" Trevor asked.

Andrea had no luck whatsoever muffling her amusement at that one, and Shaun gave a hearty roar of laughter.

Trevor laughed hesitantly, trying to figure out the joke.

"A *connoisseur* is someone who's got really good taste," Andrea explained.

"I think mac and cheese tastes really good," Trevor said earnestly.

"There we go then," Andrea said cheerfully. "Two votes for mac and cheese."

"Look out!" Shaun said, turning and nearly tripping over Trevor, who was standing directly behind him. "I'm going to be boiling water, so be careful."

There was a moment of tension, and Andrea could see him regret his strong voice as Trevor's chin trembled and he started to slump out of the kitchen.

"You don't have to go that far," Shaun said swiftly, before Andrea could remind herself that it wasn't her place to comfort the little boy.

"Here," Shaun suggested, finding a footstool. "Why don't you sit here and tell me what to do next."

"I can't read," Trevor confessed shyly, taking the box. Andrea pulled a chair up next to him.

"You can make it up," Shaun suggested. "I'll do whatever you tell me."

Trevor stared at him, glanced at Andrea for support, then looked down at the box tentatively. "Um… first you have to make the water hot."

Andrea directed him to the cabinet for a pot of the correct size. Shaun filled it in the farm-style sink and figured out how to light the gas stove without her assistance. "What's next?"

Trevor pretended to consult the box. "It has to bubble. Then add noodles."

Shaun retrieved the box and dumped the noodles into the water once it started boiling. "How long do they cook?" he asked, returning the box.

Trevor considered. "One hun-red minutes."

Andrea giggled and, reading the box over his shoulder, held up eight fingers for Shaun.

Shaun set the timer. "Yes, boss."

Trevor giggled. "We need the bowl with holes in it."

Andrea pointed out the cabinet for the colander and Shaun found it quickly.

Drunk with his new power, Trevor commanded, "Put it on your head!"

Shaun obediently did so, to Andrea's delight.

Trevor nearly fell off his stool chortling and Andrea giggled helplessly. Her initial impression of Shaun had been of an aloof man in a business suit. But with his jacket off, his sleeves rolled up, and a colander on his head, there was no way to take him too seriously.

While the noodles boiled, Trevor directed Shaun through a series of increasingly ridiculous tasks, laughing harder with each antic until his commands were completely unintelligible and Andrea's sides hurt from laughter.

The timer finally hauled them back and Shaun burnt his tongue testing a noodle, then drained them and mixed in the sauce.

They took their bowls into the dining room and Trevor threw himself onto his hyper-colored noodles.

Andrea was glad for his enthusiasm; if he had not been so busy trying to get her attention and tell her things through his mouthfuls of food, she knew she would be gazing in helpless longing across the table at Shaun. She thought she'd done a decent job so far of playing herself off as just a friendly neighbor who knew his son, not a helplessly smitten idiot who couldn't stop imagining him taking his shirt off.

Her train of thought was not helped by her hawk, who was keeping up a monotonous chorus of *Ours, ours, ours* in the back of her head, despite several pleas to just *stop*.

It was hard enough not to watch Shaun eat.

The way his jaw worked, and the amusement in his eyes as he put more noodles into Trevor's bowl after the first was vacuumed up… Andrea made herself look back at Trevor and stop thinking about Shaun's eyes.

After his third refill, Trevor began to look glazed-over, his hysteria ebbing away to a tired stupor.

"I think it's time for bed, kiddo," Shaun suggested. "Finish that last bite."

"Let me help clear up," Andrea insisted, standing and gathering the empty bowls.

"Don't wanna go to bed," Trevor protested, eyes heavy and slow.

"You're going to anyway," Shaun said firmly.

Trevor looked like he might protest and Andrea backed carefully into the kitchen. She knew better than to get in the way of a test of wills between parent and child.

It was weird and intimate, watching them navigate each other. She knew that Shaun couldn't have been in Trevor's life much; she had lived next door to Trevor for two years and had never seen his father. They were clearly just starting to build trust… and already it was apparent that there was a beautiful bond growing there.

As attracted to Shaun as Andrea could not deny that she was, she was happier yet to see Trevor with a parent that would care about him. She had always adored the sweet little boy, and wished a better life for him.

She was putting the dishes in the dishwasher, listening to Trevor's whine and Shaun's growl without being able to hear any words, when there was an unexpected soft *thump* and a very growl-like growl.

She put the pan in the bottom tray of the dishwasher and looked up as Shaun, looking rather wild around the eyes, came into the kitchen.

"Thank you for your help unlocking the house and showing me around, I will have to make you a real dinner at some point, it was lovely to meet you, Trevor will see you at preschool tomorrow morning."

Without really understanding how or why, Andrea let him herd her out of the kitchen and out onto the front porch.

"I… uh… thank you for dinner," she said, baffled. "Good..."

The front door closed firmly in her face.

"… Night."

Andrea stared at the door for a long moment, trying to make sense out of any of it.

Ours, her hawk muttered unhelpfully.

She turned away slowly, glancing back over her shoulder at the house.

They aren't ours, she said firmly.

Even if she already wanted them to be.

CHAPTER 7

"You have to go to bed now," Shaun insisted, grateful that Andrea had taken the dishes to the kitchen and wasn't witnessing his complete inability to do a basic parenting task like convince a completely exhausted kid to go to bed. "Finish that bite."

Perhaps recognizing that the macaroni in his spoon was all that was between him and the horrors of bed, Trevor sucked a single noodle off of it and spent a good minute defiantly chewing it.

"You're just trying to waste time," Shaun said crossly. "Put it all in your mouth."

Trevor got another single noodle into his mouth.

Shaun recognized the challenge, and knew that Trevor was testing him. And what was he going to do? Throw him over his shoulder and haul him off to bed?

"Mommy let me stay up and watch TV," Trevor said slyly, watching his face.

Shaun could feel his temper, stretched like an abused rubber band and threatening to snap. "I am not your mother," he growled. "And I am not going to do things the way she did. And you are going to finish that bite and you are going to go to bed and Andrea is going to go home. Right. Now."

Trevor's eyes got big in his face and he froze, spoon still suspended in front of his mouth. His face got redder and redder, and then, like mercury, he shifted into a solid, fluffy little lion cub swimming in little boy clothing. The spoon clattered to the table and sent the final few cheesy noodles spinning in every direction.

Standing on the chair with his tail fluffed up and his front paws, too big for his frame, on the table, lion-Trevor opened his mouth and gave a wail of surprise that turned to a growl.

Shaun swore, then remembered that Trevor still had ears. He resorted to his own growls when he failed to find safe words that did the situation any justice at all.

A clank of pots from the kitchen drove panic into Shaun's heart.

He had to get Andrea out of here.

Even if he had considered telling her about himself, it was one thing to confess to being a shifter, and quite another to expose a five-year-old as what most people fearfully considered a freak of nature. Trevor's secret was his own to protect.

And he couldn't even *spell* protect yet.

"Wait *here*," he told the lion cub. "Don't move."

Andrea was putting the last dish into the dishwasher as he came into the kitchen, and her warm smile as she stood nearly made him forget why he was there.

Trevor.

Trevor was a lion.

"Thank you for your help unlocking the house and showing me around, I will have to make you a real dinner at some point, it was lovely to meet you, Trevor will see you at preschool tomorrow morning."

Shaun let the words tumble from him as he herded her directly for the front door.

While she was still thanking him, puzzled, for the dinner, he shut the door on her and dashed back to the dining room.

Trevor had given in to sleep at last, and was lying in a boneless heap on the clothing he had squirmed out of.

A boneless, *furry* heap.

Shaun hadn't started shifting until puberty; he hadn't even known that shifting this young was possible.

Bad enough that he didn't know the first damn thing about being a father, now he was the father of an unpredictable *shifter* child.

But looking down on the slumbering cub, Shaun could find no regret.

He was glad this had happened with him, not with Harriette; surely she would have brought something like this up if it was something Trevor had done before?

Probably, this was the first time Trevor had shifted, all worked up after too long a day of traveling and his whole life being dumped upside down.

Shaun knelt and gathered the limp cub into his arms, cradling the creature against his shoulder.

Trevor's mother had abandoned him. He was stuck with a father he barely knew. He'd missed the day at preschool that he'd desperately wanted to attend. Add a late dinner and an argument to that, and Shaun didn't blame him for wanting to escape into some other form.

"I'd protect you from all of this if I could," Shaun said, holding the lion cub close. "I should have... tried harder to make it work, gotten a better lawyer. I should have been here for you more."

Trevor stirred in his sleep, nuzzling his whiskered nose against Shaun's neck.

He shifted back to a little boy halfway up the stairs, and barely came awake as Shaun awkwardly tried to dress him in a pair of superhero pajamas.

"Daddy?"

"Yeah?" Would he have questions about being a shifter? Shaun braced himself.

"Do you like Miss Andrea?"

That wasn't the question Shaun was prepared for. "Yes," he said helplessly, thinking of her laughing golden eyes and gorgeous curves. "I like her a lot."

Our mate, his tiger reminded him with a purr.

"I don't want you to like her," Trevor said with unexpected fierceness, his blue eyes suddenly wide open and intense.

Shaun froze in the act of tucking the blanket around Trevor's neck.

"She's your teacher," Shaun reminded his son plaintively. "Don't *you* like her?"

"I like her as a teacher," Trevor said, as if the distinction was clear. "That's all you should like her, too."

Shaun felt like his chest had been carved hollow. Every half-formed idea he'd had about telling Andrea he was a shifter, and her mate, was suddenly, abruptly dead.

His tiger gave a yowl of despair.

Trevor was the only thing in their world that could have kept him from Andrea.

For someone who wasn't even four feet tall, it was a lot of power.

Before he could stop himself, Shaun vowed, "I won't then. I promise."

The words were like a vice around his heart.

CHAPTER 8

ndrea counted paintbrushes out into paper cups and dug the scissors out of the back of the cabinet, then stared at the list of things left to collect for several moments without reading a single word.

"Use your sounds if the word seems complicated," Patricia teased her, limping in through the storage room door to switch out the poster for the next letter behind her chair. "A sounds like ah or aye. B sounds like buh…"

Andrea blushed. "Thanks, Miss Patricia," she said mockingly, shaking her head. She gathered up the rest of the supplies she needed efficiently, and followed Patricia out to set up the room for the onslaught of preschoolers.

"I met Trevor's dad," she said as casually as she could, placing the supplies at each desk.

Patricia glanced over at her suspiciously and Andrea felt her traitorous cheeks heat again. "Do tell!"

"Just briefly," Andrea protested. "I helped him unlock the house. It has a tricky deadbolt. And I watched Trevor for Harriette some-times, so I knew how to work it. That's all. Just unlocked the house for him, and showed him where the light switches were." She made herself shut her mouth.

Patricia's laugh was as golden as her hair. "Oh, you got it bad," she teased. "Is he a dish?"

"Such a dish," Andrea admitted. "The most gorgeous, steel-gray eyes. And these *shoulders*…" She caught herself making vague shapes with her hands and put herself back to work putting art supplies at each spot.

"And?"

"And the jaw. And the legs. And the suit. And the smile…" Andrea sighed to remember and her hawk gave a whistle of anticipation.

"And?!" Patricia insisted. "Have you got a date?"

"No!" Andrea protested. "All I did was unlock his house." How many times could you say unlock in one conversation before you sounded like an idiot? "Well, we did have dinner. But it was just a box of macaroni and cheese."

"Mmm, unlock his house," Patricia said suggestively. "It sounds like you did."

They both giggled like schoolgirls, and then the bell at the front door jingled cheerfully and the first of the children began to arrive.

Andrea debated telling Patricia about how her hawk was insisting that Shaun was her mate; she had told Patricia she was a shifter, and Patricia's boyfriend Lee was a bear shifter. Were *they* mates? Certainly their attraction had been mutual and immediate, but Andrea didn't know for sure, and wasn't willing to risk driving a wedge into what appeared to be a fairy tale romance if Patricia *wasn't* Lee's mate.

Attraction can happen without being mates, she told her hawk firmly. *You're just confused because it's been a long time since there was anyone in town worth being interested in.*

None of her logic could save her when Shaun walked in with Trevor.

He was not wearing a suit, but he may as well have been, he was so neatly pressed and put together. Andrea was keenly aware of her worn jeans and stained t-shirt. She was also keenly aware of her nethers, which were as obnoxiously interested in him as her hawk was. Her whole body seemed to hum with need.

She was trying to decide if her voice would wobble if she offered her usual cheerful good morning, when Trevor spotted her and waved, drawing the attention of his dad.

Andrea had no voice left at all.

Shaun's gaze was like a shot of sunlight after rain, and Andrea had to force herself not to bolt across the room into his arms.

You don't even know if you'd be welcome there, she reminded herself with clenched teeth. It had certainly *seemed* like he was interested in her, but the unceremonious way he had shown her out left her feeling terribly unsure.

We know, her hawk muttered.

She wasn't the only one who noticed him, either.

"Hel-lo!" trilled one of the mothers dropping off a daughter. Her prominent wedding ring didn't stop her from eyeing him appreciatively and obviously as she played with her styled hair.

Andrea had to turn away before she rushed to defend what wasn't even hers. She stalked, instead, to a creative play station being abused by Aaron, one of the other little boys, and knelt to encourage and demonstrate more gentle play.

"You weren't kidding," Patricia said, settling beside her as the door jingled behind them with the parents leaving. "Dish indeed!"

The children were oblivious to the reference and Andrea scowled at her friend. "Aren't you supposed to be staying off of your ankle?"

"I'm sitting!" Patricia insisted with a warm laugh. "See?"

"Can we play stand-and-sit?" Aaron begged.

"If Andrea wants to," Patricia said with a smile for Aaron and a sly sideways grin for Andrea.

Andrea wanted very different things, but a game of stand-and-sit would distract her for a little while, so she gathered the interested children and started the rowdy singing exercise with them.

CHAPTER 9

To Shaun's relief, Trevor was still a little boy in the morning, and didn't bring up the topic of his unexpected shift.

Shaun watched the boy devour a granola bar and a box of raisins for breakfast. He was going to have to go shopping today as soon as he dropped Trevor off. And bleach the fridge before he stocked it.

"Do you ever wish you were an animal?" he asked leadingly, helping himself to another granola bar.

"I *am* an animal!" Trevor said enthusiastically.

Shaun froze, oatmeal brick partway to his mouth. "You… are?"

"I'm a dog! A flying dog! I can sniff out danger and bite bad guys!" Trevor began to enthusiastically demonstrate his sniffing, nearly toppling his water glass and scattering raisins.

Shaun's heart returned to normal and he had to laugh, saving the water glass and retrieving the raisins that had bounced across the table. "Well, get ready for preschool, Puppydog," he suggested. "We don't want to be late."

Trevor seemed to have no memory of his shift, and Shaun had

hope that it was just a one-time thing, brought on by too much stress and uncertainty.

He could not find a good way to determine if Trevor remembered the promise he had coaxed from Shaun. It was an impossible vow, not to *like* Andrea. But wasn't he obligated to keep it anyway?

He was desperate to see Andrea again, and dreaded the apology he owed her. How was he going to explain how rude he'd been the night before? How was he going to be able to look at her and not want her more than he'd promised he would?

To his mixed relief, the preschool drop off gave him no opportunity to talk to Andrea at all. She met his eyes briefly, and before Shaun could formulate actual words, she was turning away to save some play equipment from the abuse of one of the children.

He realized belatedly that there was a woman trying to make conversation with him, batting mascara-crusted eyelashes at him.

"I have places to be," he growled, when his scowl failed to scare her off.

Green Valley had only one all-purpose grocery store, and although it was small and poorly lit, it proved to be unexpectedly well-stocked. Shaun bought a box of trash bags, considered, and dropped another box of them into his cart. Harriette had taken all of her personal belongings, but had left piles of miscellaneous things that he had no interest in keeping.

Industrial-strength cleaner went into the cart, then came out in favor of more child-friendly 'green' cleaner. Was Trevor old enough to stay out of toxic things? Shaun frowned. He would have to make sure everything was up out of reach. Should there be covers on the electrical outlets? Or was that only for toddlers?

The produce was an interesting mix of sad-looking imports and beautiful local greenhouse goods. Shaun considered a fat red tomato.

He could make Andrea a fresh spaghetti meal. He could bake bread, if the oven worked, and make sauce from scratch. Kids liked spaghetti, didn't they? They didn't have blocks of Parmesan, but the grated stuff would do.

There was a selection of local meat as well, and Shaun frowned over a choice of beautiful steaks. Did the house have a grill? Did Andrea eat meat? For that matter, did Trevor like it?

He realized with a scowl that he was automatically considering Andrea in his meal plans, and took the second steak out of his cart, then put it back in. He could offer her a neighborly dinner without breaking his vow, something to redeem himself as a cook after having to serve her a meal from a box.

"Always take the second steak," a voice beside him unexpectedly advised.

A plump, gray-haired woman was reaching past him for a package of chicken and she winked at him.

Shaun smiled warily, not sure how seriously to take the wink.

"Big strapping man like you needs his steak," she teased him. "Now, you must be new here."

"Yes, ma'am," Shaun said automatically.

She looked at him critically. "You must be Harriette's ex, Trevor's dad. Shaun, isn't it? You're living in the Reynolds' old place."

Shaun didn't know the origins of the house, but the reminder of Harriette made him frown without comment.

"You'd be right there next to Andrea, then."

Just the sound of her name made Shaun's heart rate increase. He growled something vaguely affirmative.

"I'm Marta," the old woman continued, oblivious. "I live two blocks over, by Gran's Grits. You've been there?"

"To your house?"

Marta laughed. "To Gran's! Best little restaurant in town. Of course, Harvey's isn't much competition. They've got a liquor license, though, so they do better business. Andrea works there, you know."

"At Harvey's?" Why did the sound of her name reduce him to such idiocy?

Marta chuckled again. "At Gran's. Waitresses in the afternoons after the preschool. She's quite the looker, isn't she?"

Shaun sputtered, utterly incapable of a coherent reply, and found something fascinating to inspect on a package of beef livers.

"No need to be coy with me, young man," Marta said with spice as she herded him back towards the vegetables and checked the ears of corn that were available, handing him those that passed her inspection and clearly expecting him to put them in his cart. "I know everything that goes on in this town. It's high time that girl settled down, and I don't see a ring on your finger."

As Shaun stared at her in shock, she continued breezily.

"I don't think much of your taste if you married Harriette, but we all make mistakes when we're young, and I imagine you figured that one out right fast."

Shaun was startled into giving a guffaw of laughter. "I did, at that," he agreed. It was hard not to like Marta, even if she was unnervingly straight-spoken. He reached up and got her a plastic produce bag at her imperious gesture.

She began to fill it with apples, tapping each one next to her ear to check for freshness. "I'm making you a pie, young man," she declared. "And you be sure to share it with your neighbor, you hear?"

Then she was pushing her squeaking cart away from Shaun, leaving him to bemusedly wander over to select a gallon of milk and a flat of eggs alone.

His smile quickly faded as he remembered his promise to Trevor.

Marta may not have seen a wedding ring, but that didn't mean he was free to follow his heart.

CHAPTER 10

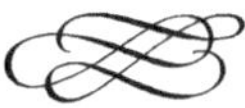

"Saw your young man at the grocery store," Marta told Andrea as she slid into the diner booth and took a copy of the laminated menu.

Andrea blushed.

"He's not my young man," she protested.

She thought about how Shaun had smiled at her, and wondered if he *could* be.

The idea put butterflies in her stomach and fire low in her belly.

Then she remembered how he'd shut the door on her face, and she shook her head.

"What can I get you?" Andrea asked quickly, fishing in her apron pocket for her pad.

"What's the special?" Marta asked.

Andrea found the pad and flipped it to a new page. "Oh, right. Corned beef sandwich and coleslaw."

"Does it look good?"

"I had one before my shift and it was the best sandwich Old George has ever made. A little salty," Andrea said candidly. "Soda machine is still down."

Marta handed back the laminated menu. "Special and iced tea, with plenty of sugar, like your new neighbor."

"He's not my… er… oh." Whatever else Shaun wasn't, he *was* her neighbor.

Marta laughed kindly as Andrea fled with her order.

Andrea had never been so glad of her reputation as an airhead. She managed to mix up refills, and nearly dumped a pitcher of ice cubes into Stanley's lap; only shifter reflexes enabled her to catch the pitcher after she dropped it. She had to ask one of her customers to repeat their order after she caught herself staring at a bowl of macaroni and cheese, daydreaming about how Shaun had looked with a colander on his head, hamming it up for his son.

Ours, ours, ours, her hawk continued to hum in the back of her head whenever she thought of Shaun, not helping her concentration in the slightest.

She didn't believe in mates… did she? It was more likely just a heady combination of hormones, wistful loneliness, and an utterly gorgeous new neighbor. She'd have to be stone dead not to be interested in him under normal circumstances, and add to that the fact that she'd been living basically like a nun since she'd come back from college… well, it was no wonder she was weak-kneed when she thought about him.

That made much more sense than magic and destiny.

No matter how much she longed for magic and destiny.

CHAPTER 11

Shaun wasn't really watching out of the window for his hot new neighbor. He just happened to notice that all of Andrea's lights except her porch light were out when he tucked Trevor into bed, and just happened to be sitting in the most uncomfortable chair in the living room with his laptop where he could see out the window to her front porch. And he just happened to be looking up from the work he was supposed to be doing when she came home, wearing an old-fashioned diner uniform.

The laptop was nearly unseated as he struggled out of the low, poorly-sprung chair with a curse.

It wasn't that he was desperate to see her again, or have her alone to himself. It was just that he needed her help.

That was all.

He was out on his own porch in a flash, clearing his throat and calling quietly, "Andrea?"

He didn't want to be too loud and wake Trevor, but Andrea must have good ears, because she paused with her hand on her open door. "Shaun?"

Hearing his name from her lips was a new kind of unsettling. Shaun had to clear his throat again.

"I wanted to apologize," he said in a rush. "I wanted to get Trevor right up to bed last night, he was so tired, and I was rude with you, I'm sorry. I'm not very comfortable with this being a dad thing yet."

"Oh!" Andrea said quietly. "Oh, don't worry about it. Of course I understand."

Shaun plowed on. "I was also wondering if you know why some of the lights in the house won't turn on. Trevor had a lot of trouble going to sleep without the hall light on. A *lot* of trouble."

"Let me guess," Andrea pulled her door shut and came to the closest edge of the porch. "He was up seven times, because he was scared, he was thirsty, he had to pee, he couldn't sleep without the light, he didn't have the right stuffy, he was itchy, and he wanted one more hug."

Shaun gave a gruff laugh. "Nailed it. Except that he had to go number two and that took approximately an hour."

"You might want to try a ticket system," Andrea said, leaning on her railing. The uniform didn't show off nearly as much as the previous day's tank top, but she was still all distractingly stacked curves and easy grace.

"A… ticket system?" Shaun dragged himself back to the conversation.

"Tell him he gets two tickets to get up after bed. Once he's used them up, he can't get out of bed again. Kids love tickets, and it will make him really consider whether or not his current reason for hopping up is worth using his ticket. Sometimes they are tired enough that just that extra moment of thought is enough stillness that they can let their body fall asleep."

"You know a lot about kids," Shaun said, a little enviously.

"I have a certificate in early education," Andrea said with a shrug. "But mostly I've learned this stuff from Patricia. She knows everything."

They gazed at each other across the tiny hedge and the two sets of porch railings until Shaun couldn't remember why he'd first called to her.

Then she looked down and cleared her throat. "You, ah, had a problem with your lights."

"Lights," Shaun agreed. "Right, lights. The light over the stairs and upstairs hallway, the upstairs bathroom, and the master bedroom."

"Sounds like you blew a fuse. Happens in these old houses all the time. I'll show you where the fuse box is." Andrea sounded all business, and Shaun had better control of himself by the time she had walked to the sidewalk and back onto his lawn.

She walked into his house like she owned it. "I babysat for Trevor a lot," she said as she showed him where the fuse box was tucked in beyond the shelves in the laundry room. She pointed out the correct switch and threw it.

"That should do it. But you ought to replace this other fuse."

"So it doesn't trip so easily?" The laundry rooms wasn't large, and Shaun had to stand close to Andrea, terribly aware of how badly he wanted to touch her, and how careful they were to not brush against each other, and not quite look at each other.

Andrea shook her head. "The opposite, actually. Some of these fuses don't match the wire gauge. It's something people do way too much – if they find that they are blowing circuits, they put in a bigger fuse so it doesn't trip so much. But the wiring just isn't robust enough for what they are trying to do, and they've taken out their safety net. Fuses trip for a reason."

Shaun had to stare. She wasn't just hot and great with kids, she was smart and capable. The whole package. Everything he'd ever wanted in a woman. And their timing was just so wrong.

"Is there an electrician in town I can hire?" Shaun said, swallowing down his desire.

Andrea was startled into looking straight at him, and even in the dim utility room, her unusual golden-brown eyes were bright. "You don't need an electrician. It's actually a really easy thing to do. I… could show you."

"Really?" Shaun wasn't thinking about that kind of electricity any more, only the electricity that was humming between them.

"Yeah," Andrea whispered.

"It's a little… frightening," Shaun murmured, no longer talking about the fuse box at all.

"Yeah," Andrea whispered.

For a long moment, the faint buzz of the laundry room light was the only sound.

Then Andrea gave a helpless little whimper and stepped towards him, tipping her head up for the kiss that Shaun was already leaning into.

CHAPTER 12

Andrea wasn't even sure what the conversation topic was anymore.

Shaun was so close, and so gorgeously tall and broad, and he smelled like earth after rain and like musk and like everything she had ever wanted.

She would have promised him anything at that moment, up to and including rewiring his entire house, and when he made the smallest of sways towards her, she could not help making a noise of helpless desire and moving to meet him.

His mouth was exactly what she'd been lying awake at night imagining, hot and fierce and demanding.

Her arms slipped up around his neck without resistance and the feeling of his arms around her, drawing her close, was like coming home. Andrea had been able to tell that he was built well through his tailored clothing, but now, pressed wantonly up against him, she could tell that had been the tip of the iceberg.

The man was ripped. The shoulders that filled out his shirts were knotted with muscles, and the arms under the shirt sleeves were thick and strong.

Without breaking their kiss for breath, he was lifting her off her feet and sitting her up on the washing machine so he wasn't bending over so far. Andrea hooked a leg around him to hold him close, while she tried with lust-clumsy fingers to unbutton the shirt that was keeping her from the amazing planes of his chest.

Shaun seemed to be suffering no such clumsiness; he had already gotten the buttons down the front of her uniform undone, and was pushing it back with his fingers so he could move his kisses down her neck and into the swells of flesh waiting below.

He nibbled and licked at her breasts and Andrea buried her fingers in his thick blond hair and bit back the cries she wanted to utter. She spread her legs wider and squirmed against him, just at the right height to feel the bulge of his lust for her. She felt she might go mad with desire, and there was entirely too much clothing between them still.

Clearly feeling the same, Shaun retreated reluctantly from her cleavage and finished the job that Andrea hadn't been able to concentrate on. She wasn't sure if he actually unbuttoned anything or simply tore it off, but he was shirtless at last, and working at his belt.

Andrea slipped off her bra, secretly glad when seeing the freedom of her breasts made Shaun fumble his pants and take his own turn being stumped by a button. She reached down to release the button and unzip him slowly, walking fingers down to touch him through the silky boxers he was wearing.

His whole body went rigid. One hand, which had been reaching for her nearest breast, closed reflexively around it as he gave a guttural moan.

Andrea gasped.

If they had been eager until now, it became frenzied.

Shaun jerked down his pants and underwear, wrenching his shoes off without untying them. Andrea tried to wriggle out of her uniform, to find her apron hopelessly knotted behind her, too tight to shimmy down off her hips or lift up over her head. Shaun gave it a tug that made stitches pop, then sensibly stopped, lifted up the skirt and pulled her soaking underwear down past her shoes.

Then, finally, he was pulling her onto the thick length of his cock, and she was wrapping her legs around him to get him deeper, crying out in pleasure and need.

The washer was noisy and clanked with every frantic motion, and when the cold concrete floor seemed unappealing, Shaun, still buried inside of her, carried her to the only slightly less uncomfortable kitchen table for several lingering thrusts, then into the living room, where they made it no further than the start of the carpet before he was laying her down to drive into her until her world exploded in brilliant sensation and he was crying out and jerking his release into her.

For several long, panting moments, they continued to move together, the after-effect of her orgasm leaving Andrea's limbs tingling and weak.

Shaun finally groaned and collapsed beside her and they lay and waited for their hearts to return to beating normally.

"Oh look," Andrea finally said, giggling helplessly. "The light over the stairs is working now."

CHAPTER 13

*P*retending that his world hadn't just been dumped upside down, Shaun craned his neck around to verify Andrea's observation. Sure enough, the light over the stairs was on now.

Somehow, after a round of sex like that, he was half expecting to find that they had taken the power out for an entire block.

He was caressing Andrea automatically, tracing the tantalizing lines of her neck and her perfect curves and he made himself stop as soon as he realized what he was doing.

It was somehow more intimate than their frantic love-making had been, and he was already swamped in doubts.

There are no doubts, his tiger told him, sated and content.

We promised, Shaun countered.

He sat up, keenly aware of Andrea's lush body still sprawled beside him. Even after *that*, he still craved her, and it was a challenge not to fall upon her with kisses and carry her off to his bedroom as his prize, even if he wasn't capable of doing more than curling around her for sleep for a while.

Perhaps sensing Shaun's second thoughts, Andrea sobered and sat up, brushing her loose hair back shyly. "I… ah… that wasn't exactly how I was planning to help you with the electricity." She turned her attention to the knotted straps of her apron, not meeting Shaun's eyes.

"Here, let me help you," Shaun said before he could stop himself.

Andrea turned away and held her hair aside so that he could work at the impressive knot they'd managed to make. It took all of his self-control not to stroke her bare skin while he worked, and he was amused to realize that her blush showed at the back of her neck through the natural tan of her skin.

"Thank you," he said, as he released the tangled fabric at last. "I… just… thank you."

"You're welcome," Andrea said shyly, pulling the uniform up over her arms and giving him a sidelong glance.

Shaun recognized that he was in deep water. He wanted to pull her close and never let her go, to ask her to marry him on the spot.

But he'd made a *promise*.

"I don't want you to get the wrong idea," he said firmly. "This was great, and you are…" calling her hot seemed both crude and painfully inadequate. "Amazing."

Her intense eyes made talking to her distracting and Shaun had to look down, realizing he was still completely naked. "But this is a weird time," he confessed, meaning it in several ways. "Trevor's just been abandoned by his mom, and he needs stability right now, not a dad who's navigating some sort of…"

Mate, his tiger tried to supply.

"Relationship," Shaun said firmly.

"Oh, sure," Andrea said too quickly. "I completely understand. This doesn't have to be… a thing. I mean, it was a thing. Just a thing."

"Yeah," Shaun said, not sure if he was glad she was being so accepting, or if he hurt that she was agreeing so quickly. "Just a thing."

Andrea giggled then, a warm, comfortable sound. "Helluva thing, though," she said honestly as she stood. "I've got to find my under*things*."

See? Shaun told his tiger in triumph. *She's being completely reasonable about this. No ridiculous hangups about mates and destiny. It's just a thing.*

But neither he, nor his tiger, was completely convinced.

CHAPTER 14

Andrea walked as slowly up her front walk as she knew how, hoping she would catch the attention of Shaun without having to actually go to his door.

To her joy, she was still unlocking her door when she heard the creak of his steps on his porch.

"Andrea?"

"Shaun!" Andrea realized she sounded far too eager and cleared her throat. "I, ah, have something for you."

Shaun was silent for a moment and Andrea rushed on. "I was at Ted's Hardware and picked up the fuse you needed."

"You didn't have to do that," Shaun protested.

"It was a couple of bucks," Andrea said dismissively. "And I was there anyway." That was a lie. She'd had no other purpose at Ted's but to pick up the fuse and hope that she ran into Shaun so she could give it to him.

"Thank you," Shaun said, sounding gruff in the shadows of his ill-lit porch. "I… really appreciate it."

"I also wrote you up some instructions, in case I didn't run into you," Andrea said shyly. "Let me go grab them."

In the stillness of her own empty house, Andrea took a deep

breath and reminded herself that what had happened was just a *thing*. This was not courtship, and she wasn't really trying to catch his attention or angling for a repeat of the night before.

She was just being neighborly.

And sort of *hoping* that the *thing* happened again.

She tripped back down her walk more briskly than she'd walked up it, and vaulted over his gate to close the distance to his house.

"I may have had a little too much fun writing this," she confessed, suddenly shy to hand over the pages. "Here's the replacement fuse, and I brought a flashlight, in case you didn't have one."

"A flashlight?" Even looking confused, Shaun was devastatingly handsome. "There's a light in the laundry room."

"You have to turn off the power to the house before you switch out a fuse," Andrea scolded him. "It's here in part one, in big letters."

Shaun laughed. "Of course. I'm an idiot," he said sheepishly.

"The jury's still out on that," Andrea teased him. "You want me to give you a hand?"

"Yeah," Shaun breathed, and they were suddenly talking about the other kind of electricity.

He was going to kiss her, Andrea was suddenly sure. He was going to kiss her again and all she could think about was the way his skin smelled and the way his bare chest had felt under her fingers and how he'd *filled* her.

He swallowed, instead of leaning in. "Yeah," he repeated firmly. "That would be great."

Andrea stuffed her memories back into the past where they belonged. "Let's go play with electricity," she said in her best enthusiastic preschool teacher voice.

CHAPTER 15

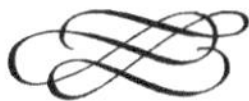

"That's the ground, we don't have to mess with that, there's the hot, and that's the return. Some of these old houses aren't color coded reliably, but mostly red or black is hot, white is the return, and bare or green is ground. You're lucky; I think the guy who wired my house got a deal on black wire, because it's arbitrarily used as ground in a bunch of places, and that can get confusing."

Andrea deftly unscrewed the first connection while Shaun held the flashlight over her head. He was hard as a rock and if she backed up an inch, she'd figure out exactly how badly he wanted her.

"Now your turn," she said, turning and brushing up against him.

For a moment, Shaun's brain completely shut off.

Andrea patiently put the screwdriver into his hand as if she hadn't noticed his rock hard cock. "It's not scary, I promise. All the power to the house is off and nothing can hurt you." She slipped the flashlight out of his hand and held it pointed at the box. "Go ahead and unscrew the next part."

Shaun took a deep breath and awkwardly unscrewed the last connection on the fuse, nervous under her scrutiny, and tense with his need for her.

Andrea showed him how to rock the fuse out of the base, and handed him the new one. "Just press it into place."

It wasn't what he wanted to press into place, but Shaun obediently popped the fuse in and when Andrea nudged him, then replaced the wires into the new connections, twisting the screws in tightly.

"Done!" Andrea said cheerfully. "Let's just put the panel cover back up, and go throw the switch!"

"That was it?" Shaun said bemusedly. "I thought there would be a lot more to it."

They lifted the panel cover into place and Shaun screwed it down.

"How'd you learn to do this?" he asked, tightening each screw carefully.

"I inherited my parents' house when they died; none of my extremely successful siblings had any use for an aging house in the small town they didn't want to come back to. And I couldn't afford a plumber or an electrician, so I learned a lot on YouTube."

Shaun recognized this as a dangerous moment.

It was the start of an actual conversation, the kind of thing where they talked about their families and ended up bonding about shared middle school experiences.

Though probably, her experiences didn't include turning into a tiger in the locker room of a boarding school unexpectedly.

"Shaun?"

His promise haunted him.

His son didn't want him to like Miss Andrea. Not seriously like her. And he owed Trevor so much, for so many years of his life that he'd missed. He couldn't break that promise and dissolve the trust they were just beginning to build. Not even for a woman who set him on fire with a single golden glance.

Our mate, his tiger insisted.

It's just… physical, he replied, barely able to form words because she was standing close in the tiny room, and the flashlight was casting her curves into sharp relief.

"Shaun?" she repeated, and it was almost a whine, as full of need as his own body.

The flashlight and screwdriver clattered to the floor as he reached for her and she moved to meet him.

If they made love any less urgently than they had the night before, it was not by much.

He carried her all the way to the couch as she wriggled out of her t-shirt, kissing every inch of skin as she exposed it, and was shucking off his pants before she got her bra off. She wrestled him out of his shirt as he did the same with her shorts, frequently at odds as their limbs tangled. Then, finally, he was buried in her again and she was clawing at his shoulders as he drew her into an orgasm that shuddered around his cock.

It was with great effort that he was able to resist joining her in the throes of pleasure, but he paced himself carefully and was able to raise her up again, her gorgeous body arching in a second agony of bliss below him as he finally released.

The couch was too narrow to comfortably lie next to each other, and Shaun feared that smothering her with his weight would put a crimp in their neighborly friendship, so he only gave himself a moment to catch his ragged breath before he rose up and attempted to reassemble his clothing.

Andrea lay panting only a few breaths longer, then sat up to clean herself and do the same.

"Daddy?"

Trevor's thin, tired voice from the top of the stairs made them both freeze.

"Daddy, why are all the lights off?"

"I was just working on the electricity, kiddo," Shaun said loudly as Andrea grimaced and yanked her shirt over her head as quietly as possible. "I'll fix it in just a second and come up and tuck you back in."

Trevor seemed to accept that, and padded sleepily back into his room.

"I'll flip the breaker on my way out," Andrea whispered as she crept for the front door, her bra stuffed into a pocket.

Then she was gone, and after only a moment, the lights sprang back to life.

CHAPTER 16

It was odd to have Shaun on *her* porch for once, and Andrea had to stare for a moment.

He was so handsome in the afternoon sun, with his neatly trimmed blond hair and gray eyes. He had clearly not shaved that morning; a dust of stubble made Andrea want to reach out and stroke his perfect jaw.

"Your flashlight," Shaun said, handing it over. "We… ah… left it on last night, so I replaced the batteries for you."

"You didn't have to do that," Andrea protested.

"You didn't have to buy me a fuse," Shaun reminded her.

"Daddy!" Trevor's voice was happy and demanding from across the wide yard. "Come push me more! I'm going too slow!"

Andrea had to laugh.

Shaun managed to look both pleased and put upon. "I swear, the kid never gets tired of the swing. I should tear that rusty old thing down."

"You're loving every minute of it," Andrea accused him.

Shaun's smile, slow and sheepish, was all the admission he needed to give.

"Daddddddyyyyyy!"

"Better go," Andrea said with a smile of her own that she knew must look foolish. "*Dinosaurus Trevorus* is calling."

"There was one other thing. I meant to ask last night, but… ah…"

Shaun was not the sort of guy that Andrea would expect to see blushing, but she was glad that she'd been able to witness the adorable phenomena. Even the tips of his ears were pink.

"Ah, indeed," Andrea said with a grin.

"Dinner," Shaun said desperately. "I wanted to make you dinner. A real dinner. To prove that my culinary talents are somewhat above boxed noodles in primary colors. And to thank you for your help."

Andrea's heart was in her throat. Not a date, she reminded herself. It wasn't a date. "I'd love to," she said, feeling shy. "My next night off is Thursday."

"Thursday," Shaun said, pouncing on the word. "Yes, Thursday. Are you allergic to anything? Vegetarian?"

"I'm easy," Andrea said, then sorely regretted her choice of words. "I mean… ah… anything sounds good. My own culinary talents are pretty much limited to boxes and sandwiches, so I won't be picky."

"Daddddddyyyyyy!"

"Thursday," Shaun repeated.

"Thursday."

She watched him walk away across the lawn, his gait a graceful stride that called Andrea to follow.

She was stroking the flashlight in her hands reflexively. But it wasn't just Shaun's glorious body that she found herself desiring.

She wanted to sprint after him and push Trevor on the swing, to romp with both of them across the grass. She wanted to laugh and play with them in the front yard, not caring who saw them. She wanted Shaun to kiss her in sunlight, to hold her hand, to push her hair back from her face…

Andrea bit the inside of her cheek.

Shaun wasn't wrong, she reminded herself. Trevor was in a fragile place, so recently abandoned by a mother that Andrea had never thought was particularly good at the role anyway. Shaun was fighting an uphill battle to win the little boy's trust and find his footing as a father, and she could only complicate that bond right now.

Her hawk muttered in her ear, discontent.

I know, she agreed with it.

Rather than continue to stare out of her window after him, she resolutely turned back into her house, where she spent several long hours looking ineffectively at her laptop keyboard, listening long-ingly to the laughter from the yard next door.

CHAPTER 17

"What are you making, Daddy?" Trevor was in full-on superhero dog mode, a red cape draped over his back as he crawled into the kitchen with his nose in the air. "It smells like gardens."

"I'm making spaghetti," Shaun told him. "Miss Andrea is coming over for dinner, remember? I hope you like spaghetti."

"I like spaghetti," Trevor said skeptically. "But I don't like sauce."

Shaun stopped stirring. "How can you like spaghetti if you don't like sauce?" At least he hadn't protested Andrea's inclusion in the meal.

"I like the noodles," Trevor said, as if it was obvious. "And I like cheese sprinkle. But *not* sauce."

Shaun wondered if this was the sort of parenting battle he should pick. Surely most of the nutrition was in the sauce. But noodles and 'cheese sprinkle' at least had good protein, and Trevor seemed to do a good job eating his vegetables most of the time. Sauce was probably not a hill Shaun needed to die on.

"No sauce for Superdog," Shaun agreed, stirring the sauce again carefully. "In fact, no spaghetti for Superdog. Only little boys at the dinner table."

Trevor sat back on his heels and gave a little roar. "What about lions? Can I be a lion at the dinner table?"

Shaun's blood ran cold and he stopped stirring again. "No," he said swiftly. "Not at the dinner table." Would he have to cancel his dinner at the last moment? Pack Trevor up and retreat to the city to find a preschool that specialized in shifter children? Was there even such a thing?

"How about a horse?" Trevor said, neighing.

Shaun tried to take comfort in the fact that he was clearly cycling through animals to pretend to be. Probably he wouldn't shift again. Probably. It was just a coincidence that he'd picked a lion.

"Nope," he said as lightly as he could, giving the sauce a careful stir.

"A cow?" Trevor mooed convincingly and giggled.

"Not a chance," Shaun said.

Trevor continued to moo until there was a knock on the door. Shaun felt his chest seize.

"I'll get it!" Trevor cried, rising to his feet and scampering away.

He had no reason to be so nervous, Shaun told himself. It wasn't a date. It was just a neighborly dinner, nothing more.

"She brought *pie*," Trevor called from the front door.

"You didn't have to do that," Shaun said, coming to the kitchen door and stopping.

Andrea was dressed convincingly casually, in a checked country shirt with rolled up sleeves and blue jeans with knees worn white. "Gran had one leftover last night, and I shouldn't eat it all myself!" She chewed on her lip and gave a shy, crooked smile.

Shaun had never seen anything more gorgeous or perfect.

"She brought pie!" Trevor repeated rapturously.

"My one baking failure," Shaun confessed as Andrea brought the pie into the kitchen. "I can bake bread, and make a decent cake when the circumstances demand it. But pie has always eluded me."

"You made bread!?" Andrea said joyfully. "I thought I smelled it, but decided I was delirious. And oh, the spaghetti smells *heavenly*. You, Mr. Powell, are quite the catch, let me tell you."

She said it lightly, teasing, but clearly recognized at the same time that Shaun did the danger of the statement. For a moment, they simply looked at each other, eyes full of conflicted longing.

Trevor, looking between them suspiciously, quickly said, "I want Miss Andrea to come see my new shelves. Not you, Daddy. Just Miss Andrea."

"I've got to watch the sauce," Shaun said gruffly, turning back to the stove. "It will be about thirty minutes, still."

"I'd love to see your shelves," Andrea agreed, taking Trevor's hand and disappearing up the stairs with him.

Listening to them play was a terrible mixed joy. Andrea's clear laughter, Trevor's non-stop chatter, just far enough away that he could hear the sound of it but not make out any words, filled the house.

It sounded like a home.

It sounded like *his* home.

"It's not a date. It's not a courtship. It's just a dinner," Shaun reminded himself fiercely as he cut open the package of spaghetti noodles. "A neighborly dinner."

Trevor liked Miss Andrea, but he clearly didn't want his father to have more to do with her than he already did. Whether he remembered the promise he had coaxed from Shaun or not, his preference was clear, and Shaun was trapped.

CHAPTER 18

"Oh, Trevor, your room looks amazing!"

Shaun had clearly spent some time cleaning and organizing, and a stack of new shelves with fabric cubes had absorbed a massive amount of the clutter. Andrea suspected that there had also been judicious use of trash bags.

The play house had been re-assembled in a new, larger configuration. "That's Daddy's seat," Trevor pointed out, indicating a pillow inside the tent. "You can sit there."

"Are you going to sell me stuffies today?" Andrea prompted.

"No, I'm not a seller today," Trevor said cheerfully. "Today I'm a super dog. We're hiding out from the bad guys and looking for clues."

"Oo," Andrea indulged. "What kinds of clues should we look for?"

His imaginative play required a great deal of earnest explanation and complicated backstory, and Andrea gave it half her attention as she tried to figure out why the new shelves made her feel so hopeful.

"Oh!" she said suddenly.

"Right!" Trevor said eagerly. Apparently her revelation had

been timed well to his conversation. "It's a clue! Now we know where the secret base is!"

"That's awesome," Andrea told him, in part as an answer, in part in response to her own realization.

If they were really moving at the end of the semester, in just a month, was it likely that Shaun would be buying new shelves and storage? Or had he reconsidered?

Had he reconsidered because of *her*?

Maybe she just had to be patient, maybe her hawk was right, and they were meant to be together, just not *yet*.

She could wait, for a guy like Shaun, for the relationship she was sure they could have.

"Five minutes!" Shaun called from downstairs.

She could wait five minutes, she thought and had to laugh, even though Trevor didn't understand why.

"Okay, Daddy!" Trevor called, but when he prepared to launch back into their play, Andrea stopped him.

"Don't you think we should clean up a little and then go set the table?"

Trevor considered this skeptically, then reluctantly agreed. They dumped the toys that had migrated out back into their fabric boxes and tromped together down the stairs.

"I want to set the table," Trevor announced at the kitchen door as if it was his own idea. He gathered up carefully counted handfuls of silverware as Shaun dumped a large pot of steaming water and noodles into the sink where the colander was waiting.

"Can I help?" Andrea asked, lingering behind.

"The bread can go to the dining room," Shaun suggested. "And the butter is there." He gestured with an elbow.

Andrea gathered both up, inhaling a deep, appreciative whiff of the fragrant bread, and took them to the dining room.

"I want you to sit there," Trevor said, indicating a chair at the end. "And Daddy sits here. I want to sit beside *you*."

Andrea raised an eyebrow.

"Don't you think your dad ought to sit a little closer? He can't reach the bread from there."

"He has long arms," Trevor said breezily.

"Let's put him across the table from us, instead of way down at the end," Andrea suggested. "It will make it easier to pass things."

"Okay," Trevor said agreeably.

He was moving the silverware down to the newly allotted space when Shaun came in with the pot of spaghetti.

"I didn't want sauce!" Trevor wailed, wide-eyed in alarm.

"No worries," Shaun said quickly. "I put aside a bowl of noodles for you before I mixed the rest up. I just didn't have enough hands to carry it all at once."

"Wouldn't your dad look funny with more hands?" Andrea suggested.

Trevor giggled.

Andrea tried not to think about what Shaun might *do* with more hands, and helped Trevor set out the napkins while his father got another load of food and dishes from the kitchen.

"This is the most amazing spaghetti I've ever seen," Andrea said, doing her best not to sound flirtatious as he dished it up. "What brand is this sauce?"

Shaun scoffed, "Brand? I made these from fresh tomatoes and onions."

"I hate onions," Trevor added, sprinkling a small mountain of Parmesan cheese onto his bowl of noodles.

"Good to know," Shaun said.

Andrea half-wished that she'd left him in the seat Trevor had originally picked for him. It was too easy to gaze across the table at him.

Shaun, on the other hand, was able to watch Trevor, who was making a production of the long noodles.

The bread was as amazing as it smelled, with a thick, chewy crust and a soft, pillowy center. Andrea closed her eyes and sighed at the perfect texture and flavor.

"You know, that's one thing Green Valley just doesn't have," she said with regret. "A decent bakery."

"I'm going to have to make you—" Shaun stopped himself.

Andrea wondered what he'd meant say, but Trevor jealously

tried to get her attention as he slurped a noodle from his bowl. "Look at me, Miss Andrea. Look at me!"

Andrea turned her attention to him, exclaiming theatrically over Trevor's noodle manipulations and encouraging him to eat them as well.

Conversation remained light and frivolous as they finished their meals, and Andrea swept the last of her sauce up with a last decadent slice of the bread.

"I'm going to have to get your dad to push me home in a wheelbarrow," Andrea joked. "I'm too full to walk!"

"Me too!" Trevor said, mimicking her leaning back in her chair. "Daddy, you have to carry me."

"Who's going to carry me?" Shaun asked with laughter.

Andrea stood as he did, and helped gather up the dishes.

"You don't have to help," Shaun told her. "I've got this."

Andrea made the mistake of meeting his eyes, and her fingers brushed his as he took the plates she was holding from her.

It was ridiculous what this man did to her calm with a simple glance and the merest touch.

Then Trevor remembered something. "Pie!" he said, sitting bolt upright in his chair. "There's pie!"

Shaun raised an eyebrow at him and backed away from Andrea inconspicuously. "Weren't you just saying how full you were?"

"No life is too full for pie," Andrea said. "Especially Gran's pumpkin pie."

"I'm not too full," Trevor promised. "I have an empty spot, right here." He pointed at his side. "It needs pie."

Andrea sat back down beside him. "My empty spot is here," she said.

Her first instinct was to touch over her heart, but she caught herself just in time and pointed to an elbow instead.

While Shaun retreated to the kitchen for the pie, she teased Trevor about eating food and letting it fill up her arms and legs. "You've always had a hollow leg," she laughed, poking him on the knee and making him squirm and giggle.

Keep it casual, she reminded herself. *It's just a thing. Twice a thing, and two dinners.*

Ours, her hawk muttered.

She was able to keep things convincingly light-hearted as they worked through pie, and left quickly when she noticed that Trevor was flagging.

"I want you to tuck me in," Trevor started to whine.

"Maybe next time, little lion," Andrea said, and when Trevor looked like he was about to throw a fit over it, quickly stalled him by saying, "I have to find more clues on my way home so we can find the bad guys before preschool tomorrow, Superpuppy!"

Shaun looked at her with consternation, walked her to the door, and they argued politely and briefly over who would keep the remainder of the pie. Andrea finally gave in and walked home with it cradled in her arms like a consolation prize.

His door closing behind her, leaving her out in the darkness and quiet by herself, felt like all the wrong things.

CHAPTER 19

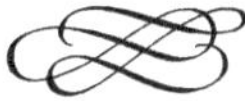

"This time, we're going to stay in bed for good," Shaun reminded Trevor wearily.

Bedtime remained the greatest test to his patience as a parent.

Some nights, Trevor fell easily asleep, giving Shaun a chance to meet Andrea as she returned from closing up at Gran's Grit, or catch her eye through the windows that looked across at each other and wave her over.

They kept the charade of keeping things casual, always with an excuse at hand for Andrea's visit after Trevor's bedtime. The aging house gave him plenty of questions to ask, and there was always the topic of Trevor.

Shaun did not have to fabricate the many questions he had about how to deal with the boy. He had not guessed how complicated a five-year-old could be. Every time he was close to despair over Trevor's childishness, the boy would come up with something incredibly deep and introspective that made him re-evaluate his understanding of his son. When Shaun was ready to roar into tiger form at the frustration and impatience that Trevor unleashed in him, the boy would do something so vulnerable and affectionate that Shaun could hold no grudge.

Andrea's advice was without fail measured and understanding, and she was sympathetic to his troubles and ready with laughter and perspective.

And after she had listened, never showing the slightest impatience, there was a moment of tension that always ended with a kiss and scramble for skin.

Those nights were the best.

But most nights, unfortunately, were a battle of wills with a five-year-old that managed to be as tenacious as Shaun's most cutthroat business associates.

Duct tape was a tempting option.

"Daddy?"

Shaun's heart sank.

Trevor's voice was so tentative and helpless that he could not resist turning in the doorway.

"What is it?" he asked, trying not to sound as frustrated and conflicted as he felt.

"Can I have one more hug?"

Shaun was undone, and he walked back in to gather Trevor into his arms and hold him tight.

"Now you have to go to sleep. For real," he scolded, releasing the reluctant boy. He tucked a stuffy into his arms. "Good night."

He shut the door behind him and waited there for the inevitable call to return. Would it be water this time? A trip to the potty? He stood there in anxious anticipation until he realized that it had been long enough there was a chance the boy was asleep.

Don't get too excited, he told himself. *Could be a false alarm.*

He crept away from Trevor's bedroom door like a thief in his own house, to what had been the guest bedroom. He hadn't been able to stomach the idea of sleeping in Harriette's bed, so this had been the best choice.

It also happened to look over into Andrea's bedroom.

He looked down from the window to see that her porch light was off, which meant she was already home from work. A glance at the clock made Shaun grimace. It was so late that there was little chance that anything would happen that night; as he watched, the last light streaming from her downstairs windows flicked off.

Shaun waited, hand on the curtain, until Andrea's silhouette danced into her bedroom, backlit by the hall light beyond until she flicked it off. There was a moment of darkness, then she bent to turn on the lamp by the bed, leaving the harsher overhead fixture off. Shaun caught her face in a moment of soft, warm illumination until she turned away from it.

He ought to stop watching. Or turn on his own light so that she knew he was there. Certainly he shouldn't continue to stare through her window like some kind of creepy stalker.

But Shaun was frozen, watching helplessly as she reached behind her to untie her apron. She gave a little hitch to her hips and twirled the loose tie as she looked over her shoulder in his direction.

Shaun grinned to realize she knew he was there and settled back onto the bed. It groaned alarmingly, and he shot a worried look to the hallway. There were no sounds from Trevor's shut door.

When he turned back, Andrea was unbuttoning her uniform, spending unnecessary time with each fastener before she slipped it off her shoulders and let it fall.

She was wearing lacy undergarments, to Shaun's mixed regret. Clearly she had been hoping for an invitation over. Had she been lingering downstairs, waiting for Trevor to go to sleep, maybe for hours?

With a mischievous, sideways look, she bent over more than necessary to pull her socks and sensible shoes from her feet. The curve of her ass was an invitation, her legs a promise.

She stood up slowly from her task, gliding her own hands along the curves of her body. The memory of the feel of those contours under his hands made Shaun clench his fingers reflexively. He was demandingly hard, and could not quite resist reaching to rub at the bulge in his pants.

Maddeningly, she turned away to unclasp her bra, holding it away from her to drop it onto the floor very obviously, but denying him a look at her gorgeous breasts.

Then she was bending forward to slip her underwear off, her

perfect ass giving just a glimpse of the treasure past it as she kicked the lacy confection off her foot.

Shaun growled out loud before he could stop himself, and his own touch through his pants seemed painfully inadequate.

She turned at last, giving him an eyeful of her inviting body… just before she leaned forward across the window seat, breasts jiggling, and swept the curtains closed across the window.

Shaun lay back on the bed, groaning in need, hand clenching over his hungry package.

He had never craved anyone like this in his life. The more that he tasted of her intoxicating skin, the more he wanted to devour it. Instead of finding satisfaction in their lovemaking, he was finding that it only made him want more of her.

He didn't just want stolen moments of sex and tantalizing glimpses of a life he didn't share — clothing or not.

He wanted to lay her down in a bed and make love to her for hours, not just steal a few moments of pleasure on the living room floor.

He wanted *her*. *All* of her.

So have her, his tiger growled in his ear. *She is ours…*

On cue, there was a needy cry from down the hall and the creak of a door.

"Daddy?"

His need washed away in a flood of more immediate concerns.

His desires could wait. But if Trevor didn't get to sleep soon, tomorrow was going to be miserable for everyone.

He considered the duct tape again briefly, then went to tuck the boy in again.

"Trevor is absolutely blooming," Patricia said quietly near Andrea's ear. "And it's not hard to see why."

It was one of those miraculous lulls in the preschool, where each student was raptly involved in their own project, or quietly helping their neighbor's efforts, with no shrill cries for help or tears of frustration. Trevor was showing Clara how to hold her scissors and demonstrating his own shaky technique with enthusiasm.

Andrea could not help blushing. She had not told Patricia about their passionate encounter in the laundry room, nor the following night, on Shaun's hideous couch. Every few nights in the weeks since then, she had found herself on his porch with some excuse, bringing by a replacement part and instructions for installing it, or answering some question about how to deal with some minor behavior of Trevor's.

They never talked about themselves or their plans, keeping what little conversation they had to upkeep of Shaun's old house or tricks for keeping up with an increasingly energetic five-year-old.

"His dad really loves him," she said. Only after she heard the words out loud did she wonder if it didn't sound wistful. "It's great to see how well Trevor is responding," she added firmly, hoping it sounded professional and not defensive.

She was *glad*, she reminded herself. Shaun was clearly right about not adding a romantic relationship to complicate what he was building with his son. Trevor was opening up to the other children, and starting to form bonds of friendship.

Who knew how adding a girlfriend to the mix would stunt that progress.

"So, what's he like?" Patricia prodded.

Andrea shrugged. "He seems nice," she said vaguely, wishing that a conflict would break out between students to draw her away from the uncomfortable topic.

Nice didn't even really touch on what she thought of him. He was kind and gentle with Trevor, and smart, if hopelessly inept with home repair. Even if the sex weren't amazing, she would have treasured those brief moments of conversation that they shared, and she liked him more with every word he spoke. It melted her heart every time that she saw him hugging Trevor goodbye or greeting him with an unabashed kiss on the head.

"What does he do for a living? How long is he staying?" Patricia managed to sound completely innocent, even with her sidelong look of pure mischief.

"I have no idea what he does," Andrea said honestly. She ignored the question about how long he was staying; it hurt her chest to remember that they might still be leaving with the end of the semester.

"Hmm," Patricia said thoughtfully. "We should ask Trevor."

Andrea gave her a suspicious look. "Are you suggesting we pump a five-year-old for information?" she asked, grinning despite herself.

Patricia's eyes were dancing. "Why else have a job like this?" she mimicked. "They're so easy to bribe at this age. Cookies and pennies will unlock any vault they guard."

Andrea laughed out loud, recognizing her own words from just a few months earlier when Patricia had first started seeing Clara's father.

Then Aaron put his hand up. "Miss Patricia! Miss Andrea! I cut the handle off!" he cried, near tears.

Andrea made Patricia stay in her seat to rest her ankle and went to salvage the art project with tape.

Was there a scotch tape that would work on hearts, she wondered. Because if she continued this way, she was undoubtedly going to need her own repairs.

CHAPTER 21

*S*haun shifted uncomfortably and wondered if it would be too obvious if he rearranged the furniture in the living room so that a less painful chair could be used to spy on Andrea's porch in the evening. He had figured out her work schedule within a few weeks, but was so desperate not to miss her that he spent extra agonizing time in the vantage point.

Maybe I should just buy a new chair, he thought.

But buying new furniture felt like a commitment to the house.

He could explain away the improvements to the wiring as a necessary safety upgrade; he didn't want Trevor in a house that wasn't up to snuff for any length of time. But a chair — especially one to surveil the neighbor like some kind of pathetic stalker — seemed like an admission he wasn't ready to make.

He spent the days that Trevor was in preschool dividing his time between catching up on work items too critical to leave to underlings and trying to tame the yard.

Wiring and plumbing might be out of his experience, but he could run a lawn mower and manage the tools he found in the back shed, and he could convince himself that it was work necessary to sell the house. It didn't take long to clip back the growth that had threatened to take over the swingset, and a fresh coat of paint made it look much less like a horror movie prop. The biggest challenge there had been keeping Trevor distracted from it long enough to let the paint dry.

Having a five-year-old underfoot was difficult in ways that Shaun had never anticipated, and rewarding to such a depth that he actively resented the years he had missed whenever he let himself think about it.

The sound of Andrea's gate squeaking set his thoughts aside and had his heart racing in anticipation.

He made himself sit an extra count of ten before rising from the detested chair, not wanting to seem too eager, and went to the porch.

Andrea was already leaning on her porch rail. "I wrote you up that stuff I was telling you about wire gauge," she said, holding a piece of paper but not offering to pass it across to him. "So you can check the other fuses, too." Instead of leaning just a little bit further to hand it to him, she gave a little questioning hitch of her shoulder.

Shaun meant to stop their quiet, desperate evenings. His head knew he couldn't just continue to string her along indefinitely, and Trevor seemed no closer to opening up to the idea of inviting her into their family than he had when Shaun first admitted that he *liked* Andrea.

He knew he ought to cool things off, before they got more knotted together than they already were. Before he hurt her any more than he knew he was going to.

But his tiger was breathing down his neck with need. *Our mate,* he reminded Shaun unnecessarily; she was frankly irresistible, and every night that Trevor was cooperative about bed Shaun spent watching their porches from the terrible chair agonizing over his willingness to take advantage of Andrea's good heart and the sweet body she offered him without strings.

He was nodding before he remembered he shouldn't be and Andrea vanished from the pool of light on her porch towards her front gate.

Maybe after tonight he'd break things off.

Then she was standing on his porch handing over a few folded sheets of printer paper and he knew he wouldn't be able to. "Thanks," he said sincerely. "I really like the instructions you've been writing up for me. You're... a great writer." Her instructions were all written out in clear, funny detail, complete with simple sketches.

When Shaun was missing her, he read them over and over again, like they were pages of love letters and not directions for home improvement.

Andrea ducked her head, and Shaun could see her blush in the faint light of their porch lights. "Thanks," she said. "I've... always wanted to be a writer."

"You should be," Shaun said. "The way you put things is just perfect. Even I understood what is supposed to happen."

"Even you!" Andrea teased. But she looked tremendously pleased and embarrassed.

"Why aren't you?" Shaun pressed.

"Why aren't I what?" Andrea looked confused. Did his presence have the same stupefying effect on her that she had on him?

"A writer? You're really good at it."

Andrea chewed on her lower lip. "I... I don't know," she admitted reluctantly. "I guess that I just have these ideas in my head that just seem better than what I end up writing down."

"What kinds of things do you want to write?" Shaun asked.

It was odd, just chatting.

It felt like violation of their agreement, and like the indulgence of something even more satisfying.

"Fantasy," Andrea admitted. "Big thick, epic fantasy novels like I used to read as a kid."

"You make it sound so shameful," Shaun teased her. "I was expecting you to say you wanted to write bodice-ripping erotica."

Andrea's laugh was rich and real, not a cultivated affectation. "Maybe I will, at that."

It was the perfect opening. "If you're looking to do some research..."

Andrea's smile was as real as her laugh. "An offer I can't refuse," she purred, and Shaun was holding the door open for her without a second thought.

He was bending to kiss her, because he was utterly helpless not to, when he was drawn up short.

"Daaaaaaddddddddy! I had a bad dreeeeeaaaaaammmmm!"

Trevor's distress was a splash of cold water on Shaun's desires and he and Andrea skittered apart, looking guilty.

"Miss… Miss… Andrea?" Trevor was standing at the top of the stairs looking down at the two of them. He was blinking in confusion... and completely naked.

"Hi, honey," Andrea said with a big smile. "I was helping your dad with some wiring questions."

Shaun held up his folded papers as if Trevor was a judge asking for evidence.

"Can you tuck me back in?" Trevor asked in a small, tired voice.

"Of course," Shaun said. "Andrea was just going."

"Not you!" Trevor cried, face crumpling. "I want Miss Andrea to tuck me in."

The two grown-ups exchanged a complicated look, Andrea asking for permission and offering consolation for the slight, Shaun granting the permission and accepting Trevor's undiplomatic preference.

"Of course, sweetie," Andrea said at once.

All three of them walked up the carpeted stairs, but when Shaun went to help get Trevor back into his discarded pajamas, he was rudely pushed away. "Just Miss Andrea!" the boy insisted, wrapping his arms around the woman possessively.

Shaun might have protested, but his eyes fell on a pillow that had fallen to the floor beside Trevor's bed. What at a glance had appeared to be a frayed seam was clearly not upon closer inspection.

The pillow had been slashed in several parallel lines.

As if by needle-sharp claws.

CHAPTER 22

Shaun darted out of the room with one of the pillows clutched against him, looking unexpectedly wild-eyed, and left Andrea alone with Trevor clinging to her.

"Tell me about your dream," Andrea invited, rocking the boy in her arms.

"I was a monster," Trevor said. "In a world of monsters, and… there were empty rooms. I couldn't find something."

"That sounds pretty scary," Andrea said gently, smoothing his blond hair back from his forehead. "Did you get to do any fun monstery things like smash cars with your giant feet?"

Trevor giggled into her shoulder. "I was a *little* monster," he said.

"Oh, a little monster," Andrea said. "That could still be fun if you got to eat cookies. What else happened?"

He shook his head. "I don't remember now."

"That's okay. That means it can't scare you now," Andrea suggested.

She started to let go of him and he clung harder. "I want you to babysit me again," he said. "Daddy can go away and you can watch me, like you did when Mommy was here."

"I liked babysitting," Andrea agreed. "We always had a lot of fun, didn't we. But aren't you cold? Let's get dressed in your PJ's, silly naked boy."

Trevor sighed and obediently let Andrea help him into his abandoned clothing.

In so many ways, it had been much easier with Harriette here. More nights than not, Trevor's mother had appointments to show houses or talk business, and she'd been happy to throw a few dollars at Andrea to watch Trevor.

It wasn't good pay, but Andrea felt amply rewarded by Trevor's affection, and she had always found him to be a sweet and obedient boy, drinking up any attention she paid him like a thirsty plant. It wasn't like she had other plans for her evenings.

And she'd never once had inappropriate ideas about Harriette.

She'd tried to like the woman, and though Andrea had never exactly succeeded in that attempt, their relationship had also never been *complicated*.

Not like her not-a-relationship with Shaun.

"That's more like it," she told Trevor encouragingly. "Now come get the biggest hug in the smallest world and I'll cover you in blankets and chase out all the bad dreams."

Almost staggering in exhaustion, Trevor slowly complied, and he was unconscious by the time Andrea quietly crept out of the room.

Downstairs, Shaun was pacing, and he looked badly disturbed.

"I'm... sorry," he said haltingly.

"Oh, there's nothing to worry about," Andrea assured him.

Shaun frowned, and his jaw worked.

"It's not weird that Trevor asked for me," she added. "I'm the novelty. You don't need to feel like he doesn't love you or anything." Did her voice catch a little, on the word love?

Shaun's expression only grew darker.

Andrea cast about for something else that might be worrying him. "Is this because he was naked?" Andrea asked. "I assure you, that is *completely* normal. We had one little girl last year who stripped naked and went streaking through the parents right in the middle of our Halloween party, her mom chasing after her waving her costume around."

Shaun gave a short, gruff laugh. "I'm… really grateful for everything," he said.

Andrea bit her lip, confused by the dismissal in his voice, and searched his face for the invitation she was expecting.

She found only distance and doubt, and when she reached out in an automatic attempt to comfort him, he didn't sway towards her like he did on other nights.

She let her hand drop back to her side.

"I… should get home," she offered, hoping he would have a better suggestion.

"Thanks again," was all he said.

So she went home… and wondered why the place felt less like home than ever.

CHAPTER 23

"He's *five*, Dad."

At the other end of the phone, there was thoughtful silence, then concession. "That's early for shifting," Shaun's father agreed.

"I'm not sure what to make of it," Shaun said, hoping he didn't sound as despairing as he felt. "Is this my fault? Is it too much stress?"

"Son, you always have tried to shoulder more than your share of the blame for things. That's why you end up in these situations."

Shaun tried to decide if that was a compliment framed as a criticism, or a criticism framed as a compliment.

There was another pause. "You said he was a lion cub?" Shaun recognized the sly, pleased tone in his father's voice.

Shaun sighed. "Yeah, Dad. A lion cub. Like you."

Damien Powell had always been disappointed that Shaun had taken after his mother and grown up to be a tiger shifter. Looking back on his childhood, the lion-themed nursery and the lion toys he'd received for holiday gifts until puberty seemed to lack subtlety.

"And he's never shifted before?"

"I guess not. It wasn't like Harriette really kept me updated on him, but I think this was the sort of thing she would bring up."

"Never thought much of that woman," Damien said candidly.

Add that to the list of ways he'd disappointed his father.

"I *called* to find out if anyone in our family had ever shifted that early."

"It's earlier than I've ever heard of," Damien said dismissively. "Most shifters figure out what they are at puberty, like you did, and like your sister did."

"Should I be worried?"

"I wouldn't be," Damien said, with the same confidence that had carried him through two marriages and shot him to the top of the engineering management industry. "It's only happened twice, it sounds like. Under pretty extenuating circumstances, both times."

Shaun clung to that hope. "You don't think it will happen again?"

"I'd avoid letting him get that tired in public, but you're probably okay."

"Dad…" Shaun's courage failed him.

"Spit it out, Son."

Shaun closed his eyes. "Was Mom your mate? Or Linda, when you remarried?"

"My *what?*"

"Your mate."

On the other end of the line, Shaun could hear his father lean back and give a roar of laughter.

Then Damien sobered.

"Wait, you're serious?"

"Very serious," Shaun said, thinking of the way Andrea felt like something he'd lost and never realized was missing.

"You don't think that Harriette was your mate, do you Son?" There was something like horror in his father's voice. "Is she giving you some destiny song and dance to try to get back together with you?"

Shaun's knee-jerk reaction was disgust and revulsion. Trying to equate any part of the bond he had with Andrea to his relationship with Harriette felt wrong at a bone-deep level.

"No. Hell, no." Shaun was not sure he had ever sworn in front of his father before. "Not for a moment."

"Good," his father said firmly. "I hope you see that gold-digger for the shallow bi—"

"Dad!" Shaun reprimanded. "I won't speak ill of Trevor's mother."

Damien was silent.

Shaun could not quite keep himself from adding, "Even when I'm thinking it really loudly."

Another roar of laughter followed.

Shaun found himself wondering if this was the first time he had made his father laugh twice in one phone call. He felt like this whole conversation ought to come with some sort of adulting award.

"So if it's not Harriette making you wonder about mate nonsense, who is it?" Shaun's father finally asked.

"No one," Shaun said, regretting his impulse to bring it up. "I haven't got time for a relationship."

He remembered the words on his divorce court papers, condemning him as too busy for the demands of parenthood or marriage.

As if he had sensed the direction of Shaun's thoughts, Damien asked, "How's the business going?"

Shaun had been grateful to find that most of what he needed to do could be done from Green Valley. But the longer he stayed, the more he found himself delegating. He couldn't be at a meeting in person, so it made more sense to have one of his managers in control of that client's paperwork, until he was only managing a handful of low-pressure clients himself.

And he didn't miss it.

He thought that he'd loved his business because he used it to escape the misery of his marriage, and later it was the only thing of interest in his rattlingly empty life. But he hadn't done more than glance over his portfolios and he was weeks behind on his research reading.

"That bad?" Damien asked dryly as he realized that he'd been silent too long.

"No… it's just. I'm thinking about stepping down."

"*That* bad?" His father *would* assume the worst.

"No," Shaun snapped. "The business is doing fine. And it's doing fine without much of me. I'm not hurting for money, and it might be nice to do something else for a while."

Not hurting for money was an understatement. Lucky markets timed to a period of his life when he was particularly aggressive about the business meant that he looked brilliant in ledgers. He might only have millions to his father's billions, but by Green Valley standards, he could live like a king for a century and still leave a respectable trust to ensure that his son was never a pauper.

"Something else like…?"

"Green Valley doesn't have a bakery," Shaun said impulsively.

He didn't think that the sound his father made qualified as a third laugh; it was too choked and skeptical.

"You'd seriously stay in that ridiculous, cow-filled country town and be a *baker*?"

Shaun cursed himself silently. He could have just said that he wanted to spend more time with Trevor. But at least the idea of his son doing something as pedestrian as opening a bakery was distracting his father from the question about mates.

"It was great to catch up with you, Dad," he said caustically. "Thanks for the advice. I've got to go pick Trevor up from preschool pretty soon here. We'll talk again soon."

"Wait!"

Shaun paused in the act of taking his cellphone from his ear. "Yes?" he finally said.

There was a moment of silence on the line. "I haven't seen Trevor since he was a baby. Do you think he'd appreciate a visit with his grandfather?"

Shaun could not help the slow smile that crept over his face. He didn't even care if this new interest in Trevor was because he had turned out to be a lion shifter. "Yeah, Dad. I think he'd like that."

Damien cleared his throat. "We'll have to arrange something

then," he said formally. There was another moment of silence, and he reluctantly added, "And you've always been a very, ah, adequate baker. Your cinnamon rolls would be a solid seller. I could put you in touch with some people I know in the food sales industry."

The silence this time was shock on Shaun's part. It was as unqualified a compliment as he'd ever gotten from his father.

"It's still just an idea," he felt obligated to say. "I haven't decided what I'm doing yet."

"Sure," Damien said gruffly. "Go pick up that boy of yours, then."

Shaun hung up in befuddlement.

That conversation had not gone anything like he had expected it to.

CHAPTER 24

"Can I get you a refill?" Andrea offered.

She ignored the coughing fit that Devon had two tables down.

"I'd love one." Shaun was startled into looking up at her, and for one brief moment, Andrea accidentally met his gaze.

"Can I have more chocolate milk?" Trevor asked eagerly, interrupting what would have become entirely too long a stare.

Shaun's silvery eyes turned to his son. "I think you should wait and eat your food," he said reluctantly. "You don't want to fill up on that."

He glanced at Andrea, this time for support, and Andrea gave a subtle nod of encouragement.

He's working so hard to be a good dad, she reminded herself. Even if she wanted more, she couldn't argue with Shaun's reasons for keeping their relationship strictly physical. There was no romance, no hand-holding, no flirting, no professions of love. They didn't share anything personal, and Andrea never left anything at his house or stayed the night.

And that ought to be enough, Andrea told herself firmly,

moving on to offer a refill to Devon's iced tea as well, ignoring his smirk.

Her hawk still mournfully insisted that there ought to be more, that they were mates and should be sharing one nest.

Andrea hated to admit how much she wanted the same thing, and how much she still hoped there might be more someday.

"Evening, Tawny," Andrea said, jerking her attention away from her juvenile longing.

Tawny Summer was half of the local post office, and had been delivering mail to all of Green Valley as long as Andrea could remember. Andrea led her to one of the booths. "Get you something to drink?"

She had to ask again because she was watching Shaun, past Tawny, as he said something that made Trevor laugh so hard that the little boy nearly fell out of his chair.

She delivered the refills without making eye contact with Shaun or Devon, and startled when Tawny asked her quietly, "What's wrong, Andrea?" as Andrea was taking her food order.

"Wrong?" Andrea said brightly. "Nothing's wrong. Everything is just… fine. Perfect. Just… thinking over a story or two. Being my usual air-headed self, I guess." She gave a trill of laughter that sounded false to her own ears and to her sulking hawk.

She escaped to the kitchen, where Old George gave her a knowing look and prompted her for the food orders she had taken and forgotten in her apron pocket.

Trevor bolted down his dinner for the promise of dessert, and Andrea had to keep herself from stepping in and reminding him to chew.

It was easier to watch Trevor than it was to watch Shaun. She wasn't sure how a man could be sexy eating a diner burger, but she suspected that Shaun would be sexy blowing his nose. It was surprisingly intimate to watch him eat, in much the same way that is was weirdly hot teaching him about wiring and showing him where the trash pickup corner for their block was.

She brought them the pie — apple for Shaun and pumpkin for Trevor — and refused to linger, choosing instead to laugh with

Tawny about her magazine delivery woes and chat with Stanley about how her book (wasn't) going.

Other than topping off their water glasses and asking with false cheerfulness how their meal was, she avoided Shaun's table until they had left, Trevor chattering cheerfully about his favorite cartoon characters as if they were close personal friends.

See? she told her hawk. Trevor was blooming under his father's affection. Shaun was right to keep a relationship with her from interfering with that.

I see wasted opportunity, her hawk snipped.

We'll go flying tonight, Andrea promised. Everything was better when they had a chance to spread their wings and feel the wind in their feathers.

She gathered up the bill and money from Shaun's table and took it to the register. She did the math twice and stared at the tip he'd left in dismay. $30 for a meal that cost less than that was a ridiculous tip. It was the kind of tip you left when you were trying to make up for something.

Like when you were feeling guilty for using someone.

There was a sour taste in the back of her mouth as Andrea cleared the other tables and distantly said goodbye to the regulars.

It's just a thing, she reminded herself, with increasing bitterness. *You knew that from the start.*

When the last chairs had been put on the tables and she had mopped the floors, Andrea gave the cat one last pat, locked the front door and slipped out the back. There weren't many places in Green Valley that weren't open to prying eyes, but Gran's Grits had a private back alley with a tall fence extending around the dumpster.

Andrea took the trash bags from the diner to the dumpster, locking the door behind her, and looked around cautiously. It was nearly sunset; the sky was starting to turn golden and red. Andrea could hear distant sounds of kids shouting to each other. Someone was taking the last moments of daylight to mow a lawn. A screen door banged and a dog started barking several blocks away.

Andrea slipped carefully out of her shoes and pulled her

uniform off over her head. She folded it neatly around her purse and tucked everything under the back step, carefully out of sight.

The she spread her arms and closed her eyes and gave a little hop into the air. Her hawk gave a keen of delight, and then they were flying swiftly to the top of the fence around the dumpster as a small red-tailed hawk. She paused there to surveil again, drinking in the sharper avian sight.

There was no one around, and none of the sounds nearby changed, so she spread her wings and soared up into the evening sky, leaving everything behind for a little while.

CHAPTER 25

Shaun left the diner feeling frustrated and confused.

He'd thought it would be a good idea to see Andrea at work, to prove that they could be friends and coexist in this tiny town.

Trying not to watch her too obviously, and being careful not to meet her amazing eyes for too long, had proven to be more effort than he'd anticipated, and he could see that she was finding it as difficult as he was. They'd figured out a perfect rhythm to the preschool drop off and pick up — a convincing mix of friendly and professional in front of other people. Trevor was innocently oblivious to any additional tension, and if Miss Patricia's glance was a little amused and knowing, neither Shaun nor Andrea gave it any weight.

But the diner had been… different.

Shaun thought it was just the surprise of seeing him, but Andrea didn't shed the tension that settled over her as the visit continued, and he could barely keep his eyes off of her. He was badly tempted to pull her into his lap and kiss her. He wanted to flirt with her, and tease her the way they did when they were alone together.

Knowing that he couldn't was galling, and he found himself

being short with Trevor's youthful antics and questionable table manners.

His conversations with Andrea had gotten shorter and more uncomfortable as the meal progressed, until he was keenly aware that it probably appeared to an outsider as if they were having some kind of falling out.

"Daddy?"

Shaun shook himself back to the now, and slowed down as he realized that he was trying to walk at a regular, grown-up pace with Trevor's hand in his own. It was only a few short blocks between Gran's Grits and their house; it had seemed foolish to drive.

"What is it, kiddo?"

Trevor seemed oddly subdued. Had Shaun been too tough on him about elbows on the table and sitting still?

"I don't think I like Granite's Grids."

"What don't you like about it?" Shaun had to ask, with the tiniest chuckle for how he had mangled the name.

"Miss Andrea seemed weird," Trevor said suspiciously.

Shaun had hoped their tension wouldn't be obvious to the boy. "She seemed fine to me," Shaun lied.

"I didn't like it," Trevor insisted stubbornly.

They walked in silence for a moment.

"Are we moving away forever?"

Shaun's heart gave a little hiccup. "Yeah, we're moving back to Minneapolis when preschool is over," he said. He had nursed the idea of a bakery in Green Valley for nearly a week, loving the idea the more he thought about it. He'd even gone as far as investigating the available rentals in the tiny town. But he hadn't mentioned the concept to anyone outside of his father, and while he didn't talk about leaving at the end of the semester, he'd never mentioned that they might not.

"Why?" Trevor's whine was quiet and intense.

Because of the miserable longing he had caught in Andrea's eyes. Because of the way he couldn't stop wanting her. Because of the impossible choice he had to make between being the father that Trevor deserved and the mate he wanted to be for Andrea.

Because maybe the distance could make him crave her less.

"My work is in Minneapolis," Shaun lied for a second time in that conversation. "And they have great schools there. You're going to Kindergarten next year, you know."

Trevor was quiet for a moment, then began to whine. "My legs are tired. Will you carry me?"

Shaun stopped and bent to gather the slight boy into his arms. Trevor slipped arms around Shaun's neck.

"I love you, Daddy," he mumbled into Shaun's collar.

Shaun squeezed him tight, as if it would keep his chest from hurting. "I love you too, slugger."

The little boy fell asleep on their walk home, and Shaun could only cradle him helplessly and wonder how something so small and fragile feeling could mean so much and cause so much pain and joy all at once.

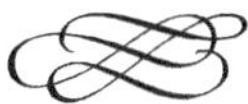

*A*ndrea flew like a shot, straining her wings to go as high as she could, and then tumbled acrobatically back down among the puffy, sunset-stained clouds. Green Valley was just a series of lines and squares below her, familiar rooftops fading into the greater patchwork of the fields around it and the wild forests that wrinkled over the hills.

For a long while, the sheer joy of flight drove everything else from her mind.

But finally, she tired, and settled into an easy glide just over the treetops.

Despite herself, Shaun slipped back into her mind.

What they had, their *thing*, was simply unsustainable.

She had made the classic mistake of wrapping her heart up with her body, and giving both of them to Shaun.

He'd wanted the one, which was admittedly gratifying, but had eschewed the other, leaving Andrea with a strange, empty aching hole where her heart had been.

Would something more have happened if Trevor hadn't needed his father's undivided affection?

Andrea couldn't bring herself to resent the little boy. She would have been happy for Trevor to rediscover his father even if she hadn't fallen for him herself, and she loved that the stability of a loving parent was having such a positive effect on him.

Her hawk was as heartbroken as she was, still sadly convinced that Shaun was destined to be theirs, but uncertain how to resolve that with the emotional distance lying between them.

Neither of them was paying the slightest attention as the sun sank below the horizon, turning the sky deep violet.

Neither of them heard the silent wings of the owl above them, or was aware of its presence until it was close enough that the backdraft of its wings fluttered her feathers as it struck, driving wicked claws deep into her.

Andrea shrieked in agony, twisted, and dived, shaking loose from the bigger bird and tearing herself off its claws by sheer force of will.

As fast as she could, she was diving away, the owl snatching at her tail feathers.

She was smaller and more maneuverable, but the owl was stronger and faster. It could also see in the dark and wasn't injured.

I'm not your prey! Andrea tried to insist, flapping frantically, but the owl didn't appear to hear her.

She rolled to the side as the owl dove at her again, claws scratching at her angled wing.

Pain burned through her wing, and her breath was coming short and hot. The initial strike had slowed her more than she had realized, and when she zigged, the owl met her with outstretched claws and a cry of triumph as it closed around her.

It wasn't the best grab, mostly one of her legs and a good portion of her tail, but Andrea failed to roll out of the grip this time.

The lights of Green Valley were below them, and Andrea could see her yard from here, all green shadows and safety. She didn't have to get far, if she could get away again.

It would serve you right if I shifted now and we both fell out of the sky, Andrea thought fiercely, but she knew they were too high; the fall would kill her as surely as the owl would, and there was not enough time to shift back before she hit the ground.

The owl was beating its broad wings, hauling her back from her goal. Andrea fought desperately, pecking and beating her agile wings. The owl struggled to keep them aloft, and they dipped lower. Andrea rolled free again, flying like an arrow in the direction of her house for a short distance until the owl inevitably caught her again.

CHAPTER 27

Shaun tucked Trevor back into bed after the third trip to the bathroom and the second drink and the seventeenth hug at least, and tried not to gnash his teeth too obviously.

A glance at the hall clock confirmed that he had certainly missed Andrea's return from the diner.

Not that he had a clue what he was going to say. Was he going to break things off completely? Tell her his dilemma and see if she had sage child advice that could fix everything? Make some transparent excuse to get her into his house and out of her clothes and pretend he could keep doing this forever?

He hurried down the stairs as quickly and quietly as he could anyway.

To his surprise, Andrea's porchlight was still on, though she usually turned it off when she came home. None of the interior lights were on, either.

Shaun went out and stood on his own porch, looking over at hers as if he could will her to come home.

Green Valley apparently had no kind of nightlife, and by ten o'clock, the whole place was reduced to quiet insects and night birds. He could hear the far-off highway if the wind was right, and there was a dog barking several blocks away. Someone yelled and it fell silent.

There was a strange cry from above, and Shaun looked up to see a dark shape — no, two of them — struggling in the sky on a collision course for his house.

He watched in fascination as the larger bird beat broad, silent wings, clearly trying to subdue its prey, which was not at all done fighting. The smaller bird was clawing and beating wings at what looked like an owl, and feathers from both of them were flying off in flurries like snow.

It was like a moment from a National Geographic special and Shaun reached for his phone before he realized that it was too dark to capture any of it. His tiger's night vision was the only reason he could see it at all.

The smaller bird was clearly wounded and overpowered, so Shaun found himself cheering silently for it as it managed to twist away and drunkenly drop several stories towards him. It was a small hawk, he realized and the larger bird, a huge owl, was on it again just before it could get to the ground. It screamed as the claws closed on it again.

That was it for the hawk, he thought, wondering if he could scare the owl off and get the smaller bird to some kind of bird rehab in time.

Do it, his tiger flared unexpectedly at him. *Now!*

He dashed down the porch steps at the urgency of the command, and picked up a landscaping rock, hurling it without thinking at the owl.

It struck true and the owl gave a cry of pain and tumbled away, releasing the hawk.

Then, to his utter astonishment, the hawk shifted into a girl — no, into Andrea! — and fell out of the sky.

She landed on her feet but fell at once to her knees, and from there toppled onto her face.

Shaun was frozen for only a moment, then he was racing across the dark lawn to where Andrea lay. The owl, which had been hovering overhead, fled.

"No, no, no," he said as he reached her and rolled her carefully over.

She was naked, and slick where he touched her. Bleeding. She was bleeding from everything. It was dark and colorless in the unlit night, over her chest, down her arms, on her legs.

"No, no, no," he repeated, gathering her into his arms. He couldn't do anything for her out here.

Her eyes opened, glinting in the darkness. "Wrong yard," she said, coughing wetly. "Sorry," she whispered, and her eyes screwed shut in pain as Shaun lifted her up and carried her up the steps.

In the light of the house, it was even worse: the blood was bright red and everywhere.

He laid Andrea gently onto the couch, not caring if she ruined the horrible thing. Pressure. He needed to put pressure on the wounds.

He collected a handful of kitchen towels and hurried back to find her sitting up.

"Lie back," he insisted. "You should not be sitting."

"It's… not as bad as it looks," she said, voice tight with the lie. "I… heal fast."

To be fair, the bleeding did seem to have slowed remarkably. But she was ghost white, and when she tried to stand, failed miserably.

"Down," Shaun commanded, and she sank obediently back into the terrible throw pillows.

"I'm fine," she insisted. "I heal really fast. I'm a…"

"A shifter," Shaun finished for her with a growl. "I know how fast a shifter can heal, and I know you need to lie down a little longer at least."

Her eyes widened in sudden understanding. "Of course you do," she said with a hiccup of pained laughter. "I'm so stupid."

"The jury's still out," Shaun told her lightly, pressing a towel into the puncture wound on her collarbone that appeared to be the worst. It was hard to tell, as covered as she was in bloody scratches and gouges.

CHAPTER 28

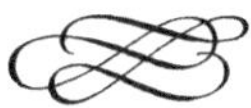

$\mathcal{A}$ndrea let Shaun clean her up, too weak to stop him, and felt unspeakably foolish.

Of *course* he was a shifter, with that powerful physique and that unsettling silvery gaze.

She'd been so busy trying to handle her own body's reaction to him that she hadn't thought too hard about his animal magnetism being an *actual* animal feature. He was graceful like a cat, and had the confidence of a predator.

"What are you?" she had to ask.

"Tiger," he answered gruffly. "Not that I've had a chance to shift since we came here, of course. I don't have the kind of form that can flit around the neighborhood looking inconspicuous."

Andrea hissed as he used a damp towel to wipe the worst of the blood from her arm. That would be where the owl had raked her wing. The few places that were still oozing blood he rinsed with hydrogen peroxide and put bandages over — tape over gauze in some places, superhero bandaids over the most minor. She knew that spectacularly colorful bruises would join the tapestry before tomorrow.

"Did you know that I was—"

"No."

Andrea wondered if she imagined that he sounded short. Was he angry that she'd kept the secret from him?

Then she remembered that he'd kept the same secret from her, and would have punched him if it didn't hurt so badly to lift her arms.

"Let me get you a shirt," Shaun said.

"I don't want to bleed all over your clothes," Andrea said. She grimaced. "Or your couch, or your floor." The whole place looked like a murder scene.

"I'll get it cleaned before Trevor gets up in the morning." Shaun found a shirt in the laundry room and helped her button it over herself. It was colorful, and loose enough that it didn't chafe over her raw wounds.

"Hydrogen peroxide," Andrea said, as she let Shaun roll up the comically long sleeves for her.

He paused. "Did I miss a spot?"

"Oh, no! I'm fine. It's just that hydrogen peroxide gets blood out of fabric. Test it first, of course, but it lifts most bloodstains without harming couches and rugs."

Shaun gave a gruff chuckle, switching sleeves. "You know the weirdest things!"

"I am a font of useful information," Andrea told him wryly. She was already starting to feel her energy return. She was undeniably tired, and in seventeen kinds of miserable pain, but she was pretty sure she wasn't going to die now.

She hadn't been so sure of that when her feet had touched the ground.

Shaun gave her sleeve a final roll and fussed over it an unnecessary moment without looking at her.

"Shaun?" Andrea had to ask. "When we met, the first time, did you… are you… have you ever heard about mates?"

"Fairy tales," Shaun said dismissively. He looked straight into her eyes then, and his gaze was so deliberate and direct that Andrea couldn't disbelieve him.

"Of course," Andrea said, glad she had an excuse for sounding faint.

She couldn't bear to look into his eyes and see his indifference, so she looked away, and found herself looking at a stack of moving boxes, folded flat and leaning against the wall.

Her chest felt too tight for her lungs.

They hadn't spoken about his plan to move back to the city with Trevor at the end of the semester since their first meeting, but when it didn't come up again, Andrea had simply assumed that Shaun had changed his mind. That she had changed his mind.

Because she loved him.

Because he loved her.

Because they were mates.

But of *course* the idea of mates was just foolishness. Of *course* it was all just a ridiculous fantasy. A ridiculous fantasy that Andrea hadn't wanted to believe in… but now that the hope of it was removed, she felt like someone had taken away something she hadn't realized was dear to her.

Inside her, her hawk gave a keen of pain more intense than any of her wounds.

CHAPTER 29

$\mathcal{I}$t took every ounce of Shaun's self-control to hold Andrea's gaze, and he was glad when she finally looked away so he could breathe again.

He had only watched one heart break before — Trevor's when Harriette had abandoned him.

But he had never caused one to shatter himself.

This was the kindest way, he tried to convince himself.

He didn't want to leave lingering hopes or unmeant promises. He wasn't going to string her along for a decade or more, waiting for Trevor to grow up. She deserved the freedom to find happiness elsewhere.

Inside, his tiger yowled in protest.

He wanted to kiss away all the pain in her face, to cradle her in his arms and take it all back, but he remembered his promise to Trevor and instead, he started collecting up the blood-soaked towels to start a load of laundry.

Andrea cleared her throat and stood carefully, swaying only slightly. "I should get back to my house," she said.

"Are you okay to do that?" Shaun asked, glad his arms were full of towels so he didn't try to catch her.

"I'm fine," Andrea said firmly. She gave a little sound that might have been an attempt at a laugh. "I guess I was lucky this happened before a weekend. I'll be back up to speed by Monday for preschool."

"What about the diner?" Shaun asked, because it was a conversational sort of thing to do.

Andrea grimaced as she tested the range of motion in her arm. "I could tell Gran I lost an argument with a lawnmower, but I think I'll go with the flu." She coughed dramatically and winced as it clearly caused more pain than she had anticipated. "Painful cough, aching limbs. Delirium. Wouldn't want any customers catching it."

"Can I do anything for you?"

To Shaun's own ears it sounded cold and uninviting, and Andrea drew herself up and matched him with her own chilly, "No, I don't need any more help."

She thawed enough to add sincerely. "Thank you for… this. For every*thing*."

Her gesture encompassed the bandaging, and the cleaning, and Shaun wondered if it didn't also included all the places that they had made love in the living room over the past few weeks.

She limped to the door and turned. "Goodbye, Shaun," she said firmly.

Shaun recognized that she *knew*.

She knew that this goodbye was a real goodbye.

And then she was gone, taking half his heart.

CHAPTER 30

*A*ndrea was glad it was the weekend for more than one reason.

She spent a long sleepless night, in too much pain to find rest in any position, and wept her pillow wet for entirely different reasons.

In the morning, she made a pitiful call to Gran's Grit, her voice so rough from crying that she knew it would be convincing. Old George accepted her excuses with a total of three words in response, and she hung up to weep in the shower as the last of the dried blood swirled down the drain.

She had finally started to believe her hawk, that she and Shaun were mates. That if she was patient, they were meant to be together. Really together, not just the desperate, hungry lovemaking that happened irregularly when it was possible with perfect discretion. If she couldn't have him yet, she at least had some hope that someday she would.

She had convinced herself that he would stay in Green Valley, that someday they would truly be *together*, that he *loved* her.

But now she knew for sure that he was leaving at the end of the semester, and that it would be forever.

Even if they could be great together, Shaun thought mates were fairy tales.

He was probably right.

She would have to be an idiot to believe anything else, and she cried helplessly when she realized that she had been that idiot.

When her hot water in the shower finally ran out, she dried off and surveyed herself in the mirror.

The damage from the owl had reduced to scabs, raw and angry red from the shower, but no longer bleeding. The worst of them still made her flinch in pain, and her suspicion that she would be bruised spectacularly had been correct.

It had been a closer encounter than Andrea liked to admit.

And part of her wished the owl had simply finished its work.

She left her towel on the bathroom floor and spent the day fitfully napping and crying on her couch. She went to the refrigerator several times and identified nothing edible, so she ate nothing.

When darkness fell, she curled on the living room floor with her laptop and stared at the screen until it went to sleep, then bent her head in defeat.

Andrea woke with her muscles screaming in pain because of her awkward sleeping position on the floor, but her head and her heart were numb.

She stretched and shook herself, metaphorically and physically, and went to the kitchen for a pain pill and a glass of water. She opened the fridge and mechanically made herself a pile of fluffy eggs with cheese and toast.

After she ate it all, bite after automatic bite, she took an efficient shower and hung her towel on the rack, then stared at her reflection.

The bruises were fading, and the scratches and punctures looked more like recent scars than fresh wounds. But she looked… grim.

You'll scare little children with that face, she scolded herself, and she made herself smile until it was halfway convincing.

If her eyes still had dark circles under them, it was nothing a little careful makeup wouldn't hide. Maybe she could blame the red eyes on allergies.

She dressed, washed her dishes, and started a load of laundry, opening all the curtains in the house that didn't face the neighbor as she worked.

Shaun, she reminded herself. *Your neighbor, Shaun, whom you will inevitably have to face again.*

But not today.

She set her laptop on the kitchen table, which faced out into the side yard, and worked until lunchtime, when she dutifully made herself a plate with a sandwich, a pile of chips, and a pickle. She switched the laundry to the dryer.

Each time she passed a mirror, she forced herself to smile, hoping that she could train herself into something convincing and automatic by the next day.

At dinner time, she opened a can of soup and nearly let it over-boil as she stared through it, then tried to eat it while it was hot enough to scald her.

The burning on her tongue was good practice for not letting herself cry.

She folded the laundry after she washed the dishes, and put every item of clothing back in her closet, straightening the house as she went.

It was a good day, she told her reflection as she straightened from spitting toothpaste in the sink.

It didn't feel like a good day, it only felt like a day.

She made herself smile. It had been long enough since she had cried that her eyes were not cherry red anymore, even if the circles under her eyes had not faded much.

She felt calm, and ready, and strangely bereft of any nervousness at all. She could think about seeing Shaun when he dropped off Trevor without quailing. She felt empty and distant, completely without fear.

You have no power over me, she quoted to her reflection, then paused thoughtfully. What could you do if you had no fear?

An idea dawned on her, and she returned to her laptop, writing feverishly until nearly dawn.

CHAPTER 31

*A*ndrea looked like she hadn't slept, Shaun thought. But she didn't look as frighteningly pale as she'd been before, and the marks on her arms looked like old scars or minor scrapes. He was painfully relieved; he'd spent the weekend helplessly worried for her, gazing at the tiny gaps in her curtains like a stalker, cataloging when her lights went on and off to convince himself that she wasn't bleeding out in a corner somewhere.

And she still looked better than he did. When they accidentally looked at each other, she smiled convincingly and held his gaze for just long enough that it didn't look like she'd been avoiding him.

He longed to escape, but Patricia had asked him to stay for a moment, along with all the other parents, while the kids sang a quick song.

Andrea was trying to keep them in the drunken line they had started in, while Patricia stood and said sweetly, "Thank you all for staying a few minutes! I have a very exciting announcement, and the kids wanted to tell you about it." She looked abashed and excited and amused as she sat at the piano. "They wrote this themselves."

The song, started raggedly but enthusiastically, began with "You're invited!" then wandered into wedding metaphors that were as hard to understand as they were to follow, and ended with, "Miss Patricia is marrying Clara's Dad!"

Everyone applauded and laughed, and Patricia, blushing happily, stood up and added, "I would like to invite you all to our wedding, the week after the preschool closes, up at our house. I particularly would like all the kids to be our flower-bearers. There are invitations with dates and directions in everyone's cubbies."

"We're going to be in a wedding!" one of the kids shouted excitedly.

"But we don't have to get married!" another responded in relief, and all the parents laughed some more as they gathered their children and lunchboxes and invitations.

Shaun found Trevor in the dispersing crowd and Patricia caught him before he could escape. "I'd really love to have you at our wedding," she told Trevor directly.

Trevor looked solemnly back. "I have to come," he said seriously.

"Hold on, slugger," Shaun stopped him. "We were planning to be gone by then." He had already listed the house, and had been planning to leave the very day that preschool let out.

Trevor looked at him in near-panic. "Daddy, I *have* to go. It's really important." His lower lip was quivering and he looked as if he were wavering between pitching a fit and simply crying.

Shaun looked at him with consternation, afraid for a moment that he was going to shift. Once the danger of that seemed to be past, he tried miserably to weigh his own need to flee Green Valley as quickly as possible against Trevor's clear desire to spend one last celebration with his preschool friends.

"It's only an extra week," he told himself as much as Trevor. He turned to Patricia. "We would love to attend. Thank you."

Patricia gave him a sunny smile. "I'm so happy to hear that!" she said, before limping to talk to another parent.

When Shaun finally escaped with Trevor, he was too grateful for the boy's sulky silence to question it.

CHAPTER 32

"Oh no you don't," Andrea said, fiercely, herding the last stubborn goat into the garage. "You were not on the guest list."

She brushed her hands off after she shut the door on the marauding animals, and gave a groomsman a high five as she headed back into the house.

She paused and drew in a deep breath before she went to find the rest of the wedding party.

The last thing Andrea wanted to do was ruin Patricia's wedding, and loose goats were already trying to do the job.

"I am not going to cry," she repeated to herself in the mirror hanging in what was serving as the girls' quarter of the house. The giant mansion was being remodeled, and most of the walls in this wing had been torn out. The construction materials had all been shoved into corners and mirrors and curtains had been hung so that the bridesmaids and party members could dress and prepare in peace.

"I always cry at weddings," Tawny told her, coming to check her own white hair in the mirror next to Andrea. "There's no shame in it."

Andrea gave her practiced smile to Tawny's reflection and didn't correct the older woman about the reason for her pending tears. She didn't need to explain that she craved her neighbor so badly that she had trouble eating, or that she slept in his shirt on her window seat every night because it was as close to him as she could be.

"A bridesmaid, at my age," Tawny was saying bemusedly, smoothing down her dress.

Patricia had taken pity on her wedding party and selected simple, flirty dresses in breathable, festive fabrics. Andrea could actually imagine wearing the dress again, not just burning it as soon as the ceremony was over like her last bridesmaids dress.

"How could I choose anyone else?" Patricia asked, coming into the room like a ray of sunshine. Her dress was simple and sleeveless, with just the barest hints of ruffles and flowers and lace. Her golden hair was up in a knot surrounded by artful curls and strands of white flowers. "Even if you weren't a dear friend, you've been bringing me my mail for years, and it's time you were part of my news, instead of just bringing it to me."

They exchanged a warm hug, careful of coiffes and clothing, and Patricia turned her gaze to Andrea.

Don't ruin her wedding by breaking down, Andrea reminded herself fiercely, and she knew her smile was too wide and too false, so she rushed to gush, "You look so gorgeous, Patricia! Like a goddess!"

If Patricia wasn't fooled by her ridiculous act, she was willing to play along. "The boot is the very best part," she laughed, lifting her skirt to show off the ankle brace she was wearing. It had been several weeks since the car accident that had hurt her ankle, but Lee was very protective of her, and insisted that she wear it as long as the doctor said, wedding or not. "It's a good thing we'll be walking down the aisle very slowly."

"You should have put off the ceremony until you could wear heels," her mother said mournfully, sweeping in through the curtained doorway. "Maybe a winter wedding that wouldn't be so awfully hot. And really, can't someone chase off those stray goats?"

But her complaining was warm and kindly meant and Patricia laughed her off.

"I put the goats in the garage," Andrea said. "They should be out of the way for the ceremony!"

"The photographer is here to take some preparation photos in here," Patricia's mother said. "I wanted to make sure everyone was decent."

Andrea obligingly smiled for the handful of staged photos that the photographer led them through, and begged off as quickly as she could to go coordinate the preschoolers that were starting to arrive.

She spotted Trevor before she saw Shaun, and her heart began to pound in her chest despite her best attempts to remind herself that she was not going to ruin Patricia's wedding by having a breakdown.

Shaun was as agonizingly good-looking in a suit as she remembered, and looked as lost as Trevor. He clung to his son's hand as most of the population of Green Valley swirled around gossiping and chattering. Andrea's pity for him overwhelmed her pain, and she approached them with her smile carefully in place.

"Trevor, you certainly look sharp! All the other kids are over there getting their baskets ready. Find your name!"

As Trevor scampered away, she dared to look up at Shaun. If she looked at a spot by his ear, instead of his eyes, she found that it wasn't as bad as she'd feared. "You'll probably find some kindred spirits over on the groom's side of things. Look for the formally dressed cityfolk over by the pool who look like they've never been to a wedding with gate-crashing goats."

Shaun gave a bark of surprised laughter. "I don't know, I think the goats sound more fun."

"They're very friendly goats," Andrea agreed.

Shaun leaned close and whispered, "Are we sure they aren't shifters who didn't get invitations?"

Andrea giggled. "That could only be the case if Patricia hadn't invited the *entire* town. They're Mrs. Davis' goats from a mile or two down the road. She's out of town visiting her sister in California."

"I guess she sent proxy guests, since she couldn't be here."

This wasn't so bad, Andrea told herself. She could joke with Shaun like nothing had ever happened between them. As raw as her heart was, there was still something wonderful about just being near him. Maybe they could actually be friends.

Until he moved away with Trevor forever.

Then he said her name, "Andrea…" and it didn't matter what he was going to say after that, everything hurt too much and her ridiculous longing for him threatened to utterly swamp her. It was *good* that he was moving away, because the pain of being so close to him and so completely far away was more than she could bear.

"I have to go get the kids in order!" she said brightly to his ear, running over whatever he was going to say.

Her forced smile was so much a fixture of her face now that she wondered if she'd sleep this way, and she turned away, willing tears out of her eyes because she was absolutely not going to ruin Patricia's wedding.

CHAPTER 33

*S*haun watched Andrea flee with a sinking heart.

For a moment, he'd believed her beautiful smile, distracted by the way her hair had been perfectly piled on her head with flowers, and the striking gold of her eyes against the summery yellow of her dress.

"Andrea," he'd started, not even sure where to take the conversation. Praise her for her sensibility? Confess that he hadn't slept a night through without waking to think about her?

The mask crumbled, only for a moment, and he saw an echo of his own pain in her gorgeous eyes before she was turning away and fleeing. He trailed after her numbly, telling himself that he was only going to check on Trevor and drop off his gift before he found his seat.

Trevor was standing with Clara at the edge of the yard where a gorgeous table was laid out under a canopy. There was a tower of frothy cupcakes and a pile of beribboned presents that Shaun added his own offering to.

"Where's the wedding cake?" Trevor was asking earnestly.

"We're having cupcakes," Clara said enthusiastically. She was wearing a pink dress that was half ruffles. "You can't have a perfect wedding without perfect cupcakes! There's strawberry and chocolate and lemon and vanilla!"

She pointed out how they were each designated with colored roses on each one. "I'm going to have *vanilla*," she said raptly.

Shaun looked at the staid group of suited individuals, and back at the boisterous Green Valley attendees. Mingling with either group sounded like some level of hell and he was glad to see that people were finally beginning to sit.

"I'm going to go find my seat," he told Trevor. "You do what Miss Andrea tells you, alright?"

Trevor didn't answer, staring thoughtfully at the tower of cupcakes.

"Cupcakes aren't until after the wedding," Shaun reminded him firmly.

When Trevor continued to be silent, Shaun said sharply. "Promise me you won't eat any cupcakes until after the wedding."

Clara took Trevor's hand as he nodded solemnly. "Come on, I'll show you the rings I get to carry. There are going to be bubbles, too." As they walked away, the little girl stage-whispered, "Grandma has cookies in her purse."

Shaun sighed, and went to be seated.

The usher took one look at him and sat him in the more thinly settled groom's side of the outdoor seating area without prompting. Shaun didn't correct him, glancing at the bride's side of the aisle in bemusement. He was pretty sure there was a homeless guy in the back row sleeping across three seats and there was an ancient woman in a wheelchair wearing a sequined flapper dress. He recognized the big bald man from Gran's Grits, as well as half of the people who had been eating there. One of them was carrying the old cat who had been sleeping in the diner window.

He was leaving Green Valley, he reminded himself. He didn't belong on that side of the aisle.

Gradually, everyone was seated, and they chatted comfortably as they waited for the ceremony to begin.

And waited.

Though it was still early in the day, the sun was sweltering, and the sunshade was most over the wedding dais, not over the guests. Shaun was sweating, and watching others fanning themselves and plucking at their formal clothing. The preacher looked like he might faint. The groom, Lee, was pacing, and his groomsmen looked bored.

Finally, Andrea herself came out and walked up the aisle alone.

It put all kinds of uncomfortably perfect ideas in Shaun's head, watching her walk down the garland-adorned aisle with flowers in her hair.

"Sorry folks," she said with the same perfectly composed smile she had been flashing to Shaun since her encounter with the owl several weeks ago. "We seem to be missing a pair of rings. We're hoping to track them down and get started shortly."

The guests broke into murmured speculation as she walked briskly back down the aisle, Lee on her heels.

A terrible thought occurred to Shaun as he remember how interested Trevor had been in the whole procedure of a wedding, and that Clara had taken him to see the rings.

Then the goats trotted back onto the scene.

CHAPTER 34

"You can't go in there," Andrea protested. "It's bad luck!"

"I think that losing the ring already qualifies as bad luck," Lee reminded her with a look that indicated he had no intentions of backing down. "I'll take my chances."

"Groom incoming!" Andrea cried, recognizing a losing battle when she saw one.

There was scrambling, and Patricia's mother gave a cry of protest.

Clara was in Patricia's lap, sobbing her heart out, and she looked up tearfully at Lee's entrance. "I didn't mean to lose them, Daddy!" she cried, releasing Patricia. "They were there when I showed Trevor, and then when we went back to look, they weren't."

Lee enfolded Clara into his big arms and held her tight. "It's okay, cub. We'll find them."

"Maybe a goat ate them," Patricia's mother hypothesized grimly.

"Wait," Andrea said suddenly. "Wait, you showed Trevor? Where *is* Trevor?"

The rest of the children were being shepherded by a wild-eyed Tawny, but Andrea hadn't seen Trevor with the others when she had left them blowing bubbles and practicing the scattering of their (already-badly-bruised) flower petals.

Clara only shrugged, still crying into Lee's shoulder.

Andrea cursed, using words inappropriate for a preschool or a wedding, as she recalled Trevor's increased social withdrawal over the last few weeks of school. She'd been so busy trying to hold herself together, and had so much baggage regarding that Trevor's dad, that she hadn't pursued his unusual intensity on the subject of the wedding, or noticed that he had retreated to having only Clara as a friend.

Dread in her throat, Andrea went back out onto the lawn — to find absolute chaos.

In the few moments she'd been inside, the wedding had imploded. Half the guests were chasing stray goats, including a handful of over-exuberant pre-schoolers who were doing more harm than good as they shrieked and raced around waving their arms and loudly calling orders at everyone. The goats were snatching at garlands as they scampered fearlessly out of reach; they clearly had no desire to be penned in the garage again. One of them was on the dais eating the flowers from the arch. Another had been 'captured' by a tiny old lady who clearly had no idea what to do with it now, and it was dragging her around behind it.

As Andrea stood in wide-eyed appraisal of the anarchy unfolding across the wide lawn, Shaun found her.

"Andrea," he said, voice a growl of near-panic. "It's Trevor."

Andrea groaned. Did Shaun have to be so distractingly hot? They were in the middle of a crisis and she *still* got all twisted up in wanting him.

"I was afraid of that," she said, dragging herself back to the moment. "He hid the rings?"

"Probably, but Andrea…"

"Did he let the goats out?"

"Probably, but Andrea…"

"Did he eat the cupcakes?"

"Andrea!"

Andrea finally stopped, as Shaun lowered his voice and pulled her off to one side, glowering at the people who had turned at his exclamation. "He's been shifting."

Andrea stared at him.

"Shifting?" she breathed. "So young?"

"I'm not sure he knows," Shaun hissed, glancing around them. "He did it the first night we were here, and again the night he had the bad dream, but he doesn't talk about it and doesn't seem to remember the next day."

Andrea slapped a hand on her forehead and tried not fall into hysterical laughter. "So, we're possibly looking for a tiger cub with stolen rings."

"Lion cub," Shaun corrected. "Like my dad. Guess it skipped a generation."

Andrea closed her eyes to focus. "You said that each time, he was really stressed out, right? So we've got to find him and keep him *calm.*"

"Despite the fact that he's got to know he's in the most trouble he's ever been in his life."

Andrea cracked an eye to peek at Shaun. He was so good-looking it was sometimes hard to look directly at him, but his expression of frustration and worry and — even now! — affection made Andrea want to drop every guard she still had in place and draw him into her arms for comfort.

"If he's this hell-bent on causing trouble, I imagine we'll find him in the thick of the chaos," Andrea said thoughtfully.

On cue, there was a crash from the tent with the gifts and the cupcakes, and the fringes of the milling crowd descended on this new source of entertainment like locusts.

With judicious use of her elbows, Andrea wove her way through the people. "Excuse me," she said. "Coming through. Maid of Honor, move it!"

Just as she finally broke through, she stepped in something that squished, and looked down in horror to recognize a sun-softened cupcake. "Oh, no…"

The tower had been tipped, and several hundred cupcakes were scattered between the edge of the crowd and Trevor, who was glowering defiantly from under the table from beneath the short tablecloth.

Beside her, Shaun gave a sigh of relief.

Trevor was still in human form.

"Alright, my friends!" Andrea called in her loudest, most child-friendly voice. "We're going to get this all cleaned up and back to our seats! Take a cupcake with you and let's get back to having a wedding! Let's have some space, here!"

The old lady with the goat pulled it past towards the garage, arms awkwardly around its white neck and people began to obediently pick up cupcakes and retreat.

Andrea had never been so glad that Patricia had taught her the secret of that voice and once the majority of the people had given them an illusion of privacy, Andrea sat down across from Trevor. Shaun crouched beside her, watching and waiting.

For a long moment, all three of them were quiet.

Then Trevor said quietly, "I didn't eat any of the cupcakes before the wedding."

Shaun sagged to a sitting position beside Andrea and laughed helplessly.

CHAPTER 35

*L*aughing was all that Shaun could think to do, he was so tangled up in humiliation and sorrow and pity for Trevor.

"Trevor, sweetie, did you take the rings?"

Andrea managed to make the question sound perfectly reasonable and not at all accusing. Shaun was quite sure he would not have been able to do the same.

But before Trevor could answer, a flurry of gold curls and pink ruffles descended on them. "My cupcakes!!" Clara wailed, running straight between them. She put her hands on her hips and glowered at Trevor. "How could you?! Why *would* you?!"

Trevor's expression of defensiveness didn't change. "I did it for you," he said solemnly to Clara. "So your dad wouldn't get married."

"Trevor!" Shaun could not keep himself from saying, outraged and humiliated.

But Trevor was at least creeping out from underneath the table.

Clara descended on him furiously, pounding on him with her tiny fists. "How could you!!"

Andrea started to stand, saying firmly, "Clara…"

Clara fell into a weeping puddle of pink lace.

Trevor looked utterly befuddled and knelt beside her before Shaun could stop him.

"I didn't want your Dad to stop loving you," Trevor said plaintively as Clara tried to push him away.

She stopped crying and stared at him, still holding him at arms' length. "That's stupid. You're stupid!"

"Clara," Andrea said again, warning and strangled laughter in her voice.

Clara looked past Trevor at Andrea. "Well, he is. My Dad is never going to stop loving me. I *want* Miss Patricia to be my Mom." Her voice went up an octave. "I want my *cupcakes!*"

"I'm sorry," Trevor said in a quavering but determined voice that made Shaun want to scoop him up and comfort him. "I thought... I thought..." he looked back at Shaun then, a heartbroken, lost look that cut Shaun to the bone. "I thought he might not love you anymore."

Before Shaun could find the breath to speak, Clara punched Trevor in the arm. "He can love more than one person, stupid."

"We don't call people stupid, Clara," Andrea reminded her automatically.

Trevor looked intensely at Clara, clearly trying to decide if he should believe her. Then he turned to Shaun for a single moment, and flickered his gaze immediately past him to Andrea.

"Miss Andrea?"

"Yes, Trevor?" Andrea stood, and opened her arms to the boy.

He hesitated, clearly wanting to run to her, but swayed in place instead.

"Are you mad at me?"

"Oh, Trevor, no. I'm sure you thought you were doing the right thing, even if it wasn't. We all make mistakes."

"I don't want you to go away."

"Oh, sweetie, I'm not going anywhere," Andrea promised.

"But we are! We're going away forever and ever and not ever coming back."

It occurred to Shaun that to a five-year-old, going away was the same as if they remained stationary and everyone around them went away. Trevor fell forward into Andrea, who knelt to wrap arms around him and murmur reassuringly near his ear.

Shaun felt the ground drop away from beneath him as all the pieces to the puzzle finally fell into place.

Trevor hadn't wanted Shaun to not like Miss Andrea because he was afraid that he would lose his father's love, the little boy was afraid of losing *Andrea's* love.

It seemed ridiculously obvious, upon reflection.

Andrea had been the anchor in Trevor's life the past two years. *Andrea* was the parent figure he could trust, even if she had been parenting from next door.

And what had Shaun done? He hadn't been there at all, until just these past few months. He was still, comparatively, a stranger to the little boy. And he'd swept in like a bull in a china shop and declared that he was going to take Trevor away from the only person he trusted. In Trevor's eyes, it probably looked like it was because he and Andrea had fallen out — exactly as Shaun and Harriette had, and probably Harriette and whoever had replaced him. In Trevor's limited experience, people only got close for a short time, and then fell apart and *he* was the one who suffered for it.

He watched Andrea cradle Trevor in her arms and felt like his chest might crack. He'd been so caught up in his relationship to Trevor, and his not-a-relationship with Andrea that he'd never really considered the bond that was already in place, or thought about the fallout of tearing them apart.

He knelt beside the pair, keenly aware of the damage he'd already done, and of the audience that had not dispersed very far away at all.

"Clara's right," he said gruffly, hoping his voice would carry only to Trevor and Andrea. "People love more than one person all the time."

"Are you sure?"

Trevor had his arms wrapped tightly around Andrea, and he was spattered in cupcake frosting. His little lost voice as he lifted his head to look at Shaun was everything Shaun had ever wanted to protect him from.

"I'm sure," Shaun said. "I love you and I love Miss Andrea."

Andrea's head snapped up, and she stared at Shaun over Trevor's head. There were tears streaking her cheeks and Shaun was gutted to realize she had been crying with Trevor.

Trevor sniffed. "But you still love me lots?"

"I will always love you, cub," Shaun said. "Always and lots."

"Even when I do bad things?"

"Especially then," Shaun promised. "Though I may not like the bad things. Will you still love me if I do bad things?"

Startled by this shift of power, Trevor furrowed his brow at Shaun. "Yes?" he said uncertainly.

"What do you think about staying in Green Valley?" Shaun proposed.

"What about your work?" Trevor asked suspiciously.

"Maybe it's time for new work," Shaun said thoughtfully. "Maybe a bakery in Green Valley?"

"We could stay?" Trevor asked eagerly. "Next door to Miss Andrea?"

"If I haven't messed things up with Miss Andrea too badly," Shaun said wryly.

By this point, Patricia had come limping onto the scene. Clara was sobbing more quietly now, and Trevor had stopped crying.

Behind Patricia, her mother was wringing her hands and exclaiming over everything. "The cupcakes! The rings! Goats! I *knew* this was all too fast! Can we reschedule? Oh disaster!"

The two children looked at Patricia with chagrin and anxiousness. Trevor's arms tightened around Andrea.

But there was only amusement on Patricia's face. "Goodness, this was a lot of a cupcakes," she said, picking her way through the sticky minefield with her rustling skirt held up. She settled down next to Clara and Trevor without care for the frosting that peppered the lawn.

"Your dress!" Clara said in alarm.

"Your *dress!*" echoed Patricia's mother in even greater dismay.

Shaun wasn't watching the dress, he was watching Andrea over Trevor's blonde head.

She looked fragile and heartsick and hopeful.

"Trevor, honey, do you know where the rings are?" Miss Patricia managed to sound both firm and forgiving all at once.

Trevor turned his head back to bury it in Andrea's dress.

"You're not in trouble," Shaun said, just as Miss Patricia said the same thing. They exchanged a brief, amused look.

"He should be in trouble!" Clara said indignantly, outrage cutting off her sobs. "He ruined the wedding!"

Patricia opened her arm to Clara and the little girl crawled over into her lap. "He didn't mean to," she said gently.

"Yes I did!" Trevor said immediately, lifting his head. Several people who were watching had to stifle giggles. Shaun was divided between pride for his honesty and keen embarrassment.

Trevor continued less confidently. "But I thought… I thought… I wanted your dad to always love you."

"He always will," Patricia assured him cheerfully.

Trevor considered. "Okay," he said at last. "I'm sorry, Clara."

Clara gave him a look that indicated her forgiveness would not be so simple for Trevor to get.

"Can you show me where the rings are now?" Patricia asked.

Trevor nodded, scrubbed at his eyes, and then got to his feet as a few of the people who had been pretending not to watch the drama unfold stepped forward to help Patricia stand.

"I threw them in the swimming pool," Trevor confessed. "In the deep end."

Shaun groaned.

Clara glared at her classmate mistrustfully and deliberately moved to the other side of Patricia as they walked away.

CHAPTER 36

$\mathcal{A}$ndrea stood as Patricia led Trevor and Clara back to the house to find the rings and was gratefully aware of most of the attention from the guests following them away.

She was also keenly aware of Shaun, who was looking only at *her*.

She gathered up a handful of cupcakes without looking back, and tipped the tray back to upright. The cupcakes looked very sad and smooshed on the empty tray.

"Andrea."

His voice was low and quiet; if Andrea had not had keen hearing courtesy of her hawk, she would not have heard him at all.

Her heart fluttered in her chest, full of hope and longing and terror.

"Andrea," he repeated, when she couldn't make herself turn.

"I guess I didn't have to worry about ruining Patricia's wedding after all," she said, as lightly as she could. "I could not have done so masterful a job anyway." She wondered as she spoke if it was too much of a tease. Shaun must be feeling awful about the disaster and responsible for Trevor's behavior. He was already keenly sensitive about being a good dad.

She heard him step closer, could feel his closeness and anxiety. She wanted to comfort him, almost as much as she wanted to stomp on his foot and punch him.

"You know the worst part?" Shaun asked, picking up more mournfully lopsided cupcakes to add to the ugly display.

"You mean the part where the rest of the preschool finds out the cupcakes were ruined?" Andrea ventured lightly. "There's going to be a tiny person riot." She wasn't sure if anyone would even eat these poor things, but it saved them from being stepped on.

"He would believe Miss Patricia when she said the same thing I did, but he wouldn't believe me."

Miss Patricia didn't say she loved me. Andrea had his words on a loop in her head, and already she was fearing that she'd imagined it. She was so uncertain she felt a little sick to her stomach, and she bent to pick up more of the cupcakes.

"I'm really bungling this," Shaun said mournfully, joining her in her hunt.

Andrea had to laugh. "Who says 'bungling' anymore?" She wanted to ask what he was bungling, and really didn't, all at the same time.

"Someone who's been trying really hard not to swear since he got custody," Shaun said frankly. "It's a struggle, let me tell you."

"If you don't make a big deal out of it, probably, he won't catch it. Except when he does." Andrea remembered too well her first year at the preschool, constantly stopping herself, and the frequent shame of hearing 'Miss Andrea said it!' Fortunately, Patricia had been very patient about it.

"Andrea?"

Andrea swallowed hard and tried to dodge the conversation she knew was coming. She wasn't ready for it, still felt like her heart was in a cage of pins. If she let it hope, it would only get hurt. "You aren't bungling being a dad, if that's what you're worried about," she told him swiftly, reaching for one of the better-looking cupcake refuges under the table. "You're doing a great job. Every parent here is glad they aren't you today, and every one of them knows how close they came to being you because these kids can be feral little proto-monsters at this stage and it's a miracle any one of them survives to adulthood."

She stood to put her gathered cupcakes on the tray, and Shaun stood to put his own beside it.

"That's not what I'm bungling," Shaun said quietly. "Or at least, that's not *all* I'm bungling."

Andrea was keenly aware of how close he was standing, and of the tremble in her legs. She was also conscious of the people milling around them, sometimes popping in with stray cupcakes to add to the dismal tower, pretending not to listen in, or engaging in their own muted conversations just out of earshot.

She was saved having to find a reply by Patricia's mother, who came bustling up nearly in tears. "Oh, Andrea, I think we're finally ready. The rings are back, we need you."

"Oh thank goodness," Andrea couldn't help saying, and she snatched up a napkin for her frosting-sticky fingers and fled back to the house.

Shaun made his way back to his seat with the other guests. Everyone seemed more amused than dismayed by Trevor's antics, and the mood was light-hearted and cheerful. He got many long looks, but most of them were accompanied by knowing smiles and friendly nods, as if he had just been accepted into some secret circle of parents-of-occasionally-terrible-children.

He smiled back tentatively as he took his seat, and put his jacket on the seat next to him to save it for Trevor.

The music started up on the little sound system and Shaun had a moment of gratitude that Trevor had chosen to destroy something less expensive. It could have been worse, he told himself.

He could have flushed the rings instead of throwing them into the swimming pool. One of the groomsmen had damp hair, and had undoubtedly had to dive in and retrieve the rings.

Then Andrea appeared at the end of the aisle, holding flowers and leading the straggling string of preschoolers behind her.

Sunlight gleamed on her upswept dark hair and turned her skin to honey. She was wearing high heels that couldn't make her look tall and walking very slowly and deliberately out of respect for the train behind her. As she passed, gazing straight ahead, Shaun thought she wobbled and flushed, but the capering children behind her had most of the audience's laughing attention.

A dozen preschoolers were waving bubble wands and throwing petals as they skipped at highly variable speeds down the aisle.

Trevor was one of the slower ones, stopping frequently to carefully blow bubbles. He waved to Shaun as he passed.

"Keep moving, kids," an older woman dressed as a bridesmaid reminded them, looking amused and a little overwhelmed.

Clara walked last of the children, satin pillow tucked under one arm as she carried the rings in determined little fists. She was scowling, and Shaun found himself pitying Trevor the job of winning her forgiveness.

Last of all was Patricia, walking slowly enough that her limp wasn't noticeable even though there were glimpses of her boot beneath her skirt. As she proceeded to the dais, eyes full of laughter fixed on her husband-to-be, the children were released out into the audience by Andrea and scurried to their families, loudly declaring what they'd just done.

"I blew bubbles! Hundreds of them!"

"I had flower petals! Mine were pink!"

Trevor was silent but smiling, and he was the only kid to filter into the groom's side of the wedding, where he climbed directly into Shaun's lap.

Once the other children had been hushed by their parents, the music was turned down and the officiant began.

Shaun spent the ceremony watching Andrea, who stood to one side patiently, holding Patricia's bouquet.

CHAPTER 38

*A*ndrea was uncomfortably aware of Shaun's gaze throughout the ceremony. He had managed to sit where he had a clear view directly to where she stood, and she tried not to fidget or stare back. She wasn't used to heels, and she was still reeling over his declaration to Trevor that he loved her.

What did it mean? What happened next? Was he really going to stay in Green Valley? The For Sale sign in front of his house made her chest tighten every time she saw it. And a *bakery*? He was thinking about opening a bakery here?

She had to jerk herself back to the wedding and prompt Clara to reluctantly hand over the rings. The little girl dropped the satin pillow as she unwrapped her fingers from her treasures.

The audience chuckled, and then clapped when she picked it up and raised it in triumph.

Patricia and Lee exchanged rings, and then a passionate kiss as their marriage was declared complete by the bemused-looking officiant.

Everyone clapped and cheered and someone turned the music back up as the ceremony broke out into a general garden party.

Andrea gave Patricia a big hug and returned the bouquet to her for the toss.

Everyone wanted to hug Patricia, and shake Lee's hand, and congratulate them, including not only this class of preschoolers, but several of the graduated classes, so there was a mob of little girls and boys to wade through.

After another round of photographs, Andrea made her way back to the cupcake table, to find that someone enterprising had cleared it off and bought everything the small local grocery had to offer; there were several tins of shelf-stable cookies, and a big generic birthday cake with most of the decoration scraped off and replaced with Lee and Patricia spelled out in M&Ms. Someone had already cut several pieces out.

"There were going to be vanilla cupcakes," Clara pouted, materializing by her elbow. "Trevor ruined everything."

"He thought he was doing something nice for you," Andrea reminded her. "He tried to look out for you."

Clara muttered something with the word stupid in it, and Andrea put a hand on her shoulder and squeezed. "Yeah, sometimes it looks pretty stupid from the outside, but you have to understand that Trevor's mom just left him all alone. He's been scared. And sometimes we do things we don't think all the way through when we're scared."

Clara looked up at her skeptically. "He's not alone! He has his dad!"

His dad, Andrea remembered achingly, looking down at the little golden-haired child. Teaching preschoolers big concepts like empathy was one of the hardest parts of her job. They were so wrapped up in themselves at this age, and had such straightforward ideas about how things must work.

As she was considering this, she suddenly heard Patricia's clear voice calling, "Heads up, Andrea!"

Just as she looked around in alarm, the bouquet caught her directly in the face and she automatically put out her hands to catch it before it could fall to the ground, staggering backwards and nearly falling over with the effort of it in her unfamiliar heels. Shifter reflexes were all that saved her dignity.

Laughter and applause greeted her as she regained her balance. Clara giggled. "That means *you'll* get married next!" she explained. "You *have* to!"

Andrea scanned the audience, and glared at Patricia, who gave her a clearly unrepentant grin and a little wave.

She turned back to the table of desserts, determined to salvage at least a decent cookie from the event, to find Clara staring down Trevor.

He was holding a single perfect cupcake. Its white rose pronounced that it was one of Clara's coveted vanilla treats. Shaun was standing beside him, looking only at Andrea.

"I didn't want to make you mad," Trevor said sheepishly to Clara. "And I saved you one."

Clara glared at him a long moment, then thoughtfully accepted the cupcake. "I'll share it with you," she said graciously. "But I get the frosting."

Trevor smiled. "Okay!"

Hand in sticky hand, they skipped away into the garden towards the sound of other children laughing and playing.

"I didn't expect her to forgive him so easily," Shaun said, watching them go.

"Kids are easy," Andrea said, turning to the table of treats because she wasn't sure how else to avoid staring at Shaun. "A little sugar goes a long ways."

She surveyed the choices, and Shaun came to stand beside her. "Does it work with bigger people, too?"

Andrea gave him a sideways glance. "Are you trying to apologize?"

Shaun looked quickly around to make sure no one was standing too close. "I should never have told you that you weren't my mate," he said quietly.

Andrea felt like the ground had fallen away under her feet and gripped the bouquet so hard that the plastic doily bit into her hand.

CHAPTER 39

Shaun half-expected Andrea to turn and beat him with the bouquet she was holding; he could feel the anger and betrayal from her in waves.

After a moment, she sighed. "I know why you did."

Shaun realized that he still hadn't really apologized. "It's not a good excuse," he said firmly. "I'm… sorry."

"What do you want to do now?" Andrea asked quietly, moving to one side as a group of people came to pick over the desserts.

Shaun looked down at the flowered crown of her head and discarded the most inappropriate of the ideas that occurred to him. "Do you know I've had three people ask me when I was going to marry you? And that was before you caught the bouquet."

Andrea gave a hiccup of a giggle. "I didn't *really* catch it," she corrected. "Patricia threw it at my head when I refused to *try* to catch it. Anyway, you don't have to marry me."

"I was thinking about a date," Shaun offered.

Andrea looked up at him, golden eyes surprised. "A date for a wedding?" she asked in astonishment.

Looking down at her, Shaun could picture just that Andrea all in white. Andrea on the dais exchanging rings with him. Andrea glowing at him the way Patricia was at Lee. Kissing Andrea and making her his wife. Peeling Andrea out of a wedding gown on a bed scattered with rose petals...

He cleared his throat. "I meant a lunch date," he said regretfully.

"Like, at a restaurant? Out in public?"

"Gran's Grits has a great selection of hot sandwiches," Shaun said with what he hoped was a winning grin.

"Sounds romantic," Andrea murmured ironically.

"I thought Trevor could come with us," Shaun added, knowing it was the nail in the romance coffin.

Andrea looked at him speculatively.

"I… want to get to know you," Shaun admitted. "And I want Trevor to get to know you, too."

"Trevor probably already knows me better than you do," Andrea reminded him.

"Trevor probably knows you better than he knows me," Shaun confessed without shame. "I don't want him to have crazy ideas that I'll stop loving him if I …" he stopped as a couple elbowed their way to the table beside them. Apparently official cake cutting had been abandoned and the cake had become a free-for-all. All that was left of the M&Ms names were two Es.

Andrea was looking at him with an expression of half-hope and half-heartbreak. "You're… serious about this?" she asked faintly.

Not touching her was taking all of Shaun's self-control. His tiger was convinced that if he just kissed her, she would understand everything.

"So serious," he said, fearing it sounded grim. "How about tomorrow for lunch?"

"Andrea! We're taking wedding party photos with the car!" Patricia's mother looked like she had done several rounds with the goats; her hair was flying away in all directions and her eyes were wild. "We need you!"

Andrea turned to follow, then paused. "Lunch tomorrow sounds great. I'll see you at noon."

CHAPTER 40

It was odd to be at Gran's Grits in something other than her uniform, and Andrea slid into the crinkly bench seat opposite to where Trevor was squirming next to Shaun.

"Soda machine is still down," Devon said, offering her a menu she already had memorized.

"Iced tea is fine," Andrea said, with a wry smile.

"Me too," Shaun said, not looking away from Andrea. His openly appreciative gaze was a little unnerving after several months of pretending they weren't looking at each other.

"Me three!" Trevor piped up.

"Milk for Trevor," Shaun interceded.

"Mommy let me drink sliced tea," Trevor muttered.

Shaun frowned. "Mommy did a lot of things I don't agree with," he reminded Trevor firmly.

Trevor looked solemnly back and Andrea felt momentarily like an outsider.

"I'll get your drinks," Devon said with a cough, walking swiftly away.

"I didn't have preschool today," Trevor blurted with a glance at Andrea, as if he had just realized it.

"No preschool during the summer," Andrea reminded him. "Do you know what you want for lunch?"

"Will you read it to me, Daddy?"

Shaun narrated the children's portion of the menu, Andrea exclaiming over the most delicious of the options.

"What are you in the mood for?" Shaun asked her, once Trevor had settled on a hot dog with curly fries.

Andrea raised her gaze to his face, unprepared for the mischief in his eyes. She slowly smiled, then looked sightlessly back at her menu, her thoughts for the moment swamped with other things she was suddenly in the mood for.

After a moment, she said, "I'm thinking about a chicken fried steak. Gran's gravy is not to be missed."

"Breakfast for lunch? A bold move," Shaun said approvingly. "I was considering a burger, but those omelets are tempting me."

"Old George does make a great omelet," Andrea encouraged.

Trevor had to get on that bandwagon, and demanded the child's pancake platter instead of the hot dog.

"What's a platter?" he asked, after Devon had taken their order.

"It's like a plate," Shaun explained.

"But bigger," Andrea added. She tore the end of the wrapper off her straw and carefully pushed the rest of the paper off, leaving a corrugated shell. She winked at Trevor, then used her straw to put a drop of her water onto it, making it squirm like a living thing as the folds of paper absorbed the liquid and expanded.

"Woah!" Trevor exclaimed, and he immediately tried to follow her lead with his own straw wrapper.

Shaun donated his straw to the cause after Trevor soaked his, and they laughed together... like a family, Andrea thought, watching him with warmth in her belly. Like they belonged together.

She looked up from Trevor's antics to find Shaun looking intensely across the table at her.

Heat rose in her cheeks, but she made herself look back.

"How's the writing going?" he asked, while Trevor entertained himself soaking straw wrappers.

"I actually got a chapter written last week," Andrea confessed. "And I have most of the outline fixed up, so I have an idea where the plot is going to go."

"How's it feel?"

"It's a little complicated," Andrea said thoughtfully. "It's harder work than I expect it to be. Hard to make myself do it, I mean. It feels like there are more important things I should be doing, like it's just a hobby, and it's hard to make myself focus. So I've been setting a timer, and that seems to work really well. Just 30 minutes at a time, and if I want to keep working I can. Usually I do."

Shaun nodded sagely. "Yeah, sometimes starting *is* that hardest bit," he agreed, giving her an intense look.

Andrea found it hard to breathe around the hope in her throat. "I noticed you'd taken down the For Sale sign at your house," she said, playing with her straw.

"Trevor's friends are here," Shaun said, with a sidelong look at Trevor, who was now making the soggy straw wrappers act out some kind of epic adventure involving a firetruck on the laminated menu. "And Green Valley kind of grows on you after a while."

"Fungus grows on things, too," Andrea said lightly. She was trying very hard not to take Shaun's reason for staying personally.

"I've always liked mushrooms," Shaun said merrily. He was smiling across the table at her and then he added the words that Andrea hadn't want to admit she was waiting for. "And this is where my mate is."

Andrea's hawk gave a trill of triumph and when Shaun offered his hand across the table, she cautiously put her fingers in his.

Almost at once, Devon was there with their order, and she had to pull her hand back as they moved Trevor's menu and wrapper detritus to make room for their plates and condiments.

"That's not a platter of pancakes," Trevor complained. "That's just a plate." But he fell into it with relish.

"If you're still hungry afterwards, we'll get you a hot dog, too," Shaun promised.

Andrea put hot sauce on her gravy, and that led to a discussion of food tastes. "If you want really hot food, there's a Thai menu at

Harvey's that is the closest thing you'll find without driving to the Twin Cities," Andrea told him.

"Our next date," Shaun said confidently. "Tomorrow night?"

"Got a sitter lined up?" Andrea countered.

Trevor looked from one of them to the other, his mouth full of syrupy pancakes, and Andrea tried not to squirm as he finally seemed to realize what was happening.

"Are you going to leave me alone?" the little boy asked into the abruptly tense silence.

"Never alone," Shaun promised. "And never for long. I was thinking Miss Tawny might come hang out with you while Miss Andrea and I go out and eat super spicy food for dinner."

"I don't like spicy food," Trevor conceded with a shrug, and he returned to his pancakes like that was the end of the discussion.

Andrea dared to look into Shaun's face again, and saw a mirror of her own relief.

It was the last piece of the puzzle slipping into place. Trevor had accepted sharing the two of them.

One nest, her hawk said, deeply content.

"If Tawny's not available, I will gladly take a home-cooked meal instead," Andrea said practically. "It's honestly been torture smelling what comes out of your house some nights."

"Every night for the rest of your life, if you like," Shaun said expansively. "And I am dying to make you my cinnamon rolls. You did say sugar helped with apologies. But they have to be eaten fresh, in the morning, after rising all night."

"Are you serious about the idea of a bakery?" Andrea had to ask. The picture of Shaun in an apron, covered in flour, was so unexpectedly appealing. Almost as appealing as eating fresh cinnamon rolls with him in the morning.

"I am," Shaun said thoughtfully. "It's not the direction I expected to take my life, but the more I think about it, the more I like it."

He glanced sideways at Trevor, who was dipping his last square of pancake in a puddle of syrup with intense concentration. "The first thing I'll make, though, is a batch of cupcakes for Lee and Patricia."

"**O**h look, the lights work again," Andrea said, giggling helplessly as she looked up at the ceiling.

Shaun dropped beside her on the bed, panting and sweating, and gathered her up into his arms. "I'm seeing lights," he gasped into her hair.

"We're going to have to get back to work," Andrea said, making no motion to do so. "Patricia is going to quiz us about how much we got done when she drops Trevor off."

Shaun made lazy patterns on her arms, content for the moment simply to cradle her and enjoy the quiet house. "Good thing there was nobody in the house next door. We were probably quite disruptive. Maybe we shouldn't sell it after all."

"We could let Trevor use it as a playhouse," Andrea laughingly proposed. "Make him move there when he's a teenager. We'll call it the lion's pride." They had both been glad when Trevor continued not to remember being a lion, and he hadn't shifted again, but they knew those days were in their future.

Shaun sobered and propped himself up on one arm to gaze down at her.

She was such a goddess, sprawled naked in his bed — his bed, not the guest bed, and not the creaking monstrosity that the house had come with. This was his house now, filled with his furniture, home to his mate.

"What is it?" Andrea asked gently, looking up at him with sated golden eyes. "What are you thinking?"

Shaun smiled. "It's a secret," he said. "I can't tell you yet."

"Argh!" Andrea reached over to grab a pillow to hit him with and he pounced on her arm before she could wind up for it.

As he kissed her from wrist to shoulder, he was sorely tempted to tell her early.

Only knowing how much Trevor wanted to be a part of it kept him quiet.

As he kissed his way up her neck, Andrea sighed regretfully. "If you keep doing that, we're never going to get out of this bed," she reminded him. "I'll go get the crimp tool from my garage and we can get the bathroom water hooked back up."

Shaun smiled to watch her roll out of the bed and slip her clothes back on. "I'll make us a snack," he offered, not moving.

"Excellent idea," Andrea said in her best preschool teacher voice. "It's hard to work hard with an empty tummy."

Shaun was chopping up an apple in the kitchen, still grinning over the anticipation of his surprise for her, when he heard her shriek.

Dropping the apple but keeping the knife, he scrambled for the front door, and paused on the front porch.

Andrea was standing at her front gate with her arms wrapped around Tawny. An open envelope was crumpled in one hand, a small stack of papers in the other. At the sight of Shaun, she released the dazed-looking Tawny.

"I did it!" she cried, waving the papers. "I did it!!"

As Tawny continued on her mail delivery route, Andrea scampered up Shaun's front walk, and threw her arms around him with no care for the knife he was holding. "I did it!!"

Careful not to accidentally decapitate her, Shaun hugged her back. "Did you sell your book?" he guessed wildly.

Andrea shook her head, dark hair spilling back from her happy face as she stepped back and hugged the papers to her chest. "Even better! I sent Midwestern House Living Magazine a few sample articles about home repair—the ones I wrote for you, actually— and they want me to do a monthly article! With illustrations! For *money*!"

"You talented vixen!" Shaun said, unable to help laughing with her. "Were you going to tell me you submitted to them?"

"I'd forgotten," Andrea confessed. "I submitted them online months ago. When… when you told me you weren't my mate and I was stupid enough to believe you."

Shaun was grateful to see that the humor and joy didn't leave her face. She had forgiven him the unforgivable. He had to bite his tongue from the impulse again to tell her what he and Trevor had planned and was grateful when Patricia pulled up in the car and got out to open the door and unstrap Trevor from the back seat.

"Is it now?" Trevor asked eagerly, pelting up the front walk. "Is it now?"

"Is what now?" Andrea asked, still bouncing on her toes and hugging the contract to her chest.

"Hang on," Shaun told Trevor. "I don't want to do this wielding a kitchen knife at her."

Trevor giggled.

Andrea gave him a curious look, then looked down the walk to where Patricia and Clara were standing by the car, not leaving, but not offering to walk up to the house. "What's up your sleeve?"

Trevor chortled and made a show of looking up his short sleeves. "Nothing here!" he said, and he looked at Shaun expectantly.

"Be right back," Shaun said. He took the knife to the kitchen and put it down with a deep breath. Then he reached into his pocket, where the small box had been burning a hole since the morning and took a deep breath. Several times, Andrea had nearly discovered it, one of several reasons he had rushed out of his pants earlier.

In the quiet house alone for a brief moment, he paused and looked around.

He had walked into this place ready to hate it, ready to hate everything about this small town and his too-close neighbor.

The uncomfortable furniture was all gone now, the space waiting for the new pieces he had ordered — with Andrea's input. He knew more now about how a house was built and put together than he had ever expected, thanks to her.

And it wasn't just a house anymore, it was a home.

His home, and Trevor's, and Andrea's.

He curled his fingers around the box and walked back out onto the porch to make it official.

⁓

*A*ndrea eyed Trevor suspiciously. "You and your dad are up to something," she accused. "And you told Clara." She glared down the walkway at Patricia, who grinned and waved, but didn't approach.

But she also didn't leave.

Trevor squirmed. "It's a secret!" he protested, much as Shaun had earlier.

Then the front screen door squeaked and Shaun came out onto the porch. He filled up the space, his height not just impressive in comparison to Andrea's short stature.

He is a fine mate, her hawk said smugly.

We could have done worse, Andrea agreed.

Then Shaun smiled at her, and, as it always did, her heart lifted in anticipation. She wasn't sure what they were up to, but she had a suspicion.

It was a suspicion that was confirmed when Shaun knelt at her feet and opened a tiny box with a sparkling ring inside. "Will you marry m—" he started.

Before he could finish, Trevor was throwing his arms around her. "Will you be my mom?" he demanded.

There was sometimes a moment in flight when a gust of wind caught under Andrea's wings, when all she had to do was glide and all the air beneath her lifted her straight for the sun.

This was like that moment: all the love she had ever wanted concentrated in a shot of joy so intense it brought tears to her eyes.

"Oh," she said helplessly. "Oh."

Her faint suspicion had not prepared her for how it would feel, Shaun looking up at her with love, Trevor pressing himself into her side.

"Is she going to say yes?" Trevor asked anxiously.

"I'm hoping so," Shaun told him.

"Why hasn't she yet?"

"I'm getting there," Andrea said, choked. "Give me a minute."

Trevor's voice was thin and uncertain. "Doesn't she want to be my mom?"

"I'm right here," Andrea reminded him. "And yes, I want to be your mom. Yes, I will marry your dad."

Trevor released her to go to the edge of the porch and holler down the walkway. "She said yes!"

As Patricia and Clara exclaimed and applauded, Shaun stood, gathering her into his arms as he kissed her. He lifted her easily up onto the railing of the porch and bruised her lips with his demanding mouth.

It didn't matter who saw them, it didn't matter who else was there.

Only his arms mattered, and his love, and the fact that she had come home at last.

Right next door.

DANDELION SEASON

CHAPTER 1

awny Summers eased the mail truck to the curb in front of Shaun Powell's house, wincing and smiling at the squeal of the touchy brakes that broke the peaceful quiet of the small town of Green Valley.

Even squeaky brakes couldn't dampen the day.

It was spring, and it was gloriously spring as if to make up for the late winter. Blue sky spread above trees glittering with early shades of green and lawns that were springing emerald from the ugly, dull brown that had covered them for so many months.

Cheerful birds sang love songs for each other from every corner, and somewhere not far away, children in the park were hollering happily about their new freedom from the indoors.

Best of all, it was Tawny's last day of work. This was her very last delivery, in fact.

She would never have to drive the clunky mail truck again, or dread Christmas, or get trapped talking to Stanley for three hours about how badly the mail service had gone down since that new-fangled Internet started causing diabetes or whatever he had last read.

It was an ending without fanfare. Her replacement had been

training for two weeks, and everyone kindly said they would miss her on her route, but otherwise, it had been a day like any other.

Tawny opened the sticky truck door and swung down to the pavement.

It even *smelled* like spring, and Tawny inhaled happily.

Starting tomorrow, she would be wrist-deep in soil, planting the greatest garden she had ever had. She'd spent every evening for the last month planning every inch of her little plot, ordering seeds and researching varieties. Several trays of tiny green sprouts were crowded on her kitchen table and the piano under desk lamps, waiting for their new homes in the ground.

The only work she had to continue to do was teach piano on weekends to help stretch the retirement checks a little bit further.

The last package was strapped in the very back of the truck, and Tawny's knees protested climbing up to get it.

The *last* package, she reminded her knees.

Tawny frowned down at the address label. There was no return address, but the postage cancellation was from right here in Green Valley.

It was unusual for someone to ship something within the town. If it had been a different address, Tawny might have assumed one of the town seniors had gotten confused and accidentally shipped a gift to themselves.

But Shaun Powell, and his wife Andrea, were young and Andrea was not *that* much of an airhead.

It was Express mail, too, with a guaranteed date and time of delivery. Who would blow that kind of money to ship a box a few blocks?

It was a light box, for the size, and Tawny carried it easily down the path and up the porch to the house. She knocked on the door, and was surprised when it swung open under her knuckles.

"Shaun?" she called hesitantly into the dark house. All of the curtains were drawn and It smelled like fresh sweet rolls. That would be Shaun's handiwork.

"Andrea?" Tawny called. After a moment, she added, "Trevor?"

At six years old, it was most likely that Trevor had left the door open.

It disturbed her sense of order to have to leave her last package without a signature, but Tawny sighed and reached for her scanner, setting the box down just inside the door.

As she was bending over to scan it as delivered, the lights in the house suddenly flicked on, and a chorus of voices shouted, "Surprise!"

Tawny jolted upright and put a hand to her throat. "What?!"

"Happy retirement!" a familiar voice congratulated. Patricia, belly round with pregnancy, was sitting on the couch, and dozens of Green Valley residents crowded forward to draw Tawny into the streamer-strewn house as the curtains were flung open.

"We're going to miss you!"

"Thank you for your service!"

"I've got big shoes to fill." That was her replacement, an earnest young man with red hair.

"You never lost a single one of my letters!"

"Christmas deliveries won't be the same without you!"

"You won't miss the catalogs!"

She was buffeted with hugs, and Tawny had to blink back tears of emotional joy as Trevor came forward to lead her to a cake, frosted like a canceled postage stamp. The sweet rolls she had smelled were just one of the offerings on the loaded table; an entire neighborhood potluck had been laid out.

"You folks didn't have to do this," she protested as a paper plate of cake was pressed into her hands. "It's not like I'm moving away or going anywhere."

"You'll always be an establishment of Green Valley," Patricia told her, rising awkwardly to give her own encumbered hug. "We're just celebrating how much we've appreciated you. And how happy we are that you'll be enjoying a well-earned retirement."

Someone put a paper crown on her, and there were gifts, to Tawny's flustered pleasure. A ribbon-adorned wheelbarrow to replace her rusted one was filled with wrapped packages—most of them in official post office packaging.

She sighed theatrically. "You know it's a federal offense to use this packaging for purposes other than its intended application," she teased them.

She was sitting on the broad couch, carefully unwrapping what was clearly a spade covered in post office shipping bags from Shaun and Andrea, when the sound of a throat clearing made her look up at the doorway with an automatic smile.

A finely dressed stranger stood there at the door no one had bothered to close. He was a large older man, with broad shoulders under an expensive looking button-down shirt, and he had a close-cropped beard that was a much white as it was blond.

Even as Tawny had a naughty moment to wonder if they had hired a good-looking stripper for her party, he caught sight of her, and the glare melted from his face into soft astonishment.

CHAPTER 2

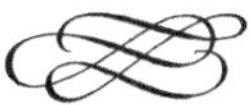

amien Powell glowered at the mail truck parked in front of his son's house. There was no sign of the mailman, despite the fact that the boxy thing was idling. He had to park across the street, and although he could not so much as hear any traffic in any direction, he still found himself practicing the rant that he wanted to deliver to the careless driver.

"Waste of taxpayer money," he growled, approaching the door to Shaun's house. "No wonder stamps cost so much."

It was wide open, to his surprise, and the house was humming with celebratory people. A banner trimmed in official post office tape declared, "Happy Retirement, Tawny!" Another waste of federal money.

He cleared his throat crossly just as his gaze fell on the subject of the banner—and the subject of his rant—sitting on the couch in a post office uniform.

The woman was unwrapping a gift with long, careful fingers, and her beautiful face was carved with affectionate lines of humor and flushed with joy and embarrassment. A ridiculous paper crown was perched on her soft waves of silver hair, and her eyes were warm and brown.

Everything about her was utterly perfect, and every word of Damien's carefully composed tirade vanished.

Inside, Damien's lion gave a contented sigh. *There she is*, he said firmly.

Who? Damien demanded. He wasn't used to feeling out of the loop.

Before his lion could answer, there was a boyish shriek of joy.

"Grandpa Powell!"

Trevor streaked from the crowd to throw himself at Damien, who caught him automatically and tossed him into the air.

"Oh, Dad! We forgot you were coming today."

"I can see that," Damien said gruffly.

Shaun was carrying a tray of warm cookies from the kitchen and Damien had a moment of sudden, irrational jealousy.

He was the one who ought to be bringing food for his mate.

Wait, what?

Our mate, his lion agreed.

How utterly unexpected.

"What did you bring me Grandpa?" Trevor was investigating every pocket that he could reach, little fingers tickling. "Do I get a present?"

"Is this your party?" Damien asked Trevor archly.

"They're my cookies," Trevor said slyly.

"Only very good grandsons who mind their manners get presents," Damien said severely. He then slipped the electronic toy from an unmolested pocket and palmed it to Trevor, who squealed in delight and disappeared to unlock its mysteries.

He turned back to consider the woman holding court on couch. She was looking away now, talking earnestly with a little girl holding a paper plate of sweets in two careful hands.

Her profile was elegant, her posture perfect.

"I can introduce you around," Shaun said dubiously, having added his platter of cookies to the spread.

Damien understood the tone.

These were not his type of people, with their country clothes and their noisy children underfoot. This was not his type of party, a potluck with paper plates. The party soundtrack was a child playing Chopsticks on an upright piano—but they had started on the wrong keys, and rather than finding the right notes, they were simply playing it over and over again incorrectly.

But watching his mate soberly take an offered sweet roll from the giggling girl made Damien unexpectedly want this to be his type of party.

"I'd like that," he said gruffly.

Shaun raised a skeptical eyebrow.

Shaun looked like this was his sort of event. Gone were the business suits that he had worn for so long. Now he wore jeans and a t-shirt, and an apron from his bakery, emblazoned with a red stylized cinnamon roll. He needed a haircut, Damien thought critically. He was dangerously close to hairnet territory.

"Alright, then," Shaun said agreeably, smothering his surprise. "This is Stanley."

Damien regretted taking Shaun's offer within five sweaty handshakes, three endless conversations about the price of farm supplies and pork, one skeptical child, and two giggling housewives who didn't seem to care about the wedding rings they were wearing.

Shaun peeled one of the women off of him and finally led him to the distasteful potluck table where Damien's mate was piling a plate with questionable offerings.

"Sorry about that. Gillian's shameless," Shaun was saying, but Damien had eyes only for Tawny.

She turned to look at them with a smile crinkling around her eyes as Shaun introduced him. "Tawny, this is my Dad, Damien Powell. Dad, this is…"

Damien moved smoothly forward and took her free hand in his own. "This is the lady of the hour," he said, with all the practiced charm at his disposal. "Let me add my congratulations."

Her hand was gentle and unexpectedly strong as she hesitantly accepted his handshake, and Damien didn't want to let it go.

For a long moment, the chaos of the party around them seemed to be distant and unimportant. The only thing that mattered was here, in the most beautiful brown eyes that Damien had ever gazed into.

"Thank you," she said, and her slow smile was friendly and shy at the same time. The color of her blush made her complexion look youthful, and there was a garden of life and energy in her eyes.

Then a playful scream and running footsteps penetrated Damien's attention, and a small, unexpected form ricocheted off the back of his knees, driving him a step forward into Tawny and sending the plate of her potluck food spilling down her uniform blouse.

Damien stared at her, aghast and mortified, as he regained his balance.

She was covered in red meatball sauce, pieces of vegetable, a small puddle of ranch dressing, a selection chocolate-covered cookies, and an unidentifiable salad that appeared to be mostly composed of mayonnaise.

A child shrieked in laughter and Damien turned with a humiliated snarl.

"Enough roughhousing!"

It was a voice he usually reserved for boardroom conflicts and employees who failed him, all of his lion's power and authority behind it.

It utterly silenced the party.

Damien turned back to his mate, and registered her blooming frown of disapproval just as a child somewhere behind him burst into noisy tears.

CHAPTER 3

Shaun's father was the most gorgeous man that Tawny had ever seen, and she had to work very hard at not staring at him as Shaun led him around the house introducing him to half the town of Green Valley.

Not only was he tall and handsome, he had the most magnificent *presence* that Tawny had ever witnessed. She knew exactly where he was, even when she was taking a cookie from Clara and he was talking to Stanley behind her.

Listening to Stanley was more accurate, of course. Price of tractors being a government conspiracy was his latest rant subject, and Tawny breathed a sigh of relief when Shaun finally took pity on his father and dragged him away to meet someone else.

"They have meatballs at the table," Clara told her in conspiratory tones. "But Trevor doesn't like the sauce."

"I shall have to try it myself," Tawny told her. She settled the paper crown and rose to her feet, glancing around automatically to find that Shaun's father was talking with Gillian. The woman was playing with her jewelry and fluttering her eyelashes at him despite the fact that he was clearly twenty years older than she was ... and she was wearing a wedding ring.

Tawny smiled at her own flash of irrational jealousy. She was too old to be thinking wistfully of handsome men anyway.

Clara ran off to play a chase game with some of the other children and Tawny went to find her own food.

The potluck table groaned under the food that had been brought. Tawny recognized Marta's ubiquitous noodle salad, Stanley's grocery store vegetable tray, and Devon's meatball crockpot. Shaun's sweet rolls and cookies were already well picked over. She took up a paper plate and began to load it with tiny portions of everything—she wouldn't want to insult anyone by not trying their offerings.

She felt his approach, like the pressure before a storm broke, even before Shaun caught her attention and said, "Tawny, this is my dad, Damien Powell."

She turned and met Damien's eyes.

Despite her best intentions, she could feel her cheeks heat, and the rush of desire in her belly was unexpected... and unwelcome.

"Dad, this is..."

Before Shaun could give her name, Damien was leaning forward and offering his hand. "The lady of the hour, of course. Let me add my congratulations."

His eyes were the same silver as Shaun's, but bottomless.

Tawny smiled helplessly. "Thank you," she said breathlessly, hoping her handshake wasn't as weak as her knees felt. Everything seemed just a little surreal.

Then unexpectedly, he staggered forward into her as a toddler bounced off of him from behind. Tawny felt her loaded paper plate heave in her unprepared hand and she watched in slow motion as it dumped entirely over onto her chest.

She was frozen in horror and discomfort, cold salad and hot meatball sauce shocking through the thin material of her uniform blouse. Vegetables and cookies slid down her breasts and bounced off of her toes.

Before she could begin to process her embarrassment, Damien was turning to snarl at the tangle of children milling behind him.

"Enough roughhousing!" he commanded, with enough force to silence the entire room.

Even though it was not directed at her, Tawny was not oblivious to the unnerving power behind his words, and she frowned as one of the children began to cry.

Damien seemed to realized his error at once. "Ah, don't cry," he said desperately, looming over the child. "It's alright. You don't have to… *please* just stop."

The little girl, three-year-old Charlotte from the preschool Andrea taught at, only wailed more loudly.

Damien searched his pockets as if the answers might be there and withdrew a phone and a box of breathmints. "Do you want a Tic Tac?" he asked coaxingly.

Charlotte looked at him with widening eyes. She stopped crying, and instead shrieked at the top of her lungs, "Mommy, a strange man is giving me CANDY!"

"I'm not a strange man," Damien tried to protest.

"It's just Trevor's grandpa!" Clara said helpfully.

"Stranger danger!" another child cried. "Stranger danger!"

Tawny could not stop herself from laughing at Damien's helpless confusion as the children in the room erupted into chaos, some of them joining the *stranger danger* chant, some of them simply using the noise and pandemonium as an excuse to run around the room in excitement.

Harried parents tried futilely to contain them.

"I'm so sorry," Damien said plaintively to Tawny as the children were slowly rounded up and gradually herded out; the party was clearly winding down. He cast his gaze down at her ruined shirt.

Still laughing, Tawny reached for a napkin, and daubed at the mess uselessly. "At least this was the last day I needed to wear my uniform," she said forgivingly.

Her paper crown started to unseat at her activity, and Damien caught it and settled it more firmly on her curls, the touch strangely intimate. Tawny had to concentrate very hard on trying to get the meatball sauce from her blouse and remind herself that he was only being kind because he'd caused the accident.

"Oh, Tawny, let me get you a clean shirt," Andrea offered.

"I'll buy you a new one," Damien said promptly.

Andrea and Tawny both looked at him. Tawny had to remind herself not to drown in those silver eyes again. His perfectly groomed beard made his mouth challenging to read, but it gave Tawny something to concentrate on that didn't make her knees weak; she wasn't fond of facial hair. "You don't have to do that," she said.

"I insist," Damien said firmly.

That put Tawny's back up immediately. "It's not necessary," she said tartly. "It's just a shirt that I never planned to wear again. You've saved me the trouble of trying to keep it for sentimental reasons."

"Then I'll take you to dinner," he growled. It wasn't a request.

"Don't be ridiculous," Tawny retorted.

There was a moment of silence, and Andrea looked back and forth between them suspiciously.

"I'll take you up on that shirt, Andrea," Tawny finally said, when she could drag her eyes away from Damien's fascinating face.

"I will drive you home," Damien said, as if he was making a great concession.

"Thank you for the offer," Tawny said, shaking her head and unseating her paper crown again. She took it off and set it on the table. "But I need to return the mail truck, and I am perfectly capable of walking home. Andrea?"

With great effort, she turned on her heel and left the room, keenly aware of her trembling hands.

CHAPTER 4

*D*amien was not used to being turned down, or to having people turn their backs to him. As lovely as Tawny's backside undeniably was, he didn't appreciate the novelty of it.

Andrea shot him one suspicious look and followed Tawny, presumably to find her a clean shirt.

Damien picked up the paper crown that Tawny had abandoned and turned it in his hands. One of the children had decorated it with enthusiastic crayon and Tawny's name (he guessed), spelled T-A-N-E-E.

The guests were gone by now; even Stanley had been dragged out by a woman in salt and pepper braids, muttering about conspiracies and price fixing.

"Well, Dad," Shaun said, once he'd finished picking up the fallen food and spot-treated the rug. "That was certainly interesting."

"Tell me more about her," Damien said.

Shaun stared at him. "About Tawny?"

Damien scowled at him. "Yes, about Tawny. Where does she live? Does she have family here? What is her perfume? What kind of car does she drive?"

"She doesn't have a car," Shaun said automatically. "What's going on, Dad?"

"She wouldn't agree to dinner," Damien said with a frown. "What other evening entertainment do you have here? Theater? Symphonies? Dancing?"

"Evening entertainment? This is Green Valley, Dad. You have to drive 75 miles to find anything resembling culture. The closest thing we have to dancing is the country bar at the end of town. There isn't even a movie theater here."

This was proving more complicated than Damien had hoped.

"What's going on?" Shaun demanded suspiciously. "What are you doing?"

"She's my mate." Damien saw no reason to hide the fact or act coy about it. She would be his soon enough.

Andrea, just coming down the stairs then, gave a cackle of glee as Shaun stared at Damien in shock. "I guessed as much!" she said in delight. "Oh, poor Tawny. She doesn't even know what hit her."

"*Poor* Tawny?" Damien repeated. He realized then that the sound he was hearing was the mail truck pulling away from the curb. His mate was leaving and he ground his teeth in frustration.

Ignoring him, Shaun was shaking his head. "This is going to be the most awkward courtship in the history of shifters."

"I want to witness every moment of it," Andrea said with wicked delight. "Let's have her over to dinner."

Scowling, Damien reminded her, "She refused dinner."

"It will be different if I invite her," Andrea assured him. "I'm not terrifying like you are."

"I'm not terrifying!" Damien protested, only aware that he was glaring at her in a manner that might have been intimidating after the words left his mouth.

"You made a little girl *cry* just ten minutes ago," Shaun reminded him.

"Does she know about shifters?" Damien asked, trying to regain some control of the conversation. "And mates?"

Shaun and Andrea exchanged looks. "I don't think so," Andrea said. "I mean, in Green Valley you never know, but she's never said anything to me that made me think she knew."

"I would have guessed not," Shaun added. "But I haven't known her long."

Damien frowned thoughtfully. "I will allow you to arrange a dinner," he agreed.

Andrea gave him an amused smirk. "How gracious of you," she teased him. "Shaun, will you make a casserole? Something classy. How about a tater tot hotdish?"

Damien tried not to wince at the idea of it.

Trevor came careening into the room just then, his new toy still clutched in one hand. "I'm huuuuungry."

"You just ate two plates of potluck," Andrea reminded him. "Where do you put it, child?"

Trevor poked over the plates of food left on the table. "I'm a hungry, hungry lion," he said, snagging a cookie and the last piece of fudge.

The adults in the room all stilled, looking at him suspiciously.

The year before, Trevor had shifted twice into a young lion in moments of stress, but he seemed to have no memory of the events, and hadn't repeated the act once Shaun and Andrea had married and his life developed stability. They all hoped he would wait a little longer to manifest his shifter abilities in earnest; he was only six, and six was complicated enough without adding claws and teeth.

Trevor, stuffing his mouth full, turned at their scrutiny. "What?" he asked around his chocolate.

"Don't fill up before dinner," Shaun said gruffly, turning away to start clearing the leftovers left on the table.

Andrea slipped Trevor another cookie behind his back with a wink.

"I'll arrange something with Tawny," she promised Damien. "I'm so delighted for you." She stood on tiptoe to kiss his bearded cheek and added quietly. "And you had better be nice to her, or half of Green Valley will come after you with pitchforks."

Damien scowled at her, dismayed by the idea that she thought he would be anything less than absolutely a perfect gentleman. "I assure you, I will court her in the manner she deserves."

"That's what I'm afraid of," Andrea said with a sigh.

CHAPTER 5

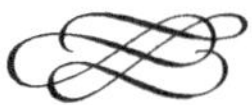

It was Tawny's first day of retirement. She hadn't remembered to turn off the alarm, but she was awake long before it rang, staring at the ceiling and thinking about Shaun's father.

Damien.

With his silvery eyes and those broad shoulders, and that deep, gruff voice that made her knees feel like jelly.

It had been a long, long time since she'd last been so affected by a handsome face and a flattering offer.

She should have let him take her to dinner, or at least drive her home.

Not for the first time, she cursed herself for being so damned independent. If she were just a little a more accommodating, if she could just be a little less stubborn, she probably wouldn't be a spinster, living alone in the tiny house she'd grown up in, wondering when life had passed her by.

There was a thump at the foot of the bed, and a familiar weight stomped up to stare at her from across her pillow.

"Good morning, Prints," Tawny said, and she reached out and pulled the black cat swiftly in for a quick cuddle. Prints was as fiercely independent as Tawny, and she tolerated only a moment of Tawny's embrace before she squirmed free with a yowl of protest.

Lady Gray, on the other side of Tawny, was grooming herself noisily, but she stopped when Tawny sat up, and both cats watched her avidly.

"I suppose you to think that the breakfast schedule shouldn't change, just because the day job is done."

Unblinking cat eyes were her only answer.

Then Tawny started to throw off the blankets, and the cats erupted into swirling chaos of pleading meows, leaping to the floor and showing her how to get out of the bedroom as if she might have forgotten overnight.

Tawny fed them and began her morning routine, nearly putting on a uniform out of habit. Instead, she chose a soft t-shirt and a pair of worn jeans. She fingered the stained shirt that she hadn't quite been able to throw away at Andrea's house, remembering all over again the smoldering look in Damien's eyes, moments before he had thrown a meal at her shirt.

Surely she'd imagined it, that look of avid interest, of hunger.

That wasn't how people looked at her.

Especially not gorgeous men wearing clothes that would have paid her bills for three months.

The sated cats chose spots on the back of the couch to groom and digest in the sunlight starting to stream in, and for a moment Tawny was tempted to join them with one of the many books in her leaning pile of books to read.

At the last moment, her stomach growled, and she realized she hadn't really had dinner last night, too flustered from her unsettling meeting with Shaun's father.

"I'm going to treat myself to breakfast out," she told the cats.

They ignored her. Tawny sighed and slipped on her shoes.

Gran's Grits was the best diner in town, in no small part due to the lack of competition.

It was a small white building, with a little porch up to a well-lit room with a handful of booths and an attempt at 50s decor that would have been more appealing if it had not actually *been* from the

50s. Gran, a tiny old lady with piercing eyes, had run the diner as long as anyone could remember, and was generally agreed to be the grumpiest person in town. She had gradually passed the day-to-day business of the diner to Old George, who wasn't particularly old, but carried on her tradition of grouchiness and never said a word he didn't have to. Gran's elderly, tiger-striped cat lived at the diner and slept in the front window most days.

Tawny slipped into one of the creaking booths and looked up in surprise to find Andrea handing her one of the plastic laminated menus.

"Andrea," she squeaked. "I didn't realize you were working here still."

Had she made a complete ham of herself the afternoon before? She remembered being mesmerized by Damien's silver gaze, but didn't remember much of what she'd said herself, besides proudly refusing his offers-that-didn't-sound-like-offers. She suspected there had been long moments of staring with inappropriate lustfulness. Had her weak-kneed attraction been as apparent to everyone else as it had been to her?

"Gran needed an extra hand," Andrea said offhandedly. "Writing is a flexible job, so I was able to come help out for a bit."

Tawny had a brief moment of relief, then Andrea grinned and slipped into the booth across from her.

"So how do you like Shaun's dad?"

"He's fine," Tawny said, trying to sound casual.

"Isn't he, though?" Andrea agreed.

"That's not what I meant," Tawny protested.

"He likes you," Andrea said teasingly.

"Oh, he doesn't," Tawny said desperately. "Don't be ridiculous."

"It's true," Andrea insisted. "He was very disappointed that you wouldn't let him buy you a shirt, or dinner, or even drive you home."

"He didn't need to do any of those things," Tawny said firmly.

"He's going to insist on doing *something*," Andrea said warningly.

"It was just an accident," Tawny insisted. "He doesn't need to do anything."

Andrea gave a knowing smirk. "It's not just about ruining your shirt," she assured Tawny. "He insists on things. And he *likes* you!"

"*I'd* like a cup of coffee," Tawny said desperately. "And I was thinking about an omelet."

"The *sausage* omelet is really good," Andrea said, her voice so suggestive that Tawny blushed scarlet. "Cream for your coffee?"

"Yes," Tawny squeaked.

Andrea flashed her one last grin and finally slid out of the booth.

Tawny put her head in her hands. It was entirely unfair for Andrea to be making her blush. She'd changed the girl's diapers when she was a baby.

"Shaun and I want you to come over for dinner this week," Andrea said, when she brought the coffee and took Tawny's order for a *vegetarian* omelet. "Are you free tomorrow night?"

Tawny looked suspiciously at Andrea. "You and Shaun?" she confirmed.

"Well, of course Trevor lives there too," Andrea said, looking completely innocent. "And Shaun's dad may still be in town."

The idea of seeing him again, of attempting to eat food in front of him and not just wear it… Tawny felt her breath catch and she tried to make herself calm down. "You aren't going to let this go, are you?"

"Nope," Andrea said cheerfully.

Tawny tried to be pragmatic about it. She should just go to dinner, to dispel the ridiculous image she'd built up in her mind. Damien Powell could not possibly be as handsome and broad-shouldered as she remembered him, and there was no chance he was really interested in her. At worst it would be a short, awkward meal and he would feel like any debt was paid and Tawny could go back to the quiet retirement she'd planned out.

"Fine," she said, hoping she didn't sound too ungrateful.

"Yes, he *is*," Andrea agreed again, and she was flitting away to refill someone's water before Tawny could correct her interpretation.

CHAPTER 6

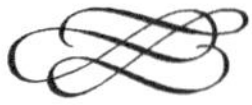

$\mathcal{D}$amien caught himself lurking at the door and made himself prowl back to the kitchen. "What time did she say she was coming?" he demanded.

"She didn't say," Andrea said, waltzing in to steal the end of a carrot from the counter.

"It's Green Valley, Dad," Shaun said. "People show up for dinner about this time. It's not an exact science."

Crunching her carrot end, Andrea grinned at him. "Nervous?"

Damien didn't bother to answer, but he heard Shaun answer for him as he growled and stalked back out of the kitchen. "Damien Powell doesn't get *nervous*, he gets *even*."

It sounded like something Damien had said once.

"Poor Tawny!" Andrea laughed.

Their teasing was suddenly irrelevant, as there was a firm tap at the front door then.

Damien did not quite run to it.

"Tawny," he said gravely, as he opened the door and saw her at last.

She was more than he'd remembered. More energy, more grace, more dancing brown eyes.

"May I come in?" she asked, after a moment, and Damien realized he was standing in the doorway gazing at her. Her cheeks were flushed.

"Of course," he said, stepping aside. "May I take your…" she wasn't wearing a coat. "Uh… pie?"

"Oh," said Tawny, looking down at it as if she'd forgotten about it. "It's still hot. I should…"

Damien was already trying to take it from her, and hissed as he jerked his fingers off the hot glass.

"Oh!" Tawny said in alarm, nearly dropping the pie. "Are you alright? Did you burn yourself?"

Chagrined, Damien blew on his fingertips. "I'm fine," he said gruffly.

"Let me put this down," Tawny said, coming into the room and looking around for a safe place to put it.

"You brought piiiiie!" Trevor hollered, skidding onto the scene.

"Don't touch it," Damien warned him, more loudly than he intended.

Trevor and Tawny both froze.

"It's hot," Damien tried to explain.

"Well, obviously," Trevor said. *Obviously* was his new favorite word this week. "What kind is it?"

Tawny finally found a safe place to put it down, slipping her hands neatly out of the hot mitts she'd been holding it with. "It's apple." She looked shyly at Damien, not quite meeting his eyes. "I hope you like it."

Trevor was dramatically sniffing. "It smells amaaaaaazing," he said, nearly toppling the little table it was on. Damien reminded himself not to yell at the boy.

"I will love it," Damien assured Tawny.

Tawny wouldn't quite meet his eyes, and her cheeks, if anything, were more red than when she'd come in. "Are your fingers okay?"

Damien obediently turned his hand palm up for inspection. "They're fine," he said reassuringly. "I heal fast."

Tawny looked like she might touch him, but Andrea came out

of the kitchen then and Tawny took a self-conscious step away instead.

"Trevor, come set the table for us, please!" Andrea called.

"Can I help?" Tawny offered.

"She brought piiiiiie!" Trevor announced.

"It's hot," Damien added.

"Well, obviously," Andrea said. "No, no, Tawny, you're our guest. Trevor, the table, please."

"It's apple pie," Trevor said helpfully, not moving.

"Trevor!" Andrea said firmly.

"Fiiiiiine."

Trevor stomped after Andrea through the kitchen to the dining room, and Damien was alone with Tawny again.

"I didn't know if you had a favorite kind," Tawny said, looking at her pie. Down the hall, silverware rattled as Trevor went through the motions of his task as if he was being tortured, Andrea reminding him of every step.

"I like apple," Damien assured her.

Tawny chewed on her lip. "It certainly smells good in here. What has Shaun whipped up this time?"

Fortunately, Damien had talked him out of something as common as a casserole. "Diablo chicken. With baby red potatoes and carrots."

"Sounds delicious."

There was an awkward moment of silence, then Tawny said brightly, "Well, I'll see if Shaun needs any help in the kitchen," and moved to leave the room.

"Wait," Damien said automatically, but he stalled out when Tawny turned her brown eyes to him expectantly.

He was a grown man, with grown children, he reminded himself, and he'd weathered two marriages. He made million dollar decisions every day without flinching.

And at the moment, he felt like an unsteady adolescent, utterly uncertain what to do next.

He wanted to tell her that she was his, that they were meant to be together. He wanted to sweep her into his arms and kiss her. He wanted to see if her hair was as soft as he remembered.

Instead, he was just staring at her, and she looked back at him quizzically with those soft eyes in her smiling face.

He had never been so grateful for Trevor's interruption as he was when the little boy escaped back into the living room, hollering behind him, "I already set the table Miss... Mom! I'm all done!"

He nearly collided with Tawny, and threw himself over the back of the couch. "Did you get to keep the mail truck, Miss Tawny?" he asked.

"No, I had to give that back," Tawny said, her smile crinkling her cheeks. "It belonged to the post office."

"I want a Mustang," Trevor volunteered. "An *orange* Mustang."

"That sounds very fancy," Tawny agreed. "I bet it would go fast."

That required Trevor to demonstrate exactly how fast it would go, Damien frowning at him thoughtfully, until Shaun came to the kitchen door.

"Dinner's ready," he said, looking between Tawny and Damien with amusement.

"Vrrrrrooooooom!" Trevor said, dashing through the kitchen to the dining room beyond.

Tawny followed him swiftly, before Damien could decide to offer her his arm or some other appropriate gesture.

CHAPTER 7

Dinner was unexpectedly pleasant.

Tawny was afraid that her wholly inappropriate attraction to Shaun's father would make her hopelessly clumsy, or that she'd be unable to make intelligent conversation in his stupifying presence. She had not mis-remembered how gorgeous and built he was, nor the mesmerizing flash of his silvery-gray eyes. If anything, he was more beautiful than she had been picturing him; his beard did absolutely nothing to detract from his physical perfection, and he was almost courtly towards her. He pulled out the chair for her, and tried to put her napkin in her lap before she took it away and did it herself.

Fortunately, Trevor kept up a steady stream of chatter and it was easy to maintain a light level of laughter and banter around his childish enthusiasm.

"Did you know *diablo* means devil?" Trevor asked earnestly. "This is *devil* chicken."

He seemed delighted by the potential evil in his food, and gleefully stabbed it and gobbled up seconds.

Tawny's pie was served for dessert, and she was flattered by everyone's appreciation.

Especially Damien's, if she was going to be honest about it.

She wasn't sure if she believed his extravagant praise for it—after all, Shaun ran a bakery and made very excellent pies himself—but his enthusiastic consumption was convincing.

"I'll leave the rest here," she offered. "It makes an excellent breakfast with a fried egg on top."

"You'll have to make that for me some day soon," Damien said.

Tawny stilled with her fork in mid-air, then laughed and forced herself to eat her next bite. He could not possibly mean that the first way she had taken it. Her cheeks heated anyway, and she got a glimpse of Shaun and Andrea exchanging amused knowing looks.

"You should make it for me!" Trevor agreed. "Mom, can we have pie for breakfast?"

"That's not for little boys," Shaun said firmly. "Just grownups."

Trevor began to whine, and Andrea stood up. "Let's get cleaned up," she said cheerfully. "It's about time for little boys to go to bed."

That made more whining, and Tawny pushed back her chair and stood up. "Let me help clear the dishes," she offered.

Damien, suddenly tall beside her, took the plate from her hands. "You're our guest," he reminded her firmly.

He handed the plate to Shaun, who looked like he might laugh, but settled for a smirk. "Let me take that," Shaun offered ironically. "Why don't you go serve Tawny a cup of coffee in the living room."

"I should..." Tawny started.

"I insist," Damien said.

For a moment, Tawny was tempted to protest on principal.

But the dinner had been so nice, after so many dinners alone, that she didn't want it to end. "Very well."

She settled herself in one of the armchairs, while Damien got cups of coffee and Trevor complained bitterly about the unfairness of bedtime before he was sleepy and thought of one hundred things that it was very important to tell Tawny.

"Don't forget to practice your intervals," Tawny reminded him. "You have a piano lesson tomorrow!"

Trevor wilted. "Yeah," he agreed reluctantly.

"Shaun and I are going upstairs to get Trevor into bed," Andrea

announced more loudly than Tawny suspected was strictly necessary. "We might be a while. Make yourselves at home!"

She herded the protesting Trevor up the stairs before her, and
Shaun gave Tawny another knowing smirk as he followed.

Then Tawny was alone in their living room for just a brief
moment before Damien came out of the kitchen with two mugs of
coffee.

"Thank you," Tawny said shyly, accepting the cup and trying
not to touch his fingers as she did so.

She failed, and the barest brush of his fingertips sent electric
shocks up her arms.

The coffee cup shook just the tiniest bit as she took her first sip.

To her surprise, he seemed more interested in hearing her
stories than telling his. At his request, she related the events of Patricia's wedding.

"There were goats everywhere, eating the decorations, being
overly friendly with the guests. Kids—of the human kind—were
running around everywhere trying to catch them and mostly
getting in the way. And the rings were nowhere to be found. I
thought Patricia's mother was going to have a heart attack on the
spot."

"Who would blame her?" Damien said with a chuckle. "That is
not how weddings are generally ordered."

"And then! Oh, right into that chaos, Trevor, bless his heart, tips
the entire tower of cupcakes over."

"It was an accident?" Damien suggested.

"Not in the slightest! Shaun didn't tell you?" she asked incredulously. "Trevor tried to sabotage the whole affair to protect his
friend, Clara! He was the one who let the goats out and hid the
rings!"

"Not a word of it," Damien said. "My son and I… we haven't
been in the habit of talking much."

Tawny felt a twinge of sympathy for the brief note of regret in
his voice.

"Did they find the rings?" Damien prompted.

"Trevor had thrown them in the deep end of the swimming

pool," Tawny said, smothering a chuckle. "One of the groomsmen had to strip to his underwear and go diving to get them back."

Damien's laugh was genuine and rich. Tawny tried to convince herself she was not flattered that he found her retelling of the events amusing and failed.

Almost as flattering was the way that he watched her when she spoke.

His silver eyes were warm with appreciation, and if Tawny didn't know better, she would have guessed she'd caught his gaze lingering over the curves of her breasts and on the lines of her shoulders.

No one had ever looked at her that way.

She knew she was plain and plump and not young enough to catch eyes even if she hadn't been those first two things. She was used to people looking straight past her.

She was just a mail carrier, the local old maid.

Damien's look was so piercing, so *intense*, that Tawny wasn't sure what to do with it.

"So, what do you do?" Tawny asked, playing with her cup.

"I manage an engineering and construction company. We do big international projects, like the Desmond Mine in Brazil, and the rail line upgrade across Siberia. We're rebuilding the interstate exchange in South Chicago next summer."

Tawny had read about the Desmond Mine. The construction was supposed to be in the trillions of dollars, but she couldn't remember what they were mining. Titanium? "Mm," she said encouragingly.

"Mostly, I'm the one they call in when a project is going south and people are threatening billion dollar lawsuits."

Tawny nodded. She did not doubt for a moment that Damien was the sort who could frighten contractors back into line. "It sounds like exciting work," she said kindly.

"It's… rewarding," Damien said mildly.

Tawny wondered if he was referring to money, or if it was the thrill of a job that let him be in charge of gigantic projects and keep disgruntled contractors in line.

It occurred to her that Shaun and Andrea had been gone an awfully long time getting Trevor to bed, and the little boy's noises of protest had long since died away.

"I… should be getting home," she said, putting aside the empty coffee cup that she'd been cradling. "It's getting late."

As she stood, Damien did also, and she'd somehow managed to forget how tall he was until he was standing next to her. It stole her breath, standing that close to him.

"Let me drive you home," he said. It didn't sound like an offer.

"It's very close," Tawny said. "I can walk easily."

"Then let me walk you home," Damien said, no less a command than his first.

Tawny nearly refused, but she looked thoughtfully up at Damien and he added, "Please?" with just a hint of uncertainty.

She didn't trust her voice, but nodded.

It wasn't until they had walked out into the warm, dark spring night that she thought that she should say goodbye to Shaun and Andrea.

Then Damien took her hand, and Tawny forgot about them entirely.

Tawny's hand in his was a good start, Damien thought, when she didn't pull it away.

He wasn't sure how something could feel so exciting… and so settling, at the same time. Her fingers belonged in his.

She belonged to him.

They stood on Shaun's porch for a moment, then Tawny shyly said, "I live on Jefferson, it's just around the corner."

He let her guide them, and wondered if he imagined that she walked more slowly that necessary, savoring their promising contact.

It had cooled, and she shivered as they walked the few, easy blocks. Damien wished he had a coat to offer her.

They stopped at one of the few fenced yards in the neighborhood—in the whole town as far as Damien could tell. "This is my house," she said shyly.

Damien opened the gate and walked with her up to the porch. Tawny hesitated at the door and then unlocked it. "Don't let Lady Gray get out," she cautioned.

"You have a cat?" Damien wasn't sure how another feline was going to react to the presence of his lion.

"Two of them," Tawny explained, opening the door. "The Cat

Formerly Known as Prints is the black one. You won't see much of her, she's still mostly feral. Lady Gray is the fluffy gray one. She's pretty shy with strangers, but she might let you pet her if she thinks you have treats."

"The Cat Formerly Known as Prints?" Damien asked in amusement, going through the door and only realizing after he was inside that he hadn't actually been *invited* in.

Tawny's home was a tiny old farm-style house, warm and homey. Every surface was covered with growing things: black trays of spring seedlings and potted houseplants.

They were greeted by a black cat, who meowed accusingly from the kitchen entry.

"P-R-I-N-T-S," Tawny introduced. "She liked to walk through my lime and leave white footprints all over the porch before I took her in and she became something that resembles a domestic cat."

Damien chuckled, and crouched down to greet the creature that shared his mate's home.

He was answered with spitting hisses and a black streak that fled to the back of the house.

"Hmm," Damien said, straightening. "That went less well than I'd hoped."

Tawny didn't seem particularly surprised. "It took me two years to tame her," she offered sympathetically.

There was a moment of silence. "Would you like a cup of… ah… coffee?" Tawny offered.

"I didn't come for coffee," Damien told her, moving swiftly to intercept her.

This was it, the moment he'd been waiting for. As he had expected, her cheeks flushed and her pulse fluttered at her throat, and Damien bent to put his mouth on hers.

He didn't expect her hand, flat on his chest, pushing him away.

"You can't just assume," Tawny said tartly.

Damien blinked at her, then frowned. She wanted him, he had no doubts in his mind at all. There was hunger in her eyes, and a hitch to her breath that she couldn't quite hide.

"Tawny," he said gruffly, "may I kiss you?"

She hesitated only a moment, then squeaked, "Yes…"

This time her arms came up around his neck, and her mouth opened under his, and he drowned.

She was stronger than she looked, and her lips were sweet and alive.

All of her curves were perfect, under his hands, and she was kissing him back with all the passion he'd known was lurking under her demure facade.

She was *his*.

Damien kissed down the side of her neck, pulling her close up against him and couldn't resist nibbling and growling, just a little. He *needed* her, desire swelling through him.

"My Tawny," he said, finding the buttons of her blouse.

"Wait, wait…" Tawny was panting, and her mouth was swollen. "What are we doing?"

"I'm making love to you," Damien said firmly.

"No," Tawny protested. "I mean, I'd figured that much out, but what we doing? What… is this?"

She felt it, Damien thought. She felt the mate pull even as a human. "Tawny, you are for me. I knew from the moment I saw you that you would make me happier than anyone else in the world ever could."

Tawny stared at him, her breath still ragged. "I'm not sure what to say to that," she finally confessed.

Damien bent to kiss her, but she pulled back reluctantly. "Damien," she said slowly. "I… like you."

"I love you," Damien said promptly.

Tawny laughed at him.

He must have scowled, because she leaned forward and patted his arm like he was a pouting child. "Damien," she said gently. "I like you a *lot*. But we just met, and it's… been a long time, and I want to take it slow."

Damien had no interest in taking it slow, and his lion had even less. He wanted to claim her, now, undress her and lay her down and make her cry his name in pleasure.

But her warm brown eyes were looking at him expectantly, and

Damien wrestled himself back under control. He could be patient. He could court her the way she deserved. "Of course," he said graciously. "Tawny, may I kiss you?"

She gave a little noise that might have been excitement or protest, and he added, "Just a kiss."

When she nodded, he enfolded her in his arms again and lay his mouth on hers.

This time he kissed her slowly, deliberately, pulling her close and holding either side of her face in his hands.

He left her breathless and trembling, almost incapable of standing. "I'll bring Trevor to his piano lesson tomorrow," he said. "Would you be interested in showing me around Green Valley afterwards?"

"I… yes," Tawny said, dazed. She cleared her throat. "Trevor is my last lesson and that sounds lovely."

Damien smiled at her. "Tomorrow, then."

She walked him to the door, hands nervous, and tipped her head up for a kiss on the porch that Damien was happy to give her.

"Good night, Tawny," Damien told her, brushing her lips.

She sighed into his kiss, then took his face in her hands and said the unthinkable: "Have you ever considered shaving off your beard?"

"I have had a beard since high school," he said with a frown. She didn't like the beard? Damien looked down at her in consternation. "I cannot imagine not having one."

Tawny had clearly realized her misstep, and said swiftly, "It's a beautiful beard. Forget I said anything."

Damien did not forget things. But he could forgive anything from Tawny's earnest face, and he gave her one final, gentle kiss on the cheek. "Good night, Tawny."

"Good night," Tawny echoed.

Then Damien was back outside her gate wondering which way to go to get back to Shaun's house, because he hadn't paid the slightest attention on the walk over.

CHAPTER 9

She was an idiot, Tawny decided, looking in the mirror the next morning.

What on earth had possessed her to tell Damien she wanted to take it slow? She hadn't wanted to take it slow, she wanted to drag him into her bedroom and find out what those shoulders looked like without a shirt over them. She wanted to feel the weight of him, the heat of him...

Tawny swallowed and made herself stop following that train of thought. She was going to need another shower—a *cold* shower—if she couldn't demonstrate some self control.

She certainly didn't look much different than she had the day before.

She didn't look like she'd been kissed dizzy by a gorgeous billionaire in her front room.

She still looked boring, with her short, frizzy white hair, and her weathered face, and her short, plump, ordinary body.

She looked... retired.

If it weren't for the slight rash around her mouth, she might not have believed that it happened.

"I love you," he'd said, as if it were perfectly normal.

But Tawny didn't believe in love at first sight. She was too practical to think that it would happen to her. Especially with someone like Damien, who could snap his fingers and have gorgeous women falling all over him. Gorgeous, *young* women.

She should have said yes the night before, before he came to his senses and overcame whatever bizarre fascination he'd briefly had for her.

Lady Gray gave a grouchy meow from the bathroom door and Tawny sighed. She needed to get dressed before the first piano students arrived, not rhapsodize over memories that seemed more and more impossible the more she thought about them.

Lessons were particularly agonizing that morning; her students seemed less prepared than usual, and Tawny cared a great deal less. She watched them play scales and thought about Damien's hands. She listened to them stumble through sight-reading practice and thought about how Damien had looked at her. She corrected their posture and thought about how Damien's arms had felt around her.

Finally, the last student before Trevor's slot was fleeing from her living room, only pausing to snag a piece of chocolate from the treat jar by the door.

Tawny followed her to the porch and sat on the chair by the door. Lady Gray and Prints were nowhere to be seen; they rarely came out on lesson days and wouldn't forgive her for inviting the trespasses on their territory until their dinner was served.

She would have liked Lady Gray's sturdy warmth in her lap to make her feel less nervous. She would even have settled for having Prints lie on the porch railing next to her, pretending she didn't exist but tolerating the occasional ear scratch.

The gate rattled and Tawny found herself on her feet before she could stop herself, smoothing down her blouse, wishing she'd done something more with her hair, maybe put on lipstick.

Damien was somehow even more handsome than she'd remembered, and Tawny blushed to remember the feel of his beard against her face.

Trevor clearly had no interest in being at piano lessons on such a beautiful day and Damien was all but frog-marching him up the walk.

"Good morning," Tawny greeted them, hoping her nervousness didn't show in her voice.

Damien poked Trevor in the side. "Good morning, Miss Tawny," Trevor said with great reluctance.

"Good morning," Damien said in his knee-weakening growl, and he flashed her a devious smile as he came up the steps. "Tawny, may I kiss you?"

Whatever greetings Tawny had expected, an offer for a kiss was not among them. She gave Trevor a hasty look, but the boy was already stomping past them into the living room.

"Yes," she said shyly.

It was a swift, business-like kiss that managed to steal her breath in just that brief moment.

How many ways to kiss could there be? Tawny wondered in a daze.

At the moment, she was dying to find out.

Then Damien was slipping a small box out of his pocket. "I brought you something," he said.

Tawny stared at it. "You… got me a present?"

"Just a token," Damien said carelessly.

"You didn't have to," Tawny protested, as he put it in her hands.

"I wanted to," Damien said. He looked smugly self-satisfied, as if he was already convinced of her reaction.

Tawny's hands trembled the tiniest bit as she opened the box, excited and surprised and a little alarmed by the gesture.

She gazed into the velvet box with growing consternation. She wanted to ask if they were real diamonds, but feared the question was insulting.

Damien supplied the answer anyway. "Those are diamonds, of course."

It was a simple bracelet, Tawny supposed. If you didn't realize that the sparkling gems were real diamonds. It must have cost a small fortune.

"Thank you," she made herself say. "It's beautiful."

"For a beautiful woman," Damien said extravagantly.

Tawny tried to keep her skepticism from showing and was glad when Trevor knocked something over in the living room with a crash. "Sorry!" the little boy hollered. "It's okay!"

She smiled as naturally as she was able. "Let's get to our lesson," she said. She put the lid back onto the box and slipped it into her sweater pocket.

CHAPTER 10

Damien was pleased that Tawny looked so flustered at his arrival with Trevor, and even more pleased when she accepted his quick, no-nonsense kiss.

He resisted the temptation to turn it into more and gave her the bracelet he'd picked out for her instead.

Her reaction to it was rather less than he'd hoped.

She looked more stunned than flattered, and the gushing delight he'd expected was sadly missing. Her gratitude felt forced, and her smile looked strained. Damien frowned, wondering where the gift had gone wrong.

He strode to claim the most comfortable looking chair in the living room, casting a glance around for one of Tawny's elusive cats. He had stopped at the little grocery store in town and found a bag of cat treats that assured him that it would win any feline.

He had opened it skeptically, and almost eaten it himself on the spot.

He couldn't fail to win over Tawny's aloof housemates so armed.

"Have you been practicing your intervals, Trevor?" Tawny asked.

"Yeah," the boy said reluctantly, squirming on the bench.

"Then we'll have good fun today," Tawny said encouragingly. She took a seat beside him on the piano bench.

She started him doing a simple scale up and down the piano, correcting his posture and hand position gently. "That's good," she said approvingly. "Now we're going to play a game, since you practiced."

Damien's phone rang and he apologized as he turned it off, noting that he had missed several other calls.

Tawny made Trevor cover his eyes and guess the intervals she played, then let him quiz her in return. Finally, Trevor played from a simple page of music, slowly and stuttering, with no sense of rhythm whatsoever.

"Excellent work!" Tawny encouraged him kindly. "Keep practicing this one, remember to count, and we'll have it ready for the fall recital."

"I don't want to do a recital," Trevor complained.

Damien cleared his throat, and earned a sulky look over the little boy's shoulder.

"Okay," Trevor agreed reluctantly.

"Take a treat on your way out," Tawny reminded him. She folded up his notebook and music for him and stood up as Damien rose to his feet.

Trevor scrambled over the bench and bolted for the door, sensing freedom.

He paused at the gate when Damien waited for Tawny as she locked her front door.

"Miss Tawny's coming with us?" he asked in confusion.

"Your grandfather asked me to show him around Green Valley," Tawny said easily, tucking her keys into her purse. She looked serene and unruffled, but Damien, watching her, was keenly aware of the color in her cheeks, and the way she shyly didn't quite meet his eyes.

"Let's show him the playground!" Trevor said enthusiastically. "He can push me on the swings!"

Damien offered his elbow to Tawny. "This is Miss Tawny's tour," he said firmly to Trevor.

Tawny tucked her arm into the offered elbow, the touch of her hand sending a wave of warmth through Damien.

She smiled at Trevor peacefully. "The playground is as good a place to start as any."

Trevor led the way, pelting down the sidewalk ahead of them.

Spring sunshine beat down on the wide streets, dappling through scattered trees.

"Do you have plans for the afternoon?" Damien asked.

"I was hoping to get my starts transplanted today," Tawny said. "It's a little early, but the forecast looks warm, so hopefully we're passed the frost risk."

Damien nodded sagely. "A little early, I suppose," he agreed gravely.

"You haven't got the faintest interest in gardening," Tawny guessed.

"I like some of the things that come out of gardens," Damien offered in return.

"What do you do for fun?" Tawny asked him.

Damien blinked at her. "I like fishing," he told her.

Tawny's face suggested it was not an interest that they shared.

"Do you like reading?" she attempted.

"A little," Damien agreed, thinking of the crowded bookshelves that had lined Tawny's house. "I enjoy a good mystery."

"Agatha?" Tawny said hopefully.

"Grisham," Damien countered.

"Ah," Tawny said. "I like lighter work, but I've read a few of his. A Time to Kill was excellent."

They chatted about books for a while as they walked. "You should drop in at our book club," she suggested slyly. "We meet Monday evenings, and our book this week is Farenheit 451."

To his own surprise, Damien did not immediately come up with an excuse not to attend. "I would love to," he said instead. "I haven't read it since high school, but I'm sure I could get an ebook copy of it and brush up."

Tawny seemed to take pity on him. "You don't have to come to my book club. It's a bunch of crotchety old ladies who mostly share local gossip and swap casserole recipes. We're honestly lucky if we talk about the book at all."

"I am in dreadful need of more casserole recipes," Damien said with a straight face. "Though I'm pretty sure that most of the local gossip is about me this week, dumping a plate of food on you and making a kid cry."

"Don't be so sure," Tawny teased him back. "Marta's cousin had a mole removed this week. That might trump the crying child and meatball stain."

"Hmm," Damien said thoughtfully. "I see the bar is high. Next time I'll have to dump an entire soup tureen on you."

"Please don't," Tawny said, laughing.

"Hurry uuuuuup!" Trevor called, nearly a block away.

"Wait at the intersection!" Tawny told him in return.

Not that there was traffic to worry about. There were a few cars parked in driveways and at curbs, and Damien could hear a vehicle somewhere a few blocks away, but for the most part, the town was quiet.

They caught up with Trevor at the corner and he took Damien's hand and all but dragged them across.

"That's the post office," Tawny pointed out with a smile. "The playground is just past it, between the Catholic church and the grocery store."

Across the intersection, Trevor let go of Damien's hand and went streaking ahead. The sound of children playing could be heard just past the little gray post office.

"Do you miss it?"

"The Post Office?" Tawny confirmed. "Not a bit. I should get together for coffee with Johanna one of these days, because she was a great boss, but I'm not sorry to have my days to myself again. And it hasn't exactly been boring," she added, giving Damien a sideways glance.

"I keep threatening to retire," Damien said thoughtfully as they came around the backside of the post office and the playground opened up in front of them. Trevor was already on the other side of the field, flinging himself, belly first, over a swing.

"What would you do?" Tawny asked as they wandered across the field, weaving among big, colorfully painted tractor tires that a handful of kids were playing chase in.

Damien gave her a sideways look. "Move to the country, maybe. Attend book clubs and learn to garden."

She met his eyes, her own face thoughtful and curious, but didn't say anything.

"Cooooooome push me!" Trevor begged.

Tawny took her hand from Damien's elbow—reluctantly, Damien thought with triumph—and went to sit in the swing next to Trevor.

Damien took off his jacket, sorry that Tawny's back was to him, and reminded Trevor to sit straight and hold on as he drew back the swing.

He pushed the boy with a tiny fraction of his shifter strength, sending him flying up into the air with shrieks of laughter. He wasn't worried about Trevor holding on. The little boy may not realize that he was a shifter yet, but he was already developing the supernatural strength that his inner lion gave him.

He didn't want to give Trevor away by testing his limits too obviously, so he pushed just hard enough that the boy laughed in delight.

CHAPTER 11

Tawny could not help but smile.

Damien was clearly having as much fun as Trevor was, and the little boy was yodeling his glee as his grandfather pushed him higher into the air.

The day was glorious, and the park was filled with sunshine and laughter.

Tawny let her feet trail through the pea gravel beneath her and tilted her head up into the sunlight. She would pay for not wearing her sunhat with new freckles, she feared, but the warmth of the sun felt delicious on her face.

"Hold on," Damien suddenly said near her ear, and as Tawny squeaked in protest, he was suddenly drawing her swing back and giving her a steady push into the air.

Tawny was not sure when she had last been on a swing. At some point, you were supposed to accept that you were a dignified woman of advanced age who wasn't supposed to do childish things like swing, and Tawny had always been very good about doing what she was supposed to.

She had been dutiful at putting away her youthful dreams and embracing her role as an old maid. She adopted cats and taught piano lessons to the neighborhood kids, chose conservative clothing, went to church on the holidays. She worked her safe job and lived in her safe town, and she learned not to yearn for things she couldn't have.

Now, leaning back in the swing, holding onto the cold chains while Damien pushed her into the air until she felt like she was flying, Tawny had to marvel at how much he had changed her life in just the few short days she had known him.

The feelings he had awakened in her frightened her, but it was the giddy, breathless fear at the end of the arc of the swing, for a moment in freefall before the chains pulled her back down and right back up again.

Damien went back to pushing Trevor and Tawny let her feet drag in the gravel and slow her, still laughing helplessly.

"Four more pushes," Damien promised Trevor.

Trevor made a noise of protest, but leaned into each arc as hard as he could to make the most of them. Tawny sat for a moment on her motionless swing to catch her breath and then stood.

As they wandered from the playground, Trevor complained that they hadn't stayed nearly long enough, and couldn't they stay five more minutes, and wouldn't it be great if they *lived* here?

"You'd miss your bedroom," Damien told him matter-of-factly. "And all your games are at home."

"I could bring them here," Trevor proposed. Then he was distracted by a chewed up tennis ball that some poor dog had lost, and he kicked it down the sidewalk in front of them.

Damien slipped his hand into Tawny's and they walked that way into the tiny downtown block of Green Valley.

Tawny was keenly aware of his strong fingers twined in hers, and it wasn't the walk that left her breathless. He was so tall and confident beside her, and looked so out of place in his fine shirt and tailored coat. Beards in Green Valley tended to be wild unkempt affairs, but Damien's looked like he'd just walked out of a salon, every hair in place.

She could get used to the beard, Tawny thought. The box in her pocket tapped against her thigh, reminding her of the sparkling bracelet that Damien had given her.

She wasn't sure she could get used to the easy wealth.

Tawny pointed out the local bank, Ted's Hardware, and Gran's Grits.

Shaun's bakery was next on the tiny Main Street, and then the little brick library.

"This is where the book club is?" Damien asked thoughtfully.

"You don't have to come," Tawny reminded him. "I was only kidding."

"I don't have anything better to do," Damien said.

From anyone else, Tawny would have suspected a dig about the small town with no entertainment, but Damien meant it sincerely behind his solemn expression; he honestly, astonishingly, could not think of a better way to spend his time.

Because of her.

In other circumstances, Tawny would have suspected a scam.

But she had no money to swindle, she was no conquest of note, and more than that, she could not doubt Damien's attraction to her.

The way he looked at her, the heated gaze behind the cool face: he wanted *her*.

He was clearly not enamored of Green Valley, and Tawny was already familiar enough with his features to recognize the disdain he masked well when someone or something was just a little too 'country' for him.

But he was willing to tolerate its idiosyncrasies… for *her*.

None of this matched Tawny's self-image, but the whole thing was so delightful and flattering that Tawny didn't want to question it too closely.

"I wanted to ask you something," Damien said, as they passed by Shaun and Andrea's house and left Trevor to fly inside to share his new plan to live in the park and move all of his things there.

"Yes?" Tawny invited.

"Do you have an opening in your piano lesson schedule?" Damien asked.

"Sure," Tawny said casually. "Do you know someone in town who needs them?"

"I'd like you to teach me," Damien said, as if it were the most logical thing in the world.

Tawny stopped in her tracks. "You do not need piano lessons!"

"Why not? I learned violin as a child. Utterly hated it. But having music in one's life is important, and you still won't let me take you to dinner."

Tawny stared at him, then frowned. "You'd have to practice," she said archly.

"Shaun and Andrea have a piano," Damien said loftily. "And Trevor could use a good example."

"You're… serious?"

"Utterly."

Something about the intensity in his silvery eyes made Tawny think that he wasn't really talking about piano lessons any longer. "Alright," she agreed hesitantly, reminding herself that there was no gain for him to deceive her. "You can have the block after Trevor's, if that's convenient."

They began to walk again, Damien's hand in hers, and the rambling town tour concluded back at her front gate.

"It's twenty dollars for a thirty minute lesson," Tawny said professionally. "Pay for the whole month up front and it's ten percent off."

"I'll have my secretary cut you a check," Damien said decisively. "Tawny, may I kiss you?"

"Here?" Tawny asked with a squeak. Though no one was in view, she knew that there would be prying neighbor eyes, all up and down the block.

Damien was already cupping her face in one hand. "Well, I was thinking on the lips," he said gravely.

Tawny had to chuckle, and nodded shyly.

If it wasn't the hurricane/twister/force-of-nature kiss that he'd given her the day before, it was still a kiss that made her knees weak and set her belly on fire with need. It was a long kiss, full of tenderness, and somehow it didn't seem nearly long *enough* when he was finally pulling back and Tawny was left panting and weak.

There was another kind of kiss to add to her list.

"I'll see you tomorrow," he said, with something like triumph in his voice.

"Tomorrow?" Tawny squeaked. Had they made plans that his kiss has erased from her mind?

"At the book club," Damien reminded her.

"You don't have to come to the book club," Tawny protested with exasperation.

"It'll be fun!" Damien said, in a voice that suggested he would force it to be fun.

Tawny had no argument for that, and drifted helplessly into her house on the aftermath of his kiss.

CHAPTER 12

*D*amien arrived at the book club meeting the next evening promptly at six, and found a circle of folding chairs had been set up in a coat closet marked 'conference room.'

The librarian, a middle-aged woman like vulture, led him to the room, shook her head, and wandered out.

A table in one corner had a coffee pot and a half dozen stained mugs. The sugar container was empty, and the coffee had clearly been made last week.

Damien decided that discretion was preferable to caffeine, no matter how his sleep had suffered in Shaun's spare bedroom, and chose not to pour himself a cup.

He claimed the most sturdy looking chair, and put his jacket over the back of the one next to him, folded his hands in his lap and waited.

After a few minutes, an older woman with a long salt-and-pepper braid wandered in. She gave him a long look, poured herself a cup of coffee into a mug that declared 'I are writer' and took the empty chair on the other side of him.

"You must be Tawny's young man," she said matter-of-factly. "Trevor's grandfather."

"Damien Powell," Damien told her formally, though it hadn't been a question.

"Marta Fredrickson," she introduced herself. "You're certainly a fish out of water."

Damien blinked at her. "Yes, ma'am, I suppose I am," he growled.

"I'll say," Marta agreed. "You should know that we're all very fond of Tawny around here. You treat her poorly, and you'll have us to answer to."

Damien looked at her in astonishment. He was used to veiled threats from high powered lawyers and swearing from angry contractors. He was not used to tiny old women who clearly didn't care what he thought.

A second gray-haired woman appeared in the doorway and stopped dead at the sight of him. "Oh my!" she said in surprise, and giggled. She was carrying a box of cookies that she put down next to the questionable coffee, and then she came and sat across from Damien very cautiously, exchanging a shy look with Marta, who introduced her.

"This is May. May, you've heard about the senior Mr. Powell. Ah, Tawny! Your *boyfriend* beat you here."

Tawny paused in the doorway where she had just appeared and blushed beat red. "Oh, he's not, I'm not, we're…"

She looked enchanting, all flustered and flushed. She was wearing a sundress and a sweater, both a bright, cheerful yellow, and she was carrying a cotton shopping bag overloaded with books.

She wasn't wearing the bracelet.

Damien turned to Marta as he lifted his jacket from Tawny's chair. "You find it acceptable to embarrass Tawny and yet you warn me to treat her right? I see that your friendship is as sour an apple as you clearly are."

He used his smoothest voice, and a tight smile that showed just a hint of teeth, the threat obvious but carefully veiled.

For a moment, the room was silent, and Damien was aware that he had their full, undivided attention. He gave Marta a long, challenging look, then turned back to give Tawny a softer smile and pat the chair behind them.

"Oh my," said May, giggling nervously. That seemed to be her only conversational contribution.

"It's not, you shouldn't… it's…" Tawny looked desperately uncomfortable and Damien regretted taking the strong hand with Marta.

Then Marta gave a bark of laughter.

"Oh, Tawny, you can pick them! I like this one! He's easy on the eyes, and he's certainly not going to be a doormat."

Tawny's rosy color had not faded. "I'm so glad you approve," she said faintly. Then, more firmly. "Now that we're all here, our book this week was Fahrenheit 451."

As Tawny had promised, the topic did not stay on the book for long. It devolved quickly into current politics, as reflected in the themes of the book, then gave up even that attempt at relevance. Marta grilled Damien unsubtly about his political leanings, his religious background, his taste in food and music, and his intentions towards Tawny.

Tawny attempted to deflect Marta's attention a few times, but gave up when Damien squeezed her hand and willingly met Marta on the battlefield.

May largely giggled shyly and agreed with anyone who offered an opinion, trying not to stare at Damien too obviously.

CHAPTER 13

"*Y*ou really *didn't* have to come to my book club," Tawny told Damien as the heavy door to the library closed behind them. "I told you it wouldn't stay on topic."

"I was actually quite disappointed," Damien said coolly.

Tawny looked at him in dismay and then saw that there was a smile twitching beneath the tidy whiskers of his beard.

"I didn't get a single casserole recipe," he explained.

Tawny could not keep from laughing in relief. He was so hard to read; there had been times during his clashes with Marta that she was not sure if he was really feeling insulted, or merely giving as good as he perceived he was getting.

Marta had certainly enjoyed herself, and Tawny now suspected that Damien had as well, a suspicion confirmed when he drew her hand into his elbow told her frankly, "I like your friend Marta. She's… spicy."

"She would like that characterization," Tawny said as they swung out onto the sidewalk. "Where are we going?"

"I am seeing you home," Damien explained. "As a proper gentleman would."

They walked a block in companionable quiet, then Damien said what Tawny had been dreading. "You're not wearing your new bracelet."

Tawny almost tripped. "Oh, Damien, I love it, it's beautiful, and so thoughtful."

"But?" Damien prompted.

Tawny chewed on her lip. "It's not very practical for Green Valley," she finally said, feeling wretched and ungrateful.

Damien was quiet as they walked and Tawny felt her heart sink. Had she offended him?

Finally he made a noise that Tawny wasn't sure was a laugh. "Fair enough," he accepted. "I think you will find your next gift considerably more practical."

Tawny stopped, and Damien stopped with her. "You don't have to get me things," she said firmly.

"I *like* to get you things," Damien said, frowning at her.

Why? Tawny wanted to ask, but a dog came barking ferociously out at them from the next yard.

"Darigold, you idiot, come!" the owner hollered from the porch, as Damien angled himself in front of her protectively.

"It's just Darigold," Tawny assured him. "He likes to come out and say hello."

Darigold skidded to a stop on the sidewalk in front of them, took one look at Damien, and turned away to flee back to his own yard.

"Good dog! Sorry, Tawny!"

Tawny waved cheerfully back, and she and Damien resumed their walk.

She was relieved when he slipped his hand into hers, and wondered what her neighbor would tell the rest of the town.

The sunset cast long shadows over everything, and stained the trees and houses in pinks and oranges. The air was sweet with new green things and fresh-cut grass, and it wasn't long before they came to her front gate.

Tawny didn't want to let go of the moment. "Do you... want to come in and have a cup of coffee?"

"I would like to come in," Damien said gravely.

Tawny was unlocking her door before she recognized that he hadn't agreed to the coffee. "I might have a bottle of wine in the pantry…" she suggested as she led him in and turned on the light.

Damien kicked the door shut behind them, and growled, "Tawny, may I ki--"

Tawny didn't let him finish, throwing her arms around his neck and pressing herself up onto his mouth and against his body. It had been an entire day since he had last kissed her, and longer than that since he'd *really* kissed her.

And he could *really* kiss.

"Tawny, may I…"

Tawny didn't let him finish, but walked backwards to her bedroom, dragging him with her as she slipped her sweater off. Her mouth must have been getting used to his beard, because the burn was less on her lips and more in her loins. She wanted him, and she knew, from pressing up against him, that he wanted her no less.

"Tawny, may I…" He was fingering the buttons of her sundress.

"Please don't," she said breathlessly, and he froze in consternation.

"They are only for decoration," Tawny explained. "There's a zipper in the back. And yes, you *may*…"

Then he was sitting behind her on the bed, drawing her close up against him while he unzipped the dress and drew it off over her head. For a moment, Tawny was afraid to turn, afraid to let him see her in only her underthings. But it wasn't like her face was promising anything her body couldn't deliver, and Tawny took a breath and faced him.

All of her worries dissolved at his expression.

His silver eyes were full of hunger.

Hunger for *her*.

"Damien," she whispered, savoring the name in her mouth.

She was standing very close to him, and it wasn't close enough at all. "Damien, may I…?" She fingered his collar, and the buttons that kept her from his skin at last.

She wasn't sure how he managed it, but with clever fingers and perhaps a few lost buttons, he was shirtless at last, and his chest was everything that Tawny had suspected it was underneath, dusted with silver curls.

"Tawny, may I kiss y--"

"Yes!" Tawny said quickly, desperately.

Then he was kissing her again, and it was even more than before, more skin contact, more of his beautiful, big arms around her.

"Tawny, may I…?" He had a finger in the waistband of her underwear, and he was kissing the side of her neck. She was not entirely sure where her bra had gone. Had she taken it off herself, while he was juggling buttons?

"Yes!" Tawny gasped, trying to figure out his belt.

He took pity on her, and stripped off his own pants rather than making her solve them herself, and then they were naked, and standing, vulnerable, together.

"Tawny," he said, running big hands down her shoulders. "Tawny," he said, cupping a breast worshipfully. "Tawny…"

She had never loved her name so much as she did when he said it.

He was fully, impressively erect, and Tawny had to ask, "May I?" and touch him when he hissed a desperate agreement.

For a long moment, they simply caressed each other, gently, full of wonder and anticipation.

Then he asked again, "Tawny, may I?"

And at her wordless, eager agreement, he was laying her back down on her bed and climbing to cover her, kissing her neck as she arched to meet him.

He paused before he entered her, a tease of pressure at her wet, eager entrance. "Tawny, may I?"

"Yes!" she cried, and she continued to say so again, and again, long after he had stopped asking, as he brought her to places she'd never imagined.

CHAPTER 14

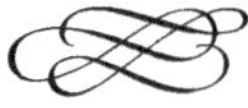

*D*amien opened his eyes to find a pair of unblinking emerald eyes fixed on him.

"Good… morning," he said in surprise.

Lady Gray fluffed up to twice her resting size, then hissed and fled.

Damien's lion chuckled.

There was sunshine spilling into the room through gaps and edges of the curtains around the window. Overstuffed bookcases lined every available wall, and a small pile of books with library tags was on the white painted bedside table. Most of them had book-marks in them.

The closet door was wide open, revealing a selection of hanging blouses and a handful of simple dresses and broomstick skirts. The shoe caddy at the bottom had three pairs of sneakers, winter boots, flowered rubber boots, and one pair of white heels that looked like they had never been worn.

A dresser in the corner had an untidy jewelry box open on the top, overflowing with cheap pieces, mostly earrings and necklaces. The bracelet he'd given her was sitting carefully apart, shut in its velvet box.

The room was small, especially compared to Damien's penthouse apartment, and teetered on the brink of dissolving into chaos.

But it had something that Damien's apartment lacked, and it took him a moment to recognize what it was.

Where his austere rooms offered a challenge, Tawny's room had only invitation.

The chair by the bed looked comfortable, even if it in no way matched the style of the rest of the furniture, and the tidy clutter looked lived-in.

Damien pulled on his clothing thoughtfully, and cataloged as much information from the room as he could.

If the books were an indication, her reading tastes were varied and eclectic, ranging from historical nonfiction to the latest in torrid vampire erotica. Her jewelry suggested that she liked small pieces with subtle humor—cats that hung from her earlobes, flowers with rainbow petals, an octopus holding teacups. Clearly, the diamonds had been a poor choice.

The photos were all old, and Damien was tall enough to see that although the bottoms were dusted, the tops were not.

One must have been her parents' wedding; a sepia affair with a young man in a WW2 military uniform. There was one of two girls in dated sixties prom dresses and Damien recognized Tawny's round-cheeked smile at once. Her hair was up in a beehive hairdo, and even in a fifty-year-old photo, he could sense her delight and embarrassment.

The only other photo of Tawny was from the early seventies or late sixties. Long brown hair fell over a beaded headband, and she was making a peace sign with one hand. The other held a cigarette.

Probably it was a cigarette.

Tawny was in the kitchen pouring a cup of coffee into a stained mug that declared 'Cat Lover.'

She startled when Damien put his hands on her waist, and put the coffee pot back on the coffee maker with a thump. "I wasn't sure how long you would sleep," she said breathlessly.

"Tawny, may I kiss you?" Damien asked, close to her ear.

"I… ah… I suppose that—"

Damien let his arms slips forward around her and kissed down the side of her neck to the collar of her t-shirt.

"Oh," Tawny whimpered as he drew her close. "There's… coffee. And sugar. The only cream I have is hazelnut."

Then she turned in his arms and kissed him like she meant it, with all the passion and hunger that he'd unlocked in her the night before.

Damien released her at last, and took the mug she had offered him. It was decorated with cartoon cats chasing yarn. Bold print declared that it was going to be a knitting day.

He accepted the sugar, but left the coffee black. "Do you knit?" he asked.

Tawny took her own cup and sat at the kitchen table. Damien took a seat opposite.

"I *learned* to knit when I turned fifty, because I thought I should. The sum total of my accomplishments are two hats, an ugly scarf, and a closet full of yarn."

Damien chuckled. "A shame. I was going to ask you to knit me a sweater. I need one desperately."

Tawny's mouth quirked into a brief smile. "I think that's above my skill set," she said honestly. "Sweaters are very challenging."

"I'm sure you would be capable of it," Damien said appraisingly.

There was a moment of silence while they each sipped their drinks. Then Tawny put her cup down firmly. "We should… talk, I think. This isn't something I usually…"

The short, sharp blare of a car horn interrupted her, and Tawny looked up with surprise.

"That sounded like it was right outside," she said, puzzled.

Damien let his mouth curl into a pleased smile. "I have a surprise for you," he said, taking her hand. "A *practical* surprise."

Tawny looked at him skeptically, but let him lead her out the front door, and from there, out to the gate.

The car he had picked out for her was waiting at the curb, the driver standing beside it. It gleamed in the early sun, every sleek line perfect. The courtesy van from the dealer was parked behind it.

Damien was aware that there were people watching from around the neighborhood, attention attracted by the honk that had summoned Tawny.

He was glad. They should witness this gift.

"What is this?" Tawny said.

"I bought you a car," Damien said, watching her face for the wave of delight to break over it.

Tawny's brow furrowed. "You bought me a car?" Her voice was unexpectedly neutral.

"Trevor said your favorite color was blue, and it's got heated leather seats, power everything, satellite radio, a back-up camera..." Tawny's face was not softening the way he had expected.

"It's for you," he explained. "You didn't have one."

"I don't need one," Tawny said coolly.

"But how much easier would it make your life?" Damien said, not sure why she wasn't properly excited. "Come, let's take it for a test drive." He snapped his fingers and the driver trotted to hand over the keys and disappear into the courtesy van.

He held the keys out to Tawny, who gazed back at him as the dealer van drove off.

She was in shock, clearly.

Damien smiled. "It handles like a dream, I promise," he said. "It will make the mail truck feel like a barge."

Tawny finally took the keys, turning them in her hand. "You bought me a BMW."

"Nothing but the best for you now. Let's take it for a drive." Damien started to open the passenger door, and turned when Tawny didn't follow.

The keys hit him square in the chest and he caught them by reflex.

"You might as well just leave cash on the dresser, you pompous jerk," Tawny said, and she had slammed the garden gate before Damien could get the car door closed and follow her.

He heard the deadbolt slide home on the house door before he even got the gate open, and he stood there in shock, trying to figure out where things had gone so wrong.

Laughter made him turn.

A wizened, gray-haired man in overalls was pushing a trash can out to the curb next door, and he was chuckling and shaking his head.

"Good luck with that one, son," the man said unsympathetically.

Damien scowled at him, less pleased with his audience than he had been. Down the block, curtains twitched aside in windows, and a woman pulling weeds a few yards down openly grinned at him.

"Hey, at least you've got a car to drive home in," the man added over his shoulder, cackling as he returned to his house.

Grinding his teeth, Damien recognized the need for a strategic retreat.

CHAPTER 15

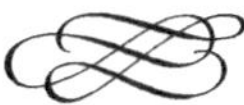

Tawny watched Damien drive away in the shiny car from the window by the door with a sigh of relief and disappointment.

She had been half-afraid that Damien was going to come up on her porch and pound on her door. And she had been half-hoping he would.

She regretted her temper already.

Not that she could possibly accept a gift like that. But she shouldn't have called him a pompous jerk, or thrown the keys like a diva in a snit. She was better than that. She was a mature woman with self-restraint.

She glanced through the open bedroom door at the tousled bed and had to laugh at herself.

There had been no self-restraint last night.

And waking up with Damien's arms around her…

Tawny realized that she desperately wanted Damien to come back. She loved how desirable he made her feel, how alive and excited.

But she knew better than to think he had any place in her life.

A *car*.

He'd known her a few days, and he'd bought her a diamond bracelet and then a *car*, the morning after she had taken him into her bed, like she was some kind of high-paid country mistress.

It only proved how little he understood anything about her.

Rather that stay in her house pretending that she wasn't waiting for him to return, Tawny abandoned her plans to finish putting starts in the garden and gathered up her house keys and a grocery bag. She would have breakfast at Gran's Grits and do her shopping first.

~

"How's the garden going, Tawny? Retirement looks like it suits you."

Tawny slipped into the booth and took off her sunhat. She was still dressed in her gardening clothes; an old shirt with rolled-up sleeves and jeans with knees that were white with wear.

She hoped her cheeks weren't too red and self-consciously tugged at the t-shirt. Damien's beard had left several rashes on her neck, and now she wished she'd worn something with a higher collar, despite the warmth of the day. "What's the special?" she said desperately. She didn't want to ask how much Andrea knew.

"Green pepper omelet with home fries. Feeling *hungry* this morning?"

Tawny sagged into her seat and looked up to meet the younger woman's dancing eyes. Andrea definitely knew too much. "The special sounds fine," she said faintly.

Andrea wrote it down with a flourish. "And to drink?"

"Coffee."

"Coming right up!"

Tawny glanced around the diner as Andrea took her order to the kitchen.

Gran's elderly gray cat was sleeping in the front window, and a few regulars were occupying other booths. She was grateful that it was a quiet morning, and wondered exactly how far the word had spread. She and Damien had certainly had plenty of audience this morning, and she knew that even just walking around town holding his hand was certain to invite speculation.

There was no easy escape from the gossip that Damien's overnight stay would cause. Tawny scowled. Or his attempt to buy her a car.

"Your coffee," Andrea said, pouring her a cup.

"Thank…"

Andrea slipped into the booth opposite from her.

"…you."

Andrea grinned. "Shaun's dad didn't come home last night. I take it that things are going well?"

"It's not going that well right now," Tawny said honestly. "I *do* like him. He's just… he's from a different world, you know? One where he's used to having all the control."

Andrea smirked. "I know the type," she said wryly. "But that's not all bad."

"He tried to buy me a car," Tawny protested.

Andrea's amusement vanished into surprise. "He didn't!"

"He did," Tawny said, angry all over again.

"Well," Andrea said slowly. "You have to understand that he's from a very different world. He's got a ridiculous amount of money, and Shaun says he likes to give extravagant gifts. We're constantly having to remind him not to spoil Trevor."

"Trevor is his grandson, so that makes some sense. But he only met me a few days ago! And who buys someone a *car?*"

"I'm not saying it was a smart gift," Andrea was quick to agree. "Just… try not to read too much into it. Have you ever heard of a love language?"

"A love language?" The idea alarmed Tawny.

"There are five kinds. Some people speak with *acts* of love—like doing a chore they know you hate, or meeting you at work with an umbrella when it unexpectedly starts raining. Some people prefer *words* of love, constantly complimenting or telling you that they care, even writing poetry or letters. Some people are all about the quality time and want to spend every moment with you. And some people use *gifts* of love. It can be awkward, if two people speak different languages, and don't recognize what the other is trying to say."

It was Andrea's use of the word love that was making Tawny so uneasy. "You're saying that Damien speaks with gifts of... love," she guessed.

"Shaun says it took him a long time to understand that about his father. He never gave compliments or showed affection, but he did give him an expensive car, and a credit card, and all the best schools. Shaun's love language leans towards acts and words, and it was hard for him to realize that Damien was saying the things he longed to hear... just in a different language."

He'd said he loved her, Tawny remembered, feeling confused.

"Can I get a refill?" someone a few booths down hollered.

"Just a minute!" Andrea responded loudly. More quietly, she continued. "Give Damien a chance," she urged. "Keep in mind that he's trying to talk to you in the language he knows best."

"You said there were five kinds of love language," Tawny said curiously. "What's the fifth?"

Andrea grinned mischievously. "Touch, of course. That's someone who expresses love with kisses and cuddles and... more."

Tawny felt her cheeks light up.

Andrea's grin only widened. "Of course, most people communicate with a combination of these five, but it's rarely a perfectly balanced equation."

"Order up!" Old George called from the kitchen.

"I think that duty calls," Tawny reminded Andrea, voice choked.

Andrea slid out of the bench seat. "I'll leave you to your breakfast," she said cheerfully. Then she impulsively leaned over the table and squeezed Tawny's hand. "You deserve to be happy, Tawny. *Enjoy this.*"

She sashayed away across the diner, leaving Tawny feeling more confused than ever. It didn't seem fair that the little girl she used to babysit was giving her relationship advice.

It was almost as odd as *needing* relationship advice.

amien was waiting in a chair in Tawny's yard when she returned, fighting down his lion's urge to pace restlessly.

She was carrying a cloth bag full of groceries and a small, sensible purse, a battered sun hat over her pale hair. Her look as he stood was conflicted.

At least it wasn't entirely unwelcoming.

"May I take that for you?" he offered.

She considered him a long moment, then handed him the heavy bag while she dug into her purse for her keys.

"About the car," she said, as she unlocked the house.

"It was inappropriate," he said promptly.

"Yes, it was inappropriate!" she scolded him. "Who buys a complete stranger a new car?"

"You're not a complete stranger!"

"I've known you less than a week!"

There was a pause while Damien chewed over the speech he had planned, and Tawny held her hand out to take the grocery bag back.

"Tawny, I... love you."

"Please reference the previous statement," Tawny said gently. "I don't know what you think it happening here, but I'm sure it isn't."

"It will," Damien said more confidently. "You're everything I've ever wanted."

She looked at him with bewilderment. "Why *me?*" she asked.

"It's… complicated," Damien started, thinking about trying to explain his lion, and the idea of mates that he'd been convinced was fantasy not so very long ago.

She frowned, and Damien recognized that a compliment would have been much more appropriate. "I… ah…"

"There were probably better answers than that," Tawny suggested dryly. Damien was relieved to see that her eyes were dancing with amusement.

"Yes," Damien agreed with chagrin. "I'm doing a terrible job of this. Will you let me start over? The whole thing, from the very beginning."

Tawny smiled slowly. "I'm afraid I don't have a plate of food for you to dump all over me this time. Should we skip that part?"

Damien put his head back and roared with laughter.

He resisted the urge to lean down and kiss her, remembering her edict not to assume. "Tawny, may I kiss you?"

His lion was convinced that all they had to do was make love to her again, to remind her what they were to each other. Neither of them was accustomed to making requests.

"No," she said firmly. "I haven't forgiven you for buying me a car yet."

Damien hadn't expected a no. People didn't tell him no. He blinked at her in confusion. "Are you going to?"

"Forgive you?" Tawny patted the side of his face. "I'll think about it. Would you like to come in and have a glass of lemonade?"

"Yes, ma'am," Damien said politely. "May I carry your groceries in for you?"

"How lovely," Tawny said archly. "What a gentleman."

She unlocked the door and led him into the house.

His phone rang as he was walking in, and he glanced at the screen as he refused the call. There were half a dozen missed calls.

"Are those all work calls?" Tawny asked, as she unpacked the groceries and managed to tuck them all into her chaotically organized cabinets.

Damien sighed. "Yes. We're gearing to move into the busiest construction season, which is when the most things go wrong."

"And you're the one they call when things go wrong."

Tawny hung the bag on hook on the back of the pantry door, and went to get the lemonade from the refrigerator. "It's a little sweet, I hope you don't mind. I like a lot of sugar in mine."

"I like sugar," Damien said, with a smile that implied he wasn't talking about the drink she was serving.

Tawny blushed, as he had hoped she would, and sat down opposite from him at the little kitchen table. "So, what are you planning to do about your work?" she asked pointedly. "Aren't they going to get angry that you aren't there to take care of things?"

"Let them," Damien said, but he felt a pang of guilt as he said it. He knew that he was making more work for everyone else, by shirking his, and that never sat well with him.

Tawny played with her lemonade glass, then lifted her chin and casually asked, "How long are you planning to stay in Green Valley?"

Damien wondered if he imagined the little defensive hitch to her voice.

They hadn't talked about a future, though he'd taken it for granted until she threw the car keys at him.

"I had only planned to come for a few days," he said thoughtfully. "Would you be interested in coming to Minneapolis with me?"

The alarm on Tawny's face was unmistakable. "That's a pretty big offer," she squeaked.

Damien frowned, then realized she might think he was frowning at *her* and tried to smile. "Then I'll arrange to stay here a little longer. I suppose I'd better start returning these calls."

Tawny smiled at him hesitantly. "I'm glad you'll be around a little longer," she said softly.

"I have a good reason to," Damien reminded her, reaching to take her hand.

He let her blush, then smiled and added, "After all, I've already signed up for piano lessons."

Tawny laughed. "You don't have to do that," she said.

CHAPTER 17

Tawny watched Damien over the edge of her book.

Nothing in Tawny's house felt big enough with Damien there.

Her bed was barely big enough for him alone; he could reach off of it in every direction easily. The two of them were crowded and competed for pillows and blankets.

Both of them could barely navigate the kitchen at the same time, and one person had to press up against the wall of the hallway if the other had to pass. Damien usually dropped a kiss on her head when that happened.

The bathroom was simply impossible, with its tiny single sink and its cluttered layout.

Even the living room felt small, with Damien claiming the largest easy chair.

And somehow, it still managed to be perfect, waking up wedged against him, using the excuse of the tiny space to steal hugs. Cooking with him in the kitchen, or washing dishes after dinner, it felt like he belonged there, close and comfortable.

Even when they simply worked together without really inter-acting like they were now, Damien tapping angrily on his laptop at emails and contracts and Tawny reading, just having him nearby felt deeply right.

He put the lid to his laptop down and looked up, and Tawny realized that her book had been in her lap for some time as she simply gazed at him in wonder.

"I was thinking chicken for dinner," she said, flustered. "I have a pack of boneless, skinless thighs. Maybe barbecue basted?"

"It sounds delicious," Damien said.

He said that about almost everything she proposed, and Tawny could not decide if he simply had no sense of taste, or if he was being polite. "I thought I might serve it with bitter greens and over-cooked liver," she added.

"Sounds… um…" Damien looked like she'd just trapped him.

Tawny laughed. "Just checking to see if you were paying attention. How does a green salad with generic dressing sound?"

"Preferable," Damien agreed.

"I can't wait until later in the summer," Tawny said, getting to her feet. "There is nothing like a salad that you harvested just a few hours before. Even with generic dressing."

Damien frowned, glancing at his laptop, and Tawny suddenly remembered that he wasn't planning to *be* there later in the summer.

He didn't *want* to be in Green Valley.

He had important work in the city, work that he was clearly barely keeping up with on the phone and on the computer.

He had not brought up the idea of Tawny going to Minneapolis since he'd sprung the idea to her several days ago and she'd nearly had a panic attack, but he sometimes frowned thoughtfully at her when he thought she didn't notice.

She went into the kitchen to start the dinner preparations, and tried to tamp down her worries.

She loved Green Valley. Her friends were here, her home, her cats, her garden. She could not imagine being happy in a city without those things.

But now she couldn't imagine being happy without *Damien*.

And where did that leave her?

"Can I help with the bitter greens and over-cooked liver?"

Tawny startled. "For such a big guy, you certainly do move quietly. Have you been taking lessons from my cats?"

Damien looked conflicted, like he was trying to decide whether or not to confess something.

"Can you tear up lettuce?" Tawny asked, taking pity on him. She set him up at the kitchen table, making a simple salad while she heated the oven and basted the chicken.

He cut peppers and cucumbers with an engineer's precision, and Tawny had to stop him from throwing away the irregular ends. "That's perfectly good food," she scolded him. "Even if it's a little ugly."

She stole one of them. "Still delicious," she pointed out.

Damien pulled her down into his lap and kissed her. "Still delicious," he agreed.

Tawny laughed, and tugged on his beard. "Still scratchy," she complained.

As she cleaned up the kitchen and checked the baking chicken, she couldn't help glancing back at Damien. He was frowning over his phone, listening to voicemails and checking email.

"More work things?" she ventured.

"My daughter, Shelley," Damien said, distracted. "She works at my company, in contracts and finance. There's some kind of contractor drama."

Tawny stopped in her tracks. "You… have a daughter?"

That was the sort of thing she ought to know, if she was in a serious relationship, Tawny was sure.

Damien seemed to realize that he'd sprung something unexpected on her, and looked up in alarm. "I… er… yes. I assumed Shaun would have… but I guess they've never been close."

"Are *you* close?" Tawny demanded, trying not feel jealous.

Damien put his phone down. "We weren't, for a long time. But recently, I've been trying to mend fences with my kids. It's going slowly, with Shelley."

Tawny shook her head, trying to tell herself that this wasn't a sign that she didn't know this man nearly as well as she thought. She slowly sat down opposite from him at the kitchen table. "Is she older or younger than Shaun?" she asked cautiously. Would he think she was prying?

"She's younger," Damien said. "After Shaun's mother, Dana, died when he was young, I married again. Linda and I divorced… ah… *mostly* amicably, when Shelley was in high school."

Tawny wondered if she looked as gobsmacked as she felt. Damien had a daughter and an ex-wife she'd never even heard of.

It wasn't as if she should have expected Damien to bring them up to her, she told herself. But it reminded her beyond a shadow of a doubt that she did not know this man, had no idea who he was outside of his charming and flattering courtship here in Green Valley.

"I didn't mean this to be a surprise," Damien said, scowling at her in that way he did whenever he thought things weren't going the way they should.

"No, I understand," Tawny was quick to assure him, hoping that her smile was convincing. "We had whole lives before we met."

"Do you have an ex-husband lurking in your past? Or kids?" Damien asked, his scowl lightening at least. Tawny wondered if he didn't sound the slightest bit jealous.

"Only pets," Tawny assured him. "And boyfriends from my youth that never lasted more than a few dates. This is Green Valley," she reminded him. "If there were skeletons in my closet, Marta or Andrea would have told you all about them, weeks ago when we met."

Damien gave a gruff laugh. "Marta told me all about the boyfriends of your youth," he confessed a little guiltily.

Tawny let her face fall to her hands. "Oh, she didn't!" But she was laughing when she lifted her head. "You have nothing to worry about," she promised him.

Damien smirked. "I am sure I don't," he said confidently.

The timer for the chicken went off then, and Tawny went to turn the pieces, wondering wryly if *she* had anything to worry about.

CHAPTER 18

"*N*ice kitty," Damien said, crouching down to make eye contact with Prints under the porch.

Prints hissed, her black fur high across her shoulders, and retreated until Damien could only see her green eyes against the shadows.

Damien tried to decide if the hiss was a little less angry than the last dozen times they had encountered each other, if the fur was a little less raised, or if the retreat was a little bit slower.

"I've got a nice treat for you," he said, waving it invitingly. "Delicious. Real salmon."

Prints stopped hissing, but didn't volunteer to come forward.

"I know you like this kind," Damien said coaxingly. He had gotten Prints to eat them from a distance, but this time, he didn't plan to simply leave the treat for her. "Come and get it…"

Prints took a single step forward and crouched down, eyes narrow and suspicious.

Damien wasn't sure how long they were going to stay like that… the sunlight was hot on his shoulders and he was beginning to think that the wretched creature really could outlast him.

He was almost glad when his phone rang and Prints took off

underneath the porch. Damien growled and tossed the treat into the darkness after her, then stood and answered the phone.

"How's Green Valley?" Shelley asked, deceptively casual. She must be in a mood, Damien guessed, not fooled by her smooth voice.

"Small, nosy, squalid, completely lacking in culture, the dining options are non-existent, and it distinctly smells like cows if there's any breeze at all."

Shelley gave a short, sharp laugh. "Well, that explains why you've been there so long." Which of course, it didn't.

"I've been busy," he told her, not bothering to explain.

"Too busy to return calls regarding a one point three million dollar goddamn change order that didn't get approved?" Shelley demanded. "What is going on, Dad?"

Damien could hear the stress in her voice and felt guilty knowing that the extra work he had dumped on her was probably the cause. "I just got off the phone with the contractor. He says our foreman approved the change order. If our guys said they could de-mobi..."

"Our foreman didn't," Shelley snapped. "He doesn't even have the authority to make that kind of approval. Which you should know!"

Damien frowned. He wasn't usually this out of the loop.

"The contractor said…"

"The contractor is a lying asshole," Shelley snapped.

Damien had to laugh. "The business is full of assholes," he agreed amicably.

Shelley was quiet a moment. "What is going on, Dad?"

"None of your goddam business," Damien said cheerfully.

He realized that there was a pair of eyes looking through a gap in the fence. A pair of young eyes, connected to the face of a boy about the same age as Trevor.

"Shi-- er, let me call you back later, Shelley."

"Don't you leave this hanging," Shelley threatened. "We've got another contract in negotiations with these jackasses…"

"Sorry, gotta go! My piano lesson starts in just a few minutes!" Damien hung up the phone as Shelley spluttered in surprise.

"You said bad words," a small voice informed him through the gap in the fence.

"Yeah, I did," Damien growled. "You shouldn't repeat them."

There was a moment of silence. "My name is Aaron," he was informed then. "It has two As. Not an E like a girl."

"Noted," Damien said gruffly.

"You're Trevor's grandpa," Aaron observed.

Damien was scrolling through his emails, deleting and forwarding anything he wasn't directly responsible for. "I am," he said briefly.

"Can Trevor come play with me?" Aaron asked plaintively. "When he's through with his piano lesson?"

"I don't see why not," Damien said with a shrug. It sounded like Trevor's lesson was winding down.

"What are you doing?" Aaron asked through the fence.

"Trying to answer emails," Damien said shortly. "Before this entire project implodes and we end up millions of dollars in the hole."

"That's a lot of money," Aaron observed. "Can I play a game on your phone?"

"Certainly not," Damien said, shocked.

"There's Trevor!" Aaron said cheerfully. "Trevor! Come over and play with me! Your grandpa said it's okay!"

Trevor came bolting off of the porch and barely paused at the gate to wave at Damien before he was skittering next door.

"Will that be okay?" Damien asked Tawny, who had come out on the porch more sedately. "Have I unleashed some unknown terror on Aaron's mother?" There were already rowdy shrieks of laughter from beyond the fence.

Tawny smiled. "It's a *known* terror; Aaron's dad will be glad for the entertainment. Trevor often goes over there after his lesson."

Damien silenced his phone and slid it into his pocket. "I trust you received the payment for my piano lessons?"

Tawny laughed. "Certified mail, yesterday. You know, you don't have to take these lessons," she said, exasperated. "It's rather ridiculous of you."

Damien came up on the porch and Tawny gave him a quick, casual kiss. "I'm already sleeping with you, clearly you don't need to butter me up anymore," she teased.

"I want to," Damien said simply.

And unexpectedly, he did.

It wasn't just that he wanted Tawny, it was that he wanted to be *with* Tawny. He wanted to sit next to her on the piano bench and laugh his way through lessons. He wanted to read the paper with her in the morning and debate with her at book club. It was awkward, living out of a suitcase in her postage-stamp house, but it was worth it.

He followed her into the house and steeled himself to be her very best student.

CHAPTER 19

Sitting so close to a gorgeous man on the piano bench was a distraction that Tawny had never had to face before. It was worse than a squirmy child. Or a sibling playing video games on a toy behind them. Or a mother talking too loudly on the phone in the kitchen.

Worse, or better. Tawny wasn't sure.

Damien listened gravely to her introduction. It was a lecture better suited for children, but Tawny had taught several adults before, and found that the material was basically universal.

She'd never been so self-conscious about it before, wondering as she explained how the piano worked if Damien would find it condescending or boring.

"Let's talk posture," she said automatically, then swallowed hard as her traitorous brain immediately thought about what he looked like underneath his clothing and imagined him sprawled across her bed. "You're sitting up straight, that's excellent. You want to adjust your seat so that your arms are relaxed, you don't want to cinch up your elbows and shoulders while you are playing." Tawny demonstrated with the *tyrannosaurus rex* impression that always made kids giggle and relax. "And you don't want to be reaching across the room for the keys."

They moved the bench until it fit Damien's tall figure, and Tawny had to perch at the very edge of the bench to reach the keys. "That's fine," she said, when Damien seemed to think he should adjust for her shorter legs. "You'll be doing most of the playing, and I'm used to compensating for kids of all sizes."

She quizzed him on musical theory and tested him on sheet music, happy to find that she wasn't going to have to start completely from scratch. "Everything you learned before will still apply," she assured him. "And you'll find that a lot of it comes back as you go."

Then, she finally let him play, starting with both hands resting on the keys, playing the first five notes of a C-major scale.

"Relax your fingers," she reminded him. "It doesn't take as much strength as you might think, to play the notes."

"That sounds easier than it actually is," Damien said, gamely running haltingly up and down the notes with a look of frustration on his face.

"Your fingers aren't used to this kind of action," Tawny said, gently resting her fingers over his. "Don't be too impatient with them."

His hands were warm, and so strong. Tawny snatched her hand back. "Keep practicing," she squeaked, as the timer she had set went off.

"That was thirty minutes?" Damien said in surprise.

"We had a lot to cover," Tawny said apologetically. "And it will seem overwhelming at first. Before your lesson next week, I want you practice sitting at the piano and getting your posture correct, and doing five repetitions of these simple up-and-downs. Watch your rhythm and concentrate on keeping even time with each note, even if some are easier than others. Do it at least five times a day, and make sure you stand up and push in the bench between practices. Next week we'll add crossovers and start on full scales. I have a worksheet on music notes that I want you to complete—it's for kids, I'm sorry, but it's important information to get into your head."

Damien was watching her with half a smile hidden in his beard, and Tawny was briefly cross at him for having it to keep his expressions from her. "Thank you, teacher Tawny," he said warmly.

"You really don't have to do this," she reminded him. "I can refund the remainder from your check."

Eyes dancing, Damien scooted closer to her on the bench, his warm thigh against hers. "I don't want a refund, but I noticed you gave Trevor a treat at the end of his lesson last week."

"I've got a jar of chocolates by the front door," Tawny told him, shivering at his proximity and unable to keep from smiling foolishly.

"Can I have my treat in kisses?" Damien asked slyly.

"There are chocolate kisses in the jar," Tawny teased him, but she lifted her mouth to him expectantly.

Then there was a boyish shriek from outside the open window, a new tenor of alarm and fear from the playful noises of before, and a strange animal yowl.

More swiftly and gracefully than Tawny would have guessed possible, Damien was vaulting over the bench and fleeing the house. "Stay here," he called desperately as he disappeared. "Please, I'll be back in a moment! *Wait here!*"

Mystified and worried, Tawny waited.

CHAPTER 20

The scene Damien found next door was exactly what he dreaded.

Aaron was descending the tree in his yard, eyes like saucers. "We were climbing the tree," he sobbed. "I know we weren't supposed to, but I'm sorry! And Trevor fell! And I won't do it again! And what *is* that? *Where did Trevor go??*"

Another parent or grandparent would have feared a different tableau—a child with a broken leg or dislocated shoulder from a fall like that.

But Trevor's clothing was scattered around the yard, and a disoriented, blinking lion cub was sitting underneath the tree, favoring one paw.

"Aaron-with-two-As, I am going to need you to take a deep breath and count to ten," Damien said, dredging his memory to remember how Andrea dealt with Trevor when he got hysterical. "As slowly as you can." He crossed the lawn and scooped Trevor carefully up with as much of his clothing as he could easily reach.

He automatically scanned the area for onlookers, and was relieved to find that Green Valley had for once decided not to provide an unwanted audience.

But the scream had not gone entirely unnoticed, and as Damien carried Trevor to the most private corner of the lawn, up next to Tawny's fence, a young man with wild eyes came bolting out of the house. "Aaron! Are you okay? What's going on?"

"Eight!" Aaron said, panting and pointing. "Nine! Ten!"

"Trevor," Damien said quietly. "It's okay now. You're okay. This is perfectly normal, and I need you to be a little boy again now."

He was fairly certain that despite his efforts at discretion, Aaron's father got an eyeful of Trevor's furry shape before he morphed back into a naked little boy.

"I was so high up!" Trevor said at once, more excited than frightened by the whole experience. "But falling was scary and there was a voice that said we ought to be something else and my wrist hurts."

Damien breathed a sigh of relief and inspected the wrist, deciding that it was sprained at worst. "We'll put a wrap and some ice on that," he said firmly. "And we'll talk about climbing trees as well."

"Are you going to tell Dad?" Trevor asked. "Are you going to tell him that I can be a…" he paused and Damien guessed that his lion was filling him in. "A lion! I can be a lion! Roar!" He made tiny claws with his small fingers.

"You didn't have a mane," Aaron said skeptically. "And you were spotted."

"You might need these," Aaron's dad added then, handing Damien the rest of Trevor's clothing.

Damien exchanged a long thoughtful look with him. He didn't look nearly as surprised by the events in his front yard as he ought to be. "Thank you," he said levelly. "Bear?" he guessed.

"Grizzly," the other man agreed with a crooked grin. "Lion seems the easy guess, given your grandson's development here. Damn, I thought I had another few years before I had to worry about this." He eyed his son warily.

"Trevor's precocious," Damien said shortly, nodding to confirm his guess. "I'm Damien Powell." He offered a hand.

"Dean James," he received in response, and they shook hands firmly.

"Now boys, listen up," Damien said, as Trevor got dressed. "This is not something that you can tell anyone about, not ever."

Aaron was looking suspiciously at his father. "Can I do that, too?"

"We won't know for a while," Dean said cautiously.

Trevor was fingering a place in his shirt where the seam had split. "Can I do it again?" it suddenly occurred to him.

"Not here," Damien and Dean said at the same time.

"It's like a secret identity," Dean said swiftly. "You can't do that out here where people can see you, like Superman can't get into his suit out in the front yard."

Trevor's blue eyes got enormous. "I'm a superhero?"

"It's like that," Damien agreed reluctantly, hoping that the parallels would be sufficient to ensure their discretion. "It has to be kept a secret."

"What about me?" Aaron whined. "I want to be a superhero."

"You're a superhero, too," Dean told him. "You're like Batman. He doesn't have powers, but he still has to keep the secrets."

"Hey," Trevor complained. "I want to be Batman."

"You're like Superman," Damien reminded him. "With the powers."

"Superman is lame," Trevor pouted. "I want to have a Batmobile."

"Is everyone alright?"

Tawny was walking across the lawn towards them.

Damien supposed he should be grateful that she had waited this long to investigate. He hadn't really expected his order for her to stay behind to be honored indefinitely.

"It's a secret!" Trevor and Aaron shouted together.

"Hey, Tawny," Dean said casually.

Damien got back to his feet. "Trevor fell out of a tree," he explained. "He's fine now."

Tawny accepted their various statements with skepticism, but nodded slowly. "You need ice on anything, Trevor?"

Trevor wriggled his wrist experimentally. "Nope," he said, looking at it curiously.

"Superpowers," Aaron said in a stage-whisper.

"So everything is just fine here," Tawny said, looking from one of them to another.

"Just great," Dean said too quickly.

Aaron took Trevor by the other hand. "We're all great!" he insisted, dragging him towards the house. "But we have to go now! Bye!"

"I'm going to… go get them a snack," Dean said with a big smile. "See you later, Tawny! Nice to meet you, Damien!"

And then it was just Tawny on the lawn with Damien.

He could tell her now, it occurred to Damien. He could tell her right now that he was a lion shifter, and that she was his mate, and he could be done with dancing around secret subjects at last.

But it felt like he'd only just won her over, like they were still in a tentative place. He didn't want to unsettle the perfect, fragile balance they had finally found. The truth about him might frighten her. Or make her angry.

He didn't want to risk either of those things.

"You know, I never did get my treat," he said, instead, and watched Tawny's cheeks redden delightfully.

CHAPTER 21

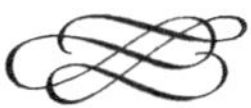

"Saw your young man outside swearing at someone on his phone," Marta said, pulling her shopping cart alongside Tawny's.

"He's not my young man," Tawny said automatically.

"Well, he's not that young, I supposed," Marta said. "But you're no spring chicken, so that's just fine."

"I mean, he's not… we're not…"

"So you keep saying," Marta said tartly. "But he's spends an awful lot of overnights at your house for someone who's not a… whatever you think you aren't."

Tawny sighed, keenly aware that her shopping cart was full of dinners for more than one.

"I take it he hasn't offered to make an honest woman out of you yet?" Marta pried.

"It's the twenty-first century," Tawny reminded her. "I don't need to be *married* to be an honest woman."

"That's what an old maid says," Marta sniffed.

"I *am* an old…" It occurred to Tawny that she didn't really feel like an old maid anymore and she trailed off.

"Not sure what *you* are or aren't, are you?" Marta said shrewdly.

Tawny sagged over the handles of her shopping cart. "Not really," she admitted.

Sometimes, she felt like she and Damien were the absolute perfect fit, like two halves of a jeweled egg. And sometimes, she felt like she was waiting for the other shoe to drop, the rest of the story, a hint of the secrets that Damien kept in his perfect beard. It was almost as if he was playing at this country life. Tawny was not oblivious to the fact that the frequency and intensity of the calls he was fielding had increased.

"Earth to Tawny," Marta said, and Tawny recognized that she had been talking and Tawny hadn't heard a word of it.

"I'm sorry, Marta," Tawny said, giving herself a shake.

"What's our book this week?"

"The Pelican Brief," Tawny said. Damien had helped them pick it.

"And your whatever he is or isn't, is he going to be there?"

"Damien said he'd be there," Tawny assured her.

"How long is he planning to stay around?" Marta asked probingly. "Doesn't he have some big shot career in the city to get back to?"

"I… don't know," Tawny confessed, a sudden pang of worry in her chest. What was she going to do when he left? He couldn't stay here indefinitely.

"You should find out," Marta said sensibly. "Now, if you aren't going to pick out some apples, kindly move your shopping cart and let someone who isn't suffering some kind of an existential crisis get some pie ingredients."

Tawny could only chuckle, and move her cart.

"See you and your young man at book club tomorrow," Marta said brightly.

CHAPTER 22

Shaun pounced on Damien the moment he opened the door.

"Trevor says he has a secret that you know and he can't tell me because he couldn't get into the Rusty Leg and I have no idea what he is talking about. Dad, what do you know about this?"

"Justice League," Damien corrected, bemused that he had picked that up from Trevor's television. "Trevor turned into a lion yesterday," he added mildly.

Andrea walked in then, not catching his words. "Is that more laundry?" she asked. "I honestly did not expect my father-in-law to be giving us practice for when Trevor goes off to college and returns only for clean clothes." Her voice was full of laughter, and she stood on her tiptoes to give Damien a fond kiss on the cheek. Damien was not sure how she had ended up so easy with him; he and Shaun were still cautiously navigating each other like the near-strangers they were.

Shaun was gripping the back of a chair with white knuckles. "He what?" he said, completely ignoring Andrea.

"Who what?" she asked.

"Trevor turned into a lion yesterday," Damien repeated.

"Oh!" Andrea said, startled. "It's been more than two years. I thought we were in the clear for a little longer. I suppose he remembers this one?"

"Clearly," Damien said regretfully.

Shaun groaned. "He's probably upstairs shifting back and forth right now. We're going to go through a fortune in shredded sheets and damaged drapes as he figures out his claws. Should we pull him out of school? There's only another few weeks..."

On cue, Trevor's voice came from up the stairs. "Grandpa? Is Grandpa Powell down there? I need his help..."

Damien exchanged a complicated look with Shaun. "Be right up, cub," he called.

But he paused. "You want to come up for this?"

Shaun raised an eyebrow at him. "You're not going to insist on doing everything yourself so it's done right?"

Damien hid a wince, Andrea frowned, and Shaun rubbed his face. "Sorry... I just..."

"You're a fine father," Damien said firmly. "And I probably have not told you that enough."

While Shaun stared back at him, gobsmacked, Damien swept past to the stairs. The compliment tasted unfamiliar in his mouth, but felt better than he had expected to admit.

Trevor was hiding in the closet when Damien arrived at his room, Shaun just a few steps behind. "It's a secret," he cried from the closet.

"Your dad is a superhero, too," Damien said firmly. "You can tell him things."

Shaun navigated the toy-strewn room and sat down on the bed. "Grandpa Powell told me," he said. "I'm excited for you."

Trevor peeked out. He was wearing clothes, but they looked worse for the wear. The neck was stretched out, and the shoulder seam gaped. There was a tear down the front that looked suspiciously like a claw mark.

"You're not mad?"

"I wouldn't be mad!" Shaun insisted. "I'm a shifter—er, super-hero—too."

Trevor's eyes went wide and he crept out. "Are we all lions?"

Shaun met Damien's eyes as he answered, "You and Grandpa are. I'm a tiger."

His tone was defensive, and Damien had a moment of chagrin.

When Shaun was a kid of Trevor's age, Damien had assumed that his son would be a lion like himself. Had he been heavy-handed in his lion-themed gifts? Did Shaun think that being a tiger was a disappointment to his father?

"We'll all drive out into the woods one day soon and go running together," Damien said, only realizing afterwards that it didn't sound like a suggestion. "If you want."

Trevor nodded enthusiastically. He came all the way out of the closet and perched on the bed next to Shaun.

"There are things you're going to have to be careful about," Shaun warned him.

"My feet are sharp," Trevor agreed solemnly.

"And you're stronger than other people," Shaun said firmly. "You can hurt them if you aren't careful. You heal fast, but they may not."

"Can I fly?" Trevor asked with perfect seriousness.

Damien chuckled.

"No," Shaun said. Then he grinned. "But your mom can."

"Miss Andrea can fly?!" Trevor nearly fell off the bed.

"She's a hawk shifter," Shaun told him.

"Like Hawkgirl?" Trevor asked avidly.

"Like a bird," Shaun clarified.

Trevor quizzed them further, about the limits of his heady new powers, and Damien was pleased that Shaun laid down sensible restrictions. They both emphasized the need to keep all of their abilities a secret.

"Can I tell Clara?" Trevor asked plaintively. "I tell Clara everything. She'd never tell bad people about me, I promise."

Damien and Shaun exchanged a look that was thoughtful. Clara's father was a shifter, and her mother knew about them, but another loose-mouthed child with information so powerful…

"Sorry kiddo," Shaun said regretfully. "The fewer people that know, the better."

"She might make me tell her," Trevor warned. "She might sit on me and make me eat dirt." Realization dawned on him. "Now that I'm a superhero, am I *stronger* than she is?"

Damien and Shaun both smothered laughter.

"You keep letting her make you eat dirt," Shaun told him, squeezing him around the shoulders. "And pretend you can't stop her, so you keep the secret as long as possible."

CHAPTER 23

$\mathcal{D}$ amien was surprised to find that he and Tawny were not the first to arrive to the book club the following day. Already, all but one of the chairs were full, mostly of middle-aged women. One sullen looking teenager sat at the edge of the group, glaring at her cellphone and typing into it. There were three plates of cookies, and the coffee smelled fresh.

The vulture-like librarian glared at them and went to rustle up more chairs as Damien insisted that Tawny take the only free seat.

She looked like she might protest, then finally sat reluctantly as Damien put his jacket across the back of the chair.

The other women grinned at them like hyenas.

"How's the garden coming along, Tawny?" one of them asked innocently.

"I'm almost done getting it in," Tawny said cheerfully. "A few more flats, and it will be done."

"Tawny wouldn't say so, but her garden is always the best in Green Valley," Marta was happy to explain. "Something blooming in every season."

"Right now there's not much blooming but dandelions," Tawny

protested, looking pleased and flattered and embarrassed. "All my spring bulbs were eaten by rabbits over the winter."

"Best tasting garden in Green Valley," one of the other women laughed.

May gave a nervous giggle and blushed when the others looked at her.

"Our book was The Pelican Brief," Tawny reminded them, as the librarian dragged two large chairs in to the increasingly tiny room.

After some rearrangement, Damien took one of the chairs like a throne, sliding in next to Tawny.

They talked about the book briefly, comparing it to other Grisham books that most of them had read and speculating about the accuracy of the law aspects of the plot.

The woman sitting next to the teenager hissed a warning at her and the girl reluctantly put the phone down. "I liked the movie better," she said darkly. "Even with Julia Roberts."

The topic immediately moved to the actress, the other movies she had done, and then to how terrible television had gotten, something they all agreed on.

From there, they began talking about cooking shows, and spring cleaning.

"I took three boxes to charity this morning," Marta pointed out proudly.

"I got rid of my husband last month," one of the others said laughingly. "Does that count?"

"Speaking of husbands," Marta said sharply. "How long are you staying in Green Valley, Damien?"

Damien felt Tawny stiffen beside him and could imagine her stricken expression.

"I haven't decided," he said as mildly as he could manage. He very casually reached over and took Tawny's hand.

In perfectly terrible timing, his phone rang then, and Damien reclaimed his hand to reach into his pocket and turn it off without looking at the screen. "I miss the days you could leave the office and they couldn't call you anymore," he said with his most charming smile.

The topic turned to technology then. Marta panned cellphones as a whole. "I wouldn't be surprised if they find out they cause cancer of the ear, or lead to baldness."

The teenager made a rude noise, muffled in a cough.

"You sound as paranoid as Stanley," one of the women told Marta. "I've been using a cellphone for ten years, and I'm healthy as a horse."

"I have a flip phone from the dark ages," Tawny said peacefully. "It does everything I need it to."

"You going to get your lady a shiny new phone?" Marta asked Damien slyly. "Top of the line, makes coffee and washes the linen?"

"Marta!" Tawny said in exasperation.

But Damien grinned at Marta. "Heard about the car, did you?"

"Everyone heard about the car," Marta told him matter-of-factly.

The room chuckled.

"If Tawny's too proud for a car, I'm not," Marta offered.

"I'd take a car," one of the other women agreed.

"Oh my," May giggled.

Tawny put her head in her hands, but her shoulders were shaking in laughter.

The stern librarian appeared at the door. "We're closing," she said briskly, then vanished.

Everyone stood, gathering up their things.

Damien easily carried the chairs back out into the library, earning a nod of approval from the librarian as she pointed out where they had come from.

When he returned to the room, Tawny was saying goodbyes to the others. The teenager had her cellphone out again and was tapping into it animatedly while her mother (Damien guessed) helped fold the remaining chairs.

"I think we talked about the book for a whole five minutes this week," he told her approvingly.

"If you count the conversation about the movie," Tawny agreed.

"You really don't have to come to my book club, even if you are really good for increasing attendance."

"I liked it," Damien said as he tucked her arm into his elbow, and he was surprised to find that it was true.

"You're full of surprises," Tawny said, shaking her head.

"Some of them good, I hope," Damien said. "Not like the car."

"Not all of your surprises are as poorly conceived as the car," Tawny agreed, laughing.

Damien stopped at the empty street corner and turned to take both of Tawny's hands in his. "I promise not to buy you a car again," he said sincerely. "Will you forgive me?"

Tawny stood up on her tiptoes to lay a kiss on his cheek. "I already did," she promised.

CHAPTER 24

Damien helping in Tawny's garden was like having all of her very favorite things together.

He was terribly distracting, with his rolled up shirt-sleeves showing off his muscled arms, and the morning sun dancing in his silver-gold hair.

"Ah," said Damien. "This is a weed I can identify. Dandelion!"

Tawny gave him a golf clap. "Very good. You'll develop that green thumb yet."

He started to kneel to pull it up, but Tawny stopped him. "Leave that one. This early in spring, it's one of the first flowers to tempt the bees in. I try to keep just a few in the beds that haven't flowered yet."

"The ways of gardening are mysterious indeed," Damien said dryly.

"With no bees, nothing gets pollinated, and there won't be any vegetables or berries later. Starve the bees now, and they won't come back later!"

"I know plenty about the birds and bees," Damien told her with a wink.

Tawny blushed. "You can pull those dandelions there, the ones that aren't blooming. And the chickweed all along there."

"Yes, Captain," Damien teased.

He knelt by the bed in question.

Tawny made herself stop gazing after him like a fool and took another flat of starts to transplant.

She was still picturing Damien's gorgeous form, in his too-nice pants and his out-of-place shirt, when he suddenly snarled in pain and alarm.

Tawny whirled around as the snarl turned animal, and to her utter astonishment, watched the clothing she had just been fantasizing about stretch and rip over golden-furred muscles.

In the blink of an eye, there was a lion, enormous and real, leaping back from the flower bed, giant jaws snapping in the air.

Without meaning to, Tawny gave a squeak of alarm, and dropped the tray of starts she was holding from fingers numb with shock.

The sound caught the lion's —*Damien's*—attention. The huge, thick-maned head swung her way and silver eyes met hers.

He opened his mouth as if he meant to say something, showing fierce teeth, and seemed to sneeze.

Tawny had to laugh, leaning weakly against the wheelbarrow.

It was only slightly hysterical laughter.

She put a hand to her forehead, shaking her head. "Oh, Damien. This makes so much sense." She thought back over his incredible presence, his unexpected strength, all the little clues and hints.

Damien sat, and cocked his big maned head at her, then shifted seamlessly back into a man.

A gorgeous, very naked man.

"I didn't mean to frighten you," he said. "This wasn't how I meant to tell you about shifters."

"I won't say it didn't frighten me to suddenly be in a very small garden with a very big lion," Tawny said, still chuckling. "But I do know about shifters. Or at least, I'd guessed."

"You knew?" Damien frowned as he stood.

"I've delivered mail in Green Valley for forty years. Once you've seen a few dozen unexpectedly naked people and exotic animals with no zoo within a hundred miles, you do put the pieces together. Either I was living in a town where people could shift, or there were a lot of secret nudists with illegal pets in the area. From there it wasn't that hard to figure out that Gran was her own cat."

Damien slowly smiled—that tiny, secret little smile that Tawny had to search for in his beard.

She brushed the dirt off of her hands and picked up the tray of starts. The flat had landed face-up, so although a few of the plants looked a little off kilter, very little damage had been done. She put it down on the wheelbarrow. "What happened? What made you change shape… er, shift?"

Damien put out a hand sheepishly. "I don't know. It hurt." He cleared his throat and added defensively, "It surprised me." There was a welt rising on his palm, red and angry.

Tawny stepped forward and took his hand, ignoring his glorious nudity with effort. "Oh, it looks like you got stung by a bee. Poor thing!"

"Are you pitying me, or the bee?" Damien asked crossly.

"Damien," Tawny said with sudden concern. "Are you allergic to bees?"

"I've never been stung before," Damien said dismissively. "But I'm a shifter, so I have a much better immune system than a human."

Tawny turned his arm over and, as she had expected, found a line of hives marching up his arm.

"You're having a shifter-strength reaction," Tawny said firmly. "I'm calling 9-1-1."

Damien grabbed her hand with his good one as she reached for her phone. "You can't do that," he said. "Hospitals can't help shifters."

"You're going into anaphylactic shock!" Tawny protested.

"I don't even know if they could help me," Damien said, starting to pant alarmingly. "But I know they'd learn a lot more about me than I care to share. Shifters in hospitals mean shifters in cages in laboratories. You have to know that."

Tawny frowned fiercely at him, not convinced. "Are you telling me you never took your kids to the doctor?" she demanded.

"A doctor we *knew*," Damien countered. "Promise you won't call 9-1-1!"

Tawny could not have documented the emotions that spilled through her if she had tried. She was angry, and frightened, and felt like her world was tilting away from her. Everything was out of control, not going at all to her careful plan. She wanted to shake Damien, and at the same time throw her arms around him and beg him to tell her that it was all going to be okay, and at the same time she wanted to push him away.

"Then promise me you won't die!" she finally retorted.

"I promise," Damien said firmly.

Tawny scowled at him. "Put your hand up above your heart. It doesn't look like the stinger is still in there. We should ice it, and get some antihistamine into you immediately. Inside. Now!"

She put herself under his good arm, and was alarmed that he let her help her into the house. His bare skin under her arm was hot to the touch.

"The couch," she said, but Damien settled to the floor and she didn't have the strength to lift him.

"I don't know if antihistamines will work," he panted. "Tawny, I'm going to shift again. My lion is stronger than I am. Promise you won't be afraid…"

"I promise," Tawny squeaked, kneeling beside him.

It was a lie; she was very afraid, but she wasn't afraid of Damien's lion, not even when the giant creature was suddenly taking up almost her entire living room floor.

He was a rich, golden color, and the paw that lay against her thigh was the size of one of her cats. She tentatively took it in her own hands, marveling at the velvety texture and the huge pads. The bee sting was invisible in the thick fur, and there was no sign of the hives that had raised along Damien's pale human skin.

The lion panted, and let his massive head thump down onto the floor, his thick mane spreading like water around him.

She wasn't afraid of the lion for a moment.

But she was still afraid.

She leaned forward, until she was curled up on his strong shoulder, face buried in the long fur, and wrapped her arms around the big cat fiercely.

It was like cuddling with a hundred willing cats, or a pile of fur coats. Warm, living fur coats.

She could hear his heartbeat, hammering irregularly but strong, and below that a rasp of a sound that wasn't quite a purr; she had heard that big cats couldn't purr, but she would have guessed this was a happy sound. One of his big paws curled gently around her.

She could never be afraid of him, not like this, but terror and adrenaline still coursed through her.

If he died…

She didn't understand what was happening between them. She told herself it was only a summer fling, a matter of convenience while Damien was visiting with his grandson. She had tried to be careful of her heart, to keep herself from reading more into his interest in her than was actually there, to keep things light and friendly and casual.

But she'd failed, so completely.

It wasn't just the way he had awakened her body, like a lily blooming after a long winter, and it wasn't just the way his kissing made her hungry for more.

It was lying in her small bed with him afterwards, twining her fingers in his and drinking up his solid warmth.

It was sharing morning coffee while they read the paper.

It was his kiss on the top of her head as they passed in the narrow hallway.

It was the way she automatically turned to tell him her observations about little things, already used to the idea that he would be close by, and that he would care what it was that she had to share.

It was the way he took her hand at book club.

Instead of keeping him at arms length, she was shaking in his…

paws. She was so afraid of losing him that she wanted to cry… and she never cried.

She was supposed to be sensible and independent.

But none of this was sensible, and she would be lost without him.

"Oh, Damien," she said into his mane, as she wasn't sure she would ever be able to say to him as a man. "Damien, I love you. Please be okay. If I lose you…"

Beneath her, the heartbeat seemed steadier, and the lion lifted his head and nuzzled her. Tawny wondered if a lion's tongue was as sandpaper in texture as a housecat's, and then he was shifting, and gathering her into his strong arms.

CHAPTER 25

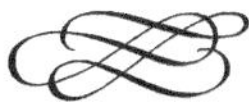

Tawny's whispered words were like honey to his ears, and Damien was shifting before he even consciously realized it, because he wanted so badly to kiss her, to hold her trembling body and tell her he was going to be fine.

"Tawny, my Tawny," he said, wrapping her in his arms. "I could never leave you. I am yours."

She cried into his shoulder for a moment, in shock and relief, and he assured her, "Look, I'm fine. The hives are almost gone. They don't even itch anymore."

Tawny inspected him critically, trailing her finger over the vanishing red spots. "Why did being a lion make the reaction stop?"

"Shifting from human to lion and back can speed up healing wounds and broken bones, sort of like the body gets itself back together the right way while it's changing. It made sense that shifting could fix a chemical imbalance as well."

"I can't believe I almost lost you to a *bee*," Tawny said, wiping her face. "Oh, I'm a disaster."

"You are beautiful," Damien told her.

Tawny snorted. "You are clearly still riddled with mind-addling histamine."

Knowing that his words would be unconvincing, Damien took her face in his hands. "Tawny, may I kiss you?"

"Yes," she said helplessly.

He kissed her soft mouth, and the dear lines around her eyes and the tears on her cheeks.

He kissed her neck, and she whimpered and clung to him.

With gentle hands, he lay her down on the floor and stripped her clothing off so he could kiss the rest of her, loving every mark of character and everything she considered a flaw.

"I love you, Tawny," he told her, and unexpected tears gathered again in her eyes. "I will never leave you."

He turned her tears to cries of pleasure, and drew her to new planes of release. After he had joined her there, they lay a long while together on the floor.

"Well," Tawny finally said, "that was certainly not the day I had planned." She looked at him wryly. "*You* are certainly nothing I had ever planned."

Damien sat up. "Tawny, there's something more."

Tawny sat up with him. "What is it?"

"Shifters have something called a mate."

"Sounds dirty," Tawny said with a wicked grin that was always surprising in her sweet face.

"You are mine. I knew from the moment I saw you that I would be yours forever. My lion knew."

Tawny looked at him curiously, her humor fading to confusion. "Like… love at first sight?" She shook her head. "I'm not sure I believe…"

"Believe it," Damian said forcefully. "Tawny," he added more gently. "I love you. I loved you from the moment I dumped a plate of food down your shirt. I will love you forever."

Tawny looked at him with pursed lips, then leaned forward and kissed him tenderly.

"Do you believe me?" Damien had to ask.

"It certainly explains a lot," Tawny said practically. "And if I can believe that you turn into a gigantic lion, it's really not such a stretch to believe in destiny. I… know I was fascinated with you from the first moment I saw you, and I know I love you now." She laid a gentle kiss on his forehead and got to her feet with a groan. "Next time, let's take this to the bed. I'm too old for floor sex!" She gathered her strewn clothing. "I'm taking a shower."

Damien had already attempted to take a shower with her in the cheerful yellow bathroom, and they had quickly discovered that it was too small for the activity to be sexy… or anything but crowded and painfully inconvenient. "I'll take the next one," he said, watching her go. "Save me some water."

He wondered if she would ever believe how gorgeous she really was to him. She had all the right curves, graceful and soft, with fascinating freckles wherever the sun hit her skin.

He stood, his own knees complaining as Tawny's had, and moved to the couch, where he leaned back and closed his eyes, feeling satisfied and triumphant.

She loved him.

He hadn't really doubted that she would, but it felt good to hear her say it, to look in her eyes and know it.

Something made him crack an eyelid and he was startled to find Prints staring at him from the opposite end of the couch.

"Your treats are in the pocket of my torn up pants outside in the garden," he told her in amusement. "This is your chance to go eat them all without having to tolerate me to get them."

But although he had not offered her anything, she approached, step by cautious step, across the couch.

Damien held still, barely daring to breath as she navigated her careful way next to him.

She sniffed his bare thigh, and Damien wondered if her sudden boldness was because she had witnessed him as a lion and now accepted him as one of her kind.

"Nice kitty," he said gruffly.

Then she crept onto his knees, crouched down possessively, and began to knead her paws.

Tawny found them this way. Damien's eyes were watering from the piercing pain of Prints' claws, but he was unwilling to disturb her tentative trust. He was stroking her gently, very slowly, and he could feel a faint purr in his kneecaps.

"How on earth?!"

Prints vanished at the exclamation, leaving a last row of deep scratches as she leaped away.

Damien frowned at them, then looked up to find Tawny gazing at him jealously.

"She never willingly sits on anyone!"

"I've been bribing her with cat treats," he explained.

"I've tried that," Tawny said, shaking her head in amazement. She had changed out of her gardening clothes, and was wearing a simple summer dress; already the day was quite hot, and Damien was not uncomfortable lounging naked on her couch.

Her hair was wild and damp around her head, like a dandelion gone to seed.

"They were very good cat treats," Damien told her with a smile. "I have some left, will they convince you to come sit in my lap, too?"

Tawny laughed at him, but came willingly to snuggle into his lap and accept his kiss.

"I was thinking, while I was in the shower," she said, playing thoughtfully with his beard. "About Minneapolis."

Damien resisted his urge to hold her tighter, hope rising in his throat. "Good things, I hope."

"I'll come with you," she said. "I… know that you have a lot at stake there. I can have a neighbor feed the cats—they're basically outdoor cats in the summer anyway, and I'll pay Stanley to come water the garden. Patricia can take the piano lessons until her baby comes."

Triumph washed over Damien. She was *his*, coming home with him, and it was settled. "I can't wait to show it to you," he said in delight. "I'll call and have the housekeeper get you a room ready and stock the kitchen. Tomorrow? Wednesday? Pack whatever you need, I can drive us up there."

She was too expressive to hide her nervousness, but Damien knew that once she was there, once she had seen what the city could be at his side, she would never leave it again.

CHAPTER 26

Tawny glared at Prints from across the garden as she finally put the last of the starts and the black cat stalked after a honeybee investigating the dandelions.

"Ungrateful turncoat," she muttered. "I spent years trying to tame you, and who do you sit on? Who do you purr for? Not me. Not the person who pays your vet bills and fills your food dish."

She sat back on her heels and pushed her hair back from her face. She had forgotten her sunhat again, and would pay for it in freckles.

And she wasn't really angry at Prints.

Tawny was very good at planning.

She had always been the one who organized things—she had started the book club, almost forty years ago, and she was usually the one who usually coordinated potlucks and fundraisers if someone fell on hard times. "Director Tawny," they had called her in school, which was nicer than saying 'bossy.' She picked a sensible, stable career that suited her strengths. She studiously saved money, she paid off her house exactly on schedule, and she retired the day her benefits kicked in.

Everything went according to a plan.

Until Damien.

Now here she was, planting late, forgetting her sunhat, and all of the plans she'd made were in pieces at her feet.

She was abandoning her book club, her garden, her cats, and running away to a city she dreaded with a man she adored.

Tawny stabbed the trowel into the dirt harder than was called for and sighed.

"Are you ready?"

Tawny turned to find that Damien was standing at the gate, looking more crisp and confident than ever. He wasn't abandoning *his* life, she thought. He was going back to it.

"I'm packed," she called, getting to her feet again. "I just wanted to get these in before I left or they were going to die. Stanley can water things, but I wouldn't trust him to transplant."

"Running water isn't a government conspiracy?" Damien said drolly.

"Oh, not the running water part," Tawny laughed. "Just all the additives they put into it for mind control or whatever. My bags are on the porch, just let me wash my hands and I'll be ready to go."

She darted into her house and drew in her breath.

It was cleaner than usual; all the library books were returned, all the house plants had been put out on the porch so they would be part of the watering cycle.

Tawny could not resist wandering through one last time. Her bed was neatly made with clean sheets, there were fresh towels in the bathroom, so that when—if—she came back, everything would be waiting for her. The washing machine had the door propped open so it wouldn't mildew while she was gone, and the cat boxes were all emptied.

She had left the front door open behind her and Lady Gray, convinced that something was up, ghosted in behind her and followed her through the house.

Tawny reached down and scooped her up, burying her face in the thick, charcoal fur. Lady Gray didn't struggle, but she also didn't purr, because being held wasn't her own idea.

"We really could take them with us," Damien said, standing in the doorway with her last bag. "I've got lots of room."

Tawny gave Lady Gray a last squeeze and put her down with a nudge to the door. "They're used to being outdoor cats, with grass and gardens and birds to hunt. They would hate it there, and make our lives miserable in payback."

Lady Gray tried to sneak back into the house and Tawny stopped her with a foot.

"Let's go," she said to Damien, trying to look brave and confident. It was easier to feel brave and confident when he was looking at her like he was: adoring and excited.

"You're going to love the city," Damien assured her. "We'll go see art museums and visit gardens. There's so much to do, and see."

Tawny smiled at him. "I'm going to love it," she said out loud, and it didn't feel like a lie. It felt like a promise. She was going to love it, because she loved this man, and that was where he belonged.

Sometimes things didn't happen according to the plan, she told herself as she locked the house and slipped the key into the flower pot by the door.

Then Damien was taking her hand in one of his, easily lifting her book-heavy suitcase with his other.

Sometimes things went better than she'd planned.

"I'll have a key made for you, of course," Damien said, as they walked from the elevator to the only door in the hallway.

"Do you own the *entire* floor?" Tawny asked in astonishment as he unlocked the door.

"I do," Damien said, opening the door and ushering her through. He decided not to mention that he owned a few of the apartments downstairs as well.

She was, as he had hoped, struck silent with awe as they walked in.

The front hall was not overly impressive, with its standard ceilings and understated style. But there was a hint of light and space ahead, and after a few steps, it opened into the vaulted living space, views of the city in two directions through floor to ceiling windows. The other two walls of the long rectangle were white shelves of carefully lit treasure.

"My whole house could fit into this room," Tawny said in awe after she had gazed at it for a few moments. "It looks like a museum."

"Come see the rest," Damien said, and he led her through the kitchen. "The refrigerator is stocked with anything you could want, please help yourself. The bar is there, pantry is there. You are welcome to use anything. If there are any ingredients you'd like, leave a note on the fridge for the housekeeper."

Tawny opened the pantry and blinked into the room beyond. "I can't imagine needing anything else," she said in wonder. She closed the door and wandered around the big stainless steel island. "What is this?" She pointed at a gleaming gadget with a computer screen.

"I have no idea," Damien confessed. "I know how to use the coffee maker and the microwave, and really nothing else."

Tawny gave him an amused look but didn't look terribly surprised. "How did Shaun get to be such a good cook?" she asked curiously.

Damien looked at her with narrow eyes, suspecting dangerous territory. "Linda, my second wife, liked to cook. Shelley had no interest in it, but Shaun took to it like a duck to water."

Tawny accepted that without question, opened one side of the monstrous fridge, considered the contents for a thoughtful moment, and closed it. "Did Linda design this kitchen?"

"Yes," Damien told her cautiously.

"It looks like it was made for someone who loved to cook," she said mildly. "I'm impressed."

Damien led her next to the media room. "It's like your own movie theater," she observed with amusement. "Oh look, there's even a popcorn maker!"

"Three kinds of disgusting butter topping for your authentic experience," Damien told her.

"I like it extra disgusting," Tawny joked.

Next were the bedrooms.

"I wanted you to have your own space," Damien said. "This is the guest room I thought you would like best."

It wasn't as close to his own room as Damien would have liked, but it was the smallest, coziest room, and he thought it would be the most comfortable. The windows here were smaller, though they had the same view of the city, and the ceiling was lower. It had a small walk-in closet, and a private bathroom with a claw-footed tub and a glass-walled shower with benches that doubled as a sauna.

"It's gorgeous," Tawny said gratefully. "I love it."

They left her suitcase there, walked past the other two guest rooms, and ended at Damien's room.

It was a room fit for a king, a vast expanse of thick-carpeted space with an enormous custom-made bed facing a wall of mirrored closet doors. The ceiling overhead was arched, cathedral style, and the bank of windows looked out over the Mississippi.

The wall opposite from the windows was lined in more of the white shelving that had been in the living area, subtle spot-lighting on each item showcased there.

"What are all these?" Tawny asked, trailing along them curiously.

"Things I've collected over the years," Damien said. "That's a Viking sword uncovered in Greenland the same year I visited. That's an Egyptian scarab that was discovered during a road project my company was heading in the 90s. It was a gift from the president at the time. That's the log book of my great-grandfather, who was there for the pounding of the cross-continental railroad spike. He was one of the engineers for the project."

"It really is a museum," Tawny observed. She didn't offer to touch anything. "Everything here, it all means something to you."

"Every piece," Damien said with a nod. "Why are you smiling?"

Tawny blushed and ducked her head.

"Tell me," he said, hoping belatedly that it sounded coaxing and not simply demanding.

"I was just wondering if it would be possible to make love on that bed without feeling like I was either on stage, or sneaking into a museum after hours."

Damien loved either idea. "Would you like to find out?" he suggested slyly.

Tawny smiled up at him, sunshine in her freckled face. "Yes," she said shyly.

CHAPTER 28

Tawny wondered how Damien managed to stay in Green Valley as long as he had.

The city was constantly in motion, there was always something to do—and it was always something important, or wonderful, or exciting.

He took her to art museums: The Art Institute, Walker Art Center, the Weisman Art Museum, until the artwork, and the names of the artists, and the long, lit hallways were all blurred together in Tawny's memories. They went to the Mill City Museum, and she learned more about flour than she ever thought possible. He took her out to see Shakespeare at the Guthrie Theater. They went to gardens, and lakes, and waterfalls, and parks.

They visited the Mall of America, mostly so that Tawny could say she had, and found acres of bookstores that Tawny could have spent entire days exploring.

Tawny stayed in the vast apartment by herself the days that Damien went to his office, rattling around feeling small and judged by the decor. Damien offered her the use of a driver to go anywhere she wanted, but her few forays out by herself seemed overwhelming and chaotic. And it just wasn't as much *fun* without him to share her observations with.

Every day, a cheerful housekeeper appeared with groceries, stocked the fridge, planned and prepared meals that needed only to be put in the oven for a programmed time, cleaned the apartment to sparkling, and disappeared.

Tawny had attempted to make friends with the woman, and thought she made some inroads, but the woman spoke only Russian, and seemed to think that conversation was keeping her from her work.

Mostly, Tawny read, took baths, missed her cats, and wondered how her garden was growing.

"I bought you a phone," Damien told her one evening, and he pushed it across the table at her like it was a live bomb. "I know how you feel about gifts, but it would make me feel better if you had a more modern device."

They were eating dinner together in the sterile, perfect dining room. It was a luscious meal, that Tawny had done nothing to make but move a pot from the fridge to the oven and set a timer. Damien occasionally reminded her that if she wanted to do more, she only had to say so, but Tawny had never enjoyed cooking *that* much, and she knew that she couldn't cook this *well*, either.

If she was being very honest, she was also more than a little intimidated by the perfect kitchen. It simply didn't look like the kind of place you could get dirty, and she was a very *messy* cook.

She took the box and opened it. The sleek machine was smaller than her ugly flip phone, but Tawny knew it would do much more. "This is probably above my level of technology," she said hesitantly. "But it's very pretty."

It felt fragile in her hands as Damien showed her how it worked. He had already programmed in his own contact information, and installed a few apps he thought she'd enjoy.

"Card games on my phone," Tawny laughed.

He was clearly anxious about her reaction; he hadn't tried to get her anything since the car, and Tawny assured him, "I love it. Thank you."

Damien showed her the calendar function. "Here, I'm going to invite you to the dinner we're going to this weekend."

He did something swiftly with his phone and Tawny almost dropped her own when it gave a pleasant little blurble and vibrated in her hand.

"And then you accept the invite, like this."

Tawny watched him add it to her calendar. "What did I just commit to?"

"It's a company dinner."

"Something fancy?" Tawny asked trepidatiously. She had already worn her best clothes the few times they'd gone out to eat, and even though she could tell that Damien wasn't picking the fanciest places, she had felt terribly outclassed.

"I'm afraid so," Damien said. "I can hire someone to assist you in buying new clothing if you'd like. My tailor only works in menswear, but I can certainly find someone to alter something for you."

He said it so casually, as if he thought it was perfectly normal to have a shopping assistant, or get clothing altered, instead of wearing whatever was good enough off the rack.

This was his life, she realized. Casual money, busy cities, phones that kept packed schedules in perfect order.

She wanted to refuse, but she didn't want to embarrass him more. "Whatever you think would be best," she agreed. "As long as it doesn't involve high heels. I nearly broke an ankle wearing those things at Patricia's wedding."

Damien laughed with her. "I assure you, there will be no goats to chase at this event," he promised.

They cleared the dishes together, and loaded the dishwasher; it was as much cleaning as Tawny ever did anymore, and she enjoyed watching Damien roll up his sleeves and help.

Damien made a few phonecalls and answered emails as Tawny curled up on one of his large, modern, geometrical couches and finished her book. Sunset over the Mississippi turned the whole room gold and rose, and she looked up from her final pages to find Damien had long since finished and was gazing at her thoughtfully.

She smiled at him slowly. "Was I making funny faces? I sometimes do, when I'm reading."

"You are very expressive," he said, amused.

"You might be, too, if you didn't have all that facial hair to hide under," Tawny pointed out. "I don't think you fully recognize your advantage here!"

"I'll take any advantage I can," Damien said, scooting closer to her on the monstrous couch. "Tawny, may I kiss you?"

Tawny tipped her face up to meet his mouth, and sighed blissfully as he wrapped his arms around her.

"Any regrets, coming to the city?" he asked, when he'd kissed her dizzy.

"Not right now," Tawny said sincerely, throwing her book aside and putting her arms around his neck.

CHAPTER 29

"Who the hell is Tawny Summers?"

Damien looked up from his computer to find Shelley standing in the open office door, puzzling down at her phone.

"Is it a contractor? Some new client?"

"No, nothing like that." Damien frowned, not entirely sure how to answer the question. Girlfriend felt inadequate and juvenile. It didn't sound anything like the domestic bliss that Tawny had brought into his life. "It's a personal matter."

"Since when do we get personal, *Dad*? And why do I want to have lunch with her?"

"She's from Green Valley," Damien said, as if that explained everything. In a lot of ways, it did.

"So she's a friend of Shaun's?" Shelley guessed. "And I'm supposed to care, why? I'm a little old to need my big brother to make friends for me anymore."

"No!" Damien said. "Well, she is sort of a friend of Shaun's, but… she's living with me."

Shelley nearly fumbled her phone. "*Living with you* living with you, or living in your apartment because there is a shortage of hotel rooms *living with you?*'

Damien sighed. "She is my mate."

Shelley was silent a moment.

"Your *what?*"

"My mate," Damien repeated.

Shelley frowned, and Damien recognized it with amusement as the same expression-masking frown that Tawny frequently called him out on.

"You always said that was a ridiculous, romantic fairy tale meant for weak-willed people who needed fantasies to get them through life."

"I was wrong," Damien said simply.

"This day could not get more surreal," Shelley said in astonishment. "I don't know what is weirder, you admitting that you were wrong, or you trying to convince me that someone from the town that smells like cows is your destined true love."

Damien couldn't help laughing, and Shelley's eyes got larger.

"And now you're laughing."

"Just have lunch with her," Damien chuckled. "You'll like her."

Shelley narrowed her eyes. "Why do you care if I like her?" she asked flatly. "It's not like we have this warm father-daughter relationship, and you've never asked me to like any of your other girl-friends."

"And I'm starting to think that was a mistake," Damien told her honestly. "That I missed out by not being a better Dad to you and Shaun."

Shelley's face went entirely unreadable. Without, Damien noted in amusement, the advantage of a beard.

"Well," she said neutrally, "I appreciate the offer. I'm really busy this week, but I'll check my calendar for next week. I'm looking forward to meeting her at the company dinner this weekend."

"Shelley…"

"Lots to do," she said briefly. "I'll have copies of the Twiller contract on your desk by this afternoon."

"Shelley…"

But she was gone, and Damien shook his head and returned to the computer in front of him.

His weeks in Green Valley had made him realize how important his family was to him, and how little he'd ever bothered to show them.

His phone gave a little beep of warning and Damien shut down his computer and packed up his files. He caught himself smiling as he dialed the phone. "I've got a surprise for you," he told Tawny, once she'd figured out how to answer it. "Be waiting downstairs."

"Aren't you mysterious," she scolded him, when he pulled up to the curb and the doorman opened the car door to let her scramble in beside him. "Where are you taking me?"

"There's a clue in the back seat," Damien told her, delighting in her excitement.

Tawny reached back and found the bag he'd left there. "A Man to Remember? I just finished reading this. I got a copy from the library and could not return it fast enough." She sounded disappointed and confused. "In fact, you kept checking to see if I'd finished it yet."

Damien grinned. "I found us a book club," he said with triumph. "The Franklin Library has a book club that meets every Thursday afternoon, and this was their book for the week."

"Oh, Damien, you sweet man! You know I've missed our book clubs!"

The Franklin Library was in Uptown, and the parking was terrible, so they arrived several minutes late and were glared at by a librarian who made the vulture from Green Valley look friendly. There were several dozen people in attendance, and as they slipped into seats near the back, a young woman leaned over to them. "Did you get the discussion syllabus?"

"Syllabus? No…"

The woman grudgingly lent them her copy of the sheet, and Tawny giggled quietly. "It's like they actually expect to talk about the *book*," she observed, handing it back.

The librarian led them on a structured analysis of the book, occasionally soliciting opinions that Damien and Tawny quickly realized were selected from only a few of the politely upraised hands.

When Tawny finally voiced her opinion that the book had terrible pacing and failed at being entertaining, she was countered with a raised eyebrow and a stiff reminder that it had won a Man Booker award.

She was subdued the rest of the meeting, which ended exactly on the hour and broke up in a hum of quiet conversation.

Damien only realized as they were walking out that he had been scowling at people, and probably had sabotaged any attempts that the book club members might have made to be friendly with Tawny.

"That… wasn't as fun as I'd hoped," he confessed to her, as they walked back to the car.

Tawny put her arm into his. "You tried!" she said encouragingly. "But there are some things that Green Valley does better, and apparently book clubs are one of those things."

Damien could think of several things that Green Valley did better, and the idea surprised him so much that he was silent until Tawny went on. "However disloyal to Gran's Grits it makes me feel, restaurants are something your city does do much better. How about taking me out to Chinese food and we can make fun of the librarian and that ridiculous syllabus and exchange recipes for tater tot casseroles, like a real book club."

Damien smiled down at her and willingly agreed.

CHAPTER 30

Tawny unlocked the door and picked her bags up. The huge door swung open on perfect hinges, and she sidled inside. It clicked locked again behind her and she walked into the living room that still felt like a museum. The only plants that Damien had in the whole apartment, as far as she could tell, were a row of hardy succulents on a short glass accent wall. The air smelled weirdly sterile compared to her own house, but the temperature was always perfect.

She put her bags down on one of the couches, first trying automatically to make them sit up straight, then deliberately letting them slouch.

Living here felt exactly like that—like she was a slouching bag in a perfect apartment.

Tawny lifted her chin. She was determined not to embarrass Damien that night, and she'd bought the nicest clothing she could afford and even splurged on a new lipstick and hairspray. She would never look young, and she would never look fashionable, but she could at least look like someone who could clean the dirt out from under her fingernails and curl her hair.

She *missed* having dirt under her fingernails.

She missed...

Tawny shook herself and went to take a shower. A note on the counter indicated that Damien would be working until it was nearly time to go, and implied that he understood she would forget to check her phone for messages.

It was an hour before she had arranged her makeup and curled her hair and put on her new clothes, resisting the urge to tuck the tags in and try to return them the next day.

The effect was not what she had hoped.

She was still herself, just with makeup and nicer clothes. She looked like someone's grandmother, caught wearing someone else's jewelry. This was a terrible idea. She was going to make a fool out of both of them. She was going to be the country bumpkin at the ball, and Damien would see her compared to all his high-class friends and socialites and wonder why he was wasting time with her.

"Tawny?"

Tawny frowned at her reflection and then had to laugh as she realized she was making the same face that Damien did when he didn't want someone to guess what he was feeling.

She was still laughing as she opened the bathroom door and found Damien, already dressed for dinner.

He was breathtaking.

It was evening, and amber light streamed in through the ridiculously large windows and turned everything to gold and glitter. He was dressed in a suit that made Tawny recognize that all of his other suits had been casual, and he filled it up like no one that Tawny had ever known, all broad shoulders and a graceful strength that Tawny would have called lion-like even if she hadn't known about his other form.

He was a king.

He was a king, and for some absurd reason, he was looking at her like she was a queen, and her laughter stilled on her lips as she blushed and her heart hammered in her chest.

"Will it do?" she asked anxiously, spreading her arms and turning in a circle.

Damien was quiet so long that Tawny began to worry she'd

picked the wrong things. "I could… maybe not wear the scarf. Is it too loud?"

"No," Damien said swiftly. "It's perfect. It's exactly right."

Tawny sagged against the doorframe with relief. "Oh thank goodness. I was second guessing my taste, and my budget, and my size, and these shoes, and look!" She held up her wrist, where she was wearing the diamond bracelet that Damien had given her a lifetime ago in Green Valley. "I have somewhere to wear it!"

His look of delight was worth every anxiety putting the bracelet on had caused Tawny as she thought about how much it must have cost.

"Perfect," Damien repeated. "Tawny, may I kiss you?"

"I'll muss you!" Tawny objected, as Damien leaned to kiss her. "Your tie is so tidy!"

"It can be fixed," Damien growled, claiming his kiss swiftly when she smiled at him and tipped her head up.

How did he manage to make everything better? Every time he looked at her, she felt like she was just where she belonged, even if nothing around her felt right.

Tawny smiled at him, and stroked his perfect beard.

"I got you something," Damien said, frowning at her because he didn't want her to see that he was nervous.

Tawny gave him a skeptical look. "Should I be afraid?"

"It might be cool when we come home," he said. There was a large box on the bed and Tawny went to open it cautiously.

"Oh," she said in awe. "It's beautiful."

It was a light wrap in fine golden wool, trimmed in pearls and embroidered with… Tawny bent to look closer. "Are those dandelions?"

"And a bee," Damien pointed out.

Tawny leaned against Damien and laughed, forgetting to be careful of their clothes and hair. "Where did you find this?" she demanded.

"I had it made," Damien said, sounding smug.

"Did they laugh when you asked for it?"

Damien snorted. "They would not dare."

"I love it," Tawny said, lifting it from the box and pulling it over her shoulders. It was deliciously soft, and light, and warmer than she expected.

"Silk and cashmere," Damien told her. The phone in his pocket buzzed and he checked the screen. "Our car is ready downstairs."

Tawny patted her hair. "Well, I'm as ready as I'm going to get."

CHAPTER 31

*D*amien could not help but gaze at Tawny as they went to the elevator.

She dressed up as well as she dressed down, and was the perfect picture of understated taste in a subtle, pearl-gray pantsuit with a pair of low dress shoes and a splash of color at her neck on a water-color silk scarf.

And she was wearing the diamond bracelet he'd given her what felt like months ago, self-consciously twisting it on her wrist.

"You look beautiful," he finally told her, as the elevator descended.

Tawny beamed at him gratefully, and the compliment was immediately worth the effort. Damien vowed to use them more frequently.

"Thank you!" She smoothed the wrap on her shoulders. "I confess, I feel a little foolish, and I'm nervous about this dinner. I hope I don't sneeze on someone important or insult the wrong person."

"You'll do fine," Damien assured her. "And if anyone is mean to you, I will shift into a lion and eat them."

Tawny laughed and hugged his arm.

Then she looked up at him curiously. "Wait, are these people shifters, too?"

"There are several shifters in the company," Damien shared. "But most of them are humans."

"Do they know about shifters?"

"Some of them, but most do not."

"It sounds like a minefield," she observed. "I shall be discrete."

The rest of the elevator ride, and the car ride to the restaurant, Tawny quizzed him about taboo topics and behavior expectations.

"No one will care if you use the wrong fork or the wrong glass," Damien promised. "And this isn't Britain, so you don't have to worry about titles."

"Small comfort," Tawny said wryly.

"You can't start worse than I did," Damien teased her, pulling up in front of the restaurant. "The first party I attended with you, I dumped an entire plate of food down your shirt and made a small child cry."

Tawny chuckled. "Let's not make it a competition," she said practically.

The valet opened her door, and Tawny made a little noise of surprise when he offered his hand to help her out, clearly not sure what to do with it.

The valet adapted, and stepped back, letting Tawny scramble out on her own as Damien came around the car to meet her.

"I'm surprised you don't have a driver," she said as the valet took the keys and vanished with the car.

"I like to drive," Damien said. "And if I ever feel like using a driver, I have a service on call."

The back half of the restaurant, a big, imposing monster called Mel's, had been reserved for the work party, and Damien led them through the tables to the back.

Tawny did a better job of not gawking than Damien would have, he suspected. She didn't try to hide her awe, but she didn't let it intimidate her, either.

"You must be Miss Summers," Jack said, descending on them once Damien's coat and Tawny's wrap had been taken.

"Oh, just Tawny, please," Tawny said swiftly, accepting Jack's hand to shake.

"I'm Jack Morning, Damien's counterpart in the design department."

"I'm afraid I have no idea what that means," Tawny said frankly. "But it's lovely to meet you."

Jack laughed. "My team draws up the plans that Damien's construction teams completely change in the field."

"If you'd design them right the first time, they wouldn't have to," Damien ribbed him, straight-faced.

"You wound me," Jack joked. "Let me introduce you to my date, Tawny."

Tawny at his side was everything Damien could have wished for. She wasn't the same conversation dominating companion that Linda had been, nor the shy, retiring type that Shaun's mother Dana had been. She was something else entirely her own: quiet, but not at all withdrawn. She was perfectly willing to admit when she didn't have any knowledge of a subject, and equally willing to argue her point when she did. She was an attentive listener, never looking bored, and she was kind and polite and unabashedly excited about everything.

Damien kept an eye out for Shelley, hoping to introduce them, but she didn't arrive until the meal was being served, and she ignored him when he tried to catch her attention.

When dinner was served, Tawny was enthusiastic about the dishes, ate gracefully, and if she was a little cautious about her manners, she picked things up quickly, and was willing to laugh at her own little clumsinesses.

"You're really taken with her," Jack observed quietly near his ear, halfway through dessert. "I've never seen you like this."

Damien scowled to cover his surprise. "I don't know what you're talking about," he growled.

"I've heard you laugh twice tonight," Jack pointed out. "And when you look at her, everything about you softens. You were actually charming with that jerk who runs permitting, and I haven't heard you swear at anyone all evening."

Damien gave a snort that didn't qualify as a third laugh. "You're exaggerating," he scoffed.

"She's not much to look at," Jack said appraisingly.

Damien could feel his lion's hackles rising. "Watch yourself," he warned.

"Peace, Damien," Jack added swiftly. "I can see the appeal. She's lively and sweet, and she's watching you the same way you're watching her. I already like her better than your last wife."

Damien was saved having to forgive him by the start of the speeches.

The speaker, fortunately, kept it brief and funny, and by the time the desserts were cleared, they were released from the tables to return to mingling.

Damien caught Shelley's eye at last, and drew Tawny over to meet her.

"Dad," she said coolly.

"Shelley," Damien greeted her.

Tawny extended her hand without prompting. "I'm Tawny," she said warmly. "It's so nice to meet you, Shelley."

Shelley shook her hand. "It's Michelle," she corrected.

Tawny blushed, and Damien was tempted to kick Shelley in the ankle because she was clearly just being unfriendly. Was she offended that Damien had failed to tell her about Tawny earlier? He remembered belatedly how rattled Tawny had been to find out about Shelley.

Tawny recovered, and gracefully said, "Of course, Michelle."

"*Shelley*," Damien said firmly. "Tawny is from Green Valley, where Shaun has settled down with Trevor."

"So I've *heard*," Shelley said shortly, giving Damien an unappreciative look.

"I teach Trevor piano lessons," Tawny offered. "He's a sweet boy."

"I'm sure he is," Shelley said unhelpfully. Damien suddenly wondered if she'd ever actually met Trevor.

"I taught Shaun's wife Andrea when she was a little girl, too,"

Tawny added nervously. When Shelley didn't immediately answer, Tawny asked desperately, "Do you work for Damien's company?"

"She's in finances and contracts," Damien said for her.

"That sounds fascinating," Tawny said too enthusiastically. Then she laughed at herself, and added, "But then, I found sorting mail satisfying work, so my bar is pretty low."

"It's interesting work," Shelley said, but Damien thought she said a little more warmly, her expression softening. "Never a dull moment."

No one could resist Tawny's genuine sweetness for long, he thought triumphantly.

"Tawny hasn't been here long, maybe you could show her around a little, meet her for lunch?" Damien said innocently, as if he hadn't already suggested it to Shelley.

Tawny smiled. "I'd really like that," she agreed.

Shelley's face was unreadable, but Damien thought she seemed confused. She didn't have many friends, he realized.

Or at least, not many that he knew about. But how well did he really know her?

"I'd like that, too," Shelley finally said. "I'll give you a call this week and arrange something."

"I have a phone number! I have no idea what it is!" Tawny fished her phone from her purse and gave Shelley her contact information, laughing over her confusion with the device.

They parted amicably, and Shelley even smiled.

Damien frowned back thoughtfully as he led Tawny to the coat check for their outerwear. "I never had a good relationship with my kids," he confessed, equally quiet. "But I've been getting to know Shaun and Trevor, and I'm realizing how much I've missed." He hesitated as he helped Tawny adjust her wrap, wondering how much to put into words about how he wanted to mend his broken family, and how it was Tawny who had opened his heart.

"And you'd like me to smooth the way," Tawny guessed.

"Am I that easy to read now?"

"I'm starting to figure you out," Tawny said cheerfully. "And her expressions are *just* like yours. She's not sure about having lunch with your country mistress, and you're too afraid to have lunch with her yourself. Is she a lion shifter like you?"

Damien was so surprised by her self-depreciating title and the accusation that he was afraid that he didn't have a chance to answer before she was waving at the traffic. "Oh, there's your car!"

He took the keys from the valet numbly as Tawny scrambled into her side of the car. They had never talked about what they were. *Girlfriend* didn't seem quite right, and he'd never put a name to what more they were.

She is our mate, his lion said, perfectly content.

Country mistress, she'd said, like she was some paid companion. Did she *know* what she meant to him? Did she believe what he'd told her about mates? She didn't really think that he was buying her company, did she? She had certainly been reluctant to accept his gifts at first.

Tawny sighed as he settled into the driver's seat beside her. "That was a lovely dinner," she said cheerfully. "But absolutely exhausting. I feel like I've had to be switched on to eleven all night just trying to keep up, and these may not be heels, but my feet are still killing me. Do you think this outfit would look alright with sneakers next time?"

Damien let her chatter on as he pulled out into the familiar city traffic towards his apartment building. She was still winding down as they took the long elevator ride up, and she kicked off the detested shoes as Damien unlocked the door for her.

"I am taking the world's shortest shower so that I don't get makeup all over the sheets, and then nothing is going to keep me from straight to sleep and staying in bed until noon," Tawny said.

"Tawny," Damien said, catching her hand.

She smiled up at him, so warm and happy that it did something deep in his chest and temporarily washed away his doubts.

"Tawny, are you having fun here?"

She hesitated just a moment, and the doubts all came surging back.

"I am having fun," she said firmly. "I… miss Green Valley, and my cats, and my neighbors. But I *am* having fun." She said it as if she were having fun by sheer force of will, then her face softened. "And *you* are here," she added gently.

Damien cupped her face, her dear, sweet face, in both of his hands, and kissed her slowly.

"Mm," she said, when he released her. "Okay, I can think of one thing that could keep me from going straight to sleep," she suggested slyly.

CHAPTER 32

Tawny had all but forgotten about lunch with Shelley when her phone rang a few days later.

"Yes?" she answered, once she'd swiped three time in vain and finally accepted the call. "This is Tawny."

"This is Shelley Powell." She sounded like she looked, all business and crisp efficiency.

"Oh, Shelley! How are you?"

"Fine," Shelley said politely. "I wondered if you'd be free for lunch today. I was thinking The Capital."

"That sounds lovely," Tawny said promptly, with no idea what The Capital was.

It proved to be an impressive building that was even more grand on the inside, when Damien's on-call driver took her to the front steps. Tawny spent several moments feeling small and underdressed, then lifted her chin and marched to the hostess.

It couldn't be worse than the city book club.

She was ushered to a table where Shelley was already seated, talking heatedly on her phone. The hostess offered her a menu that puzzled Tawny until she realized that the numbers beside the descriptions were prices without dollar signs. Exorbitant prices. Her credit card, already stretched by frivolous book purchases and the pantsuit she could barely afford for the company dinner, would be weeping this month.

Damien had insisted she take a debit card to his account "for emergencies."

Tawny wondered if lunch with his daughter counted as an emergency.

A server asked for her drink order as Shelley signed an apology and continued her conversation.

"Just water," Tawny insisted. She could put the lunch on her own card if she was careful.

"I'm very sorry about that," Shelley said as she finally concluded her call. "I swear, these subcontractors don't even read their contracts."

Tawny chuckled despite her nervousness. "I think your father said that exact thing earlier today."

Shelley looked at her without laughing. "So what is it you do, Tawny?" she asked conversationally.

"Happily retired," Tawny said cheerfully. "But I was the mail carrier for Green Valley until last month."

Shelley looked rather confused as the server returned with their drinks.

"Just water" turned out to be something bottled in glass, and Tawny wondered wryly what it was going to cost as the server poured a glass of wine for Shelley.

They chatted awkwardly about how Tawny was enjoying the city so far, and Tawny tried to stay friendly and cheerful, without betraying how nervous she felt, or how intimidated she felt by Shelley's effortless elegance. She wanted to Shelley to like her, and was sincere about her desire to help Damien reconnect with her.

"You're really not what I expected," Shelley said, once their food order had been taken. She didn't comment on Tawny's selection of the cheapest option on the menu.

Tawny chuckled, not sure how to take that. "I didn't ever expect to eat lunch in a place like this," she confessed. "And if you had told me earlier this spring that I would be dating someone like your father, I would have laughed you out of town."

"You aren't his usual type," Shelley agreed, chilly in tone, but thoughtful in expression.

Tawny couldn't quite hide her wince. It shouldn't surprise her that he had a *type*. A *younger* type, if she had to guess; Damien would not look out of place with supermodel arm candy. There were several tables nearby with men who looked older than he was making eyes at dates half her age. And after all, she hadn't even known about Shelley and her mother until just more than a week ago. She should have know that he would have other women as well. Had he been married more than twice? What did she really know about him?

"Well," she said, not sure how else to respond. "Maybe his usual type wasn't cutting it anymore."

Shelley nearly choked in her wine trying not to laugh, and Tawny caught just a glimpse of a real smile cross her face.

"I'm not a gold-digger, if that's what you were worried about," Tawny said frankly. "I've spent more time trying to get him not to buy me things than anything else. In case it was your inheritance you were concerned for."

She wondered, after she said it, if it didn't cross the line between funny and rude.

But Shelley genuinely laughed then. "I don't need Dad's money," she said earnestly. "And I don't want it any more than you do."

Their food was served then, tiny portions on giant scarlet square plates drizzled with multi-colored sauces.

"I think that if something is listed in the menu description, they should serve you more than one eyedropper full of it," Tawny observed skeptically. Then she took a curious bite. "Oh, wow."

Conversation as they ate found an easy rhythm. They started by talking about their favorite foods, which led Tawny to talk lovingly about her garden and the joy of fresh vegetables, which led to comparing hobbies. Shelley apparently loved designing clothing and from there, they began discussing books, a topic that Tawny could wax passionate about for hours.

Shelley insisted on ordering dessert for both of them, and did so without requesting a menu, so Tawny was nervous about how much it might cost. She might have to use Damien's debit card after all.

"Your dad…" she started to say, just as Shelley began, "My dad…"

They laughed. "You go first," Shelley said firmly.

"Your dad has been mending fences with Shaun since he came to Green Valley and started getting to know Trevor, and I think he'd really like to do the same with you."

"Well, if he's expecting kids, he can get over that," Shelley said, Damien's scowl familiar on her face. "I can't stand them."

"No," Tawny said hastily. "I don't think he's angling for more grandchildren… he just wants something more like a family than a collection of strangers and coworkers that share blood."

Shelley shook her head thoughtfully. "You know, as much as dad hates Green Valley, it sure has stuck to him."

Tawny felt like her chair had been pulled out from underneath her. "He hates Green Valley."

"Everything about it," Shelley told her. "He said it had no culture and smelled like cows."

Tawny wished she had Damien's gift for hiding her expressions, and was glad when Shelley's phone rang.

"I'm sorry Tawny, I have to take this," she said.

Tawny hadn't wanted to admit how much she was hoping that their visit to the city was just that—a visit.

She missed her town. She missed the tiny stores and the nosy neighbors. She was hurt to think he thought it had no culture, even if she had to admit he was right, and she ached to think about leaving it forever.

Homesickness turned the rich dessert to ash in her mouth, and Tawny had to take a long sip of the undoubtedly-expensive water to wash it down.

Shelley hung up. "I'm so sorry," she apologized. "This is a three billion dollar contract and I needed to talk to our lawyers about some of the wording before it went out for signatures."

Tawny smiled at her brightly. "Don't worry about it," she said.

"What were we talking about?"

"Your father," Tawny said. The thought of him steadied her. The way he frowned when he wanted to mask his emotions. The way he lowered his defenses with her and the way he looked when he said he loved her. His shoulders, and his big hands, and the beard she had once thought she hated.

"You're not really happy here, are you," Shelley guessed. "Even though you like my dad."

"I don't want to complain," Tawny said faintly.

"It's not complaining to be honest about what you want."

Tawny couldn't answer. To be honest, she wanted to go *home*.

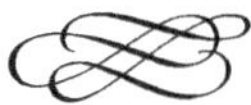

*D*amien had grown accustomed to returning to an apartment filled with light and music. Once Tawny had overcome her fear of the intimidating stereo system, she declared her undying love for it, and it was rarely silent. Damien was never sure what style of music he would come home to, but it had turned his return from work from a mandatory part of his day, to the time he loved the most.

That, and the way that Tawny greeted him, with smiles and kisses and a book in one hand.

But this time, the lights were turned down low, and the apartment was quiet.

He turned into the kitchen, and saw Tawny's phone on the counter with a bus schedule. Just as he was furrowing his brow and trying to decide what to make of that, he heard quiet steps from the room behind him.

"Planning on making a trip?" he asked as he turned, and was surprised to find not Tawny, but Shelley, holding a half-full glass of red wine, gazing into one of the display cases.

"What's this?" she asked curiously.

Damien didn't have to ask what she was looking at. He turned on the lights. "That's the paper crown that Tawny was wearing when I met her."

Shelley finally saw him. "What did you do to your face?!"

"I shaved off my beard."

"Why? How?"

"I went to my usual barber," Damien said, as casually as he could. His face felt naked, like everything he was feeling must be written across it.

"Why?"

"For Tawny."

Shelley was silent for a long moment. "I like her," she finally said. "She's... good for you."

"I trust you had a good lunch," Damien said.

"We did," Shelley agreed, but Damien found himself frowning thoughtfully at her face. Something else was going on behind her serene expression. Was it... pity?

Tawny wore her emotions no deeper than her skin, every feeling emblazoned across her features. But he and Shelley were cased in emotional armor, thick and resilient. It did nothing, he realized, to protect them from hurt or anger. But it isolated them from the potential for better things.

Like a decent relationship with each other.

How much anger and resentment could have been avoided if they had just talked to each other? If he had made an effort to connect with her, if he'd ever thought to reach out?

"Shelley," he said thoughtfully.

"Did you know that she hates it here?"

"I know," Damien said. He'd have to be blind, not to see past Tawny's brave smiles and cheerful determination. He'd bought her some houseplants, but he could tell that they didn't fill the same place in her heart that her garden had. He had even mentioned getting a cat. Tawny had laughed and said she couldn't imagine a cat getting hair on his couch, or scattering kitty litter in the bathroom.

She didn't even like to cook in his kitchen.

A sudden thought sent him back to the kitchen counter. It was an interstate bus schedule, not the city bus. A bus to Green Valley was circled.

Damien's stomach fell all the way to the ground floor.

She was gone.

"Did you know she was going?" Damien asked Shelley.

"I had no idea until I got here."

"She didn't feel like she belonged here," Damien told Shelley frankly. "She must have gone home."

Home.

It wasn't until he said the word that he recognized exactly how much Green Valley had started to feel like a home. It wasn't Tawny's tiny house that evoked the feeling, it was the quaint little town, with its colorful cast of characters. Maybe Green Valley didn't have museums and dinner parties and culture, but Damien was realizing that he didn't want those things.

He wanted quiet mornings reading the paper with Tawny. He wanted lazy afternoons drinking lemonade with Tawny. He wanted languid evenings and leisurely conversations. He even wanted the piano lessons, and the book club—the *Green Valley* book club—and pulling weeds and bee stings.

With *Tawny*.

Shelley said tentatively, "Tawny… she's different than mom was, isn't she. How you feel about her."

"She's my mate," Damien said gently. "My lion never cared who else was in my life as long as I was happy. But Tawny… Tawny matters to him, too. I don't love her any *more* than I loved your mother, or Shaun's either. But… it's different. We're *aligned* in a way that I never expected."

He wondered if Shelley was talking to her own lioness, she was so quiet for a moment.

Finally, Shelley nodded firmly. "I guess there's only one more question I have, then."

Damien was scowling out the window across the room. He couldn't see the streets below them, but he kept imagining Tawny, lost and heartbroken, wandering them. "What's the question?" he asked.

"Why are you still here?"

Damien looked at her with furrowed brow.

"Tawny's out *there*, so go get her!" Shelley walked to the island where Tawny's unwanted phone was sitting. "She circled the bus she planned to take, it doesn't leave for 15 minutes, and buses are always late. Go see if you can catch her."

She didn't have to suggest it twice.

CHAPTER 34

Two blocks in Green Valley would have been a matter of a few minutes of walking, waving at a few neighbors, and stopping to pet one of the neighborhood cats.

Two blocks in Minneapolis were much larger than they looked on the tiny, crowded map, and they were dense with people to navigate. Tawny ended up waiting through two lights at one of the intersections, not realizing that the blinking yellow crossing signal meant hurry forward rather than stop and wait, intimidated by impatient cars and honking drivers.

It was noisy and hot, and by the time Tawny arrived at the Greyhound station, her shoulders ached. Probably, she should have left the books to be shipped.

It wasn't worse than deciding to walk her route with packages had sometimes been, but she was glad to arrive at the station and put her bag at her feet as she stood in line for a ticket.

Probably her phone would have allowed her to buy a ticket, she realized belatedly, but by then she was only a few people from the start of the line and she preferred having a printed ticket to some mysterious screen on her phone that she would never find again.

Ticket in hand, Tawny realized she'd have nearly an hour to

wait until the bus took her to the Green Valley stop. She had a moment of nervousness, looking out over the crowded room.

It was the scene in a movie, lacking only the ominous music.

The laminate floor was cracked and dingy. One of the banks of lights was off-color, and faintly flickering.

In one corner, it looked rather like a drug deal was going down between a few dozen rough looking characters. A collection of bikers lingered in one corner, defying the heat with their full body leather.

"Hey lady, got a dollar?"

The man, lurking at her elbow, had a wild look in piercing blue eyes below unruly eyebrows. His beard made Damien's look down-right puny, and Tawny was pretty sure it had never been combed. What little hair remained on his head had possibly never been combed either. He wore old, mismatched clothing, and his feet were bare. He reminded her of a stray dog that was expecting to be kicked—one that might just bite her preemptively.

Tawny started to clutch her purse closer, then swiveled when another gruff voice demanded, "What's going on here?"

One of the terrifying bikers was looming over her, covered in tattoos and piercings.

Tawny had only a moment to think that it would have all been much easier if she had just had a car and been able to drive herself home to Green Valley.

That's when she realized that she'd left her new phone on the table in Damien's apartment.

CHAPTER 35

*D*amien pulled alongside the curb marked 'No Parking' and left his car there, damn the fine and the sidelong looks. He was not going to let Tawny escape.

And he certainly wasn't going to let her take the night bus to Green Valley alone. He would drive her to Green Valley if he had to wrestle her into the car by force.

The thin crowd parted before him as he stalked into the station, instinctively fearing the lion he barely had leashed inside.

Neither of them liked the tenor of the crowd in front of the station. It was late, and this was a rough, unpredictable bunch. Damien could feel the resentment from the other, lesser, alphas nearby. These were people who had everything to prove, and little to lose, and he could feel the turf war that was already simmering in the background.

He snarled to think of Tawny, sweet, innocent Tawny, spending any time here. She didn't know the first thing about cities after dark. She wouldn't know to keep her purse close, or her head down. She'd come without her phone, without any protection whatsoever.

His imagination supplied an image of her, cornered, afraid, and he nearly took the final door off its hinges as he strode into the dingy station. If anyone had dared to scare her, or worse, to mug her, or harm a single silver hair on her head, he would tear their limbs off.

A quick glance of the station showed that it was more thinly populated than the sidewalk outside, and Damien spotted Tawny at once. The back of her head was a bright spot, and she was sitting between two people. The leather-clad man next to her had a completely shaved head, covered in dark tattoos. On her other side there appeared to be a bewhiskered scarecrow, leaning disturbing close to her.

Damien closed the distance between them swiftly, fists curling in preparation for conflict, and came around the row of steel chairs to face them.

The biker was flipping through a book that Damien immediately recognized as a cookbook Tawny had been excited about. The homeless man curled up on her other side was reading what appeared to be a knitting magazine.

Damien's first thought was that they had stolen her books and she was too afraid to move, but Tawny's smile as she looked up and saw him vanquished the idea in a moment.

"Damien!" she cried cheerfully. "This is Ben, and Leroy." Ben and Leroy each gave a narrowly suspicious nod as Tawny rose to her feet. "I forgot my phone at your apartment, did you happen to bring it? What happened to your face?! Damien, your *beard!*"

She did not appear to be in any kind of trouble.

She did, however, seem to be quite dismayed. "What did you do to your beard?"

"I shaved it off. For you," Damien said crossly.

"But, I loved it," she said plaintively. "You aren't *you* without it."

"You told me you hated facial hair!"

"You changed my mind!"

"You changed my mind, too," Damien told her. "Look, I know you aren't happy here. I've put in my two weeks notice. I will live anywhere you want. Please don't leave me." He was keenly aware of the attention from Leroy, the biker who had stood up next to Tawny with his arms crossed, and Ben, who still seemed to be trying to hide behind the knitting magazine and avidly watch them at the same time.

Tawny blinked at him. "Leave you? Didn't you get my text message? Patricia had her baby! A beautiful little sister for Clara. I knew you were going to be busy the next few days, and I wanted to go see her as soon as possible. I was planning to pack up some boxes to bring back with me, and talk to Patricia's husband about what it would cost to fix up the house to sell."

"I didn't get a text," Damien said, pulling both his phone out of his jacket pocket and hers.

"I'll show you," Tawny promised, taking her phone and unlocking it with her fingerprint. There was an open text conversation, with her message typed out… and not sent. "Oh, good grief."

A chuckle escaped before Damien could stuff it back down.

"Don't laugh!" Tawny protested. "I told you this phone was above my technology level."

"I'm not laughing at you," Damien told her. "I'm just… relieved you're alright." He politely did not glance at her questionable companions. "Wait, sell your house?"

"You hate Green Valley," Tawny said, not quite meeting his eyes.

"I don't hate Green Valley!" Damien protested.

"You told Shelley it has no culture and smells like cows!"

"It does sometimes smell like cows! But… I don't find that… exactly objectionable. Tawny, I want to be where you are. I want to be where *you're* happy."

"But *you're* not happy in my house."

Leroy, who had been watching the exchange with growing perplexity. "So get a new house," he suggested.

There was a moment of silence.

"I don't hate Green Valley," Damien said, thoughtfully this time.

Tawny said hesitantly, "Madison has some culture. It's not too far away to go out for dinner or theater sometimes."

"There are some nice houses up in the hills in Patricia and Lee's neighborhood," Damien suggested.

The hope in Tawny's eyes was a beautiful thing. "Green Valley does have a vastly superior book club," she pointed out.

"Tawny, will you buy a house with me? Something we'll both like, near Green Valley, where the cats can be inside-outside cats and the kitchen isn't too big and shiny. Something with a garden."

Tawny threw her arms around him at last. "Yes. Yes, please. Oh, can we?"

Damien kissed her soundly and set her back on her feet. "Let me drive you to Green Valley to see the new baby, and we'll start looking at listings this week."

"I already paid for a bus ticket…" Tawny started to say, but her eyes were twinkling.

"I am not letting you take the night bus…"

She slipped her hand into his. "I'd rather go with you, Damien."

Leroy tried to hand her back the cookbook. "No, you keep that, Leroy," she told him. "The ladies love a man who can cook."

Ben made no attempt to hand back her magazine, folding it into himself defensively. He did shake Tawny's hand, though, and mumble his thanks.

CHAPTER 36

The trees along the driveway were thick with green leaves and an unruly front lawn was already ankle-deep in grass and clover, with bright dandelions everywhere. An unkempt flower bed bloomed with lilies and irises.

A For Sale sign was hanging from the porch.

Tawny eyes it thoughtfully as Damien led her up to the front door and unlocked it.

The house was unlit, but early sunlight spilled in from uncurtained windows, illuminating a large, empty foyer. An open door gave a glimpse at an enormous open kitchen and dining area, everything in pale wood and chrome.

Tawny expected Damien to take her on a tour of the house. Instead, he drew her back through the foyer to the back door, which opened out onto a garden.

It was a tragedy of neglect, overgrown and tangled with weeds. Beds of perennials were choked with grass and volunteer fruit tree saplings. Top-heavy apple trees bowed low over what must have once been raised vegetable beds. The skeleton of a greenhouse was covered in tattered plastic sheeting. Moles had clearly been at the wild lawn; it was as much clover and dandelions and lumps of dirt as it was grass.

And it took Tawny's breath away.

She could just imagine what it would look like with a little care.

There was room to plant a winter's worth of potatoes, and still have rows of peas and beans and carrots. The bones of the greenhouse looked sturdy enough; maybe tomatoes and peppers were possible.

As Tawny stepped out into the space in wonder, she realized that there were rose bushes against the house, sprawling with wicked thorns over the cobblestone paths. The brambles were covered in miniature roses in all colors.

At some point, she had grabbed onto Damien's arm and she clung to him in wonder and longing as she gazed around.

"What is this?" she finally dared to ask.

"Your garden," Damien said. "If you want it," he added.

She wanted it like she had never wanted anything in her life.

Anything before him.

"Mine," she breathed.

Damien gave her a sideways glance. "I haven't signed anything y—"

"Sign it!" Tawny said without thinking twice.

Damien smiled slowly at her. "We wanted a place that was ours. Yours and mine. Something that wasn't entirely either of our worlds."

Tawny stopped drinking in the garden and turned to him seriously. "I would live in the city for you," she said solemnly. "And I don't need a garden if I have you." She took his hands in her own.

"And I would live right in Green Valley with you," Damien told her just as firmly, clasping her fingers in his. "Busybody neighbors, book clubs and all."

"This is the best of everything," Tawny said longingly. "It's just a few miles from town, there's more space for you here than in my tiny house. You'd be happier in a place like this. And Damien, this *garden.*"

"There's just one problem with it," Damien said, frowning at her. Already, his beard was coming back in, not quite enough to cover his beautiful mouth.

Tawny caught her breath, already in love with the house and its land. Was there a problem with the sale? Another buyer? A haunted graveyard? She would take ghosts if it meant having her dream garden. "What is it?" she asked trepidatiously.

"We're a ways from town, out here. You'll… need a car."

Someone else might have thought he was angry, his face was so serious and firm. But Tawny could see that his eyes were dancing.

She balled up a fist and punched him in the arm. "You can't just buy me a car," she teased.

"Can I buy you a house full of books?" Damien teased in return, just the hint of a smile at his handsome mouth.

"No," Tawny said, unable to keep from laughing. "But I'll let you buy me a garden… with a few accessories."

Damien grinned then, and when he leaned towards her, Tawny put her arms around his neck and kissed him soundly. "Marry me," he said, the moment she released his lips. Like most of what he said, it didn't sound like a request, but when she smiled at him without answering, he added, "Please?"

Tawny couldn't speak for a moment, thinking about how much her life had changed in just a handful of weeks. She could not imagine her life without this man at her side, no matter where they ended up.

It was not the retirement she had planned.

It was even better.

"Oh, Damien," she said, as he began to frown at her thoughtful silence. "Of course I'll marry you. You *need* me."

Then he was catching her up in his arms and capturing her mouth.

EPILOGUE

The garden cleaned up every bit as well as Tawny had imagined. It wasn't too late in the season to get new perennials in, and though Tawny had to buy starts, by fall, the vegetable beds were groaning with produce. Lee had his construction company put shining new panels of greenhouse glass over the frame as an early wedding gift, and fat tomatoes and peppers filled the structure.

The lawn was re-rolled and seeded, all of the dandelions tamed and the fruit trees were trimmed back to healthy branches.

Tawny stood alone near the house, looking across the lawn to where Damien stood.

It was not a wedding like Patricia's had been, with most of Green Valley, mobs of children, and stray goats, but she knew that neither she nor Damien would have enjoyed that much chaos.

It wasn't quite as spare as Shaun and Andrea's courthouse elopement, either.

They each had their closest friends and family in attendance, without even bothering with a formal wedding party. Marta and May were dressed exactly as they would for the book club, except that Marta had left her hair loose and May was wearing earrings.

Shaun and Andrea stood near Shelley with Trevor. Patricia and Lee were there also, Clara like a little golden angel next to them. Baby Victoria made quiet noises of baby protest in Patricia's arms.

Tawny smiled. There weren't babies in her future with Damien, and she wasn't sorry for that. They were having an autumn marriage, in the autumn of their lives. And how lucky was she, to have this chance to share the rest of her life with someone like Damien, who made her feel young and beautiful and ready to live.

He turned towards her then, and Tawny drew in a breath of anticipation, took a tighter grip on her bouquet, and marched down the path towards him.

"I understand you have prepared your own vows?" the preacher prompted, when she took her place opposite from the man she was marrying.

Tawny nodded, and took out the notecard she had prepared in case her nerves failed her. But after staring at it sightlessly for a moment, she put it away.

"Damien, when I met you, I thought you were the most arrogant, conceited man I'd ever laid eyes on."

The little audience gave a ripple of laughter, but Tawny continued to gaze at Damien.

"But I'm really glad that you insisted we have dinner, because underneath that amazing ego was the best thing that has ever happened to me. I am so grateful that you fell into my life, and I have never met anyone as smart and funny and sweet. Every day I'm surprised and glad that you chose me, and every day I choose you all over again. I will love you forever and look forward to spending the rest of my life with you."

Damien's face twitched into a smile.

"Tawny, when I met you, I knew at once that you were mine, forever. What I didn't realize then is how completely I would be yours. You are the wisdom and beauty in my world, and I vow to honor and protect and adore you. I will love you to the end of days and back and I am so grateful that you got past my amazing ego and let me share your life."

Tawny had to wipe away the tears that overflowed from her

heart, smiling foolishly at him, as their friends and family laughed and applauded.

They exchanged simple gold bands, Tawny's hands trembling only a little.

"By the power vested in me by the State of Wisconsin, I now pronounce you husband and wife. You may kiss the bride."

Damien gathered her into his arms, but paused with his mouth just inches away. "Tawny, may I kiss you?"

Tawny answered with her mouth, slipping her arms up around his strong shoulders as she pressed her lips to his. She finally drew back to the cheers of the small audience and Damien took her hand as they walked to accept their congratulations.

"You look so beautiful," Patricia said, hugging her around the wriggling baby. Lee shook everyone's hands, and Andrea hugged everyone and cried.

"Come eat," Shaun invited. "We've got cake to cut!"

"Cake!" Clara and Trevor chorused in excitement. They raced for the door.

Tawny lingered as the rest of the party went inside, looking over her perfect garden with a contented sigh.

"Was it everything you hoped for?" Damien asked, suddenly at her elbow.

Tawny looked up at him. His beard was thick again, short and neatly shaped. "Even more," she said.

"I wanted to get you something amazing for your wedding gift," he said, smiling down at her. There was a small, slim package in his hands, wrapped in silver paper. "I thought about getting you something big—but you wouldn't wear extravagant jewelry, and I didn't figure you'd appreciate a pony or an airplane."

"I wouldn't want a pony in my garden," Tawny agreed.

"It's a little silly," Damien warned.

"It's a book," Tawny guessed, taking it. "I love books."

She unwrapped it, turned it over to the front cover, and burst out laughing.

"The Tawny, Scrawny Lion!" she exclaimed, nearly losing her her balance as she opened the children's book.

"First edition," Damien showed her. "Signed by the artist!"

"It's better than my gift for you," Tawny said abashedly.

"Let's not make it a competition," Damien said with a smile.

"I knitted you a sweater," Tawny said sheepishly.

"You said sweaters were nigh impossible," Damien said in astonishment. "And that you hadn't knitted in fifteen years."

"And you said you wanted one," Tawny reminded him. "I hope it's not too ugly. I had to rip out both the sleeves twice."

"I will wear it every day," Damien said sincerely. "No matter how ugly it is."

"It is too heavy to wear in the summer," she warned.

"I will wear it the whole year anyway," he said. "Because you made it for me, and because I will love you in every season."

"In every season," Tawny echoed.

Then he bent to kiss her, and there they stayed, savoring each other, until a whiny voice interrupted them.

"There's caaaaaake, Grandpa! Stop kissing and come cut it."

"Please?" Clara added more politely, but no less impatiently.

Laughing, Tawny and Damien broke apart and followed them into the house, hand in hand.

∾

I hope you enjoyed the first three books of Green Valley! It's a fun little town to visit and tell stories in. Shelley Powell gets her own happy ever after next in Bearly Together – keep reading for a sneak preview or get the second Green Valley Collection!

I always love to know what you thought! You can leave a review at Amazon or Goodreads (I read them all, and they help other readers find me) or drop me an email at elvaherself@elvabirch.com.

If you'd like to be emailed when I release my next book, please sign up for my mailing list. Visit my webpage (elvabirch.com), or follow me on Facebook or Instagram. You are also invited to join Elva Birch's Reader's Retreat on Facebook, where I show off new covers first, and you can get sneak previews and ask questions. I also have signed and sketched paperbacks and hardcovers!

The cover of *Dancing Bearfoot* was designed by Layla Lawlor. The covers of this collection, *The Tiger Next Door,* and *Dandelion Season* were designed by Ellen Million.

irresistible. Start with a sampler plate in Prompted 2 for fourteen pieces of sweet-to-sizzling flash fiction, or the novella, Better Half. Breakup is a free story!

Sign up for Elva Birch's mailing list and get a free copy of Better Half!

MORE BY ZOE CHANT

Shifting Sands Resort: A complete ten-book series - plus two collections of shorts. This is a sizzling shifter romance set at a tropical island resort. Each book stands alone but connects into a great mystery with a thrilling conclusion. Start with Tropical Tiger Spy or dive in to the Omnibus edition, with all of the novels, short stories, and novellas in my preferred reading order! Shifting Sands Resort crosses over with Fire and Rescue Shifters and Shifter Kingdom.

~

Fae Shifter Knights: A complete four-book fantasy portal romp, with cute pets and swoon-worthy knights stuck in a world of wonders like refrigerators and ham sandwiches. Start with Dragon of Glass!

~

Green Valley Shifters: A sweet, small town series with single dads, secret shifters, sweet kids, and spinsters. Low-peril and steamy! Standalone books where you can revisit your favorite characters - this series is also complete with six books! Start with Dancing Bearfoot! This series crosses over with **Virtue Shifters**, which starts with Timber Wolf.

BEHIND THE SCENES...

What is Patreon?

Patreon is a site where readers and fans can support creators with monthly subscriptions.

At my Patreon, I have tiers with early rough drafts of my books, flash fiction, coloring pages, signed and sketched paperbacks, exclusive swag, original artwork, photographs…and so much more! Every month is a little different, and there is a price for every budget. Patreon allows me to do projects that aren't very commercial and makes my income stream a little less unpredictable. It also gives me a place to connect with my fans!

Come find out what's going on behind the scenes and keep me creating at Patreon! patreon.com/ellenmillion

SNEAK PREVIEW: BEARLY TOGETHER

Shelley had never spent much time thinking about weddings and true love and making babies like other girls. Wedding *dresses*, because she'd always loved fashion, but the whole idea of waiting around for the perfect guy only made her roll her eyes.

She hadn't even believed in mates until her father introduced her to his, and later casually mentioned that Shaun had married his as well. It was too ridiculous to bear.

But here they were, and her lioness was growling with avid recognition, leaving no doubt in Shelley's mind that *this* was her destiny, *this* was her mate.

If she had ever bothered to imagine meeting her mate, it would not have been like this.

She was sweaty and disheveled from having to walk to the diner, and she'd gotten unexpectedly caught in the arc of a sprinkler on her way back, so her jacket had water spots and her hair was limp.

And the most gorgeous man she'd ever laid eyes on had just looked straight into her soul and was explaining to her that she was the biggest idiot in the entire sad state.

"The… license plate?" she repeated. "The noise from my car was just a *loose license plate?*"

"That's all it was, ma'am," he said, gazing back at her in a way that would have been creepy if it had been anyone else… or if she had not been staring back at him with equal avarice. "The bolts were loose and that's the rattle you were hearing when you went over bumps. I… tightened them for you."

"Not ma'am," Shelley squeaked. She didn't want to be 'ma'am' to this man. "Shelley." It sounded like a kid's name to her ears. "Michelle." Ugh, no, too formal. "Shelley. Shelley Powell." She realized that he probably already knew her name, since she'd left it with her car key.

She was not doing much to redeem her image of intelligence.

"I'm Dean," he answered, and he offered her a hand. "Dean James, not to be mistaken for James Dean."

Shelley laughed breathlessly. Dean could certainly have been a movie star, with his broad shoulders and strong jaw. She very slowly took his hand to shake and was instantly lost.

If his gaze had left her knees feeling boneless, his handshake did things to parts not much higher, and her chest was suddenly too small for her lungs. She was dizzy, and excited, and…she was ready for this. This was coming home. Her lion was rumbling in delight.

"So, you're…" she started, just as he blushed beautifully and said, "I guess…"

"You first," she said swiftly, and by virtue of her speed, he was forced to continue.

"Are you… a… ah… lion shifter like your nephew and your father?" he said with understandable hesitation. Being wrong about an assumption like that in a world where shifters were secret would have been a stunning mistake to bring up aloud.

But *this* wasn't a mistake. He was clearly feeling the same thing, the same crazy, perfect, stomach-dropping realization she was tumbling through. He was drinking in her gaze just as she was his, and they hadn't let go of each other after the handshake. Their clasped hands hung just above the countertop. If the counter had not been between them, Shelley was not sure what they would be doing now, but she would bet that it would start with a kiss from those amazing lips, and once the thought occurred to her, she couldn't shake it.

"I am," she finally remembered to confirm, because it seemed impossible that there was anything he didn't know about her. "And… you?"

"Bear," Dean said faintly, like he was imagining the same kiss. "I'm… a bear. Grizzly."

It was the stupidest conversation, dragged out a stupid amount of time, because Shelley couldn't keep a thought in her head that wasn't kissing this man. "I'm a lawyer," she said impulsively, then thought it sounded like she was bragging and blushed. "I mean… I just don't want you to think I'm an idiot. Because of the… license plate."

"Happens all the time," Dean lied kindly.

"You're just being nice," Shelley told him suspiciously.

"Yeah," Dean agreed with a smile.

"Do I owe you anything?"

"No, no charge for tightening your... license plate."

They were still clasping hands over the greasy counter.

"I'm never going to live this down, am I?" Shelley guessed sheepishly.

"It'll be one of those inside jokes that we have."

"You mean, it will actually be funny someday, instead of just horribly humiliating?"

"I promise," Dean breathed.

There was a moment of silence, then they both tried to say, "So, you're…"

This time Dean was fastest. "You first."

"You're my mate," Shelley said boldly. It was thrilling to her own ears. This beautiful man, with his strong hands and his piercing eyes: he was *hers*.

His grin was like a bolt of lightning. "That's what I was going to say," he said.

"It's… it's nice to meet you," Shelley said. Nice was so insufficient! "I… would you like to get dinner or something?" Dinner was the last thing she wanted to do with this man; she wanted to wrap herself around him and see if he tasted the way she was imagining.

She let go of his hand, but only because he was coming around the counter, and she would finally be able to…

"Daddy! Daddy!"

Shelley stumbled backwards instead of taking the step forward that she had intended.

A curly-haired boy about the same age as Trevor bolted into the room like a whirlwind, smelling like leaves and mud puddles. He just missed crashing into Shelley's legs, careening around her and wrapping himself around Dean possessively as the man bent and intercepted his hug.

Shelley stared in horror.

"You… have a kid?" she said hesitantly.

"This is my son, Aaron."

Everything about the mood had changed. Dean was bristling protectively, his arms around the little boy, his gaze challenging.

Shelley felt like someone had just hit her in the face, and she probably looked like it, too.

Her mate... had a kid.

Every brief, delirious fantasy she'd had about a life with Dean suddenly had a four-foot-high *nope* in the middle of it…

Continue the story in Bearly Together! or read it in the Green Valley Shifters Collection 2!